NIGHT WATCH

A Discworld® Novel

www.**booksattransworld**.co.uk

Also by Terry Pratchett

THE CARPET PEOPLE*
THE DARK SIDE OF THE SUN
STRATA · TRUCKERS* · DIGGERS* · WINGS*
ONLY YOU CAN SAVE MANKIND*
JOHNNY AND THE DEAD* · JOHNNY AND THE BOMB*
THE UNADULTERATED CAT†
(with Gray Jolliffe)
GOOD OMENS
(with Neil Gaiman)
THE DISCWORLD COMPANION†
(with Stephen Briggs)
THE PRATCHETT PORTFOLIO†
(with Paul Kidby)
THE LAST HERO†
(with Paul Kidby)

The Discworld® series:
THE COLOUR OF MAGIC*
THE LIGHT FANTASTIC*
EQUAL RITES* · MORT* · SOURCERY*
WYRD SISTERS* · PYRAMIDS* · GUARDS! GUARDS!*
ERIC* (with Josh Kirby)†
MOVING PICTURES* · REAPER MAN*
WITCHES ABROAD* · SMALL GODS*
LORDS AND LADIES*
MEN AT ARMS* · SOUL MUSIC*
INTERESTING TIMES* · MASKERADE*
FEET OF CLAY* · HOGFATHER*
JINGO*
THE LAST CONTINENT*
CARPE JUGULUM*
THE FIFTH ELEPHANT*
THE TRUTH*
THIEF OF TIME*

THE COLOUR OF MAGIC (graphic novel)
THE LIGHT FANTASTIC (graphic novel)
MORT: A DISCWORLD BIG COMIC (with Graham Higgins)†

SOUL MUSIC: The Illustrated Screenplay
WYRD SISTERS: The Illustrated Screenplay
MORT – THE PLAY (adapted by Stephen Briggs)
WYRD SISTERS – THE PLAY (adapted by Stephen Briggs)
GUARDS! GUARDS! – THE PLAY (adapted by Stephen Briggs)
MEN AT ARMS – THE PLAY (adapted by Stephen Briggs)

THE STREETS OF ANKH-MORPORK (with Stephen Briggs)
THE DISCWORLD MAPP (with Stephen Briggs)
A TOURIST GUIDE TO LANCRE a Discworld Mapp
(with Stephen Briggs and Paul Kidby)
DEATH'S DOMAIN (with Paul Kidby)
NANNY OGG'S COOKBOOK

* available in audio
† published by Victor Gollancz

NIGHT WATCH

Terry Pratchett

Doubleday

LONDON · NEW YORK · TORONTO · SYDNEY · AUCKLAND

TRANSWORLD PUBLISHERS
61–63 Uxbridge Road, London W5 5SA
a division of The Random House Group Ltd

RANDOM HOUSE AUSTRALIA (PTY) LTD
20 Alfred Street, Milsons Point, Sydney,
New South Wales 2061, Australia

RANDOM HOUSE NEW ZEALAND LTD
18 Poland Road, Glenfield, Auckland 10, New Zealand

RANDOM HOUSE SOUTH AFRICA (PTY) LTD
Endulini, 5a Jubilee Road, Parktown 2193, South Africa

Published 2002 by Doubleday
a division of Transworld Publishers

A catalogue record for this book is available from the British Library.
ISBN 0385 602642

Typeset in 11/14½pt Meridien
by Falcon Oast Graphic Art Ltd

Printed in Great Britain
by Clays Ltd, St Ives plc

1 3 5 7 9 10 8 6 4 2

NIGHT WATCH

Sam Vimes sighed when he heard the scream, but he finished shaving before he did anything about it.

Then he put his jacket on and strolled out into the wonderful late spring morning. Birds sang in the trees, bees buzzed in the blossom. The sky was hazy, though, and thunderheads on the horizon threatened rain later. But, for now, the air was hot and heavy. And, in the old cesspit behind the gardener's shed, a young man was treading water.

Well . . . treading, anyway.

Vimes stood back a little way and lit a cigar. It probably wouldn't be a good idea to employ a naked flame any nearer to the pit. The fall from the shed roof had broken the crust.

'Good morning!' he said cheerfully.

'Good morning, your grace,' said the industrious treadler.

The voice was higher pitched than Vimes expected and he realized that, most unusually, the young man in the pit was in fact a young woman. It wasn't *entirely* unexpected – the Assassins' Guild was aware that women were at least equal to their brothers when it came to inventive killing – but it never-theless changed the situation somewhat.

'I don't believe we've met?' said Vimes. 'Although I see you know who I am. You are . . . ?'

'Wiggs, sir,' said the swimmer. 'Jocasta Wiggs. Honoured to meet you, your grace.'

'Wiggs, eh?' said Vimes. 'Famous family in the Guild. "Sir" will do, by the way. I think I once broke your father's leg?'

'Yes, sir. He asked to be remembered to you,' said Jocasta.

'You're a bit young to be sent on this contract, aren't you?' said Vimes.

'Not a contract, sir,' said Jocasta, still paddling.

'Come now, Miss Wiggs. The price on my head is at least—'

'The Guild council put it in abeyance, sir,' said the dogged swimmer. 'You're off the register. They're not accepting contracts on you at present.'

'Good grief, why not?'

'Couldn't say, sir,' said Miss Wiggs. Her patient struggles had brought her to the edge of the pit, and now she was finding that the brickwork was in very good repair, quite slippery and offered no handholds. Vimes knew this, because he'd spent several hours one afternoon carefully arranging that this should be so.

'So why were you sent, then?'

'Miss Band sent me as an exercise,' said Jocasta. 'I say, these bricks really are jolly tricky, aren't they?'

'Yes,' said Vimes, 'they are. Have you been *rude* to Miss Band lately? Upset her in any way?'

'Oh, no, your grace. But she did say I was getting over-confident, and would benefit from some advanced field work.'

'Ah. I see.' Vimes tried to recall Miss Alice Band, one of the Assassins' Guild's stricter teachers. She was, he'd heard, very hot on practical lessons.

'So . . . she sent you to kill me, then?' he said.

'No, sir! It's an exercise! I don't even have any crossbow bolts! I just had to find a spot where I could get you in my sights and then report back!'

'She'd believe you?'

'Of course, sir,' said Jocasta, looking rather hurt. 'Guild honour, sir.'

Vimes took a deep breath. 'You see, Miss Wiggs, quite a few of your chums have tried to kill me at home in recent years. As you might expect, I take a dim view of this.'

'Easy to see why, sir,' said Jocasta, in the voice of one who

8

knows that their only hope of escaping from their present predicament is reliant on the goodwill of another person who has no pressing reason to have any.

'And so you'd be *amazed* at the booby traps there are around the place,' Vimes went on. 'Some of them are pretty cunning, even if I say it myself.'

'I certainly never expected the tiles on the shed to shift like that, sir.'

'They're on greased rails,' said Vimes.

'Well done, sir!'

'And quite a few of the traps drop you into something deadly,' said Vimes.

'Lucky for me that I fell into this one, eh, sir?'

'Oh, that one's deadly too,' said Vimes. '*Eventually* deadly.' He sighed. He really wanted to discourage this sort of thing but . . . they'd put him off the register? It wasn't that he'd *liked* being shot at by hooded figures in the temporary employ of his many and varied enemies, but he'd always looked at it as some kind of vote of confidence. It showed that he was annoying the rich and arrogant people who ought to be annoyed.

Besides, the Assassins' Guild was easy to outwit. They had strict rules, which they followed quite honourably, and this was fine by Vimes, who, in certain practical areas, had no rules whatsoever.

Off the register, eh? The only other person not on it any more, it was rumoured, was Lord Vetinari, the Patrician. The Assassins understood the political game in the city better than anyone, and if they took you off the register it was because they felt your departure would not only spoil the game but also smash the board . . .

'I'd be jolly grateful if you could pull me out, sir,' said Jocasta.

'What? Oh, yes. Sorry, got clean clothes on,' said Vimes. 'But when I get back to the house I'll tell the butler to come down here with a ladder. How about that?'

'Thank you very much, sir. Nice to have met you, sir.'

9

Vimes strolled back to the house. Off the register? Was he allowed to appeal? Perhaps they thought—

The scent rolled over him.

He looked up.

Overhead, a lilac tree was in bloom.

He stared.

Damn! Damn! *Damn!* Every year he forgot. Well, no. He never *forgot*. He just put the memories away, like old silverware that you didn't want to tarnish. And every year they came back, sharp and sparkling, and stabbed him in the heart. And today, of all days . . .

He reached up, and his hand trembled as he grasped a bloom and gently broke the stem. He sniffed at it. He stood for a moment, staring at nothing. And then he carried the sprig of lilac carefully back up to his dressing room.

Willikins had prepared the *official* uniform for today. Sam Vimes stared at it blankly, and then remembered. Watch Committee. Right. The battered old breastplate wouldn't do, would it . . . Not for His Grace the Duke of Ankh, Commander of the City Watch, Sir Samuel Vimes. Lord Vetinari had been very *definite* about that, blast it.

Blast it all the more because, unfortunately, Sam Vimes could see the point. He hated the official uniform, but he represented a bit more than just himself these days. Sam Vimes had been able to turn up for meetings with grubby armour, and even Sir Samuel Vimes could generally contrive to find a way to stay in street uniform at all times, but a Duke . . . well, a Duke needed a bit of polish. A Duke couldn't have the arse hanging out of his trousers when meeting foreign diplomats. Actually, even plain old Sam Vimes never had the arse hanging out of his trousers, either, but no one would have actually started a war if he had.

The plain old Sam Vimes had fought back. He got rid of most of the plumes and the stupid tights, and ended up with a dress uniform that at least looked as though its owner was male. But the helmet had gold decoration, and the bespoke armourers had made a new, gleaming breastplate with useless gold ornamentation on it. Sam Vimes felt like a class traitor every time he wore it. He hated being thought of as one of those people that wore stupid ornamental armour. It was gilt by association.

He twirled the sprig of lilac in his fingers, and smelled again the heady smell. Yes . . . it hadn't always been like this . . .

Someone had just spoken to him. He looked up.

'What?' he barked.

'I enquired if her ladyship is well, your grace?' said the butler, looking startled. 'Are you feeling all right, your grace?'

'What? Oh, yes. No. I'm fine. So is her ladyship, yes, thank you. I popped in before I went outside. Mrs Content is with her. She says it won't be for a while.'

'I have advised the kitchen to have plenty of hot water ready, your grace, nevertheless,' said Willikins, helping Vimes on with the gilty breastplate.

'Yes. Why do they need all that water, do you think?'

'I couldn't say, your grace,' said Willikins. 'Probably best not to enquire.'

Vimes nodded. Sybil had already made it quite clear, with gentle tact, that he was not required on this particular case. It had been, he had to admit, a bit of a relief.

He handed Willikins the sprig of lilac. The butler took it without comment, inserted it into a little silver tube of water that would keep it fresh for hours, and fixed it on to one of the breastplate straps.

'Time moves on, doesn't it, your grace,' he said, dusting him down with a small brush.

Vimes took out his watch. 'It certainly does. Look, I'll drop in at the Yard on my way to the palace, sign what needs signing, and I'll be back as soon as possible, all right?'

Willikins gave him a look of almost unbutlery concern. 'I'm sure her ladyship will be fine, your grace,' he said. 'Of course she is not, not—'

'—young,' said Vimes.

'I would say she is richer in years than many other primi-gravidae,' said Willikins smoothly. 'But she is a well-built lady, if you don't mind me saying so, and her family have tradition-ally had very little trouble in the childbirth department—'

'Primi what?'

'New mothers, your grace. I'm sure her ladyship would much rather know that you were running after miscreants than wear-ing a hole in the library carpet.'

'I expect you're right, Willikins. Er . . . oh, yes, there's a young lady dogpaddling in the old cesspit, Willikins.'

'Very good, your grace. I shall send the kitchen boy down there with a ladder directly. And a message to the Assassins' Guild?'

'Good idea. She'll need clean clothes and a bath.'

'I think, perhaps, the hose in the old scullery might be more appropriate, your grace? To start with, at least?'

'Good point. See to it. And now I must be off.'

In the crowded main office of the Pseudopolis Yard Watch House, Sergeant Colon absent-mindedly adjusted the sprig of lilac that he'd stuck into his helmet like a plume.

'They go very strange, Nobby,' he said, leafing listlessly through the morning's paperwork. 'It's a copper thing. Happened to me when I had kids. You get tough.'

'What do you mean, tough?' said Corporal Nobbs, possibly the best living demonstration that there was some smooth evolution between humans and animals.

'We-ell,' said Colon, leaning back in his chair. 'It's like . . . well, when you're our age . . .' He looked at Nobby, and hesitated. Nobby had been giving his age as 'probably 34' for years; the Nobbs family were not good at keeping count.

'I mean, when a man reaches . . . a certain age,' he tried again, 'he knows the world is never going to be perfect. He's got used to it being a bit, a bit . . .'

'Manky?' Nobby suggested. Tucked behind his ear, in the

place usually reserved for his cigarette, was another wilting lilac flower.

'Exactly,' said Colon. 'Like, it's never going to be perfect, so you just do the best you can, right? But when there's a kid on the way, well, suddenly a man sees it different. He thinks: my kid's going to have to *grow up* in this mess. Time to clean it up. Time to make it a Better World. He gets a bit . . . keen. Full of ginger. When he hears about Strongintfearm it's going to be very hot around here for— 'morning, Mister Vimes!'

'Talking about me, eh?' said Vimes, striding past them as they jerked to attention. He had not in fact heard any of the conversation, but Sergeant Colon's face could be read like a book and Vimes had learned it by heart years ago.

'Just wondering if the happy event—' Colon began, trailing after Vimes as he took the stairs two at a time.

'It hasn't,' said Vimes shortly. He pushed open the door to his office. ' 'morning, Carrot!'

Captain Carrot sprang to his feet and saluted. ' 'morning, sir! Has Lady—'

'No, Carrot. She has not. What's been happening overnight?'

Carrot's gaze went to the sprig of lilac, and back to Vimes's face. 'Nothing good, sir,' he said. 'Another officer killed.'

Vimes stopped dead. 'Who?' he demanded.

'Sergeant Strongintfearm, sir. Killed in Treacle Mine Road. Carcer again.'

Vimes glanced at his watch. They had ten minutes to get to the palace. But time suddenly wasn't important any more.

He sat down at his desk. 'Witnesses?'

'Three this time, sir.'

'That many?'

'All dwarfs. Strongintfearm wasn't even on duty, sir. He'd signed off and was picking up a rat pie and chips from a shop and walked out straight into Carcer. The devil stabbed him in the neck and ran for it. He must've thought we'd found him.'

'We've been looking for the man for *weeks*! And he bumped

into poor old Stronginthearm when all the dwarf was thinking of was his breakfast? Is Angua on the trail?'

'Up to a point, sir,' said Carrot awkwardly.

'Why only up to a point?'

'He – well, we assume it was Carcer – dropped an aniseed bomb in Sator Square. Almost pure oil.'

Vimes sighed. It was amazing how people adapted. The Watch had a werewolf. That news had got around, in an underground kind of way. And so the criminals had evolved to survive in a society where the law had a very sensitive nose. Scent bombs were the solution. They didn't have to be *that* dramatic. You just dropped a little flask of pure peppermint or aniseed in the street where a lot of people would walk over it, and suddenly Sergeant Angua was facing a hundred, a *thousand* criss-crossing trails, and went to bed with a terrible headache.

He listened glumly as Carrot reported on men brought off leave or put on double shift, on informers pumped, pigeons stooled, grasses rustled, fingers held to the wind, ears put on the street. And he knew how little it all added up to. They still had fewer than a hundred men in the Watch, and that was including the canteen lady. There were a million people in the city, and a billion places to hide. Ankh-Morpork was *built* of boltholes. Besides, Carcer was a nightmare.

Vimes was used to the other kinds of nut jobs, the ones that acted quite normally right up to the point where they hauled off and smashed someone with a poker for blowing their nose noisily. But Carcer was different. He was in two minds, but instead of them being in conflict, they were in competition. He had a demon on *both* shoulders, urging one another on.

And yet . . . he smiled all the time, in a cheerful chirpy sort of way, and he acted like the kind of rascal who made a dodgy living selling gold watches that go green after a week. And he appeared to be convinced, utterly convinced, that he never did anything really wrong. He'd stand there amid the carnage, blood on his hands and stolen jewellery in his pocket, and with an expression of injured innocence declare, 'Me? What did *I* do?'

And it was believable right up until you looked hard into those cheeky, smiling eyes, and saw, deep down, the demons looking back.

. . . but you mustn't spend too much time looking at those eyes, because that'd mean you'd taken *your* eyes off his hands, and by now one of them held a knife.

It was hard for the average copper to deal with people like that. They expected people, when heavily outnumbered, to give in or try to deal or at least just *stop moving*. They didn't expect people to kill for a five-dollar watch. (A hundred dollar watch, now, that'd be different. This was Ankh-Morpork, after all.)

'Was Stronginthearm married?' he said.

'No, sir. Lived in New Cobblers with his parents.'

Parents, thought Vimes. That made it worse.

'Anyone been to tell them?' he asked. 'And don't say it was Nobby. We don't want any repeat of that "bet you a dollar you're the widow Jackson" nonsense.'

'I went, sir. As soon as we got the news.'

'Thank you. They took it badly?'

'They took it . . . solemnly, sir.'

Vimes groaned. He could imagine the expressions.

'I'll write them the official letter,' he said, pulling open his desk. 'Get someone to take it round, will you? And say I'll be over later. Perhaps this isn't the time to—' No, hold on, they were dwarfs, dwarfs weren't bashful about money. 'Forget that – say we'll have all the details of his pension and so on. Died on duty, too. Well, near enough. That's extra. It all adds up.' He rummaged in his cupboards. 'Where's his file?'

'Here, sir,' said Carrot, handing it over smoothly. 'We are due at the palace at ten, sir. Watch Committee. But I'm sure they'll understand,' he added, seeing Vimes's face. 'I'll go and clean out Stronginthearm's locker, sir, and I expect the lads'll have a whip-round for flowers and everything . . .'

15

Vimes pondered over a sheet of headed paper after the captain had gone. A file, he had to refer to a damn *file*. But there were so many coppers these days . . .

A whip-round for flowers. And a coffin. You look after your own. Sergeant Dickins had said that, a long time ago . . .

He wasn't good with words, least of all ones written down, but after a few glances at the file to refresh his memory he wrote down the best he could think of.

And they were all good words and, more or less, they were the right ones. But in truth Stronginthearm was just a decent dwarf who'd been paid to be a copper. He'd joined up because, these days, joining the Watch was quite a good choice of career. The pay wasn't bad, there was a worthwhile pension, there was a wonderful medical scheme if you had the nerve to submit to Igor's ministrations in the cellar and, after a year or so, an Ankh-Morpork trained copper could leave the city and get a job in the Watches of the other cities on the plain with instant promotion. That was happening all the time. Sammies, they were called, even in towns that had never heard of Sam Vimes. He was just a little proud of that. 'Sammies' meant watchmen who could think without their lips moving, who didn't take bribes – much, and then only at the level of beer and doughnuts, which even Vimes recognized as the grease that helps the wheels run smoothly – and were, on the whole, trustworthy. For a given value of 'trust', at least.

The sound of running feet indicated that Sergeant Detritus was bringing some of the latest trainees back from their morning run. He could hear the jody Detritus had taught them. Somehow, you could tell it was made up by a troll:

> 'Now we sing dis stupid song!
> Sing it as we run along!
> Why we sing dis we don't know!
> We can't make der words rhyme prop'ly!'

'Sound off!'
                    'One! Two!'
'Sound off!'
                    'Many! Lots!'
'Sound off!'
                    'Er . . . what?'

It still irked Vimes that the little training school in the old lemonade factory was turning out so many coppers who quit the city the moment their probation was up. But it had its advantages. There were Sammies almost as far as Uberwald now, all speeding up the local promotion ladder. It helped, knowing names, and knowing that those names had been taught to salute him. The ebb and flow of politics often meant that the local rulers weren't talking to one another, but via the semaphore towers, the Sammies talked *all the time*.

He realized he was humming a different song under his breath. It was a tune he'd forgotten for years. It went with the lilac, scent and song together. He stopped, feeling guilty.

He was finishing the letter when there was a knock at the door.

'Nearly done!' he shouted.

'It'th me, thur,' said Constable Igor, pushing his head round the door, and then he added, 'Igor, sir.'

'Yes, Igor?' said Vimes, wondering not for the first time why anyone with stitches all round his head needed to tell anyone who he was.*

'I would just like to thay, sir, that I could have got young Thtronginthearm back on his feet, thur,' said Igor, a shade reproachfully.

---

* The Igor employed by the Watch as forensic specialist and medical aide was quite young (in so far as you could tell with an Igor, since useful limbs and other organs were passed on among Igors as others might hand on a pocket watch) and very modern in his thinking. He had a DA haircut with extended quiff, wore crêpe soles and sometimes forgot to lisp.

Vimes sighed. Igor's face was full of concern, tinged with disappointment. He had been prevented from plying his . . . craft. He was naturally disappointed.

'We've been through this, Igor. It's not like sewing a leg back on. And dwarfs are dead set against that sort of thing.'

'There's nothing thupernatural about it, thur. I am a man of Natural Philothophy! And he was still warm when they brought him in—'

'Those are the rules, Igor. Thanks all the same. We know your heart is in the right place—'

'*They* are in the right *places*, sir,' said Igor reproachfully.

'That's what I meant,' Vimes said, without missing a beat, just as Igor never did.

'Oh, very well, sir,' said Igor, giving up. He paused, and then said: 'How is her ladyship, sir?'

Vimes had been expecting this. It was a terrible thing for a mind to do, but his had already presented him with the idea of Igor and Sybil in the same sentence. Not that he disliked Igor. Quite the reverse. There were watchmen walking around the streets right now who wouldn't have legs if it wasn't for Igor's genius with a needle. But—

'Fine. She's fine,' he said abruptly.

'Only I heard that Mrs Content was a bit worr—'

'Igor, there are some areas where . . . Look, do you know *anything* about . . . women and babies?'

'Not in so many wordth, sir, but I find that once I've got someone on the slab and had a good, you know, rummage around, I can thort out most thingth—'

Vimes's imagination actually shut down at this point.

'Thank you, Igor,' he managed, without his voice trembling, 'but Mrs Content is a very experienced midwife.'

'Jutht as you say, sir,' said Igor, but doubt rode on the words.

'And now I've got to go,' said Vimes. 'It's going to be a long day.'

He ran down the stairs, tossed the letter to Sergeant Colon, nodded to Carrot and they set off at a fast walk for the palace.

After the door had shut one of the watchmen looked up from the desk where he'd been wrestling with a report and the effort of writing down, as policemen do, what ought to have happened.

'Sarge?'

'Yes, Corporal Ping?'

'Why're some of you wearing purple flowers, sarge?'

There was a subtle change in the atmosphere, a suction of sound caused by many pairs of ears listening intently. All the officers in the room had stopped writing.

'I mean, I saw you and Reg and Nobby wearing 'em this time last year, and I wondered if we were all supposed to . . .' Ping faltered. Sergeant Colon's normally amiable eyes had narrowed and the message they were sending was: you're on thin ice, lad, and it's starting to creak . . .

'I mean, my landlady's got a garden and I could easily go and cut a—' Ping went on, in an uncharacteristic attempt at suicide.

'You'd wear the lilac today, would you?' said Colon quietly.

'I just meant that if you wanted me to I could go and—'

'Were *you* there?' said Colon, getting to his feet so fast that his chair fell over.

'Steady, Fred,' murmured Nobby.

'I didn't mean—' Ping began. 'I mean . . . was I where, sarge?'

Colon leaned on the desk, bringing his round red face an inch away from Ping's nose. 'If you don't know where *there* was, you weren't there,' he said, in the same quiet voice. He stood up straight again. 'Now me an' Nobby has got a job to do,' he said. 'At ease, Ping. We are going *out*.'

'Er . . .'

This was not being a good day for Corporal Ping.

'*Yes?*' said Colon.

'Er . . . standing orders, sarge . . . you're the ranking officer, you see, and I'm orderly officer for the day, I wouldn't ask otherwise but . . . if you're going out, sarge, you've got to tell me where you're going. Just in case anyone has to contact you, see? I got to write it down in the book. In pen and everything,' he added.

'You know what day it is, Ping?' said Colon.

'Er . . . twenty-fifth of May, sarge.'

'And you know what that means, Ping?'

'Er . . .'

'It means,' said Nobby, 'that anyone important enough to ask where we're going—'

'—knows where we've gone,' said Fred Colon.

The door slammed behind them.

The cemetery of Small Gods was for the people who didn't know what happened next. They didn't know what they believed in or if there was life after death and, often, they didn't know what hit them. They'd gone through life being amiably uncertain, until the ultimate certainty had claimed them at the last. Among the city's bone orchards the cemetery was the equivalent of the drawer marked Misc, where people were interred in the glorious expectation of nothing very much.

Most of the Watch got buried there. Policemen, after a few years, found it hard enough to believe in people, let alone anyone they couldn't see.

For once, it wasn't raining. The breeze shook the sooty poplars around the wall, making them rustle.

'We ought to have brought some flowers,' said Colon, as they made their way through the long grass.

'I could nick a few off some of the fresh graves, sarge,' Nobby volunteered.

'Not the kind of thing I want to hear you saying at this time, Nobby,' said Colon severely.

'Sorry, sarge.'

'At a time like this a man ought to be thinking of his immortal soul viz ah viz the endless mighty river that is History. I should do that, if I was you, Nobby.'

20

'Right, sarge. Will do. I see someone's doing it already, sarge.'

Up against one wall, lilac trees were growing. That is, at some point in the past a lilac had been planted there, and had given rise, as lilac will, to hundreds of whippy suckers, so that what had once been one stem was now a thicket. Every branch was covered in pale mauve blooms.

The graves were still just visible in the tangled vegetation. In front of them stood Cut-Me-Own-Throat Dibbler, Ankh-Morpork's least successful businessman, with a sprig of lilac in his hat.

He caught sight of the watchmen and nodded to them. They nodded back. All three stood looking down at the seven graves. Only one had been maintained. The marble headstone on that one was shiny and moss-free, the turf was clipped, the stone border was sparkling.

Moss had grown over the wooden markers of the other six, but it had been scraped off the central one, revealing the name:

JOHN KEEL

And carved underneath, by someone who had taken some pains, was:

How Do They Rise Up

A huge wreath of lilac flowers, bound with purple ribbon, had been placed on the grave. On top of it, tied round with another piece of purple ribbon, was an egg.

'Mrs Palm and Mrs Battye and some of the girls were up here earlier,' said Dibbler. 'And of course Madam always makes sure there's the egg.'

'It's nice, the way they always remember,' said Sergeant Colon.

The three stood in silence. They were not, on the whole, men with a vocabulary designed for times like this. After a while, though, Nobby felt moved to speak.

'He gave me a spoon once,' he said, to the air in general.

'Yeah, I know,' said Colon.

'My dad pinched it off me when he come out of prison, but it was my spoon,' said Nobby persistently. 'That means a lot to a kid, your own spoon.'

'Come to that, he was the first person to make me a sergeant,' said Colon. 'Got busted again, of course, but I knew I could do it again then. He was a good copper.'

'He bought a pie off me, first week I was starting out,' said Dibbler. 'Ate it *all*. Didn't spit out *anything*.'

There was more silence.

After a while Sergeant Colon cleared his throat, a general signal to indicate that some sort of appropriate moment was now over. There was a general relaxation of muscles.

'Y'know, we ought to come up here one day with a billhook and clear this lot up a bit,' said the sergeant.

'You always say that, sarge, every year,' said Nobby as they walked away. 'And we never do.'

'If I had a dollar for every copper's funeral I've attended up here,' said Colon, 'I'd have . . . nineteen dollars and fifty pence.'

'Fifty pence?' said Nobby.

'That was when Corporal Hildebiddle woke up just in time and banged on the lid,' said Colon. 'Before your time, o'course. Everyone said it was an amazin' recovery.'

'*Mr Sergeant?*'

The three men turned. Coming towards them in a high-speed sidle was the black-clad, skinny figure of Legitimate First, the cemetery's resident gravedigger.

Colon sighed. 'Yes, Leggie?' he said.

'Good morrow, sweet—' the gravedigger began, but Sergeant Colon waved a finger at him.

'Stop that right now,' he said. 'You know you've been warned before. None of that "comic gravedigger" stuff. It's not funny and it's not clever. Just say what you've got to say. No silly bits.'

Leggie looked crestfallen. 'Well, good sirs—'

'Leggie, I've known you for years,' said Colon wearily. 'Just *try*, will you?'

22

'The deacon wants them graves dug up, Fred,' said Leggie in a sulky voice. 'It's been more'n thirty years. Long past time they was in the crypts—'

'No,' said Fred Colon.

'But I've got a nice shelf for 'em down there, Fred,' Leggie pleaded. 'Right up near the front. We need the *space*, Fred! It's standing room only in here, and that's the truth! Even the worms have to go in single file! Right up near the front, Fred, where I can chat to 'em when I'm having my tea. How about that?'

The watchmen and Dibbler shared a glance. Most people in the city had been into Leggie's crypts, if only for a dare. And it had come as a shock to most of them to realize that solemn burial was not for eternity but only for a handful of years so that, in Leggie's words, 'my little wriggly helpers' could do their work. After that, the *last* last resting place was the crypts, and an entry in the huge ledgers.

Leggie lived down there in the crypts. As he said, he was the only one who did, and he liked the company.

Leggie was generally considered weird, but conscientiously so.

'This isn't your idea, right?' said Fred Colon.

Leggie looked down at his feet. 'The new deacon's a bit, well, new,' he said. 'You know . . . keen. Making changes.'

'You told him *why* they're not being dug up?' said Nobby.

'He said that's just ancient history,' said Leggie. 'He says we all have to put the past behind us.'

'An' did you tell him he should take it up with Vetinari?' said Nobby.

'Yes, and he said he was sure his lordship was a forward-thinking man who wouldn't cling to relics of the past,' said Leggie.

'Sounds like he *is* new,' said Dibbler.

'Yeah,' said Nobby. 'An' not likely to get old. It's okay, Leggie, you can say you've asked us.'

The gravedigger looked relieved. 'Thanks, Nobby,' he said.

'And I'd just like to say that when your time comes, gents, you'll be on a good shelf with a view. I've put your names down in my ledger for them as comes after me.'

'Well, that's, er, very kind of you, Leggie,' said Colon, wondering if it was. Because of pressure of space, bones in the crypt were stored by size, not by owner. There were rooms of ribs. There were avenues of femurs. And shelf after shelf of skulls up near the entrance, of course, because a crypt without a lot of skulls wasn't a proper crypt at all. If some of the religions were right and there really was bodily resurrection one day, Fred mused, there was going to be an awful lot of confusion and general milling about.

'I've got just the spot—' Leggie began, and then stopped. He pointed angrily towards the entrance. 'You *know* what I said about him coming up here!'

They turned. Corporal Reg Shoe, a whole bouquet of lilac tied to his helmet, was walking solemnly up the gravel path. He had a long-handled shovel over his shoulder.

'It's only Reg,' said Fred. 'He's got a right to be here, Leggie. You know that.'

'He's a dead man! I'm not havin' a dead man in my cemetery!'

'It's full of 'em, Leggie,' said Dibbler, trying to calm the man down.

'Yeah, but the rest of 'em don't walk in and out!'

'Come on, Leggie, you act like this every year,' said Fred Colon. 'He can't help the way he was killed. Just because you're a zombie doesn't mean you're a bad person. He's a useful lad, Reg. Plus it'd be a lot neater up here if everyone looked after their plots like he does. 'morning, Reg.'

Reg Shoe, grey-faced but smiling, nodded at the four of them and strolled on.

'And bringing his own shovel, too,' muttered Leggie. 'It's disgusting!'

'I've always thought it was rather, you know, nice of him to do what he does,' said Fred. 'You let him alone, Leggie. If you start throwing stones at him like you did the year before last Commander Vimes'll get to hear about it and there'll be trouble. Be told. You're a good man with a, a—'

'—cadaver,' said Nobby.

'—but . . . well, Leggie, you weren't there,' said Colon. 'That's the start and finish of it. Reg was. That's all there is to it, Leggie. If you weren't there, you don't understand. Now you just run along and count the skulls again, I know you like that. Cheerio, Leggie.'

Legitimate First watched them go as they walked away. Sergeant Colon felt he was being measured up.

'I've always wondered about his name,' said Nobby, turning and waving. 'I mean . . . Legitimate?'

'Can't blame a mother for being proud, Nobby,' said Colon.

'What else should I know today?' said Vimes, as he and Carrot shouldered their way through the streets.

'We've had a letter from the Black Ribboners*, sir, suggesting that it would be a great step forward for species harmony in the city if you'd see your way clear to—'

'They want a vampire in the Watch?'

'Yes, sir. I believe many members of the Watch Committee think that despite your stated reservations it would be a good—'

'Does it look to you as if my body is dead?'

'No, sir.'

'Then the answer's no. What else?'

Carrot riffled through a stuffed clipboard as he half ran to keep up. 'The *Times* says Borogravia has invaded Mouldavia,' he announced.

'Is that good? I can't remember where it is.'

'Both formerly part of the Dark Empire, sir. Right next door to Uberwald.'

* The Uberwald League of Temperance, made up of former vampires who now wore black ribbons to show that they had completely sworn off the sticky stuff, my vord yes, and much preferred a good singsong and a healthy game of table-tennis.

'Whose side are we on?'

'The *Times* said we should be supporting little Mouldavia against the aggressor, sir.'

'I like Borogravia already,' snapped Vimes. The *Times* had printed, in his opinion, a particularly unflattering cartoon of him the previous week, and to make matters worse Sybil had requested the original and had had it framed. 'And what does this all mean to us?'

'Probably more refugees, sir.'

'Ye gods, we've got no more room! Why do they keep coming here?'

'In search of a better life, sir, I think.'

'A *better* life?' said Vimes. '*Here?*'

'I think things are worse where they come from, sir,' said Carrot.

'What kind of refugees are we talking about here?'

'Mostly human, sir.'

'Do you mean that most of them will be human, or that each individual will be *mostly* human?' said Vimes. After a while in Ankh-Morpork, you learned how to phrase that kind of question.

'Er, apart from humans the only species I've heard of there in any numbers are the kvetch, sir. They live in the deep woods and are covered in hair.'

'Really? Well, we'll probably find out more about them when we're asked to employ one in the Watch,' said Vimes sourly. 'What else?'

'Rather hopeful news, sir,' said Carrot, smiling. 'You know the Hooms? The street gang?'

'What about them?'

'They've initiated their first troll member.'

'What? I thought they went around beating up trolls! I thought that was the whole *point*!'

'Well, apparently young Calcite likes beating up trolls, too.'

'And that's good?'

'In a way, sir, I suppose it's a step forward.'

'United in hatred, you mean?'

'I suppose so, sir,' said Carrot. He flicked papers back and forth on his clipboard. 'Now, what else have I got? Oh, yes, the river patrol boat has sunk again—'

Where did I go wrong? thought Vimes as the litany went on. I was a copper once. A real copper. I chased people. I was a hunter. It was what I did best. I knew where I was anywhere in the city by the feel of the street under my boots. And now look at me! A Duke! Commander of the Watch! A political animal! I have to know about who's fighting who a thousand miles away, just in case that's going to mean riots here!

When did I last go on patrol? Last week? Last month? And it's never a proper point patrol, 'cos the sergeants make damn sure everyone knows I've left the building and every damn constable reeks of armour polish and has had a shave by the time I get there, even if I nip down the back streets (and that thought, at least, was freighted with a little pride, because it showed he didn't employ *stupid* sergeants). I never stand all night in the rain, or fight for my life rolling in the gutter with some thug, and I never move above a walk. That's all been taken away. And for what?

Comfort, power, money and a wonderful wife . . .

. . . er . . .

. . . which was a *good* thing, *of course*, but . . . even so . . .

Damn. But I'm not a copper any more, I'm a, a manager. I have to talk to the damn committee as if they're children. I go to receptions and wear damn stupid toy armour. It's all politics and paperwork. It's all got *too big*.

What has happened to the days when it was all so simple?

Faded like the lilac, he thought.

They entered the palace and went up the main stairs to the Oblong Office.

The Patrician of Ankh-Morpork was standing looking out of the window when they entered. The room was otherwise deserted.

'Ah, Vimes,' he said, without turning round. 'I thought you might be late. In the circumstances, I dismissed the committee. They were sorry, as indeed was I, to hear about Stronginthearm. No doubt you have been writing the official letter.'

Vimes flashed a questioning expression at Carrot, who rolled his eyes and shrugged. Vetinari found things out *very* quickly.

'Yes, that's right,' said Vimes.

'And on such a beautiful day as this, too,' said Vetinari. 'Although there's a storm heading our way, I see.' He turned. He had a sprig of lilac pinned to his robe.

'Lady Sybil is doing well?' he said, sitting down.

'You tell me,' said Vimes.

'Some things can't be hurried, no doubt,' said Vetinari smoothly, shuffling the papers. 'Let me see now, let me see, there were just a few points that I should deal with . . . ah, the regular letter from our religious friends at the Temple of Small Gods.' He carefully removed it from the pile and set it to one side. 'I think I shall invite the new deacon to tea and explain matters to him. Now, where was I . . . ah, the political situation in— Yes?'

The door opened. Drumknott, the chief clerk, came in.

'Message for his grace,' he said, although he handed it to Lord Vetinari. The Patrician passed it, very politely, across the desk. Vimes unfolded it.

'It's off the clacks!' he yelled. 'We've got Carcer cornered in New Hall! I've got to get down there *now*!'

'How exciting,' said Lord Vetinari, standing up suddenly. 'The call to the chase. But is it necessary for you to attend personally, your grace?'

Vimes gave him a grey look. '*Yes*,' he said. 'Because if I don't, y'see, some poor sod who's been trained by me to do the right thing is going to try to *arrest* the bugger.' He turned to Carrot. 'Captain, get on it right now! Clacks, pigeons, runners, whatever. I want *everyone* answering this shout, okay? But no one, I repeat, *no one* is to try to tackle him without a lot of backup! Understood? And get Swires airborne! Oh, *damn* . . .'

'What's wrong, sir?' said Carrot.

'This message is from Littlebottom. She sent it straight here. What's she doing there? She's Forensic. She's not street! She'll do it by the book!'

'Shouldn't she?' said Vetinari.

'No. Carcer needs an arrow in his leg just to get his attention. You shoot first—'

'—and ask questions later?' said Vetinari.

Vimes paused at the door and said, 'There's nothing I want to ask him.'

Vimes had to slow down for breath in Sator Square, and that was disgusting. A few years ago he'd've only really been getting into his stride by now! But the storm rolling over the plains was driving the heat before it, and it wouldn't do for the commander to turn up wheezing. As it was, even after pausing behind a street market stall for a few gulps of air, he doubted if he had enough wind left for a lengthy sentence.

To his tremendous relief, an entirely unwounded Corporal Cheery Littlebottom was waiting by the University walls. She saluted.

'Reporting, sir,' she said.

'Mm,' murmured Vimes.

'I spotted a couple of trolls on traffic duty, sir,' said Cheery, 'so I've sent them round to the Water Bridge. Then Sergeant Detritus turned up and I told— I *advised* him to go into the University via main gate and get up high. Sergeant Colon and Nobby arrived and I sent them along to the Bridge of Size—'

'Why?' said Vimes.

'Because I doubt if he's really going to try going that way,' said Cheery, her face a very careful picture of innocence. Vimes had to stop himself from nodding. 'And then as more people come along I'm putting them around the perimeter. But I think he's gone up and he's staying high.'

'Why?'

'Because how's he going to fight his way out through a lot of wizards, sir? His best chance is to sneak around on the roofs and drop down somewhere quiet. There's a lot of hiding places and he can get all the way to Peach Pie Street without coming down.'

Forensic, thought Vimes. Hah. And with any luck he doesn't know about Buggy.

'Well thought out,' he said.

'Thank you, sir. Would you mind standing a bit closer to this wall, sir?'

'What for?'

Something shattered on the cobbles. Vimes was suddenly flat against the wall.

'He's got a crossbow, sir,' said Cheery. 'We think he stole it from Stronginthearm. But he's not very good with it.'

'Well done, corporal,' said Vimes weakly. 'Good job.' He glanced around the square behind him. The wind was whipping at the awnings of the market stalls and the traders, with occasional looks at the sky, were covering their wares.

'But we can't just let him hang around up there,' he went on. 'He'll start taking pot shots and he's bound to hit *someone*.'

'Why would he do that, sir?'

'Carcer doesn't need a reason,' said Vimes. 'He just needs an excuse.' A movement far above caught his eye, and he grinned.

A large bird was gaining height over the city.

The heron, mumbling complaints, fought for altitude in big, sweeping circles. The city whirled around Corporal Buggy Swires as he gripped even harder with his knees, and then he swung the bird downwind and it landed with a staggering run on the top of the Tower of Art, the highest building in the city.

With a practised movement the gnome sliced through the string holding the portable semaphore in place, and leapt down after it into the compost of ivy leaves and old ravens' nests that carpeted the top of the tower.

The heron watched him with round-eyed stupidity. Buggy had tamed it in the usual gnome way; you painted yourself green like a frog and hung out in the marshes, croaking, and then when a heron tried to eat you, you ran up its beak and nutted it. By the time it came round you'd blown the special oil – that had taken all day to make, and the stink of it had emptied the Watch House – up its nostrils and it took one look at you and thought you were its mum.

A heron was useful. It could carry equipment. But Buggy preferred a sparrowhawk for traffic patrol. It was better for hovering.

He slotted the portable semaphore arms on to the post he'd secretly installed weeks ago. Then he unshipped a tiny telescope from the heron's saddlebags and strapped it on to the edge of the stone, looking almost straight down. Buggy liked moments like this. It was the only time that everyone else was smaller than him.

'Now . . . let's see what we can see,' he muttered.

There were the University buildings. There was the clock tower of Old Tom, and the unmistakable bulk of Sergeant Detritus climbing among the nearby chimneys. The yellow light of the gathering storm glinted off the helmets of watchmen who were hurrying through the streets. And there, creeping along behind the parapet . . .

'Gotcha,' he said quietly, and reached for the handles of the semaphore.

'D . . . T . . . R . . . T . . . S space H . . . D . . . N . . . G space O . . . L space T . . . M,' said Cheery.

Vimes nodded. Detritus was on the roof near the tower of Old Tom. And Detritus carried a siege crossbow that three men couldn't lift, and had converted it to fire a thick sheaf of arrows all at once. Mostly they shattered in the air because of the forces involved and the target was hit by an expanding cloud of burning splinters. Vimes had banned him from using it on people, but it was a damn good way of getting into buildings. It could open the front door and the back door at the same time.

'Tell him to fire a warning shot,' he said. 'If he hits Carcer with that thing we won't even find a corpse.' Though I'd quite like to find a corpse, he added to himself.

'Yes, sir.' Cheery pulled a couple of white-painted paddles out of her belt, sighted on the top of the tower, and sent a brief signal. There was an answering signal from the distant Buggy.

'D . . . T . . . R . . . T . . . S space W . . . R . . . N . . . G space S . . . H . . . T,' Cheery muttered to herself, as she waved the rest of the message.

There was another answering dip from above. A moment later a red flare shot up from the top of the tower and exploded. It was an efficient way of getting everyone to pay attention. Then Vimes saw the message relayed.

Around the University buildings, watchmen who'd also seen the order ducked into doorways. They knew about the bow.

There were a few seconds for the troll to work out the spelling, a distant heavy thud, a sound like a swarm of hellish bees, and then a crash of tiles and masonry. Pieces of tile rained down into the square. An entire chimney, still with a wisp of smoke coming from it, smashed down a few yards from where Vimes was standing.

Then there was the patter of dust and small bits of wood, and a gentle shower of pigeon feathers.

Vimes shook some flakes of mortar off his helmet. 'Yes, well, I think he's been warned,' he said.

Half a weathercock landed next to the chimney.

Cheery blew some feathers off her telescope and sighted on the top of the tower again. 'Buggy says he's stopped moving, sir,' she reported.

'Really? You surprise me.' Vimes adjusted his belt. 'And now you can give me your crossbow. I'm going up.'

'Sir, you said no one was to try to arrest him! That's why I sent the signal to you!'

'That's right. *I'm* going to arrest him. Right now. While he's counting all his bits to check that he's still got 'em. Tell Detritus what I'm doing, 'cos I don't want to end up as 160lbs of cocktail delicacies. No, don't keep opening your mouth like that. By the time we've sorted out backup and armour and got everyone lined up he'll have dug in somewhere else.'

The last words were delivered at a run.

Vimes reached a door and darted inside. New Hall was student accommodation, but it was still only half past ten so most of them would be in bed. A few faces looked around doors as Vimes trotted along the corridor and reached the stairwell at the far end. That took him – walking now, and rather less sure of his future – to the top floor. Let's see, he'd been here before . . . yes, there was a door ajar, and a glimpse of mops and buckets suggested that this was a janitor's cupboard.

With, at the far end, a ladder leading up to the roof.

Vimes carefully cocked the crossbow.

So Carcer had a Watch crossbow, too. They were good classic single-shot models, but they took a while to reload. If he fired at Vimes and missed, then that was the only shot he'd get. After that . . . you couldn't plan.

Vimes climbed the ladder, and the song came back.

'They rise *feet* up, *feet* up, *feet* up . . .' he hissed under his breath.

He stopped just below the edge of the open trapdoor on to the leads. Carcer wouldn't fall for the old 'helmet on stick' trick, not with only one shot available. He'd just have to risk it.

Vimes thrust his head up, turned it quickly, ducked out of sight for a moment and then came through the opening in a rush. He rolled clumsily when he hit the leads, and rose into a crouch. There was no one else there. He was still alive. He breathed out.

A sloping, gabled roof rose up beside him. Vimes crept along,

33

wedged himself against a chimneystack peppered with splinters of wood, and glanced up at the tower.

The sky above it was livid blue-black. Storms picked up a lot of personality as they rolled across the plains, and this one looked like a record breaker. But brilliant sunlight picked out the Tower of Art and, at the top, the tiny dots of Buggy's frantic signal . . .

O . . . O . . . O

Officer In Trouble. A brother is hurtin'.

Vimes spun around. There was no one creeping up on him. He eased himself around the chimneys and there, tucked between another couple of stacks and out of sight of everyone except Vimes and the celestial Buggy, was Carcer.

He was taking aim.

Vimes turned his head to spot the target.

Fifty yards away, Carrot was picking his way across the top of the University's High Energy Magic building.

The bloody fool was never any good at concealment. Oh, he ducked and crept, and against all logic that made him more noticeable. He didn't understand the art of thinking himself invisible. And there he was, furtively shlepping through the debris on the roof and looking as visible as a big duck in a small bathtub. And he'd come up without backup.

The fool . . .

Carcer was aiming carefully. The roof of the HEM was a maze of abandoned equipment and Carrot was moving along behind the raised platform that held the huge bronze spheres known throughout the city as The Wizards' Balls, which discharged surplus magic if – or more usually when – experiments in the hall below fouled up. Carrot, screened by all that, was not making such a good target.

Vimes raised his crossbow.

Thunder . . . rolled. It was the roll of a giant iron cube down the stairways of the gods, a crackling, thudding crash that tore the sky in half and shook the building.

Carcer glanced up, and saw Vimes.

'Wotcha doin', mifter?'

Buggy didn't budge from the telescope. A crowbar wouldn't have separated him at this point.

'Shut up, ye daft corbies!' he muttered.

Both men below had fired, and both men had missed because they were trying to fire and dodge at the same time.

Something hard prodded Buggy's shoulder.

'Wot's *happ'nin'*, mifter?' said the insistent voice.

He turned. There were a dozen bedraggled ravens behind him, looking like old men in ill-fitting black cloaks. They were Tower of Art birds. Hundreds of generations of living in a highly charged magical environment had raised the intelligence level of what had been bright creatures to begin with. But, although the ravens were intelligent, these ones weren't hugely clever. They just had a more persistent kind of stupidity, as befitted birds for whom the exciting panorama of the city below was a kind of daytime TV.

'Push *off*!' shouted Buggy, and turned back to the telescope. There was Carcer, running, and Vimes running after him, and *here came the hail* . . .

It turned the world white. It thudded around him and made his helmet ring. Hailstones as big as his head bounced on the stone and hit Buggy from underneath. Cursing, and shielding his face with his arms, and hammered all the time by shattering crystal balls, each one predicting a future of pain, he skidded and slid across the rolling ice. He reached an ivy-hung arch between two lesser turrets, where the heron had already taken refuge, and fell inside. Frozen shrapnel still ricocheted in and stung him, but at least he could see and breathe.

A beak prodded him sharply in the back.

'Wot's happ'nin' now, mifter?'

Carcer landed heavily on the arch between the student hall and the main buildings, almost lost his footing on the tiles, and hesitated. An arrow from a watchman below grazed his leg.

Vimes dropped down behind him, just as the hail hit.

Cursing and slipping, one man followed the other across the arch. Carcer reached a mass of ivy that led up on to the roof of the Library and scrambled up it, scattering ice below.

Vimes grabbed the ivy just as Carcer disappeared on to the flat roof. He looked round at a crash behind him, and saw Carrot trying to make his way along the wall from the High Energy Magic building. The hail was forming a halo of ice fragments around him.

'Stay there!' Vimes bellowed.

Carrot's reply was lost in the noise.

Vimes waved his arms and then grabbed at the ivy as a foot slipped. 'Bloody stay *there*!' he yelled. 'That is an *order*! You'll go over!'

He turned and started up the wet, cold vines.

The wind dropped, and the last few hailstones bounced off the roof.

Vimes stopped a few feet from the top of the ivy, worked his feet firmly into footholds in the ancient, knotted stems, and reached up for a decent hold.

Then he thrust himself up, left hand ready, caught the boot that swung towards him and carried on rising, pushing Carcer off balance. The man sprawled backwards onthe slippery hail, tried to get to his feet, and slipped again. Vimes tugged himself on to the roof, stepped forward, and found his legs skidding away beneath him. Both he and Carcer got up, tried to move, and fell over again.

From a prone position the man landed a kick on Vimes's shoulder, sending both of them sliding away in opposite directions, and then turned over and scuttled on all fours around the Library's big glass and metal dome. He grabbed the rusty frame, hauled himself upright, and pulled out a knife.

'Come and get me, then,' he said. There was another roll of thunder.

'I don't have to,' said Vimes. 'I just have to wait.' At least until I get my breath back, he thought.

'Why're you picking on me? What'm I supposed to have done?'

'Couple of murders ring a bell?' said Vimes.

If injured innocence was money, Carcer's face was his fortune. 'I don't know anything about—'

'I'm not up here to play games, Carcer. Knock it off.'

'You going to take me alive, your grace?'

'You know, I don't want to. But people think it's neater all round if I do.'

There was a clattering of tiles away on the left, and a thud as a huge siege bow was rested on the ridge of a nearby roof. The head of Detritus rose behind it.

'Sorry about dat, Mister Vimes, hard to climb up in dat hail. Jus' stand back.'

'You're going to let it *shoot* me?' said Carcer. He tossed the knife away. 'An unarmed man?'

'Trying to escape,' said Vimes. But this was starting to go bad. He could feel it.

'Me? I'm just standing here, haha.'

And there it was. That bloody laugh, on top of that damn grin. It was never far away. 'Haha' didn't come close to doing it the injustice it deserved. It was more a sort of modulation to the voice, an irritatingly patronizing chortle that suggested that all this was somehow *funny* and you hadn't got the joke.

Trouble was, you couldn't shoot someone for having an annoying laugh. And he *was* just standing there. If he ran, you could shoot him. Admittedly, it would be Detritus doing the shooting, and while with that bow it was *technically* possible to shoot to wound, the people you were wounding would probably be in the building next door.

But Carcer was just waiting there, insulting the world by his existence.

In fact he wasn't merely standing there now. In one movement he'd swung himself on to the lower slopes of the Library's dome. The glass panes – at least, the glass panes that had survived the freak hail – creaked in the iron framework.

'Stop right there!' Vimes bellowed. 'And come down!'

'Now *where* could I go?' said Carcer, grinning at him. 'I'm just waiting for you to arrest me, right? Hey, I can see your house from up here!'

What's under the dome? thought Vimes. How high are the bookcases? There's other floors in the Library, aren't there? Like galleries? But you can definitely look up at the dome from the ground floor, right? If you were careful, could you swing on to a gallery from the edge of the dome? It'd be risky, but if a man knew he was going to swing *anyway* . . .

Picking his way with care, he reached the edge of the dome. Carcer climbed up a little further.

'I warn you, Carcer—'

'Only high spirits, Mister Grace, haha! Can't blame a man for trying to enjoy his last few minutes of freedom, can you?'

I can see your house from up here . . .

Vimes hauled himself on to the dome. Carcer cheered.

'Well done, your Vimes!' he said, easing himself towards the top.

'Don't mess me about, Carcer. It'll go badly for you!'

'Badder than it's going to go anyway?' Carcer glanced down through a smashed pane. 'Long way down, Mister Vimes. I reckon a man'd die instantly falling all that way, wouldn't he?'

Vimes glanced down, and Carcer leapt.

It didn't go the way he'd planned. Vimes had been tensed for something like this. After a complicated moment, Carcer was lying on the iron latticework, one arm under him, the other outflung and being banged heavily on the metal by Vimes. The knife it had held skidded away down the dome.

'Gods, you must think I'm stupid,' Vimes growled. 'You

wouldn't throw away a knife, Carcer, if you didn't have another one!'

Vimes's face was close to the man's now, close enough to look into the eyes above that chirpy grin and watch the demons waving.

'You're hurting me, and that's not allowed!'

'Oh, I wouldn't want anything to happen to *you*, Carcer,' said Vimes. 'I want to see you in front of his lordship. I just want to hear you *admit* something for once. I just want to see that bloody cheeky grin wiped off your face. Sergeant Detritus!'

'Sah!' shouted the troll, from his distant ridge.

'Make a signal. I want people up here now. Me and Carcer are just going to stay nice and quiet here, so's he doesn't try any tricks.'

'Right, sir.' With another distant clatter of doomed tiles, the troll disappeared from view.

'You shouldn't have sent Captain Carrot away,' muttered Carcer. 'He doesn't like watchmen bullying innocent civilians—'

'It is true that he has yet to master some of the finer details of *de facto* street policing,' said Vimes, maintaining his grip. 'Anyway, I'm not hurting you, I'm protecting you. Wouldn't like you to fall all that way.'

Thunder rumbled again. The sky wasn't just storm-black now. There were pinks and purples in the clouds, as though they were bruised. Vimes could see the clouds moving like snakes in a sack, to an endless sullen rumbling. He wondered if the wizards had been messing about with the weather.

Something was happening to the air. It tasted of burned metal and flints. A weathercock on top of the dome began to spin round and round.

'I didn't think you was stupid, Mister Vimes . . .'

'What?' said Vimes, looking down suddenly. Carcer was smiling cheerfully.

'I said I didn't think you was stupid, Mister Vimes. I know a clever copper like you'd think I'd got two knives.'

'Yeah, right,' said Vimes. He could feel his hair trying to stand on end. Little blue caterpillars of light were crackling over the ironwork of the dome, and even over his armour.

'Mister Vimes?'

'*What?*' Vimes snapped. Smoke was rising from the weather-cock's bearings.

'I got three knives, Mister Vimes,' said Carcer, bringing his arm up.

The lightning struck.

Windows blew out and iron gutters melted. Roofs lifted into the air and settled again. Buildings shook.

But this storm had been blowing in from far across the plains, pushing the natural background magic ahead of it. It dumped it now, all in one go.

They said afterwards that the bolt of lightning hit a clock-maker's shop in the Street of Cunning Artificers, stopping all the clocks at that instant. But that was nothing. In Baker Street a couple who had never met before became electrically attracted to one another and were forced to get married after two days for the sake of public decency. In the Assassins' Guild, the chief armourer became hugely, and since he was in the armoury at the time, *tragically* attractive to metal. Eggs fried in their baskets, apples roasted on the greengrocers' shelves. Candles lit them-selves. Cartwheels exploded. And the ornate tin bath of the Archchancellor of Unseen University was lifted neatly off the floor, sizzled across his study and then flew off the balcony and on to the lawn in the octangle several storeys below, without spilling more than a cupful of suds.

Archchancellor Mustrum Ridcully paused with his long-handled scrubbing brush hovering halfway down his back, and stared around.

Tiles smashed to the ground. Water boiled in the ornamental fountain near by.

Ridcully ducked as a stuffed badger, the origin of which was never ascertained, flew across the lawn and smashed through a window.

He winced as he was hit by a brief and inexplicable shower of small cogwheels, which pattered down all around him.

He stared as half a dozen watchmen dashed into the octangle and headed up the steps to the Library.

Then, gripping the sides of the bath, the Archchancellor stood up. Foaming water cascaded off him, as it would off some ancient leviathan erupting from the abyssal sea.

'Mister Stibbons!' he bellowed, his voice bouncing off the imposing walls, 'Where the   is my   *hat*?'

He sat down again and waited.

There were a few minutes of silence and then Ponder Stibbons, Head of Inadvisably Applied Magic and Praelector of Unseen University, came running out of the main door carrying Ridcully's pointy hat.

The Archchancellor snatched at it and rammed it on his head.

'Very well,' he said, standing up again. 'Now, will   care to tell m   at the   is going on? And why   Old Tom   ing repeatedly?'

'   been a   of magic, sir! I   someone up   the mechanism!' Ponder shouted, above the sound-destroying silences.*

There was a dying metallic noise from the big clock tower. Ponder and Ridcully waited a few moments, but the city stayed full of normal noise, like the collapse of masonry and distant screams.

'Right,' said Ridcully, as if grudgingly awarding the world a mark for trying. 'What was that all about, Stibbons? And why are there policemen in the Library?'

'Big magical storm, sir. Several thousand gigathaums. I believe the Watch is chasing a criminal.'

* Old Tom, the University's venerable clock, tolled not sounds but silences. They were not simply ordinary silences, but intervals of noise-absorbing non-sound that filled the world with loud soundlessness.

41

'Well, they can't just run in here without askin',' said Ridcully, stepping out of the bath and striding forward. 'What do we pay our taxes for, after all?'

'Er, we don't actually pay taxes, sir,' said Ponder, running after him. 'The system is that we promise to pay taxes if the city ever asks us to, provided the city promises never to ask us, sir. We make a voluntary—'

'Well, at least we have an *arrangement*, Stibbons.'

'Yes, sir. May I point out that you—'

'And that means they have to ask *permission*. The essential decencies must be maintained,' said Ridcully firmly. 'And I am the Master of this college!'

'On the subject of, er, decencies, sir, you are not in fact wearing—'

Ridcully strode through the open doors of the Library.

'What is going on here?' he demanded.

The watchmen turned, and stared. A large blob of foam, which up until that point had been performing sterling service in the cause of the essential decencies, slipped slowly to the floor.

'Well?' he snapped. 'Haven't you lot seen a wizard before?'

A watchman snapped to attention and saluted. 'Captain Carrot, sir. We've, er, never seen so *much* of a wizard, sir.'

Ridcully gave him the slow blank stare used by those with acute uptake-grasping deficiency.

'What's he talkin' about, Stibbons?' he said out of the corner of his mouth.

'You're, er, insufficiently dressed, sir.'

'What? I've got my hat on, haven't I?'

'Yes, sir—'

'Hat = wizard, wizard = hat. Everything else is frippery. Anyway, I'm sure we're all men of the world,' Ridcully added, looking around. For the first time he took in other details about the watchmen. 'And dwarfs of the world . . . ah . . . trolls of the world too, I see . . . and . . . women of the world too, I note . . .

42

er . . .' The Archchancellor lapsed into a moment's silence, and then said, 'Mr Stibbons?'

'Yes, sir?'

'Would you be so kind as to run up to my rooms and fetch my robe?'

'Of course, sir.'

'And, in the meantime, please be so good as to lend me *your* hat . . .'

'But you do actually have your hat on, sir,' said Ponder.

'Quite so, quite so,' said Ridcully, slowly and carefully through his fixed grin. 'And now, Mister Stibbons, in addition, right *now*, I wish *you*, in fact, to lend, to *me*, your *hat*, please.'

'Oh,' said Ponder. 'Er . . . yes . . .'

A few minutes later a thoroughly clean and decent and clothed Archchancellor was standing in the very centre of the Library, staring up at the damaged dome, while beside him Ponder Stibbons – who for some reason had elected to continue to remain hatless, even though his hat had been handed back to him – stared glumly at some magical instruments.

'Nothing at all?' said Ridcully.

'Ook,' said the Librarian.*

'You've searched everywhere?'

'He can't search *everywhere* in this library, sir,' said Ponder. 'That would take more time than actually could possibly exist. But all the mundane shelves, certainly. Um.'

Carrot turned to Ponder. 'What was the "um" for, please, sir?'

'You understand that this is a magical library? And that means that even in normal circumstances there is an area of high magical potential above the bookshelves?'

---

* Who was an orangutan, changed from his former human shape as a result of a long-forgotten magical accident. It was so forgotten, in fact, that now people were forgetting he was an orangutan. This might seem quite hard to do, given that even a small orang-utan is quite capable of filling all immediately available space, but to the wizards and most of the citizens he was now just the Librarian, and that was that. In fact, if some-one ever reported that there was an orangutan in the Library, the wizards would probably go and ask the Librarian if he'd seen it.

'I *have* been in here before,' said Carrot.

'Then you know that time with libraries is . . . somewhat more flexible?' said Ponder. 'Given the additional power of the storm, it might just be possible that—'

'Are you going to tell me he's been moved in time?' said the watchman.

Ponder was impressed. He hadn't been brought up to believe that watchmen were clever. However, he took care not to show it.

'Would that it were that simple,' he said. 'However, um, the lightning appears to have added a random lateral component . . .'

'A what?' said Ridcully.

'You mean in time *and* space?' said Carrot. Ponder felt himself getting rattled. Non-wizards shouldn't be that quick.

'Not . . . *exactly*,' he said, and gave up. 'I'm really going to have to work on this, Archchancellor. Some of the readings I'm getting can't possibly be real.'

Vimes knew that he had woken up. There had been darkness and rain and a terrible pain in his face.

Then there had been another flowering of pain on the back of his neck, and a feeling of being pulled this way and that.

And now there was light.

He could see it through his eyelids. His left eyelid, anyway. Nothing but pain was happening on the other side of his face. He kept the eye shut, and strained his hearing instead.

Someone was moving about. There was a clink of metal. A woman's voice said, 'He's awake.'

'Are you sure?' said a man's voice. 'How can you tell?'

'Because I'm good at telling if a man is asleep,' said the woman.

Vimes opened his eye. He was lying on a bench or table of some sort. A young woman was leaning against the wall next to him, and her dress and bearing and the way she leaned filed her immediately in Vimes's policeman brain as: seamstress, but one of the bright ones. The man had a long black robe and silly floppy hat that got filed under: help, I'm in the hands of a *doctor*!

He sat bolt upright.

'You lay one hand on me and I'll thump you!' he yelled, trying to swing his legs off the table. Half his head burst into flame.

'I should take it easy, if I was you,' said the doctor, gently pushing him back. 'That was a very nasty cut. And don't touch the eyepatch!'

'Cut?' said Vimes, his hand brushing the stiff cloth of an eyepatch. Memories interlocked. 'Carcer! Did anyone get him?'

'Whoever attacked you got away,' said the doctor.

'After that fall?' said Vimes. 'He must've been limping, at least! Look, I've got to get—'

And then he noticed all the other things. He'd been picking them up all the time, but only now did his subconscious present the list.

He wasn't wearing his own clothes . . .

'What happened to my uniform?' he said, and he noticed the *I told you so* expression the woman gave the doctor.

'Whoever attacked you stripped you down to your drawers and left you lying in the street,' she said. 'I found you some spare clothes at my place. It's amazing what people leave behind.'

'Who took my armour?'

'I never know names,' said the woman. 'I saw a bunch of men running off carrying stuff, though.'

'Ordinary thieves? Didn't they leave a receipt?'

'No!' she said, laughing. 'Why should they?'

'And are *we* allowed to ask questions?' said the doctor, tidying his tools.

None of this was right . . .

'Well, I mean . . . thank you, yes,' said Vimes.

45

'What's your name?'

Vimes's hand stopped halfway to his face again. 'You mean you don't know me?' he said.

'Should we?' said the doctor.

None of this was *right* . . .

'This is Ankh-Morpork, isn't it?' said Vimes.

'Er, yes,' said the doctor, and turned to the woman. 'There was a blow to the head,' he said, 'but I wouldn't have thought it was *that* bad . . .'

'Look, I'm wasting time,' said the woman. 'Who are you, mister?'

Everyone in the city knew Vimes, surely? The Guild of Seamstresses certainly did. And the doctor didn't look stupid. Perhaps this was not the right time to be totally truthful. He might just be somewhere where being a copper wasn't a good thing to be. It might be dangerous to be Vimes and, right now, he wasn't well enough to deal with it.

'Keel,' he said. The name just dropped into his mind; it had been bubbling under the surface of his thoughts all day, ever since the lilac.

'Yeah, right,' said the woman, smiling. 'Want to make up a first name?'

'John,' said Vimes.

'Appropriate. Well . . . *John*, it's like this. Men lying flat out and naked around here aren't that uncommon. And, it's a funny thing, but they don't usually want anyone to know their real name, or where they live. You won't be the first one Doctor Lawn here has patched up. My name's Rosie. And now there's a little fee, you understand? For both of us.'

'All right, all right, I know how this goes,' said Vimes, holding up his hands. 'This is the Shades, right?' They both nodded. 'Okay, then. Thank you. I haven't got any money, obviously, but once I've got home—'

'I'll escort you, shall I?' said the woman, handing him a badly styled coat and a pair of antique boots. 'I wouldn't like

46

you to be attacked by anything. A sudden loss of memory, for example.'

Vimes snapped, but very gently. His face hurt and there were plenty of other bruises everywhere, and he was dressed in a suit that smelled like a privy. He'd go up the Watch House, get cleaned and changed and make a quick report, and head on home. And this young lady could spend a night in the cells and then be handed over to the Seamstresses' Guild. They came down heavily on extortion like this. It was bad for trade.

'All right,' he said. And pulled the boots on. The soles were made of thin, damp cardboard, and they were too tight.

Dr Lawn waved his hands in a general gesture of dismissal. 'He's all yours, Rosie. You leave that patch on for a few days, Mr Keel, and with any luck you'll have a working eye. Someone took a slash at you with a sharp knife. I've done the best I can and the stitching is good, but you're going to have a nasty scar.'

Vimes raised his hand to his cheek yet again.

'And don't pick at it!' Lawn snapped.

'Come on . . . John,' said Rosie. 'Let's get you home where you belong.'

They stepped out. Water was dripping from the eaves, but the rain had eased.

'I live up past Pseudopolis Yard,' said Vimes.

'Lead on,' said Rosie.

They hadn't reached the end of the street before Vimes was aware that a couple of dark figures had fallen in behind them. He was about to turn, but Rosie clamped a hand on his arm.

'Don't bother them, and they won't bother you,' she said. 'They're just coming with us for protection.'

'Whose? Yours or mine?'

Rosie laughed. 'Both,' she said.

'Yes, you just keep on walking, kind sir, and we'll be as quiet as little mice,' said a shrill voice behind him. A slightly deeper one said, 'That's right, dearie. Just be a good boy and Aunty Dotsie won't have to open her handbag.'

'That's Dotsie and Sadie!' said Vimes. 'The Agony Aunts! Well, *they* bloody well know who I am!'

He turned.

The dark figures, both wearing old-fashioned black straw hoods, stepped back. In the gloom there were a number of metallic noises, and Vimes forced himself to relax a little. Even though they were, more or less, on the same side as the Watch, you never quite knew where you were with the Agony Aunts. Of course, that's what made them so useful. Any customer disturbing the peace in one of the local houses of good repute feared the threat of the Aunts far more than he did the Watch. The Watch had rules. And the Watch didn't have Dotsie's handbag. And Sadie could do terrible things with a parrot-headed umbrella.

'Come on,' he said. 'Dotsie? Sadie? Let's not mess about, eh?'

Something prodded him in the chest. He looked down. The thing had a carved parrot head on it.

'You must keep walking, kind sir,' said a voice.

'While you've still got toes, dearie,' said another voice.

'Probably a good idea,' said Rosie, tugging Vimes's arm. 'But I can tell you've impressed them.'

'How?'

'You're not bent double and making bubbling noises. Come along, mystery man.'

Vimes stared ahead, looking out for the blue light of Pseudopolis Yard. Somehow, it'd all make sense there.

But, when he got there, there was no blue light over the archway. There were just a few lights upstairs.

Vimes hammered on the door until it opened a crack.

'What the hell's going on here?' he demanded, to the nose and one eye that was the visible totality of the occupant. 'And get out of the way!'

He pushed the door back and strode in.

It wasn't the Watch House, not inside. There were the familiar

48

stairs, right enough, but there was a wall right across the charge room, and carpets on the floor, and tapestries on the wall . . . and a housemaid holding a tray, and staring, and dropping the tray, and screaming.

'Where are all my *officers*?' Vimes yelled.

'You leave this minute, d'you hear? You can't just come in like that! You get out of here!'

Vimes turned, and confronted the old man who'd opened the door. He looked like a butler, and had picked up a cudgel. Perhaps because of nerves, or maybe just because of general elderly tremors, the tip of the cudgel waved and weaved under his nose. Vimes snatched it and threw it on the floor.

'What is going on?' he demanded. The old man looked as bewildered as he was.

Vimes felt an odd, hollow terror welling up inside him. He darted back through the open door and into the wet night. Rosie and the Aunts had melted away in the darkness, as night people do when trouble looms, but Vimes ran on and into Kings Way, pushing aside other pedestrians and dodging the occasional carriage.

He was getting a second wind when he reached Scoone Avenue and turned into the driveway of his house. He wasn't sure what he'd find, but the place looked normal and there were torches burning on either side of the door. Familiar gravel crunched under his feet.

He went to hammer on the door, but steeled himself not to, and rang the bell instead.

After a moment the door was opened by a butler.

'Thank goodness!' said Vimes. 'It's me, man. Been in a fight. Nothing to worry about. How is—'

'What do you want?' said the butler coldly. He took a step back, bringing him more fully in the light of the hall lamps. Vimes had never seen him before.

'What's happened to Willikins?' said Vimes.

'The scullery boy?' Now the butler's tone was icy. 'If you are

49

a relative, I suggest you enquire round at the tradesmen's entrance. You ought to know better than to come to the front door.'

Vimes tried to think how to deal with this, but his fist didn't bother to wait. It laid the man out quite cleanly.

'No time for this,' said Vimes, stepping over him. He stood in the middle of the big hall and cupped his hands.

'Mrs Content? Sybil?' he yelled, feeling the terror twist and knot inside him.

'Yes?' said a voice from what Vimes had always called The Ghastly Pink drawing room, and Sybil stepped out.

It *was* Sybil. The voice was right, and the eyes were right, and the way she stood was right. But the age wasn't right. This was a girl, far too young to be Sybil . . .

She looked from him to the prone butler. 'Did *you* do that to Forsythe?' she said.

'I . . . er . . . I . . . it's . . . there's been a mistake . . .' Vimes murmured, backing away. But Sybil was already pulling a sword off the wall. It wasn't there for show. Vimes couldn't remember if his wife had ever learned to fence, but several feet of edged weapon is quite threatening enough when wielded by an angry amateur. Amateurs sometimes get lucky.

He backed away hurriedly. 'It's been a mistake . . . wrong house . . . mistaken identity . . .' He almost tripped over the fallen butler but managed to turn this into a staggering run through the doorway and down the steps.

Wet leaves brushed against him as he blundered through the shrubbery to the gateway, where he leaned against the wall and gulped for air.

That bloody Library! Hadn't he heard something, once, about how you could walk through time or something there? All those magical books pressed together did something *strange*.

Sybil had been so young. She'd looked sixteen! No wonder there wasn't a Watch House in Pseudopolis Yard! They'd only moved in there a few years ago!

The water was soaking through the cheap clothes. Back home . . . somewhere . . . was his huge leather greatcoat, heavy with oil, warm as toast . . .

Think, think, don't let the terror take control . . .

Perhaps he could go and explain things to Sybil. After all, she was still Sybil, wasn't she? Kind to bedraggled creatures? But even the softest heart would be inclined to harden when a rough, desperate man with a fresh scar and bad clothes barged into the house and said he was going to be your husband. A young woman could get quite the wrong idea, and he wouldn't want that, not while she was holding a sword. Besides, Lord Ramkin was probably still alive and he'd been a bloodthirsty old devil, as far as Vimes could recall.

He slumped against the wall and reached for a cigar and the terror twisted him again.

There was nothing in his pocket. Nothing at all. No Pantweed's Slim Panatellas but, more importantly, no cigar case . . .

It had been specially made. It had a slight curve. It had always nestled in his pocket since the day Sybil had given it to him. It was as near part of him as any *thing* could be.

'We are here, and this is now.' Constable Visit, a strict believer in the Omnian religion, occasionally quoted that from their holy book. Vimes understood it to mean, in less exalted copper speak, that you have to do the job that is in front of you.

I am here, Vimes thought, and this is then. And less conscious parts of his brain added: you have no friends here. No home here. No purpose here. You are alone here.

No . . . not alone, said a part that was much, much deeper even than the terror, and was always on watch.

Someone was watching him.

A figure detached itself from the damp shadows of the street, and walked towards him. Vimes couldn't make out the face, but that didn't matter. He knew it would be smiling that special smile of the predator who knows he has the prey under his paw, and knows that the *prey* knows this too, and also knows that the prey is desperately going to act as if they're having a perfectly friendly conversation, because the prey wants, so much, for this to be the case . . .

You don't want to *die* here, said the deep dark part of Vimes's soul.

'Got a light, mister?' said the predator. He didn't even bother to wave an unlit cigarette.

'Why, yes, of course,' said Vimes. He went as if to pat his pocket but swung around, arm outstretched, and caught a man creeping up behind him right across the ear. Then he leapt for the light-seeker in front of him and bore him to the ground with an arm across his throat.

It would have worked. He knew, afterwards, that it really would have worked. If there hadn't been two more men in the shadows, it *would* have worked. As it was, he managed to kick one of them on the kneecap before he felt the garrotte go round his neck.

He was pulled upright, the scar screaming pain as he tried to clutch at the rope.

'You hold him right there,' said a voice. 'Look what he did to Jez. Damn! I'm gonna kick him in—'

The shadows moved. Vimes, struggling for breath, his one good eye watering, was only vaguely aware of what was happening. But there were some grunts, and some soft, strange noises, and the pressure on his neck was abruptly released.

He fell forward, and then, reeling a little, struggled to his feet. A couple of men were lying on the ground. One was bent double, making little bubbling noises. And, far off and getting further, there were running footsteps.

'Lucky we found you in time, kind sir,' said a voice right behind him.

'Not lucky for some, dearie,' said one right next to it.

Rosie stepped forward, out of the gloom. 'I think you ought to come back with us,' she said. 'You're going to get hurt, running around like this. Come on. Obviously I'm not taking you back to my place—'

'—obviously,' murmured Vimes.

'—but Mossy'll find you somewhere to lay your head, I expect.'

'Mossy Lawn!' said Vimes, suddenly light-headed. 'That's him! The pox doctor! I remember!' He tried to focus one tired eye on the young woman. Yes, the bone structure was right. That chin. That was a no-nonsense chin. It was a chin that took people somewhere. 'Rosie . . . you're Mrs Palm!'

'Mrs?' she said, coldly, while the Agony Aunts giggled their high-pitched giggle. 'I think *not*.'

'Well, I mean—' Vimes floundered. Of course, only the senior members of the profession adopted 'Mrs' as an honorific. She wasn't senior yet. There wasn't even a guild.

'And I've never seen you before,' said Rosie. 'And neither have Dotsie and Sadie, and they have an amazing memory for faces. But you know us and you act as if you own the place, John Keel.'

'Do I?'

'You do. It's the way you stand. Officers stand like that. You eat well. Maybe a bit too well. You could lose a few pounds. And then there's the scars all over you. I saw 'em in Mossy's place. Your legs are tanned from the knees down, and that says "watchman" to me, because they go bare-legged. But I know every watchman in the city and you're not one of them, so maybe you're a military man. You fight by instinct, and dirty, too. That means you're used to fighting for your life in a mêlée, and that's odd, because that says to me "foot soldier", not officer. The word is that the lads took some fine armour off you. That's officer. But you don't wear rings. That's foot soldier – rings catch in things, can pull your finger off if you're not careful. And you're married.'

'How can you tell *that*?'

'Any woman could tell that,' said Rosie Palm smoothly. 'Now, step sharp. We're out after curfew as it is. The Watch won't bother much about us, but they *will* about you.'

Curfew, thought Vimes. That *was* a long time ago. Vetinari never ordered curfews. They interfered with business.

'I think perhaps I lost my memory when I was attacked,' he said. That sounded good, he thought. What he really needed now was somewhere quiet, to think.

'Really? I think perhaps I'm the Queen of Hersheba,' said Rosie. 'Just remember, kind sir. I'm not doing this because I'm interested in you, although I'd admit to a macabre fascination about how long you're going to survive. If it hadn't been a cold wet night I'd have left you in the road. I'm a working girl, and I don't need trouble. But you look like a man who can lay his hands on a few dollars, and there *will* be a bill.'

'I'll leave the money on the dressing table,' said Vimes.

The slap in the face knocked him against the wall.

'Consider that a sign of my complete lack of a sense of humour, will you?' said Rosie, shaking some life back into her hand.

'I'm . . . sorry,' said Vimes. 'I didn't mean to . . . I mean . . . look, thank you for everything. I mean it. But this is not being a good night.'

'Yes, I can see that.'

'It's worse than you think. Believe me.'

'We all have our troubles. Believe me,' said Rosie.

Vimes was glad of the Agony Aunts behind them as they walked back to the Shades. This was the *old* Shades, and Lawn lived a street's width away from it. The Watch never set foot here. In truth, the new Shades wasn't a lot better, but people had at least learned what happened if anyone attacked a watchman. The Aunts were a different matter. No one attacked the Aunts.

A night's sleep, thought Vimes. Maybe, in the morning, this won't have happened.

'She wasn't there, was she?' said Rosie, after a while. 'Your wife? That was Lord Ramkin's house. Are you in trouble with him?'

'Never met the man,' said Vimes absently.

'You were lucky someone told us where you'd gone. Those men were probably in the pay of someone up there. They're a law unto themselves, over in Ankh. Some rough man walking around with no tradesman's tools . . . well, he's to be turned off the patch, and if they rob you blind while they're doing it who's going to care?'

Yes, thought Vimes. That's the way it was. Privilege, which just means private law. Two types of people laugh at the law: those that break it and those that make it. Well, it's not like that now—

—but I'm not in 'now' now. Damn those wizards . . .

The wizards. Right! In the morning I'll go and explain! Easy! *They'll* understand! I'll bet they can send me right back to when I left! There's a whole *university* full of people to deal with this! It's not my problem any more!

Relief filled his body like warm pink mist. All he had to do was get through the night . . .

But why wait? They were open all night, weren't they? Magic didn't shut. Vimes remembered late-night patrols when he could practically see by the glows coming from some of the windows. He could simply—

Hold on, hold on. A policeman's thought had been stirring in his mind. The Aunts didn't run. They *famously* didn't run. They caught up with you slowly. Anyone who'd been, as they called it, 'a very naughty boy' would sleep extremely badly knowing that the Aunts on his tail were *slowly* getting nearer, pausing only for a cream tea somewhere or to visit an interesting jumble sale. But Vimes had run, run all the way up to Scoone Avenue, in the dark, through coach traffic and crowds of people swarming home before curfew. No one had paid him any attention, would surely not have seen his face if they did. And he certainly didn't know anyone here. He amended the thought: no one knew *him*.

'So,' he said casually, 'who told you where I'd gone?'

'Oh, one of those old monks,' said Rosie.

'Which old monks?'

'Who knows? A little bald man with a robe and a broom. There's always monks begging and chanting somewhere. He was in Phedre Road.'

'And you asked him where I'd gone?'

'What? No. He just looked around and said, "Mr Keel ran up to Scoone Avenue," and then he went on sweeping.'

'Sweeping?'

'Oh, it's the kind of holy thing they do. So they don't tread on ants, I think. Or they sweep sins away. Or maybe they just like the place clean. Who cares what monks do?'

'And nothing about that struck you as odd?'

'Why? I thought perhaps you were naturally kind to beggars!' snapped Rosie. 'It doesn't bother me. Dotsie said she put something in his begging bowl, though.'

'What?'

'Would *you* ask?'

The majority of Vimes thought: who does care about what monks do? They're monks. That's *why* they're weird. Maybe one had a moment of revelation or something, they like that kind of thing. So what? Find the wizards, explain what's happened and leave it to them.

But the policeman part thought: how do little monks know I'm called Keel? I smell a rat.

The majority said: it's a thirty-year-old rat, then.

And the policeman said: yes, that's why it smells.

'Look, I'm going to have to go and check something,' he said. 'I'll . . . probably be back.'

'Well, I can't chain you up,' said Rosie. She smiled a grim little smile, and went on: 'That costs extra. But if you don't come back, yet have *any* intention of staying in this city, then the Aunts—'

'I promise you, the last thing I want to do is leave Ankh-Morpork,' said Vimes.

'That actually sounded convincing,' said Rosie. 'Off you go, then. We're past curfew now. But why don't I think you'll be bothered by that?'

As he disappeared in the gloom Dotsie sidled up to Rosie. 'You want we should follow him, dearie?'

'Don't bother.'

'You should have let Sadie give him a little prod, dear. That slows them down.'

'I think it takes quite a lot to slow that man down. And we don't want trouble. Not at a time like this. We're too close.'

'You don't want to be out at a time like this, mister.'

Vimes turned. He'd been hammering on the closed gates of the University.

There were three watchmen behind him. One of them was holding a torch. Another was holding a bow. The third had clearly decided that activities for tonight would not include heavy lifting.

Vimes raised his hands slowly.

'I expect he wants to be in a nice cold cell for the night,' said the one with the torch.

Oh dear, thought Vimes. It's the Comedian of the Year contest. Coppers really oughtn't to try this, but they still did.

'I was just visiting the University,' he said.

'Oh, yes?' said the one without either torch or bow. He was portly, and Vimes could make out the tarnished gleam of a sergeant's stripes. 'Where d'you live?'

'Nowhere,' said Vimes. 'I've just arrived. And shall we move right along? I don't have a job and I don't have any money. And neither of those is a crime.'

'Out after curfew? No visible means of support?' said the sergeant.

'I got my legs,' said Vimes.

'At the moment, hur, hur,' said one of the men. He stopped when Vimes looked at him.

'I want to make a complaint, sergeant,' said Vimes.

'What about?'

'You,' said Vimes. 'And the Brothers Grin here. You're not *doing* it right. If you're going to arrest someone, you take charge right away. You've got a badge and a weapon, yes? And he's got his hands up, and a guilty conscience. *Everyone's* got a guilty conscience. So he's wondering what you know and what you're going to do, and what you do is fire off the questions, sharply. You don't make silly jokes 'cos that makes you too human and you keep him off balance so he can't quite think a clear sentence and above all you *don't let him move like this and grab your arm and pull it up so it almost breaks like this and grab your sword and hold it to your throat like this*. Tell your men to lower those swords, will you? The way they're waving them around, they could hurt someone.'

The sergeant gurgled.

'Right,' said Vimes. 'Oh, sergeant . . . this is a *sword*? Ever sharpen it? What do you use it for, *bludgeoning* people to death? Now, what you're going to do is, you're all going to put your weapons on the ground over there, and then I'm going to let the sarge go and I'll leg it up that alley, okay? And by the time you've got your weapons back in your hands, and believe me I'd advise you to get hold of weapons before coming after me, I'll be well away. End of problem all round. Any questions?'

All three watchmen were silent. Then Vimes heard a very faint, very close noise. It was the sound of the hairs in his ears rustling as, with great care, the tip of a crossbow bolt gently entered his ear.

'Yes, sir, I have a question,' said a voice behind him. 'Do you ever listen to your own advice?'

Vimes felt the pressure of the crossbow against his skull, and wondered how far the arrow would go if the trigger was pulled. An inch would be too much.

Sometimes you just had to take the lumps. He dropped the sword with great and exaggerated care, released his grip on the sergeant, and stepped away meekly while the fourth watchman maintained his aim.

'I'll just stand with my legs apart, shall I?' he said.

'Yeah,' growled the sergeant, turning round. 'Yeah, that'll save us a bit of time. Although for *you*, mister, we've got all night. Well done, lance-constable. We'll make a watchman of you yet.'

'Yeah, well done,' said Vimes, staring at the young man with the bow. But the sergeant was already taking his run-up.

It was later. Pain had happened.

Vimes lay on the hard cell bed and tried to make it go away. It hadn't been as bad as it might be. That mob hadn't even been able to organize a good seeing-to. They didn't understand how a man could roll with the punches and half the time they were getting in their own way.

Was he enjoying this? Not the pain. He'd pass on the pain. In fact he'd passed out on the pain. But there was that small part of him he'd heard sometimes during strenuous arrests after long chases, the part that wanted to punch and punch long after punching had already achieved its effect. There was a joy to it. He called it the beast. It stayed hidden until you needed it and then, when you needed it, out it came. Pain brought it out, and fear. He'd killed werewolves with his bare hands, mad with anger and terror and tasting, deep inside, the blood of the beast . . . and it was sniffing the air.

' 'ullo, Mister Vimes, haha. I was wondering when you'd wake up.'

He sat up sharply. The cells were barred on the corridor side, but also between cells as well, on the basis that those caged ought to know they were in a cage. And in the next cell, lying with his hands behind his head, was Carcer.

'Go on,' said Carcer cheerfully. 'Make a grab for me through the bars, eh? Want to see how long it takes before the guards arrive?'

59

'At least they got you too,' said Vimes.

'Not for long, not for long. I smell of roses, me, haha. Visitor to the city, got lost, very helpful to the Watch, so sorry to have bothered them, here's a little something for their trouble . . . You shouldn't of stopped the Watch taking bribes, Mister Vimes. It means an easier life all round, haha.'

'Then I'll nail you some other way, Carcer.'

Carcer inserted a finger in his nose, wiggled it around, withdrew it, inspected its contents critically and flicked them towards the ceiling.

'Well, that's where it all goes runny, Mister Vimes. You see, I wasn't dragged in by four coppers. I didn't go around assaulting watchmen, or trying to break into the University . . .'

'I was knocking on the door!'

'I believe you, Mister Vimes. But you know what coppers are like. You look at 'em in a funny way, and the buggers'll fit you up for every crime in the book. Terrible, what they can pin on an honest man, haha.'

Vimes knew it. 'So you got some money,' he said.

'O'course, Mister Vimes. I'm a crook. And the best part is, it's even easier to be a crook when no one knows you're a crook, haha. But coppering depends on people believing you're a copper. A turn-up for the books, eh? You know we're back in the good old days, haha?'

'It seems that way,' Vimes admitted. He didn't like talking to Carcer, but right now he seemed to be the only real person around.

'Where did you land, if I may ask?'

'In the Shades.'

'Me too. Couple of blokes tried to mug me where I lay. Me! I ask you, Mister Vimes! Still, they had some money on them, so that worked out all right. Yes, I think I'm going to be very happy here. Ah, here comes one of our brave lads . . .'

A watchman walked along the passage, swinging his keys. He was elderly, the kind of copper who gets given the jobs where

60

swinging keys is more likely than swinging a truncheon, and his most distinguishing feature was a nose twice the width and half the length of the average nose. He stared at Vimes for a moment, and then passed on to Carcer's cell. He unlocked the door.

'You. Hop it,' he said.

'Yessir. Thank you, sir,' said Carcer, hurrying out. He pointed to Vimes. 'You wanna watch *that* one, sir. He's an animal. Decent people shouldn't be locked up in the same cells, sir.'

'Hop it, I said.'

'Hopping it, sir. Thank you, sir.' And Carcer, with a leery wink at Vimes, hopped it.

The jailer turned to Vimes. 'And what's your name, hnah, mister?'

'John Keel,' said Vimes.

'Yeah?'

'Yeah, and I've had my kicking. Fair's fair. I'd like to go now.'

'Oh, you'd like to go, would you? Hnah! You'd like me to hand over these keys, hnah, and give you five pence from the poor box for your, hnah, trouble, eh?'

The man was standing *very* close to the bars, with the grin of one who mistakenly thinks he's a wit when he's only half a one. And if Vimes's reflexes were quicker, and he'd bet they were even now, it'd be the work of a second to pull the old fool forcibly into the bars and spread his nose even further across his face. No doubt about it, the psychopaths had it the easy way.

'Just freedom would do,' he said, resisting temptation.

'*You* ain't going anywhere, hnah, 'cept to see the captain,' said the jailer.

'That'd be Captain Tilden?' said Vimes. 'Have I got that right? Smokes like a bonfire? Got a brass ear and a wooden leg?'

'Yeah, an' he can have you *shot*, hnah, how d'you like *them* bananas?'

The cluttered desk of Vimes's memory finally unearthed the

inadvertent coffee mat of recollection from under the teacup of forgetfulness.

'You're *Snouty*,' he said. 'Right? Some bloke broke your nose and it never got set properly! And your eyes water all the time which is why they gave you permanent jail duty—'

'Do I know you, mister?' said Snouty, peering at Vimes through suspicious, running eyes.

'Me? No. No!' said Vimes hastily. 'But I've heard people talk about you. Practically runs the Watch House, they said. Very fair man, they said. Firm but fair. Never spits in the gruel, never widdles in the tea. And never confuses his fruit, either.'

The visible parts of Snouty's face contorted into the resentful scowl of someone who can't quite keep up with the script.

'Oh yeah?' he managed. 'Well, hnah, I've always kept a clean cell, that's very true.' He looked a little nonplussed at the development, but managed another scowl. 'You stay there, mister, and I'll go an' tell the captain you woke up.'

Vimes went back and lay on the bunk, staring at the badly spelled and anatomically incorrect graffiti on the ceiling. For a while there was a raised voice from upstairs, with an occasional intrusive 'hnah!' from Snouty.

Then he heard the jailer's footsteps on the stairs again.

'Well, well, well,' he said, with the tone of someone looking forward to seeing a third party get what was coming to them. 'Turns out the captain wants to see you *right away*. Now, are you gonna let me shackle you, hnah, or do I call the lads down?'

Gods protect you, Vimes thought. Maybe it was true that the blow that had spread Snouty's nose across his face had scrambled his brain. You had to be a special kind of idiot to try to handcuff a dangerous prisoner all by yourself. If he'd tried it with Carcer, for example, he'd have been a dead idiot five minutes ago.

The jailer opened the door. Vimes stood up and presented his wrists. After a second's hesitation, Snouty handcuffed him. It always paid to be nice to a jailer; you might not get handcuffed behind your back. A man with both hands in front of him had quite a lot of freedom.

'You go up the stairs first,' said Snouty, and reached down and picked up an efficient looking crossbow. 'And if you even try to walk fast, mister, I'll shoot you, hnah, where you die slow.'

'Very fair,' said Vimes. 'Very fair.'

He walked up the steps very carefully, hearing Snouty's heavy breathing right behind him. Like many people of limited intellectual scope, Snouty took what he *could* do very seriously. He'd show a refreshing lack of compunction about pulling that trigger, for one thing.

Vimes reached the top of the stairs and remembered to hesitate.

'Hnah, turn left, you,' said Snouty behind him. Vimes nodded to himself. And then first on the right. It was all coming back to him, in a great wave. This was Treacle Mine Road. This was his first Watch House. This was where it all began.

The captain's door was open. The tired-looking old man behind the desk glanced up.

'Be seated,' said Tilden coldly. 'Thank you, Snouty.'

Vimes had mixed memories of Captain Tilden. He had been a military man before being given this job as a kind of pension, and that was a bad thing in a senior copper. It meant he looked to Authority for orders and obeyed them, whereas Vimes found it better to look to Authority for orders and then filter those orders through a fine mesh of common sense, adding a generous scoop of creative misunderstanding and maybe even incipient deafness if circumstances demanded, because Authority rarely descended to street level. Tilden set too great a store by shiny breastplates and smartness on parade. You had to have some of that stuff, that was true enough. You couldn't let people slob around. But although he'd never voice the view in public, Vimes liked to see a bit of battered armour around the place. It showed that someone had been battering it. Besides, when you were lurking in the shadows you didn't want to gleam . . .

There was an Ankh-Morpork flag pinned to one wall, the red faded to threadbare orange. Rumour had it that Tilden saluted it every day. There was also a very large silver inkstand, with a gilt regimental crest on it, occupying quite a lot of the desk; Snouty polished it every morning and it shone. Tilden had never quite left the army behind.

Still, Vimes retained a soft spot for the old man. He'd been a successful soldier, as these things went; he'd generally been on the winning side, and had killed more of the enemy by good if dull tactics than his own men by bad but exciting ones. He'd been, in his own way, kind and reasonably fair; the men of the Watch had run rings around him, without his ever noticing.

Now Tilden was giving him the Long Stare With Associated Paperwork. It was supposed to mean: we know all about you, so why don't you tell us all about yourself? But he really wasn't any good at it.

Vimes returned it blankly.

'What is your name again?' said Tilden, aware that Vimes was the better starer.

'Keel,' said Vimes. 'John Keel.' And . . . what the hell . . . 'Look,' he said, 'you've only got one piece of paper there that means anything, and that's the report from that sergeant, assuming he can write.'

'As a matter of fact I have *two* pieces of paper,' said the captain. 'The other one concerns the *death* of John Keel, what?'

'What? For a scrap with the Watch?'

'In the current emergency, that would be quite sufficient for the death penalty,' said Tilden, leaning forward. 'But, ha, perhaps it won't be necessary in this case, because John Keel died yesterday. You beat him up and robbed him, what? You took his money but you didn't bother with the letters, because your sort can't read, what? So you wouldn't have known that John Keel was a *policeman*, what?'

'*What?*'

Vimes stared at the skinny face with its triumphantly bristling moustache and the little faded blue eyes.

And then there was the sound of someone industriously sweeping the floor in the corridor outside. The captain looked past him, growled, and hurled a pen.

'Get him out of here!' he barked. 'What's the little devil doing here at this time of night, anyway?'

Vimes turned his head. There was a skinny, wizened-looking man standing in the doorway, bald as a baby. He was grinning stupidly, and holding a broom.

'He's cheap, sir, hnah, and it's best if he comes in when it's, hnah, quiet,' Snouty murmured, grabbing the little man by a stick-thin elbow. 'C'mon, out you get, Mister Lousy—'

So now the crossbow wasn't pointing at Vimes. And he had several pounds of metal on his wrists or, to put it another way, his arms were a hammer. He went to stand up . . .

Vimes woke up and stared at the ceiling. There was a deep rumbling somewhere near by. Treadmill? Watermill?

It was going to be a corny line, but some things you had to know.

'Where am I?' he said. And then he added: '*This* time?'

'Well *done*,' said a voice somewhere behind him. 'Consciousness to sarcasm in five seconds!'

The room was large, by the feel of the air, and the play of light on the walls suggested there were candles alight behind Vimes.

The voice said: 'I'd like you to think of me as a friend.'

'A friend? Why?' said Vimes. There was a smell of cigarette smoke in the air.

'Everyone ought to have a friend,' said the voice. 'Ah, I see you've noticed you're still handcuffed—'

The voice said this because in one movement Vimes had swung himself off the table and plunged forward—

Vimes woke up and stared at the ceiling. There was a deep

rumbling somewhere near by. Treadmill? Watermill? Then his thoughts knotted themselves most unpleasantly.

'What,' he said, 'just happened?'

'I thought you might like to try that again, lad,' said the invisible friend. 'We have little tricks here, as you will learn. Just sit up. I know you've been through a lot, but we don't have time for messing about. This is sooner than I'd like, but I thought I'd better get you out of there before it went *really* runny . . . Mister Vimes.'

Vimes froze. 'Who *are* you?' he said.

'It's Lu-Tze officially, Mister Vimes. But you can call me Sweeper, since we're friends.'

Vimes sat up carefully and looked around.

The shadowy walls were covered with . . . writing, it must be writing, he thought, but the Hubland type of writing which is only one step away from being little pictures.

The candle was standing on a saucer. Some way behind it, just visible in the shadows, were two cylinders, each as wide as a man and twice as long, set in massive horizontal bearings, one above the other. Both were turning slowly, and both gave the impression of being a lot bigger than their mere dimensions suggested. Their rumble filled the room. There was a strange violet haze around them.

Two yellow-robed figures tended the cylinders, but Vimes's eye was drawn to the skinny little bald man sitting on an upturned crate by the candle. He was smoking a foul roll-up of the sort favoured by Nobby, and looked like a foreign monk. In fact, he looked exactly the kind Vimes occasionally saw with begging bowls in the street.

'You're looking fit, Mister Vimes,' said Sweeper.

'You were in the Watch House, right?' said Vimes. 'Snouty called you Lousy!'

'Yes, Mister Vimes. Lu-Tze. I've been sweeping up there every night for the past ten days. All for two pence and all the kicks I can't dodge. Just waiting for you.'

'And you told Rosie Palm where I'd gone, too? You were the monk on the bridge?'

'Right again. Couldn't be sure she'd catch up.'

'How do *you* know who I am?'

'Don't get excited, Mister Vimes,' said Sweeper calmly. 'I'm here to help you . . . your grace. And I'm your friend because right now I'm the only person in the world who will probably believe anything you tell me about, oh, thunderstorms and falls, that sort of thing. At least,' he added, 'the only sane person.'

He watched Vimes as the man sat quite still for half a minute.

'*Good*, Mister Vimes,' said Sweeper. 'Thinking. I like that in a man.'

'This is magic, right?' said Vimes, at last.

'Something like that, yes,' said Sweeper. 'F'rinstance, just now we moved you back in time. Just a few seconds. Just so you wouldn't do anything you'd regret. Can't say I blame you for wanting to have a go at someone after all you've been through, but we don't want any harm to come to you, do we . . .'

'Hah? I almost had my hands round your throat!'

Sweeper smiled. It was a disarming little smile. 'Smoke?' he said. He fumbled in his robe and produced a ragged hand-rolled cigarette.

'Thanks, but I've got my own—' Vimes began automatically. His hand stopped halfway to his pocket.

'Oh, yes,' said Sweeper. 'The silver cigar case. Sybil gave it to you as a wedding present, right? Shame about that.'

'I want to go home,' said Vimes. It came out as a whisper. He hadn't been sleeping in the past twelve hours, merely recovering.

This time it was Sweeper who sat in silence, apart from the rumble of the cylinders.

'You're a policeman, Mister Vimes,' he said eventually. 'Well, I'd like you to believe, for a while, that I'm a sort of policeman too, all right? Me and my colleagues, we see that . . . things happen. Or don't happen. Don't ask questions right now. Just nod.'

Vimes shrugged instead.

'Good. And let's say on *our* patrol we've found you, as it might be, in a metaphorical kind of way, lying in the gutter on a Saturday night singing a rude song about wheelbarrows—'

'I don't know a rude song about wheelbarrows!'

Sweeper sighed. 'Hedgehogs? Custard? One-string fiddles? It really doesn't matter. Now, we've found you a long way from where you should be and we'd *like* to get you home, but it's not as easy as you might think.'

'I've gone back in time, haven't I? It was that bloody Library! Everyone knows the magic in there makes strange things happen!'

'Well, yes. It was mainly that, yes. It's more true to say that you, er, got caught up in a major event.'

'Can anyone get me back? Can *you* get me back?'

'We-ell . . .' said Sweeper, looking awkward.

'Wizards can if you can't,' said Vimes. 'I'll go back and see them in the morning!'

'Oh, you will, will you? I'd like to be there when you do. These ain't the wizards under decent old Ridcully, you know. You'll be lucky if they only laugh at you. Anyway, even if they wanted to be helpful they'd hit the same problem.'

'And what's that?'

'It can't be done. Not yet.' For the first time in the conversation Sweeper looked ill at ease. 'The big problem I'm facing, Mister Vimes, is that I ought to tell you a few things that I'm not, in any circumstances, allowed to tell you. But you're a man who isn't happy until he knows the facts. I respect that. So . . . if I tell you everything, can you spare me, oh, twenty minutes of your time? It could save your life.'

'All right,' said Vimes. 'But what—'

'You've got a bargain,' said Sweeper. 'Roll 'em, boys.'

The noise of the big cylinders changed for a moment and Vimes felt a very slight shock, a suggestion that his whole body had just gone *plib*.

'Twenty minutes,' said Sweeper. 'I'll answer *every* question. And then, Mister Vimes, we'll send you back from twenty minutes in the future to *now* and you'll tell yourself what you and me agree you ought to know. Which will be most of it, really. You're a man who can keep secrets. Okay?'

'Yes, but—' Vimes began.

The tone of the spinning cylinders changed slightly.

Sam Vimes saw himself standing in the middle of the room. 'That's me!'

'Yeah, right,' said Sweeper. 'Now listen to the man.'

'Hello, Sam,' said the other Vimes, staring not quite at him. 'I can't see you, but they say you can see me. Remember the smell of lilac? You thought about those who died. And then you told Willikins to hose down that kid. And, eh . . . you've got a pain in your chest you're a bit worried about but you haven't told anyone . . . That's about enough, I think. You know I'm you. Now, there's some things I can't tell you. I can know 'em because I'm in a—' The speaker stopped and looked away, as if he was taking instruction from someone offstage '—a closed loop. Er, you could say I'm twenty minutes of your life you don't recall. Remember when you had . . .'

. . . a sensation that his whole body had just gone *plih*.

Sweeper stood up. 'I hate to do this,' he said, 'but we're in the temple and we can pretty much dampen out the paradoxes. On your feet, Mister Vimes. I'm going to tell you everything.'

'You just said you couldn't!'

Sweeper smiled. 'Need any help with those handcuffs?'

'What, these old Capstick Mark Ones? No, just give me a nail and a couple of minutes. How come I'm in a temple?'

'I brought you here.'

'You carried me?'

'No. You walked with me. Blindfolded, of course. And then when you were here, I gave you a little drink . . .'

'I don't remember that!'

'Of course not. That was the purpose of the drink. Not very mystical, but it does the job. We don't want you coming back here, now, do we? This place is supposed to be a *secret*—'

'You messed up my memory? Now you see here—' Vimes half stood, but Sweeper held up his hands placatingly.

'Don't worry, don't worry, it just . . . made you forget a few minutes,' he said.

'*How many minutes?*'

'Just a few, just a few. And it had herbs in it. Good for you, herbs. And then we let you sleep. Don't worry, no one is after us. They'll never know you've gone. See this thing here?'

Sweeper picked up an open-work box that lay beside his chair. It had straps like a knapsack, and Vimes could just see a cylinder inside the box.

'This is called a Procrastinator,' said the monk, 'and it's a tiny version of the ones over there, the ones that look like your granny's mangle. I'm not going to get technical, but when it's spinning it moves time around you. Did you understand what I just said?'

'No!'

'All right, it's a magic box. Happier?'

'Go on,' said Vimes grimly.

'You wore one of these when I led you here from the Watch House. Because you were wearing it, you were, shall we say, outside time. And after we've had this little talk I'll take you back to the Watch House and the old captain won't know any different. No time is passing in the outside world while we're in the temple. The Procrastinators take care of that. Like I said, they move time around. Actually, what's really happening is that they are moving us back in time at the same time that time moves us forward. We've got others around the place. Good for keeping food fresh. What else can I tell you . . . oh, yeah. It helps keep track if you just think of things happening one after another. Believe me.'

'This is like a dream,' said Vimes. There was a clink as the handcuffs sprang open.

'Yes, it is, isn't it,' said Sweeper calmly.

'And can your magic box take me home? Move me in time all the way to where I ought to be?'

'This? Hah. No, this is strictly for small-scale stuff—'

'Look, Mr Sweeper, I've spent the last day fighting a right bastard on a roof and getting beaten up twice and sewn up once and, hah, stitched up, too. I've got the impression I should be thanking you for something but I'm damned if I know what it is. What I want is straight answers, mister. I'm the Commander of the Watch in this city!'

'Don't you mean *will be*?' said Sweeper.

'No! You told me it helps if I think of things happening one after another! Well, yesterday, *my* yesterday, I was Commander of the Watch and I bloody well still *am* the Commander of the Watch. I don't care what anyone else thinks. They are not in possession of all the facts!'

'Hold on to that thought,' said Sweeper, standing up. 'All right, commander. You want some facts. Let's take a walk in the garden, shall we?'

'*Can you get me home?*'

'Not yet. It's my professional opinion that you're here for a reason.'

'A reason? I fell through the bloody dome!'

'That helped, yes. Calm down, Mister Vimes. It's all been a great strain, I can see.'

Sweeper led the way out of the hall. There was a big office outside, a hubbub of quiet but purposeful activity. Here and there, among the worn and scratched desks, there were more cylinders like the ones Vimes had seen in the other chamber. Some of them were turning slowly.

'Very busy, our Ankh-Morpork section,' said Sweeper. 'We had to buy the shops on either side.' He picked up a scroll from a basket by one desk, glanced at the contents, and tossed it back with a sigh. 'And everyone's overworked,' he added. 'We're here at all hours. And when *we* say "all hours", we know what we're talking about.'

'But what is it you *do*?' said Vimes.

'We see that things happen.'

'Don't things happen anyway?'

'Depends what things you want. We're the Monks of History, Mister Vimes. We see that it happens.'

'I've never heard of you, and I know this city like the back of my hand,' said Vimes.

'Right. And how often do you *really* look at the back of your hand, Mister Vimes? We're in Clay Lane, to stop you wondering.'

'What? Those loony monks in the funny foreign building between the pawnbrokers and the shonky shop? The ones who go dancing round the street banging drums and shouting?'

'Well *done*, Mister Vimes. It's funny how secretly you can move when you're a loony monk dancing through the streets banging a drum.'

'When I was a kid most of my clothes came from the shonky shop in Clay Lane,' said Vimes. 'Everyone we knew got their clothes from the shonky shop. Used to be run by a foreign guy with a funny name . . .'

'Brother Soon Shine Sun,' said Sweeper. 'Not a hugely enlightened operative, but a genius when it comes to pricing fourth-hand schmutter.'

'Shirts so worn you could see daylight through 'em and trousers as shiny as glass,' said Vimes. 'And by the end of the week half the stuff was in the pawn shop.'

'That's right,' said Sweeper. 'You'd pawn your clothes in the pawn shop, but you'd never *buy* clothes from the pawn shop, 'cos there were Standards, right?'

Vimes nodded. When you got right down to the bottom of the ladder the rungs were very close together and, oh my, weren't the women careful about them. In their own way, they were as haughty as any duchess. You might not have much, but you *could* have Standards. Clothes might be cheap and old but at least they could be scrubbed. There might be nothing behind the front door worth stealing but at least the doorstep could be clean enough to eat your dinner off, if you could've afforded dinner. And no one ever bought their clothes from the pawn shop. You'd hit bottom when you did that. No, you bought them from Mr Sun at the shonky shop, and you never asked where *he* got them from.

'I went off to my first proper job in a suit from the shonky shop,' he said. 'Seems like centuries ago now.'

'No,' said Sweeper. 'It was only last week.'

Silence ballooned. The only sound was the purr of the cylinders dotted around the room.

Then Sweeper added: 'It must have occurred to you.'

'Why? I've spent most of the time here being beaten up or unconscious or trying to get home! You mean I'm out there somewhere?'

'Oh, yes. In fact last night you saved the day for your squad by aiming a crossbow at a dangerous miscreant who was attacking your sergeant.'

The silence ballooned larger this time. It seemed to fill the universe.

Eventually, Vimes said: 'No. That's not right. That never happened. I would have remembered that. And I can remember a lot about my first weeks in the job.'

'Interesting, isn't it?' said Sweeper. 'But is it not written: "There's a lot goes on we don't get told"? Mister Vimes, you need a short spell in the Garden of Inner City Tranquillity.'

It was indeed a garden, like a lot of other gardens you got in areas such as Clay Lane. The grey soil was nothing more than old brick dust, elderly cat mess and generalized, semi-rotted dross. At the far end was a three-hole privy. It was built handily by the gate to the back lane so the night-soil men didn't have far to go, but this one had a small stone cylinder turning gently beside it and the gate was barred shut.

The garden didn't get much proper light. Gardens like this never did. You got second-hand light once the richer folk in the taller buildings had finished with it. Some people kept pigeons or rabbits or pigs on their plots, or planted against all experience a few vegetables. But it'd take magic beans to reach the real sunlight in gardens like this.

Nevertheless, someone had made an effort. Most of the spare ground had been covered with gravel of different sizes, and this had been carefully raked into swirls and curves. Here and there, apparently with great thought, some individual larger stones had been positioned.

Vimes stared at the garden of rocks, desperate for anything to occupy his attention.

He could see what the designer had in mind, he thought, but the effect had been spoiled. This was the big city, after all. Garbage got everywhere. The main disposal method was throwing it over a wall. Sooner or later someone would sell it on or, possibly, eat it.

A young monk was carefully raking the gravel. He gave a respectful bow as Sweeper approached.

The old man sat down on a stone bench.

'Push off and get us two cups of tea, lad, will you?' he said. 'One green with yak butter, and Mister Vimes will have it boiled orange in a builder's boot with two sugars and yesterday's milk, right?'

'That's how I like it,' said Vimes weakly, sitting down.

Sweeper took a deep, long breath. 'And I like building gardens,' he said. 'Life should be a garden.'

Vimes stared blankly at what was in front of them. 'Okay,' he said. 'The gravel and rocks, yes, I can see that. Shame about all the rubbish. It always turns up, doesn't it . . .'

74

'Yes,' said Lu-Tze. 'It's part of the pattern.'

'What? The old cigarette packet?'

'Certainly. That invokes the element of air,' said Sweeper.

'And the cat doings?'

'To remind us that disharmony, like a cat, gets everywhere.'

'The cabbage stalks? The used sonky?'*

'At our peril we forget the role of the organic in the total harmony. What arrives seemingly by chance in the pattern is part of a higher organization that we can only dimly comprehend. This is a very important fact, and has a bearing on your case.'

'And the beer bottle?'

For the first time since Vimes had met him, the monk frowned.

'Y'know, some bugger always tosses one over the wall on his way back from the pub on Friday nights. If it wasn't forbidden to do that kind of thing, he'd feel the flat of my hand and no mistake.'

'It's not part of the higher organization?'

'Possibly. Who cares? That sort of thing gets on my *thungas*, it really does,' said Sweeper. He sat back with his hands on his knees. Serenity flowed once more. 'Well now, Mister Vimes . . . you know the universe is made up of very small items?'

'Huh?'

'We've got to work up to things gradually, Mister Vimes. You're a bright man. I can't keep telling you everything is done by magic.'

'Am I really here too? In the city? I mean, a younger me?'

'Of course. Why not? Where was I? Oh, yes. Made up of very small items, and—'

'This is not a good time to be in the Watch. I remember! There's the curfew. And that was only the start!'

---

* Named after Wallace Sonky, a man without whose experiments with thin rubber the pressure on housing in Ankh-Morpork would have been a good deal more pressing.

'Small items, Mister Vimes,' said Sweeper sharply. 'You need to know this.'

'Oh, all *right*. How small?'

'Very, very small. So tiny that they have some very strange ways indeed.'

Vimes sighed. 'And I ask you: what ways are these, yeah?'

'I'm glad you asked that question. For one thing, they can be in many places at once. Try to think, Mister Vimes.'

Vimes tried to concentrate on what was probably the discarded fish-and-chip wrapper of Infinity. Oddly enough, with so many horrible thoughts crowding his head, it was almost a relief to put them on one side in order to consider this. The brain did things like that. He remembered once when he'd been stabbed and would've bled to death if Sergeant Angua hadn't caught up with him, and how, as he lay there, he'd found himself taking a very intense interest in the pattern of the carpet. The senses say: we've only got a few minutes, let's record everything, in every detail . . .

'That can't be right,' he said. 'If this seat is made up of lots of tiny things that can be in lots of places at once, why is it standing still?'

'Give the man a small cigar!' said Sweeper jubilantly. 'That's the big problem, Mister Vimes. And the answer, our Abbot tells us, is that it *is* in lots of places at once. Ah, here's the tea. And in order for it to be in lots of places at once, the multiverse is made up of a vast number of alternative universes. An oodleplex of oodleplexes. That's like the biggest number anyone can think of, ever. Just so's it can accommodate all the quantum. Am I going too fast for you?'

'Oh, *that*,' said Vimes. 'I know about *that*. Like, you make a decision in this universe and you made a different decision in another one. I heard the wizards talking about that at a posh reception once. They were . . . arguing about the Glorious Twenty-fifth of May.'

'And what were they saying?'

'Oh, all the old stuff . . . that it would have turned out differ-ent if the rebels had properly guarded the gates and the bridges, that you can't break a siege by a frontal attack. But they were saying that, in a way, everything happens somewhere . . .'

'And you believed them?'

'It sounds like complete *thungas*. But sometimes you can't help wondering: what would have happened if I'd done some-thing different—'

'Like when you killed your wife?'

Sweeper was impressed at Vimes's lack of reaction.

'This is a test, right?'

'You're a quick study, Mister Vimes.'

'But in some other universe, believe me, I hauled off and punched you one.'

Again, Sweeper smiled the annoying little smile that sug-gested he didn't believe him.

'You haven't killed your wife,' he said. 'Anywhere. There is nowhere, however huge the multiverse is, where Sam Vimes *as he is now* has murdered Lady Sybil. But the theory is quite clear. It says that if anything could happen without breaking any physical laws, it *must* happen. But it hasn't. And yet the "many universes" theory works. Without it, no one would ever be able to make a decision at all.'

'So?'

'So what people do matters!' said Sweeper. 'People invent *other* laws. What they do is *important*! The Abbot's very excited about this. He nearly swallowed his rusk. It means the multiverse isn't infinite and people's choices are far more vital than they think. They *can*, by what they do, change the universe.'

Sweeper gave Vimes a long look. 'Mister Vimes, you're think-ing: I'm back in time, and damn me, I'm probably going to end up being the sergeant that teaches me all I know, right?'

'I've been wondering. The Watch would offer any gutter trash a job in those days, because of the curfew and all the spying. But look, I remember Keel and, yes, he did have a scar and an eye-patch but I'm sure as hell that he wasn't me.'

'Right. The universe doesn't work like that. *You* were indeed taken under the wing of one John Keel, a watchman from Pseudopolis who came to Ankh-Morpork because the pay was better. He was a real person. He was not you. But do you remember if he ever mentioned to you that he was attacked by two men not long after he got off the coach?'

'Hell, yes,' said Vimes. 'The muggers. He got this— he got *his* scar that way. A good old Ankh-Morpork welcome. But he was a tough man. Took 'em both down, no problem.'

'This time, there were three,' said Sweeper.

'Well, three's trickier, of course, but—'

'You're the policeman. You guess the name of the third man, Mister Vimes.'

Vimes hardly had to think. The answer erupted from the depths of darkest suspicion. 'Carcer?'

'He soon settled in, yes.'

'The bastard was in the next cell! He even *told* me he'd grabbed some money.'

'And you're both stuck here, Mister Vimes. This isn't *your* past, any more. Not exactly. It's *a* past. And up there is *a* future. It might be your future. But it might not be. You want to go home now, leaving Carcer here and the real John Keel dead? But there'll be no home to go to, if you could do that. Because young Sam Vimes wouldn't get a swift course in basic policing from a decent man if you did. He'll learn it from people like Sergeant Knock and Corporal Quirke and Lance-Corporal Colon. And that might not be the worst of it, by a long way.'

Vimes shut his eyes. He remembered how wet behind the ears he'd been. And Fred . . . well, Fred Colon hadn't been too bad, under the half-hearted timorousness and lack of imagination, but Quirke had been an evil little sod in his way and as for Knock, well, Knock had been Fred's teacher and the pupil wasn't a patch on the master. What had Sam Vimes learned from Keel? To stay alert, to think for himself, to keep a place in his head free from the Quirkes and Knocks of the world, and not to hesitate about fighting dirty today if that was what it took to fight again tomorrow.

He'd often thought he'd have been dead long ago if it wasn't for—

He looked up sharply at the monk.

'Can't tell you that, Mister Vimes,' said Lu-Tze. 'Nothing's certain, 'cos of quantum.'

'But, look, I know my future happened, because I was there!'

'No. What we've got here, friend, is quantum interference. Mean anything? No. Well . . . let me put it this way. There's one past, and one future. But there are two presents. One where you and your evil friend turned up, and one where you didn't. We can keep these two presents going side by side for a few days. It takes a lot of run time, but we can do it. And then they'll snap back together. The future that happens depends on you. We want the future where Vimes is a good copper. Not the other one.'

'But it must've happened!' snapped Vimes. 'I told you, I can remember it! I was there yesterday!'

'Nice try, but that doesn't mean anything any more,' said the monk. 'Trust me. Yes, it's happened to you, but even though it has, it might not, 'cos of quantum. Right now, there isn't a Commander Vimes-shaped hole in the future to drop you into. It's officially Uncertain. But might not be, if you do it right. You owe it to yourself, commander. Right now, out there, Sam Vimes is learning to be a very bad copper indeed. And he learns fast.'

The little monk stood up. 'I'll let you think about that,' he said.

Vimes nodded, staring at the gravel garden.

Sweeper crept away quietly and went back into the temple. He walked to the other side of the office. He removed a strange-shaped key from around his neck and inserted it into a small door. The door opened. Brilliant sunlight burst ahead of him. He walked on, his sandals leaving the cold flagstones and walking on to well-trodden earth in broad, hot daylight.

The river had a different course this far back in the past, and present-day residents of Ankh-Morpork would have been surprised at how pleasant it looked, seven hundred thousand years ago. Hippos sunbathed on a sandbank out in mid-stream and, according to Qu, were getting troublesome lately – he'd had to set up a little temporal fence around the camp at nights, so that any hippo trying to wander in among the tents found themselves back in the water with a headache.

Qu himself, his straw hat protecting his head from the hot sun, was supervising his assistants in a vined-off area. Lu-Tze sighed as he walked towards it.

There were going to be explosions, he knew it.

It wasn't that he disliked Qu, the order's Master of Devices. The man was a sort of engineering equivalent of the Abbot. The Abbot had taken thousand-year-old ideas and put them through his mind in a new way, and as a result the multiverse had opened for him like a flower. Qu, on the other hand, had taken the ancient technology of the Procrastinators, that could save and restore time, and had harnessed it to practical, everyday purposes, such as, yes, blowing people's heads off. It was something that Lu-Tze tried to avoid. There were better things to do with people's heads.

As Lu-Tze approached, a line of joyful, dancing monks wove their way along a bamboo replica of a street, letting off firecrackers and banging gongs. As they reached a corner the last monk turned and lightly tossed a little drum into the outstretched arms of a straw dummy.

The air shimmered, and the figure disappeared with a small thunderclap.

'Nice to see something not blowing anyone's head off,' said Lu-Tze, leaning on the vine rope.

'Oh, hello, Sweeper,' said Qu. 'Yes. I wonder what went

wrong. You see, the body should have moved forward by a microsecond and left the head where it was.' He picked up a megaphone. 'Thank you, everyone! Places for another run! Soto, take over, please!'

He turned to Lu-Tze. 'Well?'

'He's thinking about it,' said Sweeper.

'Oh, for heavens' sake, Lu-Tze! This is completely un-authorized, you know! We're supposed to prune out rogue history loops, not expend vast amounts of time keeping them going!'

'This one's important. We owe it to the man. It wasn't his fault we had the major temporal shattering just as he fell through the dome.'

'Two timelines running side by side,' moaned Qu. 'That's quite unaccceptable, you know. I'm having to use techniques that are completely untried.'

'Yes, but it's only a few days.'

'What about Vimes? Is he strong enough? He's got no train-ing for this!'

'He defaults to being a copper. A copper's a copper, wherever he is.'

'I really don't know why I listen to you, Lu-Tze, I really don't,' said Qu. He glanced at the arena and hurriedly raised his mega-phone to his lips. 'Don't hold it that way up! I said *don't* hold—'

There was a thunderclap. Lu-Tze didn't bother to look round.

Qu lifted the megaphone again and said, wearily, 'All right, someone *please* go and fetch Brother Kai, will you? Start look-ing around, oh, two centuries ago. You don't even use these very useful devices I, er, devise,' he added to Lu-Tze.

'Don't need to,' said Lu-Tze. 'Got a brain. Anyway, I use the temporal toilet, don't I?'

'A privy which discharges ten million years into the past was *not* a good idea, Sweeper. I'm sorry I let you persuade me.'

'It's saving us fourpence a week to Harry King's bucket boys, Qu, and that's not to be sneezed at. Is it not written: "a penny saved is a penny earned"? Besides, it all lands in a volcano any-way. Perfectly hygienic.'

There was another explosion. Qu turned and raised his mega-phone. 'Do *not* bang the tambourine more than twice!' he bellowed. 'It's tap-tap-throw-duck! *Please* pay attention!'

He turned back to Sweeper. 'Four more days at most, Lu-Tze,' he said. 'I'm sorry, but after that I can't hide it in the paperwork. And I'll be amazed if your man can stand it. It'll affect his mind sooner or later, however tough you think he is. He's not in his right time.'

'We're learning a lot, though,' Lu-Tze insisted. 'For a perfectly logical chain of reasons Vimes ended up back in time even *looking* rather like Keel! Eyepatch *and* scar! Is that Narrative Causality or Historical Imperative or just plain weird? Are we back to the old theory of the self-correcting history? Is there no such thing as an accident, as the Abbot says? Is every accident just a higher-order design? I'd love to find out!'

'Four days,' Qu insisted. 'Any longer than that and this little exercise will show up and the Abbot will be very, very annoyed with us.'

'Right you are, Qu,' said Sweeper meekly.

He'll be annoyed if he *has* to find out, certainly, he thought as he walked back to the door in the air. He'd been very specific. The Abbot of the History Monks (the Men In Saffron, No Such Monastery . . . they had many names) couldn't allow this sort of thing, and he'd taken pains to forbid Lu-Tze from this course of action. He had added, 'but when you do, I expect Historical Imperative will win.'

Sweeper went back to the garden and found Vimes still staring at the empty baked-bean tin of Universal Oneness.

'Well, commander?' he said.

'Are you really like . . . policemen, for time?' said Vimes.

'Well, in a way,' said Sweeper.

'So . . . you make sure the good stuff happens?'

'No, not the good stuff. The right stuff,' said Sweeper. 'But frankly, these days, we have our work cut out making sure *any-thing* happens. We used to think time was like a river, you could row up and down and come back to the same place. Then we found it acted like a sea, so you could go from side to side as well. Then it turned out to be like a *ball* of water; you could go up and down too. Currently we think it's like . . . oh, lots of spaces, all rolled up. And then there are time jumps and time slips and humans mess it up too, wasting it and gaining it. And then there's quantum, of course.' The monk sighed. 'There's *always* bloody quantum. So what with one thing and another, we think we're doing well if yesterday happens before to-morrow, quite frankly. You, Mister Vimes, got caught up in a bit of . . . an event. We can't put it right, not properly. You can.'

Vimes sat back. 'I've got no choice, have I?' he said. 'As my old sergeant used to say . . . you do the job that's in front of you.' He hesitated. 'And that's going to be me, isn't it? *I* taught me all I know . . .'

'No. I explained.'

'I didn't understand it. But perhaps I don't have to.'

Sweeper sat down. 'Good. And now, Mister Vimes, I'll take you back inside and I'll give you some background on the sergeant and we'll work out what you *need* to know from all this, and we can set up a little loop so that you can tell yourself what you need to know. No addresses, though!'

'And what'll happen to me?' said Vimes. 'The *me* sitting here now? The . . . er . . . other me walks away and *me*, this mc, you understand . . . Well, what happens?'

Sweeper gave him a long, thoughtful look. 'Y'know,' he said, 'it's very hard to talk quantum using a language originally designed to tell other monkeys where the ripe fruit is. Afterwards? Well, there will be a you. As much you as you are now, so who can say it's not you? This meeting will be . . . a sort of loop in time. In one sense, it will never end. In a way, it'll be—'

'Like a dream,' said Vimes wearily.

Sweeper brightened. 'Very good! Yes! Not true, but a very, very good lie!'

'You know, you could've just told me *everything*,' said Vimes.

'No. I wouldn't be able to tell you everything and you, Mister Vimes, aren't in the mood for games like that. This way, a man you trust – that's you – will tell you all the truth you need to know. Then we'll do a little of what the younger acolytes call "slicing and glueing", and Mister Vimes will go back to Treacle Mine Lane a little wiser.'

'How are you going to get hi— me back to the Watch House? Don't even think about giving me some kind of potion.'

'No. We'll blindfold you, twirl you round, take you the long way, and walk you back. I promise.'

'Any other advice?' said Vimes gloomily.

'Just be yourself,' said Sweeper. 'See it through. There'll come a time when you'll look back and see how it all made sense.'

'Really?'

'I wouldn't lie. It'll be a perfect moment. Believe me.'

'But . . .' Vimes hesitated.

'Yes?'

'You must know there's another little problem if I'm going to be Sergeant Keel. I've remembered what day this is. And I know what's going to happen.'

'Yes,' said Sweeper. 'I know, too. Shall we talk about that?'

Captain Tilden blinked. 'What happened there?' he said.

'Where?' said Vimes, trying to fight down nausea. Time coming back had left him with a horrible sensation that he was really two people and neither of them was feeling at all well.

'You *blurred*, man.'

'Perhaps I'm a bit tired of this,' said Vimes, pulling himselves together. 'Listen, captain, I am John Keel. I can prove it, okay? Ask me some questions. You've got my papers there, haven't you? They were stolen!'

Tilden hesitated for a moment. He was a man whose mind was ponderous enough to have momentum; it was quite hard for his thoughts to change direction.

'Who is Commander of the Pseudopolis Watch, then?' he said.

'Sheriff Macklewheet,' said Vimes.

'Aha! Wrong! Fallen at the very first fence, what? In fact, you fool, it's Sheriff Pearlie—'

'Hnah, excuse me, sir . . .' said Snouty nervously.

'Yes? What?'

'Hnah, it *is* Macklewheet, sir. Pearlie died last week. Heard it in the, hnah, pub.'

'Fell into the river when drunk,' said Vimes helpfully.

'That's what I heard, hnah, sir,' said Snouty.

Tilden looked furious. 'You could've known that, what?' he said. 'It doesn't prove anything!'

'Ask me something else, then,' said Vimes. 'Ask me what Macklewheet said about me.' And I just hope I've got the answers right.

'Well?'

'Said I was the best officer on his force and he was sorry to see me go,' said Vimes. 'Said I was of good character. Said he wished he could pay me the twenty-five dollars a month I was going to get here—'

'I never offered you—'

'No, you offered me twenty dollars and now that I've seen the mess here I'm not taking it!' Vimes rejoiced. Tilden hadn't even learned how to control a conversation. 'If you pay Knock twenty dollars he owes you nineteen dollars change! The man couldn't talk and chew gum at the same time. And look at this, will you?'

Vimes dumped his handcuffs on the desk. The gaze of Snouty and Tilden swung to them as if magnetic.

Oh *dear*, thought Vimes, and stood up and lifted the crossbow out of Snouty's hands. It was all in the movement. If you moved with authority, you got a second or two extra. Authority was everything.

He fired the bow at the floor, then handed it back.

'A kid could open those cuffs and while Snouty here keeps a very clean jail he's completely drawers at being a guard,' said Vimes. 'This place needs shaking up.' He leaned forward, knuckles on the captain's desk, with his face a few inches from the trembling moustache and the milky eyes.

'Twenty-five dollars or I walk out that door,' he said. It was probably a phrase never ever said before by any prisoner anywhere on any world.

'Twenty-five dollars,' murmured Tilden, hypnotized.

'And the rank will be sergeant-at-arms,' said Vimes. 'Not sergeant. I'm not going to be given orders by the likes of Knock.'

'Sergeant-at-arms,' said Tilden distantly, but Vimes saw the hint of approval. It was a good *military*-sounding title, and it was still on the books. In fact it was a pretty ancient pre-coppering term, back in the days when a court employed a big man with a stick to drag miscreants in front of it. Vimes had always admired the simplicity of that arrangement.

'Well, er, Sheriff Macklewheet, er, certainly gave you a most glowing reference,' said the captain, shuffling the papers. 'Very glowing. Things have been a little difficult since we lost Sergeant Wi—'

'And I'll be paid my first month in advance, please. I need clothes and a decent meal and somewhere to sleep.'

Tilden cleared his throat. 'Many of the unmarried men stay in the barracks in Cheapside—'

'Not me,' said Vimes. 'I'll be lodging with Doctor Lawn in Twinkle Street.' Well, Rosie Palm did suggest he had a spare room . . .

'The pox hnah doctor?' said Snouty.

'Yeah, I'm particular about the company I keep,' said Vimes. 'It's also just around the corner.'

He took his hands off the desk, stood back and whipped off a salute of almost parodic efficiency, the sort that Tilden had always loved.

'I'll report for duty at three o'clock tomo— this afternoon, sir,' he said. 'Thank you, sir.'

Tilden sat mesmerized.

'It was twenty-five dollars, sir, I believe,' said Vimes, still maintaining the salute.

He watched the captain get up and go to the old green safe in the corner. The man was careful not to let Vimes see him turn the dial, but Vimes was pretty certain he didn't need to. The safe had still been there when he made captain, and by then *everyone* knew the combination was 4-4-7-8 and that no one seemed to know how to change it. The only things worth keeping in it had been the tea and sugar and anything you particularly wanted Nobby to read.

Tilden came back with a small leather bag and slowly counted out the money, and was so cowed that he didn't ask Vimes to sign anything.

Vimes took it, saluted again, and held out his other hand.

'Badge, sir,' he said.

'Ah? Oh, yes, of course . . .'

The captain, entirely unnerved, fumbled in the top drawer of the desk and pulled out a dull copper shield. If he'd been that observant, he'd have noticed how hungrily Vimes's eyes watched it.

The new sergeant-at-arms picked up his badge with care and saluted yet again. 'Oath, sir,' he said.

'Oh, er, that thing? Er, I believe I've got it written down somewh—'

Vimes took a deep breath. This probably wasn't a good idea, but he was flying now.

'I comma square bracket recruit's name square bracket comma do solemnly swear by square bracket recruit's deity of choice square bracket to uphold the Laws and Ordinances of the city of Ankh-Morpork comma serve the public truſt comma and defend the ſubjects of His ſtroke Her bracket delete whichever is inappropriate bracket Majeſty bracket name of reigning monarch bracket without fear comma favour comma or thought of perſonal ſafety semi-colon to purſue evildoers and protect the innocent comma laying down my life if neceſſary in the cau*f*e of said duty comma so help me bracket afore*f*aid deity bracket full stop Gods Save the King stroke Queen bracket delete whichever is inappropriate bracket full stop.'

'My word, well done,' said Tilden. 'You *have* come well prepared, sergeant.'

'And now it's the King's Shilling, sir,' said Vimes insistently, soaring on wings of audacity.

'What?'

'I have to take the King's Shilling, sir.'

'Er . . . do we have a—'

'It's, hnah, in the bottom drawer, sir,' said Snouty helpfully. 'On the bit of string.'

'Oh yes,' said Tilden, beaming. 'It's a long time since we used that, what?'

'Is it?' said Vimes.

After some rummaging, Tilden produced the coin. It was a genuine old shilling, probably worth half a dollar now just for its silver and thus, coppers being coppers, it had always been dropped into the new copper's hand and then tugged away before it was pinched.

Vimes had taken the oath once. He wondered if taking it twice cancelled it out. But it needed to be done and you had at least to *touch* the Shilling. He felt the weight in his palm and took a small shameful pleasure in closing his fingers on it before the captain had time to drag it back. Then, point made, he released the grip.

With a final salute he turned, and tapped Snouty on the shoulder. 'With the captain's permission, I'd like a chat with you outside, please.'

And Vimes strode out.

Snouty looked at Tilden, who was still sitting as though hypnotized, the Shilling dangling from his fist. The captain managed to say, 'Good man, that. Ver' good . . . got backbone . . .'

'Hnah, I'll just go an' see what he wants, sir,' said Snouty, and scuttled out.

He had reached the end of the corridor when a hand came out of the shadows and pulled him close.

'You're a useful man to know, Snouty,' hissed Vimes. 'I can tell.'

'Yessir,' said Snouty, held half on tiptoe.

'You've got your ear to the ground, eh?'

'Yessir!'

'There's someone in every nick who knows all that's going on and can lay his hands on just about anything, Snouty, and I think you are that man.'

'Hnah, yessir!'

'Then listen here,' said Vimes. 'Size eight boots, size seven-and-a-quarter helmet, a *good* leather cape. The boots should be a good make but second-hand. Got that?'

'Second-hand?'

'Yes. Soles pretty nearly worn through.'

'Soles pretty nearly worn through, hnah, check,' said Snouty.

'Breastplate not to have any rust on it but a few dents will be okay. A *good* sword, Snouty, and believe me I know a good sword when I hold one. As for all the rest of the stuff, well, I *know* a man like you can get hold of the very best and have it delivered to Dr Lawn's place in Twinkle Street by ten this morning. And there'll be something in it for you, Snouty.'

'What'll that be, sir?' said Snouty, who was finding the grip uncomfortable.

'My undying friendship, Snouty,' said Vimes. 'Which is going to be an extremely rare coin in these parts, let me tell you.'

'Right you are, sarge,' said Snouty. 'And will you be wanting a bell, sir?'

'A bell?'

'For ringing and shouting, hnah, "all's well!" with, sarge.'

Vimes considered this. A bell. Well, every copper still got a bell, it was down there in the regulations, but Vimes had banned its use on anything but ceremonial occasions.

'No bell for me, Snouty,' said Vimes. 'Do *you* think things are well?'

Snouty swallowed. 'Could go either way, sarge,' he managed.

'Good man. See you this afternoon.'

There was a glow of dawn in the sky when Vimes strode out, but the city was still a pattern of shadows.

In his pocket was the reassuring heaviness of the badge. And in his mind the huge, huge freedom of the oath. Ruler after ruler had failed to notice what a devious oath it was . . .

He walked as steadily as he could down to Twinkle Street. A couple of watchmen tried to waylay him, but he showed them the badge and more importantly he had the *voice* now, it had come back to him. It was night and he was walking the streets and he *owned* the damn streets and somehow that came out in the way he spoke. They'd hurried off. He wasn't sure they'd believed him, but at least they'd pretended to; the *voice* had told them he could be the kind of trouble they weren't paid enough to deal with.

At one point he had to step aside as a very thin horse dragged a huge and familiar four-wheeled wagon over the cobbles. Frightened faces looked out at him from between the wide metal strips that covered most of it, and then it disappeared into the gloom. Curfew was claiming its nightly harvest.

These were not good times. Everyone knew Lord Winder was insane. And then some kid who was equally mad had tried to knock him off and would have done, too, if the man hadn't moved at the wrong moment. His lordship had taken the arrow in the arm, and they said – *they* being the nameless people of the kind that everyone met in the pub – that the wound had poisoned him and made him worse. He suspected everyone and everything, he saw dark assassins in every corner. The rumour was that he woke up sweating every night because they even got into his dreams.

And he saw plots and spies everywhere throughout his waking hours, and had men root them out, and the thing about rooting out plots and spies everywhere is that, even if there are no real plots to begin with, there are plots and spies galore very soon.

At least the Night Watch didn't have to do much of the actual rooting. They just arrested the pieces. It was the *special* office in Cable Street that was the long hand of his lordship's paranoia.

The Particulars, they were officially, but as far as Vimes could remember they'd revelled in their nickname of the 'Unmentionables'. They were the ones that listened in every shadow and watched at every window. That was how it seemed, anyway. They certainly were the ones who knocked on doors in the middle of the night.

Vimes stopped, in the dark. The cheap clothes were soaked through, the boots were flooded, rain was trickling off his chin and he was a long, long way from home. Yet, in a treacherous kind of way, *this* was home. He'd spent most of his days working nights. Walking through the wet streets of a sleeping city was his life.

The nature of the night changed, but the nature of the beast remained the same.

He reached into the ragged pocket and touched the badge again.

In the darkness where lamps were few and far between, Vimes knocked on a door. A light was burning in one of the lower windows, so Lawn was presumably still awake.

After a while a very small panel slid back and he heard a voice say, 'Oh . . . it's you.' There was a pause, followed by the sound of bolts being released.

The doctor opened the door. In one hand he held a very long syringe. Vimes found his gaze inexorably drawn to it. A bead of something purple dripped off the end and splashed on to the floor.

'What would you have done, *injected* me to death?' he said.

'This?' Lawn looked at the instrument as if unaware that he'd been holding it. 'Oh . . . just sorting out a little problem for someone. Patients turn up at all hours.'

'I'll bet they do. Er . . . Rosie said you had a spare room,' said Vimes. 'I can pay,' he added quickly. 'I've got a job. Five dollars a month? I won't be needing it for long.'

'Upstairs on the left,' said Lawn, nodding. 'We can talk about it in the morning.'

'I'm not a criminal madman,' said Vimes. He wondered why he said it, and then wondered who he was trying to reassure.

91

'Never mind, you'll soon fit in,' said Lawn. There was a whimper from the door leading to the surgery.

'The bed's not aired but I doubt that you'll care,' he said. 'And now, if you'll excuse me . . .'

It wasn't aired, and Vimes didn't care. He didn't even remember getting into it.

He woke up once, in panic, and heard the sound of the big black wagon rattling down the street. And then it just, quite seamlessly, became part of the nightmare.

At ten o'clock in the morning Vimes found a cold cup of tea by his bed and a pile of clothes and armour on the floor outside the door. He drank the tea while he inspected the pile.

He'd read Snouty right. The man survived because he was a weathercock and kept an eye on which way the wind was blowing, and right now the wind was blowing due Vimes. He'd even included fresh socks and drawers, which hadn't been in the specification. It was a thoughtful touch. They probably hadn't been paid for, of course. They had been 'obtained'. This was the *old* Night Watch.

But, glory be, the breathy little crawler had scrounged something else, too. The three stripes for a sergeant had a little gold crown above them. Vimes instinctively disliked crowns, but this was one he was prepared to treasure.

He went downstairs, doing up his belt, and bumped into Lawn coming out of his surgery, wiping his hands on a cloth. The doctor smiled absently, then focused on the uniform. The smile did not so much fade as drain.

'Shocked?' said Vimes.

'Surprised,' said the doctor. 'Rosie won't be, I expect. I don't do anything illegal, you know.'

'Then you've got nothing to fear,' said Vimes.

'Really? That *proves* you're not from round here,' said Lawn. 'Want some breakfast? There's kidneys.' This time it was Vimes's smile that drained. 'Lamb,' the doctor added.

In the tiny kitchen he prised the lid off a tall stone jar and pulled out a can. Vapour poured off it.

'Ice,' he said. 'Get it from over the road. Keeps food fresh.'

Vimes's brow wrinkled. 'Over the road? You mean the mortuary?'

'Don't worry, it's not been used,' said Lawn, putting a pan on the stove. 'Mr Garnish drops off a lump a few times a week, in payment for being cured of a rather similar medical condition.'

'But mostly you work for the ladies of, shall we say, negotiable affection?' said Vimes. Lawn gave him a sharp look to see if he was joking, but Vimes's expression hadn't changed.

'Not just them,' he said. 'There are others.'

'People who come in by the back door,' said Vimes, looking around the little room. 'People who for one reason or another don't want to go to the . . . better known doctors?'

'Or can't afford them,' said Lawn. 'People who turn up with no identity. And you had a point . . . *John*?'

'No, no, just asking,' said Vimes, cursing himself for walking right into it. 'I just wondered where you trained.'

'Why?'

'The kind of people who come in by the back door are the kind of people who want results, I imagine.'

'Hah. Well, I trained in Klatch. They have some novel ideas about medicine over there. They think it's a good idea to get patients better, for one thing.' He turned over the kidneys with a fork. 'Frankly, sergeant, I'm pretty much like you. We do what needs doing, we work in, er, unpopular areas and I suspect we both draw the line somewhere. I'm no butcher. Rosie says you aren't. But you do the job that's in front of you, or people die.'

'I'll remember that,' said Vimes.

'And when all's said and done,' said Lawn, 'there are worse things to do in the world than take the pulse of women.'

After breakfast Sergeant-at-Arms John Keel stepped out into the first day of the rest of his life.

He stood still for a moment, shut his eyes, and swivelled both feet like a man trying to stub out two cigarettes at once. A slow, broad smile spread across his face. Snouty had found just the right kind of boots. Willikins and Sybil between them conspired to prevent him wearing old, well-worn boots these da— those days, and stole them away in the night to have the soles repaired. It was good to *feel* the streets with dry feet again. And after a lifetime of walking them, he *did* feel the streets. There were the cobblestones: catheads, trollheads, loaves, short and long setts, rounders, Morpork Sixes, and the eighty-seven types of paving brick, and the fourteen types of stone slab, and the twelve types of stone never intended for street slabs which had got used anyway, and had their own patterns of wear, and the rubbles and the gravels, and the repairs, and the thirteen different types of cellar cover and twenty types of drain lid—

He bounced a little, like a man testing the hardness of something. 'Elm Street,' he said. He bounced again. 'Junction with Twinkle. Yeah.'

He was back.

It wasn't many steps to Treacle Mine Road, and as he turned towards the Watch House a flash of colour caught his eye.

And there it was, overhanging a garden wall. Lilac was common in the city. It was vigorous and hard to kill and had to be. The flower buds were noticeably swelling.

He stood and stared, as a man might stare at an old battlefield.

. . . they rise hands up, hands up, hands up . . .

How did it go, now? Think of things happening one after the other. Don't assume that you know what's going to happen, because it might not. Be yourself.

And, because he was himself, he made a few little purchases in little shops in dark alleys, and went to work.

The Treacle Mine Road Night Watch House was generally deserted around midday, but Vimes knew that Snouty, at least, would be there. He was a Persistent Floater, just like Nobby and Colon and Carrot and, when you got down to it, Vimes as well. Being on duty was their default state of being. They hung around the Watch House even when off duty, because that's where their lives took place. Being a copper wasn't something you left hanging by the door when you went home.

But I promise I'll learn how, thought Vimes. When I get back, it'll all be different.

He went around the back and let himself in by the stable entrance. It wasn't even locked. Black mark right there, lads.

The iron bulk of the hurry-up wagon stood empty on the cobbles.

Behind it was what they called, now, the stables. In fact, the stables were only the bottom floor of what would have been part of Ankh-Morpork's industrial heritage, if anyone had ever thought of it like that. In practice they thought of it as junk that was too heavy to cart away. It was part of the winding gear from a treacle mine, long since abandoned. One of the original lifting buckets was still up there, glued to the floor by its last load of the heavy, sticky, unrefined treacle which, once set, was tougher than cement and more waterproof than tar. Vimes remembered, as a kid, begging chippings of pig treacle off the miners; one lump of that, oozing the sweetness of prehistoric sugar cane, could keep a boy's mouth happily shut for a week.*

Inside the treacle-roofed stable level, chewing a bit of bad hay, was the horse. Vimes knew it was a horse because it checked out as one: four hooves, tail, head with mane, seedy brown coat. Considered from another angle, it was half a ton of bones held together with horsehair.

He patted it gingerly; as one of nature's pedestrians, he'd never been at home around horses. He unhooked a greasy clip-board from a nail near by and flicked through its pages. Then he had another look around the yard. Tilden never did that. He

---

* In the same way that ancient forests become coal, ancient swaths of natural sugar cane can become, under the pressure of millennia, what in various parts of the Disc is known as hokey-pokey, pig treacle or rock molasses. But much boiling and purification was necessary to create the thick golden syrup that was the city dweller's honey, and these days Ankh-Morpork's supplies come from the more accessible toffee beds near Quirm.

looked at the pigsty in the corner where Knock kept his pig, and then at the chicken run, and the pigeon loft, and the badly made rabbit hutches, and he did a few calculations.

The old Watch House! It was all there, just like the day he first arrived. It had been two houses once, and one of them had been the treacle mine office. Everywhere in the city had been something else once. And so the place was a maze of blocked-in doorways and ancient windows and poky rooms.

He wandered around like a man in a museum. See the old helmet on a stick for archery practice! See Sergeant Knock's broken-springed armchair, where he used to sit out on sunny afternoons!

And, inside, the smell: floor wax, stale sweat, armour polish, unwashed clothes, ink, a hint of fried fish and always, here, a taint of treacle.

The Night Watch. He *was* back.

When the first members of the Night Watch came in they found a man perfectly at ease, leaning back in a chair with his feet on a desk and leafing through paperwork. The man had sergeant's stripes and an air of an unsprung trap. He was also giving absolutely no attention to the newcomers. He particularly paid no heed to one gangly lance-constable who was still new enough to have tried to put a shine on his breastplate . . .

They fanned out among the desks, with muttered conversations.

Vimes knew them in his soul. They were in the Night Watch because they were too scruffy, ugly, incompetent, awkwardly shaped or bloody-minded for the Day Watch. They were honest, in that special policeman sense of the word. That is, they didn't steal things too heavy to carry. And they had the morale of damp gingerbread.

He'd wondered last night about giving them some kind of pep talk by way of introduction, and decided against it. They might be very bad at it but they *were* coppers, and coppers did not respond well to the Happy Families approach: 'Hello, chaps, call me Christopher, my door is always open, I'm sure if we all pull together we shall get along splendidly like one big happy family.' They'd seen too many families to fall for that rubbish.

Someone cleared their throat with malice aforethought. Vimes glanced up and into the face of Sergeant 'Knocker' Knock and, for a fraction of a second, had to suppress the urge to salute. Then he remembered what Knock was.

'Well?' he said.

'That's *my* desk you're sitting at, sergeant,' said Knock.

Vimes sighed, and pointed to the little crown on his sleeve. 'See this, sergeant?' he said. 'It's what they used to call the hat of authority.'

Knock's little weaselly eyes focused on the crown. And then they went back to Vimes's face, and widened in the shock of recognition.

'Bloody hell,' breathed Knock.

'That's "bloody hell, *sir*,"' said Vimes. 'But "sarge" will do. Most of the time. And this is your mob, is it? Oh dear. Well, let's make a start.'

He swung his feet off the desk and stood up. 'I've been looking at the feed bills for Marilyn,' he said. 'Interesting reading, lads. According to my rough calculations a horse eating that much ought to be approximately spherical. Instead, she's so thin that with two sticks and some sheet music I could give you a tune.'

Vimes put the papers down. 'Don't think I don't know where the corn goes. I bet I know who's got the chickens and rabbits and pigeons,' he said. 'And the pig. I bet the captain thinks they get fat on leftovers.'

'Yeah, but—' a voice began.

Vimes's hand slammed on the desk. 'You lot even starve the damn horse!' he said. 'That stops right now! So will a lot of other things. I know how it works, see? Mumping free beer and a doughnut, well, that's part of being a copper. And who knows, there might even be a few greasy spoons in this town *so happy* to see a copper that they will spontaneously offer him a free nosh. Stranger things have happened. But nicking the oats from Marilyn, that stops now. And another thing. Says here that last night the hurry-up wagon had eight passengers,' he said. 'Two of them I know about, .'cos one of them must've been me and I met the other man. The cells are empty this morning. What happened to the other six? Sergeant Knock?'

The sergeant licked his lips nervously. 'Dropped 'em off in Cable Street for questioning, o'course,' he said. 'As per instructions.'

'Did you get a receipt?'

'A what?'

'Your men hauled in six people who were staying out late and you handed them over to the Unmentionables,' said Vimes, with the calm that comes before a storm. 'Did they sign for them? Do you even know their names?'

'Orders is just to hand 'em over,' said Knock, trying a little defiance. 'Hand 'em over and come away.'

Vimes filed that for future reference and said: 'Now, *I* didn't get taken there 'cos we had a bit of a . . . misunderstanding. And as you can see it was a bigger misunderstanding than you thought, because I'm *not* down in the Tanty counting cockroaches, Knock. No, indeed.' He took a few steps forward. 'I am standing in *front* of you, Knock. Isn't that what I'm doing?'

'Yes, sarge,' Knock muttered, pale with fear and fury.

'Yes, sarge,' said Vimes. 'But there was another man in the cells, and he's gone too. All I want to know is: how much, and who to? I don't want any looks of cherubic innocence, I don't want any "don't know what you're talking about, sir", I just want to know: how much, and who to?'

A cloud of red, resentful solidarity settled over the faces in front of him. But he didn't need telling. He could *remember*. Corporal Quirke always had a private income from bribes; he'd been like Nobby Nobbs without the latter's amiable incompetence. An *efficient* Nobby, in fact, and you could throw into the mix bullying and brown-nosing and a delight in small evils.

Vimes's gaze fell on Quirke, and stayed there.

'I know you were on the wagon last night, corporal,' he said. 'You and Lance-Constable, er, Vimes, it says here.'

'Not worth worrying anyone if they look a decent sort,' Quirke said. And he'd said: 'How can we tell they're a decent sort, corp?'

'Well, see how much they can afford.'

'You mean we let 'em go if they're rich?'

'Way of the world, lad, way of the world. No reason why we shouldn't get our share, eh? Did you see his moneybag? Five dollars should do it. Four for me and one for you, 'cos you're learning. That's nearly three days' pay, it'll cheer up your ol' mum no end, and where's the loser?'

'But suppose he's nicked the money, corp?'

'Suppose the moon was made of cheese? Would you like a slice?'

'I think it was five dollars, corporal,' said Vimes, and watched the man's lizard eyes flash towards the young lance-constable.

'No, the man in the cell talked,' lied Vimes. 'Told me I was an idiot not to buy my way out. So, Mister Quirke, it's like this. They're crying out for good men in the Day Watch, but if you don't stand too close to the light you might pass. Get along there right now!'

'Everybody does it!' Quirke burst out. 'It's *perks*!'

'Everybody?' said Vimes. He looked around at the squad. 'Anyone else here take bribes?'

His glare ran from face to face, causing most of the squad to do an immediate impression of the Floorboard and Ceiling Inspectors Synchronized Observation Team. Only three members met his gaze. There was Lance-Corporal Colon, who could be a little slow. There was a certain lance-constable, whose face was a mask of terror. And there was a dark-haired, round-faced constable who seemed to be puzzled, as if he was trying to remember something, but who nevertheless stared back with the firm steady gaze of the true liar.

'Apparently not,' said Vimes.

Quirke's finger shot out and vibrated in the direction of the young Sam Vimes.

'He shared it! He shared it!' he said. 'You ask him!'

Vimes felt the shock run round the squad. Quirke had just committed suicide. You hung together against officers, fair enough, but when the jig was up you did not Drop Someone In The Cacky. They'd laugh at the idea of a watchman's honour, but it did exist in a blackened, twisty way. You Did Not Drop Your Mates In The Cacky. And especially you did not do it to a wet-behind-the-ears rookie who wouldn't know any better.

Vimes turned, for the first time, to the young man he'd been avoiding.

Gods, was I ever that skinny? he thought. Did I ever have that much Adam's apple? Did I really try to polish rust?

The young man's eyes were almost back in his head, only the whites showing.

'Lance-Constable Vimes, isn't it?' he said quietly.

'Yessir!' said Sam hoarsely.

'At ease, lance-constable. Did you in fact take a share of the bribe?'

'Yessir! A dollar, sir!'

'At the instigation of Corporal Quirke?'

'Er . . . sir?'

'Did he offer it to you?' Vimes translated.

Vimes watched his own agony. You Did Not Drop Someone In The Cacky.

'All right,' he said at last. 'I'll talk to you later on. Oh, you still here, Quirke? If you want to complain to the captain, that's fine by me. But if you don't get your stuff out of your locker in ten minutes I'll damn well charge you rent!'

Quirke looked around for immoral support, and found none. He'd gone too far. Besides, the Watch could see a storm of cacky when it was right overhead and were in no mood to stick their necks out for something like Quirke.

'I will,' he said. 'I *will* complain to the captain. You'll see. You'll see. I've got four years' good conduct, I have—'

'No, that was four years' Not Found Out,' said Vimes. 'Clear off.'

When Quirke's footsteps had died away Vimes glared at the squad.

'Good afternoon, lads, my name's John Keel,' he said. 'We bloody well better get along fine. Now shine up, captain's inspection in two minutes, off you go . . . Sergeant Knock, a word, please.'

The men dispersed hurriedly. Knock stepped forward, not quite managing to conceal his nervousness. After all, his immediate superior now was a man who, last night, he had kicked in the nadgers. People could hold a grudge about a thing like that. And he'd had time to think.

'I'd just like to say, sir, about last night—' he began.

'I'm not bothered about last night,' said Vimes.

'You're not?'

'Would you recommend Fred Colon for corporal? I'd value your judgement.'

'You would?'

'Certainly. He looks a solid lad.'

'He is? I mean, yes, he is. Very thorough,' said Knock, relief rising off him like steam. 'Doesn't rush into things. Wants to join one of the regiments.'

'Well, we'll give him a try while we've still got him. That means we'll need another lance-corporal. Who was that lad next to Colon?'

'Coates, sir. Ned Coates. Bright lad, sometimes thinks he knows better, but we were all like that, eh?'

Vimes nodded. His expression completely failed to give away the fact that, as far as he was concerned, there were things clinging to the underside of high branches that knew better than Sergeant Knock.

'A taste of responsibility might do him some good, then,' he said. Knock nodded, because at that point he would have agreed to absolutely anything. And his body language was saying: we're all sergeants together, right? We're talking about sergeanty things, like sergeants do. We're not bothered about anyone being kicked in the nadgers, eh? Not us! 'cos we're sergeants.

His eyes widened, and he saluted as Tilden entered the office. There was some half-hearted saluting among the squad, too. The captain acknowledged them stiffly, and looked nervously at Vimes.

'Ah, sergeant,' he said. 'Settling in?'

'Yessir. No problems.'

'Well done. Carry on.'

When the man had disappeared up the creaking stairs Vimes turned back to Knock.

'Sergeant, we don't hand over prisoners without a receipt, understand? Never! What happens to them afterwards? Do you *know*?'

'They get questioned,' said Knock. 'We takes 'em up there for questioning.'

'What kind of questions? How long it takes two men to dig half a hole?'

'What?' Knock's brow knitted.

'From now on, someone at Cable Street signs for prisoners or we bring them right back here,' said Vimes. 'It's bloody *elementary*, sergeant. You hand 'em over, you get a docket. Don't you do that down at the Tanty?'

'Well, yeah, obviously, but . . . well, Cable Street . . . I mean, you don't know what it's like here, I can see that, but with the Unmentionables round at Cable Street it's best not to—'

'Listen, I'm not telling you to kick the door down and shout "put down those thumbscrews!" ' said Vimes. 'I'm telling you we keep *track* of prisoners. When you arrest a man, you sign him over to Snouty, don't you? When he leaves, Snouty or the orderly man signs him out, doesn't he? It's basic custody

102

discipline, man! So if you hand a prisoner over to Cable Street, someone *there* gives you a signature. Understand? No one just *disappears.*'

Knock's face showed a man contemplating an immediate future that contained fewer opportunities for personal gain and a greatly raised risk of being shouted at.

'And just to make sure everyone understands, I'll ride the wagon tonight,' said Vimes. 'But first I'll take that lad Vimes out for a stroll and shake him up a bit.'

'He could do with it,' said Knock. 'Can't get his mind right. Good with his hands but you have to tell him everything twice.'

'Maybe I'll shout, then,' said Vimes. 'Vimes!'

Lance-Constable Vimes shivered to attention.

'We're going to take a stroll, lad,' said Vimes. 'Time you knew what's what.' He nodded to Knock, took his younger self by the shoulder, and marched out.

'What d'you think, sarge?' said Coates, coming up behind Knock as the sergeant glared at the departing back.

'He likes *you*,' said Knock bitterly. 'Oh, *yes*. Apple of his eye, *you* are. You're his ol' pal. *You're* being bumped up to lance-corporal.'

'Think he'll last?'

'I'll give him a couple of weeks,' said Knock. 'I've seen 'em like that before. Big men in little towns, coming here, thinking they're the bee's nose. We soon cut 'em down to size. What d'you think?'

'Dunno, sarge,' said Coates. 'Still thinking.'

'Knows his coppering, mind you,' said Knock. 'Bit too cocky though. He'll learn. He'll learn. There's ways. We'll show him. Take him down a peg. Teach him how we do things around here . . .'

Vimes always preferred to walk by himself. And now there were two of him, walking by himself. It was a strange sensation, and gave him the impression that he was looking through a mask.

'No, not like that,' he said. 'I always have to teach people to walk. You swing the foot, like this. Get it right and you can keep going all day. You're not in a hurry. You don't want to miss things.'

'Yes, sarge,' said young Sam.

It was called proceeding. Vimes proceeded along Treacle Mine Road, and felt – magnificent. Of *course* there were lots of things to worry about, but right here and now all he had to do was patrol, and it felt fine. Not much paperwork in the old Watch; in fact, come to think of it he'd probably doubled it. All he had to do right now was his duty, as he'd been taught it. He had nothing to do but be himself.

Young Sam wasn't saying much. That was good sense.

'I see you've got a bell there, lad,' said Vimes, after a while.

'Yes, sarge.'

'Regulation bell?'

'Yes, sarge. Sergeant Knock gave it to me.' I'll bet he did, thought Vimes.

'When we get back, just you swap it for someone else's. Doesn't matter whose. No one'll say anything.'

'Yes, sarge.' Vimes waited. 'Why, sarge? A bell's a bell.'

'Not that one,' said Vimes. 'That's three times the weight of the normal bell. They give it to rookies to see what they do. Did you complain?'

'No, sarge.'

'That's the way. Keep quiet, and pass it on to some other sucker when we get back. That's the coppers' way. Why did you come into the job, lad?'

'My mate Iffy joined last year. He said you got free food and a uniform and you could pick up the extra dollar here and there.'

'That'd be Iffy Scurrick stationed over in the Dolly Sisters house, then,' said Vimes. 'And you've been picking up the odd dollar, have you?'

They walked in silence for a moment. Then Sam said: 'Have I got to give that dollar back, sarge?'

'Are you *worth* a dollar?' said Vimes.

'I gave it our mum, sarge.'

'Did you tell her how you got it?'

'I didn't want it!' Sam blurted out. 'But Corporal Quirke said—'

'Was he worth listening to?'

'Dunno, sarge.'

'You don't know? I bet your mum didn't bring you up to think like that,' said Vimes. No, she bloody well didn't, he thought. She'd tan your hide, copper or not, if she knew it was a dodgy dollar.

'No, sarge. But they're all at it, sarge. I don't mean the lads, sarge, but you only have to look round the city. Our rent's going up, taxes go up, there's these new taxes all the time, and it's all just cruel, sarge, it's cruel. Winder sold us all to his mates, and that's a fact, sir.'

'Hmm,' said Vimes. Oh, yes. Tax farming. What a clever invention. Good old Winder. He'd flogged the right to collect taxes to the highest bidders. What a great idea, nearly as good as banning people from carrying weapons after dark. Because a) you saved the cost of tax collectors and the whole revenue system b) you got a wagonload of cash up front. And c) the business of tax gathering then became the business of groups of powerful yet curiously reticent people who kept out of the light. However, they employed people who not only went out in the light but positively blocked it, and it was *amazing* what those people found to tax, up to and including Looking At Me, Pal. What was it Vetinari had said once? 'Taxation is just a sophisticated way of demanding money with menaces'? Well, the tax farmers were very unsophisticated in the way they went about recouping their investment.

He remembered those da— *these* days. The city had never seemed poorer, but by the gods there was a lot of tax being paid.

Hard to explain to a kid like Sam why poncing a dollar when you got the chance was a bad thing to do.

'Put it like this, lance-constable,' as they turned the corner. 'Would you let a murderer off for a thousand dollars?'

'No, sir!'

'A thousand dollars'd set your mum up in a nice place in a good part of town, though.'

'Knock it off, sarge, I'm not like that.'

'You were when you took that dollar. Everything else is just a haggling over the price.'

They walked in sullen silence. Then:

'Am I going to get the sack, sarge?' said the lance-constable.

'For a dollar? No.'

'I'd just as soon *be* sacked, sarge, thanks all the same,' said young Sam defiantly. 'Last Friday we had to go and break up some meeting over near the University. They were just talking! And we had to take orders from some *civilian*, and the Cable Street lads were a bit rough and . . . it's not like the people had weapons or anything. You can't tell me *that's* right, sarge. And then we loaded some of 'em into the hurry-up, just for talking. Mrs Owlesly's boy Elson never came home the other night, too, and they say he was dragged off to the palace just for saying his lordship's a loony. Now people down our street are looking at me in a funny way.'

Ye gods, I remember, thought Vimes. I thought it was all going to be chasing men who gave up after the length of a street and said 'It's a fair cop, guv'nor'. I thought I'd have a medal by the end of the week.

'You want to be careful what you say, lad,' he said.

'Yeah, but our mum says it's fair enough if they take away the troublemakers and the weirdies but it's not right them taking away ordinary people.'

Is this *really* me? Vimes thought. Did I really have the political awareness of a head louse?

'Anyway, he *is* a loony. Snapcase is the man we ought to have.'

. . . and the self-preservation instincts of a lemming?

'Kid, here's some advice. In this town, right now, if you don't know who you're talking to – don't talk.'

'Yes, but Snapcase says—'

'*Listen*. A copper doesn't keep flapping his lip. He doesn't let on what he knows. He doesn't say what he's thinking. No. He watches and listens and he learns and he bides his time. His mind works like mad but his face is a blank. Until he's ready. Understand?'

'All right, sarge.'

'Good. Can you use that sword you have there, lad?'

'I did the training, yes.'

'Fine. Fine. The training. Fine. So if we're attacked by a lot of sacks of straw hanging from a beam, I can rely on you. And until then shut up, keep your ears open and your eyes peeled and *learn* something.'

Snapcase is the man to save us, he thought glumly. Yeah, I used to believe that. A lot of people did. Just because he rode around in an open carriage occasionally and called people over and talked to them, the level of the conversation being on the lines of: 'So you're a carpenter, are you? Wonderful! What does that job entail?' Just because he said publicly that perhaps taxes were a bit on the high side. Just because he *waved*.

'You been here before, sarge?' said Sam, as they turned a corner.

'Oh, everyone's visited Ankh-Morpork, lad,' said Vimes jovially.

'Only we're doing the Elm Street beat perfectly, sarge, and I've been letting you lead the way.'

Damn. That was the kind of trouble your feet could get you into. A wizard once told Vimes that there were monsters up near the Hub that were so big they had to have extra brains in their legs, 'cos they were too far away for one brain to think fast enough. And a beat copper grew brains in his feet, he really did.

Elm Street, left into The Pitts, left again into The Scours . . . it was the first beat he'd ever walked, and he could do it without thinking. He *had* done it without thinking.

'I do my homework,' he said.

'Did you recognize Ned?' said Sam.

Perhaps it was a good thing that he was leaving his feet to their own devices, because Vimes's brain suddenly filled with warning bells.

'Ned?' he said.

'Only before you came he said he thought he remembered you from Pseudopolis,' said Sam, oblivious of the clamour. 'He was in the Day Watch there before he came here 'cos of better promotion prospects. Big man, he said.'

'Can't say I recall him,' said Vimes, with care.

'You're not all that big, sarge.'

'Well, Ned was probably shorter in those days,' said Vimes, while his thoughts shouted: shut up, kid! But the kid was . . . well, him. Niggling at little details. Tugging at things that didn't seem to fit right. Being a copper, in fact. Probably he ought to feel proud of his younger self, but he didn't.

You're not me, he thought. I don't think I was ever as young as you. If you're *going* to be me, it's going to take a lot of work. Thirty damn years of being hammered on the anvil of life, you poor bastard. You've got it all to come.

Back at the Watch House, Vimes wandered idly over to the Evidence and Lost Property cupboard. It had a big lock on it which was not, however, ever locked. He soon found what he was looking for. An unpopular copper needed to think ahead, and he intended to be unpopular.

Then he had a bite of supper and a mug of the thick brown cocoa on which the Night Watch ran and took Sam out on the hurry-up wagon.

He'd wondered how the Watch was going to play it and wasn't surprised to find they were using the old dodge of obeying orders to the letter with gleeful malignancy. At the first point he made, Lance-Corporal Coates and Constable Waddy were waiting with four sullen or protesting insomniacs.

'Four, *sah*,' said Coates, ripping off a textbook salute. 'All we've apprehended *sah*. All written down on this chitty what I am giving to you at this moment in time sah!'

'Well done, lance-corporal,' said Vimes, drily, taking the paperwork, signing one copy and handing it back. 'You may have a half-holiday at Hogswatch, and give my regards to your granny. Help 'em in with 'em, Sam.'

'We usually only get four or five on a round, sir!' Sam whispered, as they pulled away. 'What'll we do?'

'Make several journeys,' said Vimes.

'But the lads were taking the pi— the michael, sir! They were laughing!'

'It's past curfew,' said Vimes. 'That's the law.'

Corporal Colon and Constable Wiglet were waiting at their post with three miscreants.

One of them was Miss Palm.

Vimes gave Sam the reins and jumped down to open the back of the wagon and fold down the steps.

'Sorry to see you here, miss,' he said.

'Apparently some new sergeant's been throwing his weight around,' said Rosie Palm, in a voice of solid ice. She refused his hand haughtily, and climbed up into the wagon.

Vimes realized that one of the other detainees was a woman, too. She was shorter than Rosie, and was giving him a look of pure bantam defiance. She was also holding a huge quilted workbasket. Out of reflex Vimes took it, to help her up the steps.

'Sorry about this, miss—' he began.

'Get your hands off that!' She snatched the basket back and scrambled into the darkness.

'Pardon *me*,' said Vimes.

'This is Miss Battye,' said Rosie, from the bench inside the wagon. 'She's a seamstress.'

'Well, I assumed she—'

109

'A *seamstress*, I said,' said Miss Palm. 'With *needles* and *thread*. Also specializes in crochet.'

'Er, is that a kind of extra—' Vimes began.

'It's a type of knitting,' said Miss Battye, from the darkness of the wagon. 'Fancy you not knowing that.'

'You mean she's a *real*—' said Vimes, but Rosie slammed the iron door. 'You just drive us on,' she said, 'and when I see you again, John Keel, we are going to have *words*!'

There was some sniggering from the shadows inside the wagon, and then a yelp. It had been immediately preceded by the noise of a spiky heel being driven into an instep.

Vimes signed the grubby form presented to him by Fred Colon and handed it back with a solid, fixed expression that made the man feel rather worried.

'Where to now, sarge?' said Sam, as they pulled away.

'Cable Street,' said Vimes. There was a murmur of dismay from the crated people behind them.

'That's not right,' muttered Sam.

'We're playing this by the rules,' said Vimes. 'You're going to have to learn why we have rules, lance-constable. And don't you eyeball me. I've been eyeballed by experts, and *you* look as if you're desperate for the privy.'

'Yeah, all right, but everyone knows they torture people,' mumbled Sam.

'Do they?' said Vimes. 'Then why doesn't anyone do anything about it?'

''cos they torture people.'

Ah, at least I was getting a grasp of basic social dynamics, thought Vimes.

Sullen silence reigned in the seat beside him as the wagon rumbled through the streets, but he was aware of whispering behind him. Slightly louder than the background, he heard Rosie Palm's voice hiss: 'He won't. I'll bet anything.'

A few seconds later a male voice, slightly the worse for drink and very much the worse for bladder-twisting dread, managed:

'Er, sergeant, we . . . er . . . believe the fine is five, er, dollars?'

'I don't think it is, sir,' said Vimes, keeping his eyes on the damp streets.

There was some more frantic whispering, and then the voice said: 'Er . . . I have a very nice gold ring . . .'

'Glad to hear it, sir,' said Vimes. 'Everyone should have something nice.' He patted his pocket for his silver cigar case, and for a moment felt more anger than despair, and more sorrow than anger. There was a future. There had to be. He remembered it. But it only existed as that memory, and that was fragile as the reflection on a soap bubble and, maybe, just as easily popped.

'Er . . . I could perhaps include—'

'If you try to offer me a bribe one more time, sir,' said Vimes, as the wagon turned into Cable Street, 'I shall personally give you a thumping. Be told.'

'Perhaps there is some other—' Rosie Palm began, as the lights of the Cable Street House came into view.

'We're not at home to a tuppenny upright, either,' said Vimes, and heard the gasp. 'Shut up, the lot of you.'

He reined Marilyn to a halt, jumped down and pulled his clipboard from under the seat. 'Seven for you,' he said, to the guard lounging against the door.

'Well?' said the guard. 'Open it up and let's be having them, then.'

'Right,' said Vimes, flicking through the paperwork. 'No problem.' He thrust the clipboard forward. 'Just sign here.'

The man recoiled as though Vimes had tried to offer him a snake.

'What d'ya mean, sign?' he said. 'Hand 'em over!'

'You sign,' said Vimes woodenly. 'That's the rules. Prisoners moved from one custody to another, you have to sign. More'n my job's worth, not to get a signature.'

'Your job's not worth spit,' snarled the man, grabbing the board. He looked at it blankly, and Vimes handed him a pencil.

'If you need any help with the difficult letters, let me know,' he said helpfully.

Growling, the guard scrawled something on the paper and thrust it back. 'Now open up, *p-lease*,' he said.

'Certainly,' said Vimes, glancing at the paper. 'But now I'd like to see some form of ID, thank you.'

'What?'

'It's not me, you understand,' said Vimes, 'but if I went back and showed my captain this piece of paper and he said to me, Vi— Keel, how d'you *know* he's Henry the Hamster, well, I'd be a bit . . . flummoxed. Maybe even perplexed.'

'Listen, we don't sign for prisoners!'

'*We* do, Henry,' said Vimes. 'No signature, no prisoners.'

'And you'll stop us taking 'em, will you?' said Henry the Hamster, taking a few steps forward.

'You lay a hand on that door,' said Vimes, 'and I'll—'

'Chop it off, will you?'

'—I'll arrest you,' said Vimes. 'Obstruction would be a good start, but we can probably think of some more charges back at the station.'

'Arrest me? But I'm a copper, same as you!'

'Wrong again,' said Vimes.

'What is thetrouble . . . here?' said a voice.

A small, thin figure appeared in the torchlight. Henry the Hamster took a step back, and adopted a certain deferential pose.

'Officer won't hand over the curfew breakers, sir,' he said.

'And this is the officer?' said the figure, lurching towards Vimes with a curiously erratic gait.

'Yessir.'

Vimes found himself under cool and not openly hostile inspection from a pale man with the screwed-up eyes of a pet rat.

'Ah,' said the man, opening a little tin and taking out a green throat pastille. 'Would you be Keel, by anychance? I havebeen

. . . hearing about you.' The man's voice was as uncertain as his walk. Pauses turned up in the wrong places.

'You hear about things quickly, sir.'

'A salute is generally in order, sergeant.'

'I don't see anything to salute, sir,' said Vimes.

'Goodpoint. Goodpoint. You are new, of course. But, you see, we in theParticulars . . . often find it necessary to wearplain . . . clothes.'

Like rubber aprons, if I recall correctly, thought Vimes. Aloud, he said: 'Yes, sir.' It was a good phrase. It could mean any of a dozen things, or nothing at all. It was just punctuation until the man said something else.

'I'm Captain Swing,' said the man. 'Findthee Swing. If you think the name is amusing, pleasesmirk . . . and get it over with. You may now salute.'

Vimes saluted. Swing's mouth turned up at the corners very briefly.

'Good. Your first night on our hurry-up wagon, sergeant?'

'Sir.'

'And you're here so early. With a full load, too. Shall we take alook . . . at your passengers?' He glanced in between the iron-work. 'Ah. Yes. Good evening, Miss Palm. And an associate, I see—'

'I do crochet!'

'—and what appear to be some party-goers. Well, well.' Swing stood back. 'What little scamps your street officers are, to be sure. They really *have* scoured the streets. How they love their . . . littlejokes, sergeant.' Swing put his hand on the wagon door's handle and there was a little noise which was nevertheless a thunderclap in the silence, and it was the sound of a sword moving very slightly in its scabbard.

Swing stood stock still for a moment and then delicately popped the pastille into his mouth. 'Aha. I think that perhaps this little catch can be . . . thrownback, don't you,

113

sergeant? We don't want to make a mockery of . . . thelaw. Take them away, take them away.'

'Yes, sir.'

'But just onemoment, please, sergeant. Indulge me . . . just a little hobby of mine . . .'

'Sir?'

Swing had reached into a pocket of his over-long coat and pulled out a very large pair of steel calipers. Vimes flinched as they were opened up to measure the width of his head, the width of his nose and the length of his eyebrows. Then a metal ruler was pressed against one ear.

While doing this, Swing was mumbling under his breath. Then he closed the calipers with a snap, and slipped them back.

'I must congratulateyou, sergeant,' he said, 'in overcoming your considerable natural disadvantages. Do you know you have the eye of a mass murderer? I am neverwrong . . . in these matters.'

'Nosir. Didn't know that, sir. Will try to keep it closed, sir,' said Vimes. Swing didn't crack a smile.

'However, I'm sure that when you have settled in you and Corporal, aha, Hamster here will get along like a . . . houseonfire.'

'A house on fire. Yes, sir.'

'Don'tlet . . . me detain you, Sergeant Keel.'

Vimes saluted. Swing nodded, turned in one movement, as though he was on a swivel, and strode back into the Watch House. Or jerked, Vimes considered. The man moved in the same way he talked, in a curious mixture of speeds. It was as if he was powered by springs; when he moved a hand, the first few inches of movement were a blur, and then it gently coasted until it was brought into conjunction with whatever was the intended target. Sentences came out in spurts and pauses. There was no *rhythm* to the man.

Vimes ignored the fuming corporal and climbed back on to the wagon. 'Turn us round, lance-constable,' he said. 'G'night, Henry.'

Sam waited until the wheels were rumbling over the cobbles before he turned, wide-eyed, to Vimes.

'You were going to draw on him, weren't you?' he said. 'You were, sarge, weren't you?'

'You just keep your eyes on the road, lance-constable.'

'But that was Captain Swing, that was! And when you told that man to prove he was Henry the Hamster, I thought I'd widd— choke! You knew they weren't going to sign, right, sarge? 'cos if there's a bit of paper saying they've got someone, then if anyone wants to find out—'

'Just drive, lance-constable.' But the boy was right. For some reason, the Unmentionables both loved and feared paperwork. They certainly generated a lot of it. They wrote everything down. They didn't like appearing on other people's paperwork, though. That worried them.

'I can't believe we got away with it, sarge!'

We probably haven't, Vimes thought. But Swing has enough to worry him at the moment. He doesn't *care* very much about a big stupid sergeant.

He turned and banged on the ironwork.

'Sorry for the inconvenience, ladies and gentlemen, but it appears the Unmentionables are not doing business tonight. Looks like *we'll* have to do the interrogation ourselves. We're not very experienced at this, so I hope we don't get it wrong. Now, listen carefully. Are any of you serious conspirators bent on the overthrow of the government?'

There was a stunned silence from within the wagon.

'Come on, come on,' said Vimes. 'I haven't got all night. Does anyone want to overthrow Lord Winder by force?'

'Well . . . no?' said the voice of Miss Palm.

'Or by crochet?'

'I *heard* that!' said another female voice sharply.

'No one? Shame,' said Vimes. 'Well, that's good enough for me. Lance-constable, is it good enough for you?'

'Er, yes, sarge.'

'In that case we'll drop you all off on our way home, and my charming assistant Lance-Constable Vimes will take, oh, half a dollar off each of you for travelling expenses for which you *will* get a receipt. Thank you for travelling with us, and we hope you will consider the hurry-up wagon in all your future curfew-breaking arrangements.'

Vimes could hear shocked whispering behind him. This was not how things were supposed to go these days.

'Sarge,' said Lance-Constable Vimes.

'Yep?'

'Have you really got the eye of a mass murderer?'

'In the pocket of my other suit, yes.'

'Hah.' Sam was quiet for a while, and when he spoke again he seemed to have something new on his mind.

'Er, sarge?'

'Yes, lad?'

'What's a tuppenny upright, sarge?'

'It's a kind of jam doughnut, lad. Did your mum ever make 'em?'

'Yes, sarge. Sarge?'

'Yes, lad?'

'I think it probably means something else as well, sarge,' said Sam, sniggering. 'Something a bit . . . rude . . .'

'The whole of life is a learning process, lance-constable.'

They got the wagon back to the yard ten minutes later, and by that time Vimes knew that a new rumour was fanning out across the city. Young Sam had already whispered things to the other officers as the curfew-breakers were dropped off, and nobody gossips like a copper. They didn't like the Unmentionables. Like petty criminals everywhere, the watchmen prided themselves that there were some depths to which they would not sink. There had to be some things below you, even if it was only mudworms.

Rosie Palm bolted the door of her flat, leaned on it and stared at Sandra.

'What *is* he?' said Sandra, dumping her workbasket on the table. It clanked within. 'Is he on *our* side?'

'You heard the lads!' snapped Rosie. 'No bribes now! And then he drags us off to Swing's bastards and *then* he won't hand us over! I could kill him! I rescued him from the gutter, got Mossy to patch him up and suddenly he's playing big silly games!'

'Yes, what *is* a tuppenny upright?' said Sandra brightly.

Miss Palm paused. She quite enjoyed Sandra's company and the extra rent certainly came in handy, but there were times she wondered whether a) she should have a talk with the girl or b) she was being very gently wound up. She suspected the latter, since Sandra was taking more money than her most of the time. It was getting embarrassing.

'It's a kind of jam doughnut,' she said. 'Now, you'd better go and hide the—'

Someone knocked on the door behind her. She motioned Sandra through the bead curtain, took a moment to pull herself together, and opened the door a fraction.

There was a very small old man standing in the hall.

Everything about him sloped hopelessly downwards. His grey moustache could have been stolen from a walrus, or a bloodhound that had just been given some very bad news. His shoulders sagged listlessly. Even parts of his face seemed to be losing the battle with gravity.

He held his cap in his hands and was twisting it nervously.

'Yes?' said Rosie.

'Er, it said "seamstress" on the sign,' the old man mumbled. 'An', well, since my ol' woman died, you know, what with one thing an' another, never bin any good at doing it for meself . . .'

He gave Rosie a look of sheer, helpless embarrassment.

She glanced down at the sack by his feet, and picked it up. It was full of very clean, but very worn, socks. Every single one had holes in the heel and toe.

'Sandra,' she said, 'I think this one's for you . . .'

*

It was so very early in the morning that 'late at night' wasn't quite over. White mist hung everywhere in the streets, and deposited droplets like tiny pearls on Vimes's shirt as he prepared to break the law.

If you stood on the roof of the privy behind the Watch House and steadied yourself on the drainpipe, one of the upstairs windows would bounce open if you hit it with the palm of your hand in *exactly* the right place.

It was a useful bit of information, and Vimes wondered if he should pass it on to young Sam. Every honest copper ought to know how to break into his own nick.

Tilden had limped home long ago, but Vimes did a quick sweep of his office and it was with great satisfaction that he did not see what he hadn't expected to be there. Down below, a few of the more conscientious officers were signing off before heading home. He waited in the shadows until the door had banged shut for the last time and there were no footsteps for several minutes. Then he made his way down the stairs and into the locker room.

He had been issued with a key to his own locker, but still oiled the hinge from a small bottle before he opened it. He had not in fact put anything in there yet but, behold, there was a rumpled sack on the floor. He lifted it up . . .

Well *done*, lads.

Inside was Captain Tilden's silver inkwell.

Vimes stood up, and looked around at the lockers, with their ancient carved initials and occasional knife marks on the doors. He pulled from his pocket the little black cloth roll he'd taken from the evidence locker earlier. A selection of lock picks glinted in the grey light. Vimes wasn't a genius with the hooks and rakes, but the cheap and worn door locks were hardly a major challenge.

Really, it was just a matter of choosing.

And afterwards he walked back through the mists.

He was horrified to find he was feeling good again. It was a betrayal of Sybil and the future Watch and even of His Grace Sir Samuel Vimes, who had to think about the politics of distant countries and manpower requirements and how to raise that damn boat that River Division kept sinking. And, yes, he wanted to go back, or forwards or across or whatever. He really did. He wanted to go home so much he could taste it. Of course he did. But he couldn't, not yet, and here he was and as Dr Lawn said, you did the job. And currently the job involved survival on the street in the great game of Silly Buggers, and Vimes knew all about that game, oh yes. And there was a thrill in it. It was the nature of the beast.

And thus he was walking along, lost in thought, when the men jumped him from the mouth of a shadowy alley.

The first one got a foot in the stomach, because the beast does not fight fair. Vimes stepped aside and grabbed the other one. He felt the knife skitter along his breastplate as he lowered his head and tugged the man hard into the helmet.

The man folded up quite neatly on the cobbles.

Vimes spun around to the first man, who was bent almost double, and wheezing, but had nevertheless kept hold of his knife, which he waved around in front of him like some kind of talisman. The point made erratic figures-of-eight in the air.

'Drop it,' said Vimes. 'I won't ask again.'

He sighed, and pulled an object out of his back pocket. It was black and tapered and made of leather filled with lead shot. He'd banned them in the modern Watch but he knew some officers had acquired them, and if he judged the man to be sensible then he *didn't* know they'd got them. Sometimes an argument had to be ended quickly, and there were worse alternatives.

He brought the blackjack down on the man's arm, with a certain amount of care. There was a whimper and the knife bounced off the cobbles.

'We'll leave your chum to sleep it off,' he said. 'But *you* are coming to see the doctor, Henry. Are you coming quietly?'

A few minutes later Dr Lawn opened his back door and Vimes brushed past, the body over his shoulders.

'You minister to all sorts, right?' said Vimes.

'Within reason, but—'

'This one's an Unmentionable,' said Vimes. 'Tried to kill me. Needs some medicine.'

'Why's he unconscious?' said the doctor. He was wearing a huge rubber apron, and rubber boots.

'Didn't want to take his medicine.'

Lawn sighed, and with a hand that held a mop he waved Vimes towards an inner door. 'Bring him right into the surgery,' he said. 'I'm afraid I'm cleaning up after Mr Salciferous in the waiting room.'

'Why, what did *he* do?'

'He burst.'

Vimes, his natural inquisitiveness suddenly curbed, carried the body into Lawn's inner sanctum. It looked little different from when Vimes had last seen it, but then he'd barely been capable of taking in details. There was the table, and a workbench, and all along one wall were racks of bottles. No two bottles were the same size. In one or two of them, things floated.

On another wall were the instruments.

'When I die,' said Lawn, inspecting the patient, 'I'm going to instruct them to put a bell on my tombstone, just so's I can have the pleasure of not getting up when people ring. Put him down, please. Looks like concussion.'

'That was me hitting him,' said Vimes helpfully.

'You broke his arm too?'

'That's right.'

'You made a very neat job of it. Easy to set it and plaster him up. Is there something wrong?'

Vimes was still staring at the instruments. 'You use all these?' he said.

'Yes. Some of them are experimental, though,' said Lawn, busying himself at his work table.

120

'Well, I'd hate you to use this on me,' said Vimes, picking a strange instrument like a couple of paddles tied with string. Lawn sighed.

'Sergeant, there are no circumstances where the things you're holding could possibly be used on you,' he said, his hands working busily. 'They are . . . of a feminine nature.'

'For the seamstresses?' said Vimes, putting the pliers down in a hurry.

'Those things? No, the ladies of the night take pride these days in never requiring that sort of thing. My work with them is more of, shall we say, a preventative nature.'

'Teaching them to use thimbles, that sort of thing?' said Vimes.

'Yes, it's amazing how far you can push a metaphor, isn't it . . .'

Vimes prodded the paddles again. They were quite alarming.

'You're married, sergeant?' said Lawn. 'Was Rosie right?'

'Er . . . yes. My wife is, er, elsewhere, though.' He picked the things up and dropped them hastily again, with a clatter.

'Well, it's just as well to be aware that giving birth isn't like shelling peas,' said the doctor.

'I should bloody well hope not!'

'Although I have to say the midwives seldom refer anything to me. They say men shouldn't fish around where they don't belong. We might as well be living in caves.'

Lawn looked down at his patient. 'In the words of the philosopher Sceptum, the founder of my profession: am I going to get paid for this?'

Vimes investigated the moneybag on the man's belt. 'Will six dollars do it?' he said.

'Why would the Unmentionables attack *you*, sergeant? You're a policeman.'

'I am, but they aren't. Don't you know about them?'

'I've patched up a few of their guests, yes,' said Lawn, and Vimes noted the caution. It didn't pay to know too much in this town. 'People with curious dislocations, hot wax burns . . . that sort of thing . . .'

'Well, I had a little brush with Captain Swing last night,' Vimes said, 'and he was as polite as hell to me about it, but I'd bet my boots he knows that this lad and his friend came after me. That's his style. He probably wanted to see what I'd do.'

'He's not the only one interested in you,' said Lawn. 'I got a message that Rosie Palm wants to see you. Well, I assume she meant you. "That ungrateful bastard" was the actual term she used.'

'I think I owe her some money,' said Vimes, 'but I've no idea how much.'

'Don't ask me,' said Lawn, smoothing the plaster with his hand. 'She generally names her price up front.'

'I mean the finder's fee, or whatever it was!'

'Yes, I know. Can't help you there, I'm afraid,' said Lawn.

Vimes watched him working for a while, and said, 'Know anything about Miss Battye?'

'The seamstress? She hasn't been here long.'

'And she's *really* a seamstress?'

'For the sake of precision,' said Dr Lawn, 'let us say she's a needlewoman. Apparently she heard there was a lot of work for seamstresses in the big city and had one or two amusing mis-understandings before someone told her exactly what was meant. One of them involved me removing a crochet hook from a man's ear last week. Now she just hangs out with the rest of the girls.'

'Why?'

'Because she's making a fortune, that's why,' said the doctor. 'Hasn't it ever occurred to you, sergeant, that sometimes people go to a massage parlour for a *real* massage, for example? There's ladies all over this city with discreet signs up that say things like *"Trousers repaired while you wait"* and a small but significant number of men make the same mistake as Sandra. There's lots of men work here in the city and leave their wives back home and sometimes, you know, a man feels these . . . urges. Like, for a sock without holes and a shirt with more than one button. The ladies pass on the work. Apparently it's quite hard to find a really good needlewoman in this city. They don't like being confused with, er, seamstresses.'

'I just wondered why she hangs around street corners after curfew with a big sewing basket . . .' said Vimes.

Lawn shrugged. 'Can't help you there. Right, I've finished with this gentleman. It'd be helpful if he lies still for a while.' He indicated the racks of bottles behind him. 'About how long will you want him to lie still for?'

'You can do that?'

'Oh, yes. It's not accepted Ankh-Morpork medical practice, but since Anhk-Morpork medical practice would consist of hitting him on the head with a mallet he's probably getting the best of the deal.'

'No, I meant that you doctors aren't supposed to hurt people, are you?'

'Only in the course of normal incompetence. But I don't mind sending him to sleepy land for another twenty minutes. Of course, if you want to wham him with the mallet I can't stop you. The last guest of Swing I treated had several fingers pointing entirely the wrong way. So if you'd like to give him a few wallops for good luck I could point out some quite sensitive areas—'

'No thanks. I'll just haul him out the back way and drop him in an alley.'

'Is that all?'

'No. *Then* . . . I'll sign my name on his damn plaster cast. So he sees it when he wakes up. In bloody big letters so it won't rub off.'

'Now that's what I call a sensitive area,' said Lawn. 'You're an interesting man, sergeant. You make enemies like a craftsman.'

'I've never been interested in needlework,' said Vimes,

hoisting the man on his shoulder. 'But what sort of things would a needlewoman have in her workbasket, do you think?'

'Oh, I don't know. Needles, thread, scissors, wool . . . that kind of thing,' said Mossy Lawn.

'Not very heavy things, then?' said Vimes.

'Not really. Why d'you ask?'

'Oh, no reason,' said Vimes, making a small mental note. 'Just a thought. I'll go and drop off our friend here while I've still got some mist to lurk in.'

'Fine. I'll have breakfast on when you get back. It's liver. Calves'.'

The beast remembers. This time, Vimes slept soundly.

He had always found it easier to sleep during the day. Twenty-five years on nights had ground their nocturnal groove in his brain. Darkness was easier, somehow. He knew how to stand still, a talent that few possess, and how to merge into the shadows. How to guard, in fact, and see without being seen.

He remembered Findthee Swing. A lot of it was history. The revolt would have happened with Swing or without him but he was, as it were, the tip of the boil.

He'd been trained at the Assassins' School and should never have been allowed to join the Watch. He had too much *brain* to be a copper. At least, too much of the wrong kind of brain. But Swing had impressed Winder with his theories, had been let in as a sergeant and then was promoted to captain immediately. Vimes had never known why; it was probably because the officers were offended at seeing such a fine genn'lman pounding the streets with the rest of the oiks. Besides, he had a weak chest, or something.

Vimes wasn't against intellect. Anyone with enough savvy to let go of a doorknob could be a street monster in the old days, but to make it above sergeant you needed a grab-bag of guile, cunning and street wisdom that could pass for 'intelligence' in a poor light.

Swing, though, started in the wrong place. He didn't look around, and watch and learn, and then say, 'This is how people are, how do we deal with it?' No, he sat and thought: 'This is how the people ought to be, how do we change them?' And that was a good enough thought for a priest but not for a copper, because Swing's patient, pedantic way of operating had turned policing on its head.

There had been that Weapons Law, for a start. Weapons were involved in so many crimes that, Swing reasoned, reducing the number of weapons *had* to reduce the crime rate.

Vimes wondered if he'd sat up in bed in the middle of the night and hugged himself when he'd dreamed *that* one up. Confiscate all weapons, and crime would go down. It made sense. It would have worked, too, if only there had been enough coppers – say, three per citizen.

Amazingly, quite a few weapons were handed in. The flaw, though, was one that had somehow managed to escape Swing, and it was this: criminals don't obey the law. It's more or less a requirement for the job. They had no particular interest in making the streets safer for anyone except themselves. And they couldn't believe what was happening. It was like Hogswatch every day.

Some citizens took the not unreasonable view that something had gone a bit askew if only naughty people were carrying arms. And they got arrested in large numbers. The average copper, when he's been kicked in the nadgers once too often and has reason to believe that his bosses don't much care, has an understandable tendency to prefer to arrest those people who won't instantly try to stab him, especially if they act a bit snotty and wear more expensive clothes than he personally can afford. The rate of arrests shot right up, and Swing had been very pleased about that.

Admittedly some of the arrests had been for possessing weaponry after dark, but quite a few had been for assaults on the Watch by irate citizens. That was Assault on a City Official, a very heinous and despicable crime and, as such, far more important than all these thefts that were going on everywhere.

It wasn't that the city was lawless. It had plenty of laws. It just didn't offer many opportunities not to break them. Swing didn't seem to have grasped the idea that the system was supposed to take criminals and, in some rough and ready fashion, force them into becoming honest men. Instead, he'd taken honest men and turned them into criminals. And the Watch, by and large, into just another gang.

And then, just when the whole wretched stew was thickening, he'd invented craniometrics.

Bad coppers had always had their ways of finding out if someone was guilty. Back in the old days – hah, *now* – these included thumbscrews, hammers, small pointed bits of wood and, of course, the common desk drawer, always a boon to the copper in a hurry. Swing didn't need any of this. He could tell if you were guilty by looking at your eyebrows.

He measured people. He used calipers and a steel ruler. And he quietly wrote down the measurements, and did some sums, such as dividing the length of the nose by the circumference of the head and multiplying it by the width of the space between the eyes. And on such figures he could, *infallibly*, tell that you were devious, untrustworthy and congenitally criminal. After you had spent the next twenty minutes in the company of his staff and their less sophisticated tools of inquiry he would, amazingly, be proved right.

Everyone was guilty of something. Vimes knew that. Every copper knew it. That was how you maintained your authority – everyone, talking to a copper, was secretly afraid you could see their guilty secret written on their forehead. You couldn't, of course. But neither were you supposed to drag someone off the street and smash their fingers with a hammer until they told you what it was.

Swing would probably have ended up face down in some alley somewhere if it wasn't for the fact that Winder had found

126

in him a useful tool. No one could sniff out conspiracies like Swing. And so he'd ended up running the Unmentionables, most of whom made Sergeant Knock look like Good Copper Of The Month. Vimes had always wondered how the man had kept control, but maybe it was because the thugs recognized, in some animal way, a mind which had arrived at thuggery by the long route and was capable of devising in the name of reason the kind of atrocities that unreason could only dream of.

It wasn't easy, living in the past. You couldn't whack someone for what they were going to do, or what the world was going to find out later. You couldn't warn people, either. You didn't know what could change the future, but if he understood things right, history tended to spring back into shape. All you could change was the bits around the edges, the fine details. There was nothing he could do about the big stuff. The lilac was going to bloom. The revolution was going to happen.

Well . . . a *kind* of revolution. That wasn't really the word for what it was. There was the People's Republic of Treacle Mine Road (Truth! Justice! Freedom! Reasonably priced Love! And a Hard-Boiled Egg!) that would live for all of a few hours, a strange candle that burned too briefly and died like a firework. And there was the scouring of the house of pain, and the—

Anyway . . . you did the job that was in front of you, like unimaginative coppers always did.

He got up around one in the afternoon. Lawn was closeted in his surgery, doing something that involved some serious whimpering on the part of something else. Vimes knocked on the door.

After a moment it was opened a fraction. Dr Lawn was wearing a face mask and holding a very long pair of tweezers in his hand.

'Yes?'

'I'm going out,' said Vimes. 'Trouble?'

'Not too bad. Slidey Harris was unlucky at cards last night, that's all. Played an ace.'

'That's an unlucky card?'

'It is if Big Tony knows he didn't deal it to you. But I'll soon have it removed. If you're going to injure anyone tonight, can you do it *before* I go to bed? Thank you.' Lawn shut the door.

Vimes nodded at the woodwork, and went out to stretch his legs and get some lunch. It was waiting for him, on a tray, around the neck of a man.

Quite a young man, now, but there was something about the expression, as of a rat who was expecting cheese right around the next corner, and had been expecting cheese around the last corner too, and the corner before that, and, although the world had turned out so far to be full of corners yet completely innocent of any cheese at all, was nevertheless quite certain that, just around the corner, cheese awaited.

Vimes stared. But why should he be surprised? As long ago as he could remember, there was *always* someone selling highly suspicious chemically reclaimed pork products in this town. The seller was very familiar. Just . . . younger.

His expression lit up at the sight of an unfamiliar face. The seller liked to meet people who hadn't yet bought one of his pies.

'Ah, sergeant . . . Hey, what's the little crown mean?'

'Sergeant-at-arms,' said Vimes. 'That's like "sergeant with all the trimmings".'

'Well, sergeant, could I interest you in a very special sausage inna bun? Guaranteed no rat? One hundred per cent organic? All pork shaved before mixing?'

Why not? thought Vimes. And his stomach, liver, kidneys and lengths of intestine all supplied reasons, but he fumbled in his pocket for some change anyway.

'How much, Mr . . . er,' Vimes remembered in time, and made a show of looking at the name on the front of the tray, '. . . Dibbler?'

'Four pence, sergeant.'

'And that's cutting your own throat, eh?' said Vimes jovially.

'Pardon?' said Dibbler, looking puzzled.

'I said, a price like that's cutting your own throat, eh?'

'Cutting my own . . . ?'

'Throat,' said Vimes desperately.

'Oh.' Dibbler thought about this. 'Right. Yeah. It *is*. You never said a truer word. So you'll have one, then?'

'I notice it says on your tray "Dibbler Enterprises, Est",' said Vimes. 'Shouldn't it say *when* you were established?'

'Should it?' Dibbler looked down at his tray.

'How long have you been going?' said Vimes, selecting a pie.

'Let's see . . . what year is this?'

'Er . . . Dancing Dog, I think.'

'Since Tuesday, then,' said Dibbler. His face brightened. 'But this is only the start, mister. This is just to get a stake together. In a year or two I'm going to be a big man in this town.'

'I believe you,' said Vimes. 'I really do.'

Dibbler looked down at his tray again as Vimes strolled off. 'Cutting my own throat, cutting my own throat,' he mumbled to himself, and seemed to like the sound of it. But then he focused more clearly on the tray and his face went pale.

'Sergeant!' he shouted. 'Don't eat the pie!'

Vimes, a few yards away, stopped with the pie halfway to his mouth.

'What's wrong with it?' he said. 'Silly me. I mean, what's *uniquely* wrong with it?'

'Nothing! I mean . . . these are better!'

Vimes risked another look at the tray. They all looked the same to him. Dibbler's pies quite often looked appetizing. Therein lay their one and only charm.

'I can't see any difference,' he said.

'Yeah, yeah, there *is*,' said Dibbler, sweat beading on his forehead. 'See? The one you got has that little pattern of pastry pigs on it? And all the others have pastry sausages? I'd hate you to think that, you know, I thought you were a pig or anything, so if you'll hand it over I'll happily give you, er, another one, that one's not the right one, er, not that it's a wrong one, but, er, with the pig and everything . . .'

Vimes looked into the man's eyes. Dibbler had yet to learn that friendly blankness that thirty years of selling *truly* organic pies would call into being.

While the man stared in horror, he took a large bite out of the pie.

It was everything that he had expected and nothing that he could identify.

'Yum,' he said and, with some concentration, eyes fixed on the luckless pieman, finished it all.

'I think it's quite possible no one else makes pies like you do, Mr Dibbler,' he said, licking his fingers in case he might want to shake hands with someone later on.

'You ate it all?' said Dibbler.

'Was that wrong?' said Vimes.

And now relief rose off the man like smoke off a greenwood fire. 'What? No! That's fine! Jolly good! Want another one to help it down? Half-price?'

'No, no, one is more than enough,' said Vimes, backing away.

'You finished every bit?' said Dibbler.

'That was right, wasn't it?' said Vimes.

'Oh, yeah. Sure. Obviously!'

'Got to be going,' said Vimes, moving on down the lane. 'I'll look forward to seeing you again when I've got less appetite.'

He waited until he was well out of sight before taking a few random turns in the network of alleys. Then he stepped into the shadow of a deep doorway and felt in his mouth for the piece of pie that had seemed curiously unchewable even by pie standards.

Usually, if you found something more than usually hard or crunchy in one of Dibbler's Famous Pork Pies, the trick was either to swallow it and hope for the best or spit it out with your eyes closed. But Vimes felt around between gum and cheek and fished out a folded piece of paper, stained with unknowable juices.

130

He unfolded it. In smudged pencil, but still decipherable, it read: *Morphic Street, 9 o'clock tonight. Password: swordfish.*

Swordfish? *Every* password was swordfish! Whenever anyone tried to think of a word that no one would ever guess, they *always* chose swordfish. It was just one of those strange quirks of the human mind.

That explained the guilt, anyway. A plot. Another damn plot, in a city full of plots. Did he *need* to know about plots? Anyway, he knew about this one. Morphic Street. The famous Morphic Street Conspiracy. Ha.

He pushed the greasy scrap into a pocket and then hesitated.

Someone was being quiet. Overlaid on the distant street noises was a sort of hollow in the sounds, filled by careful breathing. And the hairs on the back of his neck were standing up.

Quietly, he pulled the blackjack out of his rear pocket.

Now, what were the options? He was a copper, and someone was creeping up on him. If they weren't a copper, then they were in the wrong (because he was a copper). If *they* were a copper, too, then they were one of Swing's crew and therefore in the wrong (because he was a better copper than them, and so were things floating in gutters) and therefore delivering a swift bucketful of darkness had no obvious downside.

On the other hand, thieves, assassins and Swing's men, by all accounts, did a lot of creeping up on people and were probably pretty good at it, whereas the person tracking him was keeping their back so close to the wall he could hear the scraping. That meant they were probably just a member of the public with something on their mind and he was not inclined to add several ounces of lead shot simply for that reason (because he'd like to believe he wasn't that sort of copper).

He settled for stepping out into the alley and saying 'Yeah?'

A boy stared up at him. It had to be a boy. Nature would not have been so cruel as to do that to a girl. No single feature in itself was more than passably ugly, but the combination was greater than the sum of the parts. There was also the smell. It wasn't bad, as such. It just wasn't entirely human. There was something feral about it.

'Er . . .' said its pinched-up face. 'Look, tell you what, mister, you tell me where you're going and I'll stop following you, have we got a deal? Cost you no more'n a penny and that's a special price. Some people pay me a lot more'n that to stop following 'em.'

Vimes continued to stare. The creature was wearing an over-size evening dress jacket, shiny with grease and greenish with age, and a top hat that must once have been trodden on by a horse. But the bits that were visible between the two were regrettably familiar.

'Oh, no . . .' he moaned. 'No, no, no . . .'

'You all right, mister?'

'No, no, no . . . oh, ye gods, it had to happen, didn't it . . .'

'You want I should go'n' fetch Mossy, mister?'

Vimes pointed an accusing finger. 'You're Nobby Nobbs, right?'

The urchin backed away. 'Could be. So what? Is that a crime?' He turned to run but Vimes's hand fell heavily on his shoulder.

'Some people might say so. You're Nobby Nobbs, son of Maisie Nobbs and Sconner Nobbs?'

'Prob'ly, prob'ly! But I ain't done nothin', mister!'

Vimes bent down to look into eyes that peered out at the world through a mask of grime. 'How about whizzing wipers, snitching tinklers, pulling wobblers, flogging tumblers and running rumbles?'

Nobby's brow creased in genuine puzzlement. 'What's pulling wobblers mean?' he said.

Vimes gave him a similar look. Street parly had changed a lot in thirty years.

'That's stealing trifles . . . small items. Isn't it?'

'Nah, nah, mister. That's "tottering nevils",' said Nobby, relax-

132

ing. 'But you ain't doin' badly, for someone who's new. What's oil of angels?'

Memory flicked a card.

'A bribe,' said Vimes.

'And a dimber?' said Nobby, grinning.

'Easy. Could be a head beggar, could be just a handsome man.'

'Well done. Bet you don't know how to fleague a jade, though.'

Once again, from a dusty recess, a memory unrolled. This one stuck in your mind.

'Dear me, do you know that? What a shame in one so young,' said Vimes. 'That's when you want to sell a broken-down horse and have to make it a bit frisky in front of the punters, and so you take some fresh raw hot ginger, lift up its tail, and push the ginger—'

'Cor,' said Nobby, suddenly impressed. 'Everyone says you're a real quick learner, and that's true enough. You could've been born here.'

'Why're you following me, Nobby Nobbs?' said Vimes.

The urchin held out a grubby hand. Some street language *never* changes.

Vimes pulled out sixpence. It shone in Nobby's palm like a diamond in a chimney-sweep's ear.

'One of 'em's a lady,' he said, and grinned. The hand stayed out.

'That was a bloody sixpence I just gave you, kid,' Vimes growled.

'Yeah, but I got to think of—'

Vimes grabbed the lapels of Nobby's greasy coat and lifted him up, and was mildly shocked to realize that there was practically no weight there.

Street urchin, he thought. Urchin sounds about right – spiky, slimy and smelling slightly of rotting seaweed. But there's hundreds of them round here, clawing a living off the very margins, and as I recall Nobby was one of the sharpest. And as trustworthy as a chocolate hammer. But that's okay. There's ways to deal with that.

'How much,' he said, 'for you to work for *me*, all the time?'

'I got customers to think of—' he began.

'Yeah, but I'm the one holding you up in one hand, right?' said Vimes.

With his oversized boots dangling a foot above the ground, Nobby considered his position. 'All the time?'

'Right!'

'Er . . . for something like that I've got to be looking at a lordship every day . . .'

'A dollar? Guess again!'

'Er . . . half a dollar?'

'Not a chance. A dollar a *week*, and I won't make your life the utter misery which, Nobby, I assure you I can do in so many little ways.'

Still dangling, Nobby tried to work all this out. 'So . . . I'll be kind of like a copper, right?' he said, grinning artfully.

'Kind of.'

'Number One Suspect says it's a good life being a copper, 'cos you can pinch stuff without getting nicked.'

'He's got that right,' said Vimes.

'An' he says if anyone gives you lip, you can bop 'em one and chuck them in the Tanty,' Nobby went on. 'I'd like to be a copper one day.'

'Who's Number One Suspect?'

'That's what our mam calls Sconner, our dad. Er . . . payment up front, yeah?' Nobby added, hopefully.

'What do *you* think?'

'Ah. Right. No, eh?'

'Correct. But I'll tell you what . . .' He lowered Nobby to the ground. Light as a feather, he thought. 'You come with me, kid.'

Ankh-Morpork was full of men living in lodgings. Anyone with a spare room rented it out. And, in addition to the darning and stitching that was turning Miss Battye into one of the highest earning seamstresses in the city, they needed something else that women were best able to supply. They needed feeding.

There were plenty of hot-chair eating places like the one Vimes headed for now. It sold plain food for plain men. There wasn't a menu. You ate what was put in front of you, you ate it quick, and you were glad to get it. If you didn't like it, there were plenty who did. The dishes had names like Slumgullet, Boiled Eels, Lob Scouse, Wet Nellies, Slumpie and Treacle Billy – good, solid stuff that stuck to the ribs and made it hard to get up out of the seat. They generally had a lot of turnip in, even if they weren't supposed to.

Vimes elbowed his way to the counter, dragging Nobby behind him. A chalked sign said 'All You Can Eat In Ten Minutes For 10p'.

Beneath it, a large woman was standing bare-armed by a cauldron in which uncertain things bubbled in grey scum. She gave him an appraising look and then glanced at his sleeve.

'What can I do for you, sergeant?' she said. 'What happened to Sergeant Knock?'

'Comes in here a lot, does he?' said Vimes.

'Dinner and supper.' Her look said it all: second helpings, too, and never pays.

Vimes held up Nobby. 'See this?' he said.

'Is it a monkey?' said the woman.

'Har har, very funny,' moaned Nobby, as Vimes lowered him again.

'He's going to come in here for one square meal every day,' said Vimes. 'All he can eat for ten pence.'

'Yes? And who's paying, may I ask?'

'Me.' Vimes plonked a half-dollar on the table. 'That's five days in advance. What's the special today? Slumgullet? It'll put hairs on his chest, when he gets a chest. Give him a big bowl. You might make a loss on this deal.'

135

He shoved Nobby on to a bench, placed the greasy bowl in front of him, and sat down opposite.

'You said a lady,' he said. 'Don't mess me about, Nobby.'

'Have I got to share this, sarge?' said Nobby, picking up a wooden spoon.

'It's all yours. Make sure you eat up every bit. There may be a test later,' said Vimes. 'A woman, you said.'

'Lady Meserole, sarge,' said Nobby indistinctly, through a mouthful of mixed vegetables and grease. 'Posh lady. Everyone calls her Madam. Come from Genua a few months ago.'

'When did she ask you?'

'This morning, sarge.'

'What? She just stopped you in the street?'

'Er . . . I've got a kind of gen'ral contract with her, sarge.'

Vimes glared. It was better than speaking. Nobby wriggled uneasily.

'Fact is, sarge, she . . . er, caught me snickering her nolly last month. Hell's bells, sarge, she's got a punch on her like a mule! When I come round, we got to talking, and she said a keen young lad like me could be useful as, like, an ear on the street.'

Vimes continued to glare, but he was impressed. Young Nobby had been a gifted pickpocket. Anyone who caught him in the act was quick indeed. He turned up the ferocity of the glare.

'All right, sarge, she said she'd turn me over to the Day Watch if I didn't,' Nobby confessed, 'and you go straight to the Tanty if a nob lays a complaint against you.'

That's bloody true, thought Vimes. Private law again.

'I don't want to go to the Tanty, sarge. Sconner's in there.'

And he used to break your arms, Vimes remembered. 'So why's a fine lady interested in me, Nobby?' he said aloud.

'Didn't ask. I told 'er about you an' the hurry-up wagon and the Unmentionables and everything. She said you sounded fascinatin'. An' Rosie Palm's paying me a measly penny a day to keep an eye on you, too. Oh, an' Corporal Snubbs at Cable Street, he's payin' me one half-penny to watch you, but what is

136

a half-penny these days, say I, so I don't watch you much on his account. Oh, and Lance-Corporal Coates, I'm getting a penny from him, too.'

'Why?'

'Dunno. He asked me this morning, too. A penny job.' Nobby belched hugely. 'Better out than in, eh? Who d'you want me to watch for you, sarge?'

'Me,' said Vimes. 'If you can fit me into your busy schedule.'

'*You* want me to follow you?'

'No, just tell me what people are saying about me. Keep an eye on who else is following me. Watch my back, sort of thing.'

'Right!'

'Good. Just one more thing, Nobby . . .'

'Yes, sarge?' said Nobby, still spooning.

'Give me back my notebook, my handkerchief and the four pennies you whizzed from my pockets, will you?'

Nobby opened his mouth to protest, dribbling slumgullet, but closed it when he saw the glint in Vimes's eye. Silently, he produced the items from various horrible pockets.

'Well done,' said Vimes, getting up. 'I'm sure I don't have to tell you what'll happen to you if you try the old dippitydoodah on me again, do I, Nobby?'

'No, sarge,' said Nobby, looking down.

'Want another bowl? Have fun. I've got to go to work.'

'You can rely on me, sarge!'

Oddly enough, thought Vimes as he walked back to the Watch House, I probably can. Nobby would nick anything and dodge anything but he wasn't *bad*. You could trust him with your life, although you'd be daft to trust him with a dollar.

He purchased a packet of Pantweed's Slim Panatellas from another street trader. Carrying them around in their cardboard packet didn't feel right at all.

There was a buzz in the main office as he strolled in. Watchmen were standing around in little groups. Sergeant Knock spotted Vimes and trotted over.

'Bit of a do, sir. Had a break-in last night,' he reported, with just a hint of smirk.

'Really?' said Vimes. 'What did they steal?'

'Did I say they stole anything, sir?' said the sergeant innocently.

'Well, no, you didn't,' said Vimes. 'That was me jumping to what we call a *conclusion*. Did they steal anything, then, or did they break in to deliver a box of chocolates and a small complimentary basket of fruit?'

'They stole the captain's silver inkstand,' said Knock, impervious to sarcasm. 'And it was an inside job, if you want my opinion. The door upstairs was forced but the main doors weren't. Must've been a copper what done it!'

Vimes was amazed at the forensic expertise shown here. 'My word, a copper *stealing*?' he said.

'Yes, a terrible thing,' said Knock earnestly. 'Especially since you showed us the way yesterday, about being honest and everything.' He glanced past Vimes, and shouted. 'Attention! Officer present!'

Tilden was coming down the stairs. The room fell silent, except for his hesitant steps.

'No luck, sergeant?' he said.

'Not so far, sir,' said Knock. 'I was just telling Sergeant Keel here what a terrible thing has happened.'

'It was engraved, you know,' said Tilden mournfully. 'Everyone in the regiment chipped in what they could afford. This really is very . . . upsetting.'

'A man'd have to be a right bastard to steal something like that, eh, sergeant?' said Knock.

'Absolutely,' said Vimes. 'I see you're pretty well organized on this one, sergeant. Have you looked everywhere?'

'Everywhere except the lockers,' said Knock. 'That's not something we'd do lightly, rummaging through a man's locker. But we're all here now, and Captain Tilden's here to see fair play, so although it's very distasteful I'll ask you, captain, for permission to rummage.'

'Yes, yes, if you must,' said Tilden. 'I don't like the idea. It is really quite dishonourable, you know.'

'Then I think, sir, to show that we're doing this fairly,' said Knock, 'us sergeants ought to be searched first. That way no one can say we don't take it seriously.'

'Come now, sergeant,' said Tilden, with a little smile, 'I hardly think *you* are suspected.'

'No, sir, fair's fair,' said Knock. 'We'll set a good example, eh, Sergeant Keel?'

Vimes shrugged. Knock grinned at him, pulled out a bundle of keys and beckoned to Lance-Corporal Coates.

'You do the honours, Ned,' he said, beaming. 'Me first, o'course.'

The door was unlocked. The contents of Knock's locker were the usual unsavoury mess of lockers everywhere, but there was certainly no silver inkstand. If there were, it would have turned black after a single day.

'Well done. Now Sergeant Keel's, please, Ned.'

Knock's friendly beam fixed on Vimes as the policeman fumbled with the lock. Vimes stared back, face blank as a slate, as the door creaked open.

'Oh dear, what have we here?' said Knock, without even bothering to look.

'It's a sack, sarge,' said Coates. 'Something heavy in it, too.'

'Oh dear me,' said Knock, still staring at Vimes. 'Open it up, lad. Gently. We don't want anything to get damaged, eh?'

There was a rustle of hessian, and then:

'Er . . . it's half a brick,' Ned reported.

'What?'

'A half brick, sir.'

'I'm saving up for a house,' said Vimes. There were one or two sniggers from the assembled men, but some of the faster thinkers were suddenly looking worried.

They know, thought Vimes. Well, lads, welcome to Vimes's

139

Roulette. You spun the wheel and now you've got to guess where the ball is going to go . . .

'Are you *sure*?' said Knock, turning to the open locker.

'It's just a sack, sarge,' said Ned. 'And half a brick.'

'Is there a loose panel or something?' said Knock desperately.

'What, in a sack, sarge?'

'Well, that seems to be *our* lockers,' said Vimes, rubbing his hands together. 'Who's next, Sergeant Knock?' Round and round the little ball goes, and where it stops, nobody knows . . .

'Y'know, person'ly, I think the captain's right, I don't think any of the men would—' Knock began, and faltered. Vimes's stare could have hammered rivets.

'I believe, sergeant, that since we have begun this, it should be concluded,' said Tilden. 'That is only fair.'

Vimes took a couple of steps towards Coates and held out his hand. 'Keys,' he said.

Coates glared at him.

'The keys, lance-corporal,' said Vimes.

He snatched them from Coates's hand, and turned to the line of lockers.

'Right,' he said. 'Let's start with the well-known arch-criminal, Lance-Constable Vimes . . .'

Door after door was opened. The lockers, while possibly of interest to anyone studying the smells of unwashed clothing and the things that could grow on neglected socks, failed to produce a single silver inkstand.

It did turn up *The Amorous Adventurs of Molly Clapper* in Corporal Colon's locker, however. Vimes stared at the crude and grubby engravings like a long-lost friend. He *remembered* that book; it had gone around the Watch House for years, and as a young man he had learned a lot from some of the illustrations, although a good deal of what he'd learned had turned out to be wrong.

Fortunately, Captain Tilden's view was blocked and Vimes shoved the greasy book back on the shelf and said to the red-eared Colon: 'Studying theory, eh, Fred? Good man. Practice makes perfect.'

Then he turned, at last, to Coates's locker. The man was watching him like a hawk.

The scratched door creaked open. Every neck craned to see. There was a stack of old notebooks, some civilian clothing and a small sack of what, when it was tipped out on to the floor, turned out to be laundry.

'Surprised?' said the lance-corporal.

Not half as much as you, Vimes thought.

He winked at Coates, and turned away. 'Can I have a word with you in your office, captain?'

'Yes, sergeant, I suppose so,' said Tilden, looking around. 'Oh, dear . . .'

Vimes gave the man some time to climb the stairs, then followed him into his office and tactfully closed the door.

'Well, sergeant?' said Tilden, collapsing into his chair.

'Have you looked *everywhere*, sir?' said Vimes.

'Of course, man!'

'I mean, sir, perhaps you put it in a desk drawer? Or the safe, perhaps?'

'Certainly not! I sometimes put it in the safe at weekends, but I'm . . . sure I didn't do that last night.'

Vimes noted the subtle uncertainty. He was doing a bad thing, he knew. Tilden was nearly seventy. At a time like that, a man learned to treat his memory as only a rough guide to events.

'I find, sir, that when a busy man has a lot on his plate he can do things that subsequently slip his mind,' he said. I know I do, he added to himself. I could put my house keys down in a bare room and not find them thirty seconds later.

'We've all been under a lot of pressure lately,' he added, knowing that Tilden frequently fell asleep during the afternoon until Snouty coughed very loudly outside the door before taking him his cocoa.

'Well, that's true,' said Tilden, turning desperate eyes to him.

'All this curfew business. Very . . . unsettling. Forget my own head if it wasn't nailed on, what?'

He turned and looked at the green safe.

'Only had it a couple of months,' he muttered. '*I suppose* I . . . look the other way, will you, sergeant? May as well sort this out . . .'

Vimes obligingly turned his back. There was some clicking, and a creak, and then an intake of breath.

Tilden got to his feet, holding the silver inkstand. 'I believe I've made a fool of myself, sergeant,' he said.

No, I've made a fool of you, thought Vimes, fervently wishing he hadn't. I'd intended to drop it into Coates's locker, but I couldn't . . .

. . . not after what I found in there.

'Tell you what, sir,' he volunteered, 'we could say it was a kind of test.'

'I don't tell lies as a rule, Keel!' said the captain, but added, 'I appreciate the suggestion, nevertheless. Anyway, I *know* I'm not as young as I was. Perhaps it's time to retire.' He sighed. 'I have to say I've been considering it for some time.'

'Oh, don't talk like that, sir,' said Vimes, far more jovially than he felt. 'I can't see you retiring.'

'Yes, I suppose I should see things through,' Tilden mumbled, walking back to his desk. 'Do you know, sergeant, that some of the men think you are a spy?'

'Who for?' said Vimes, reflecting that Snouty delivered more than cocoa.

'Lord Winder, I assume,' said Tilden.

'Well, we all work for him, sir. But I don't report to anyone but you, if that's any help.'

Tilden looked up at him and shook his head sadly. 'Spy or not, Keel, I don't mind telling you that some of the orders we've been getting lately have . . . not been thought out properly, in my opinion, what?'

He gave Vimes a glare as if defying him to produce the red-hot thumbscrews there and then.

142

Vimes could see how much the admission that abduction and torture and conspiracy to criminalize honest citizens might not be acceptable government policy was costing the old man. Tilden hadn't been brought up to think like that. He'd ridden off under the flag of Ankh-Morpork to fight the Cheese-Eaters of Quirm or Johnny Klatchian or whatever enemies had been selected by those higher up the chain of command with never a second thought about the rightness of the cause, because that sort of thinking could slow a soldier down.

Tilden had grown up knowing that the people at the top were right. That was why they were at the top. He didn't have the mental vocabulary to think like a traitor, because only traitors thought like that.

'Haven't been here long enough to comment, sir,' said Vimes. 'Don't know how you do things here.'

'Not like we used to,' mumbled Tilden.

'Just as you say, sir.'

'Snouty says you know your way around remarkably well, sergeant. For someone new to the city.'

That was a sentence with a hook on the end, but Tilden was an inexperienced angler.

'One nick is pretty much like any other, sir,' said Vimes. 'And, of course, I've visited the city before.'

'Of course. Of course,' said Tilden hurriedly. 'Well . . . thank you, sergeant. If you could, er, explain things to the men? I'd be grateful . . .'

'Yes, sir. Of course.'

Vimes shut the door carefully behind him and went down the steps two at a time. The squad below had barely moved. He clapped his hands like a schoolteacher.

'C'mon, c'mon, you've got patrols to go to! Get moving! *Not you, Sergeant Knock – a word in the yard, please!*'

Vimes didn't bother to wait to see if the man would follow him. He went out into the late afternoon sunshine, leaned against the wall, and waited.

Ten years ago, he'd have— correction, ten years ago, if he was sober, he'd have taught Knock a few lessons about who's boss with several well-aimed punches. And that was certainly the custom *these* days. Scraps between watchmen hadn't been uncommon when Vimes was a constable. But that wouldn't do for Sergeant Keel.

Knock stepped out, inflated with mad, terrified bravado.

When Vimes raised his hand, the man actually flinched.

'Cigar?' said Vimes.

'Er . . .'

'I don't drink,' said Vimes. 'But you can't beat a good cigar.'

'I . . . er . . . don't smoke,' mumbled Knock. 'Look, about that inkstand—'

'D'you know, he'd gone and put it in that safe of his?' said Vimes, smiling.

'He had?'

'And then forgotten about it,' said Vimes. 'Happens to us all, Winsborough. A man's mind starts to wander, he's never quite certain of what he's done.'

Vimes maintained the friendly grin. It was as good as raining blows. Besides, he'd given Knock his correct name. The man never used it in public, for fear of the panic it might cause.

'Just thought I'd put your mind at rest about it,' said Vimes.

Sergeant Winsborough Knock shifted uneasily from one foot to the other. He wasn't certain whether he'd got away with something, or had just ended up getting deeper into something else.

'Tell me more about Lance-Corporal Coates,' said Vimes.

Knock's face was, for a moment, an agony of calculation. And then he adopted his usual policy: when you think there's wolves on your trail, throw someone off the sleigh.

'Ned, sir?' he said. 'Hard worker, of course, does his job – but a bit tricky, between you and me.'

'How? And you don't have to call me "sir", Winsborough. Not out here.'

'He reckons Jack's as good as his master, if you know what I mean. Reckons he's as good as anyone. Bit of a troublemaker in that respect.'

'Barrack-room lawyer?'

'That sort of thing, yes.'

'Rebel sympathies?'

Knock turned his eyes up innocently. 'Could be, sir. Wouldn't like to see the lad in trouble, o'course.'

You think I'm a spy for the Unmentionables, thought Vimes. And you're throwing Coates to me. The other day you were pushing him for promotion. You little worm.

'Worth keeping an eye on, then?' he said aloud.

'Yessir.'

'Interesting,' said Vimes, always a worrying word to the uncertain. It certainly worried Knock, and Vimes thought: my gods, perhaps Vetinari feels like this *all the time* . . .

'Some of us, er, go round to the Broken Drum after the shift's over,' said Knock. 'It's open round the clock. I don't know if you—'

'I don't drink,' said Vimes.

'Oh. Yes. You said,' said Knock.

'And now I'd better pick up young Sam and get out on patrol,' said Vimes. 'Nice to have this little talk with you, Winsborough.'

He strode past, taking care not to look back. Sam was still waiting in the main office, but was sucked into his wake as he swept past.

'I say, who's the skirt up there with old Folly?'

The prefects looked up. On the raised platform at the end of the noisy hall Doctor Follett, Master of Assassins and *ex officio* headmaster of the Guild School, was in animated conversation with, indeed, a lady. The vivid purple of her dress made a splash of colour in the vast room, where black predominated, and the elegant whiteness of his hair shone like a beacon in the darkness.

It was a Guild of Assassins, after all. Black was what you wore. The night was black and so were you. And black had such style, and an Assassin without style, everyone agreed, was just a highly paid arrogant thug.

The prefects were all over eighteen and, therefore, allowed to visit parts of the city that the younger boys weren't even supposed to know about. Their pimples no longer erupted at the sight of a woman. Now, their eyes narrowed. Most of them had already learned that the world was an oyster that could be opened with gold if a blade did not suffice.

'Probably a parent,' said one of them.

'I wonder who's the lucky boy?'

'I know who she is,' said 'Ludo' Ludorum, head of Viper House. 'I heard some of the masters talking earlier. She's Madam Roberta Meserole. Bought the old house in Easy Street. They say she made a pile of money in Genua and wants to settle down here. Looking for investment opportunities, apparently.'

'*Madam?*' said Downey. 'An honorific or a job description?'

'In Genua? Could be both,' said someone, to general laughter.

'Folly's certainly plying her with champagne,' said Downey. 'They're on their third bottle. What *have* they got to talk about?'

'Politics,' said Ludo. 'Everyone knows Winder isn't going to do the decent thing, so it'll be down to us. And Folly's annoyed because we've lost three chaps up there already. Winder's pretty cunning. There's guards and soldiers everywhere you look.'

'Winder's a scag,' said Downey.

'Yes, Downey. You call everyone a scag,' said Ludo calmly.

'Well, everyone is.'

Downey turned back to the table and a movement – or, rather, a lack of movement – caught his eye. Towards the far end one young Assassin was sitting reading, with a book stand positioned in front of his plate. He was intent on it, an empty fork halfway to his mouth.

With a wink at the others, Downey selected an apple from the bowl in front of him, stealthily drew his arm back, and let fly with malicious accuracy.

The fork moved like a snake's tongue, and skewered the apple out of the air.

The reader turned a page. Then, eyes never leaving the print, he delicately brought the fork up to his mouth and took a bite out of the apple.

The rest of the table looked back at Downey, and there were one or two chuckles. The young man's brow furrowed. Assault having failed, he was forced to try scathing wit, which he did not have.

'You really are a scag, Dog-botherer,' he said.

'Yes, Downey,' said the reader levelly, his eyes still intent on the page.

'When are you going to pass some decent exams, Dog-botherer?'

'I really couldn't say, Downey.'

'Never killed anyone, right, Dog-botherer?'

'Probably not, Downey.' The reader turned another page. That little sound infuriated Downey even more.

'What's that you're reading?' he snapped. 'Robertson, show me what the Dog-botherer is reading, will you? Come on, pass it up.'

The boy next to the one currently known as Dog-botherer snatched the book off the stand and threw it along the length of the table.

The reader sighed and sat back as Downey gave the pages a cursory flick.

'Well, look here, you fellows,' he said. 'Dog-botherer is reading a *picture book*.' He held it open. 'Colour it in yourself with your paints or crayons, did you, Dog-botherer?'

The former reader stared up at the ceiling. 'No, Downey. It was hand-coloured to his instructions by Miss Emelia Jane, the sister of Lord Winstanleigh Greville-Pipe, the author. It says so on the frontispiece, you will note.'

147

'And here's a lovely picture of a *tiger*,' Downey ploughed on.
'Why're you looking at pictures, Dog-botherer?'

'Because Lord Winstanleigh has some interesting theories on the art of concealment, Downey,' said the reader.

'Huh? Black and orange tiger in green trees?' said Downey, turning the pages roughly. 'Big red ape in green forest? Black and white zebra in yellow grass? What's this, a manual on how not to do it?'

Again there was a round of chuckles, but they were forced. Downey had friends because he was big and rich, but sometimes he was embarrassing to have around.

'As a matter of fact Lord Winstanleigh also has an interesting point to make on the dangers of intuitive—'

'This a Guild book, Dog-botherer?' Downey demanded.

'No, Downey. It was privately engraved some years ago and I succeeded in tracing a copy in—'

Downey's hand shot out. The book whirled away, causing a table full of younger boys to scatter, and landed at the back of the fireplace. The diners on the top tables looked round, and then turned back in disinterest. Flames licked up. For a moment, the tiger burned brightly.

'Rare book, was it?' said Downey, grinning.

'I think it may now be said to be non-existent,' said the one known as Dog-botherer. 'That was the only extant copy. Even the engraved plates have been melted down.'

'Don't you ever get upset, Dog-botherer?'

'Oh yes, Downey,' said the reader. He pushed his chair back and stood up. 'And now, I believe, I will have an early night.' He nodded at the table. 'Good evening, Downey, gentlemen . . .'

'You're a scag, Vetinari.'

'Just as you say, Downey.'

Vimes thought better when his feet were moving. The mere activity calmed him down and shook his thoughts into order.

Apart from the curfew and manning the gates, the Night Watch didn't do a lot. This was partly because they were incompetent, and partly because no one expected them to be anything else. They walked the streets, slowly, giving anyone dangerous enough time to saunter away or melt into the shadows, and then rang the bell to announce to a sleeping world, or at any rate a world that had been asleep, the fact that all was, despite appearances, well. They also rounded up the quieter sort of drunk and the more docile kinds of stray cattle.

They think I'm a spy for Winder? thought Vimes. Spying on the Treacle Mine Road Watch? It's like spying on dough.

Vimes had flatly refused to carry a bell. Young Sam had acquired a lighter one, but out of deference to Vimes's crisply expressed wishes, kept the clapper muffled with a duster.

'Is the wagon going out tonight, sarge?' said young Sam, as the twilight faded towards night.

'Yes. Colon and Waddy are on it.'

'Taking people to Cable Street?'

'No,' said Vimes. 'I told them to take everyone to the Watch House and Snouty'll fine 'em half a dollar and take their name and address. Perhaps we'll have a raffle.'

'We'll get into trouble, sarge.'

'The curfew's just to frighten people. It doesn't mean much.'

'Our mum says there's going to be trouble soon,' said Sam. 'She heard it in the fish shop. Everyone says it's going to be Snapcase at the palace. He listens to the people.'

'Yeah, right,' said Vimes. And I listen to the thunder. But I don't *do* anything about it.

'Our mum says everyone'll have a voice in the city when Snapcase is the Patrician,' Sam went on.

'Keep the voice down, kid.'

'The day'll come when the angry masses will rise up and throw off their shekels, the fishmonger says,' said Sam.

If I *was* a spy for Swing, that fishmonger would be gutted, Vimes thought. Quite the revolutionary, our mum.

He wondered if it was at all possible to give this idiot some lessons in basic politics. That was always the dream, wasn't it? 'I wish I'd known then what I know now'? But when you got older you found out that you *now* wasn't *you* then. You then was a twerp. You then was what you had to be to start out on the rocky road of becoming you now, and one of the rocky patches on that road was being a twerp.

A much better dream, one that'd ensure sounder sleep, was not to know now what you didn't know then.

'What's your dad do?' he said, as if he didn't know.

'He passed away a long time ago, sarge,' said Sam. 'When I was little. Run down by a cart when he was crossing the street, our mum said.'

What a champion liar she was, too.

'Sorry to hear that,' said Vimes.

'Er, our mum says you'd be welcome round to tea one night, what with you being all by yourself in a strange city, sarge.'

'Would you like me to give you another tip, lad?' said Vimes.

'Yes, sarge, I'm learning a lot.'

'Lance-constables do not invite their sergeants round to tea. Don't ask me why. It's one of those things that does not happen.'

'You don't know our mum, sarge.'

Vimes coughed. 'Mums are mums, lance-constable. They don't like to see men managing by themselves, in case that sort of thing catches on.'

Besides, I know she's been up in Small Gods these past ten years. I'd rather put one hand flat on the table and give Swing the hammer than walk down Cockbill Street today.

'Well,' said Sam, 'she says she's going to make you some Distressed Pudding, sarge. She makes great Distressed Pudding, our mum.'

The best, thought Vimes, staring into the middle distance. Oh, gods. The very best. No one has ever done it better.

'That'd be . . . very kind of her,' he managed.

'Sarge,' said Sam after a while, 'why are we patrolling Morphic Street? It's not our beat.'

'I switched beats. I ought to see as much of the city as possible,' said Vimes.

'Not a lot to see in Morphic Street, sarge.'

Vimes looked at the shadows. 'Oh, I don't know,' he said. 'It's amazing what you see if you concentrate.' He pulled Sam into a doorway. 'Just whisper, lad,' he said. 'Now, look down there at the house opposite. See that doorway with the deeper shadow?'

'Yes, sarge,' whispered Sam.

'Why's it such a deep shadow, d'you think?'

'Dunno, sarge.'

''cos someone in black is standing in it, that's why. So we're going to walk a little further and then we'll just turn around and go back round the corner. We're heading back to the station like good boys because our cocoa's getting cold, see?'

'Right, sarge.'

They ambled back around the corner, and Vimes let them walk sufficiently far up the street that the footsteps died away naturally.

'Okay, this is far enough,' he said.

Give Sam his due, Vimes thought, he knew how to stand still. He'd have to teach him how to unfocus himself, too, so that you could very nearly fade out of sight on a cloudy day. Had Keel taught him that? After a certain age, memory was indeed an untrustworthy thing . . .

The city's clocks chimed the three-quarter-hour.

'What time's curfew?' Vimes whispered.

'Nine o'clock, sarge.'

'Must be nearly that now,' said Vimes.

'No, it's only just gone a quarter to nine, sarge.'

'Well, it's going to take me a few minutes to get back. I want you to sneak back after me and wait at the corner. When it starts, you come running and banging that bell of yours.'

'When what starts, sarge? Sarge?'

151

But Vimes was walking noiselessly down the road. He made a note to tip Snouty a dollar. These boots were like foot gloves.

Torches spluttered on the junction, destroying the night vision of anyone who looked in that direction. Vimes padded around its dark penumbra and sidled along the buildings on the far wall until he was level with the door. Then he swung around the frame and shouted.

'You're *nicked*, chum!'

'——!' said the shadow.

'And that's offensive language, sir, such as I would not wish my young lance-constable to hear!'

Behind him he heard Lance-Constable Vimes advancing at a run, ringing his bell madly and shouting, 'Nine o'clock and all's not well at all!' And there were other sounds, too, the ones Vimes had been half-listening for, of doors slamming and distant footsteps hurrying away.

'You bloody fool!' said the struggling figure in black. 'What the hell are you playing at!' He pushed at Vimes, who nevertheless tightened his grip.

'That, sir, is assault upon a Watch officer,' said Vimes.

'*I'm* a Watch officer too, you damn flatfoot! From Cable Street!'

'Where's your uniform?'

'We don't wear uniforms!'

'Where's your badge!'

'And we don't carry badges!'

'Hard to see why I shouldn't think you is a common thief then, sir. You was casing that house over there,' said Vimes, happy in the role of big, thick, but horribly unshakeable copper. 'We *seen* you.'

'There was going to be a meeting of dangerous anarchists!'

'What kind of a religion is that, sir?' Vimes patted the man's belt. 'Oh, dear, what have we here? A very nasty dagger. See this, Lance-Constable Vimes? A weapon, no doubt about it! That's against the law. Carried after dark, which is even more against the law! And it's a *concealed* weapon!'

'What do you mean, concealed?' screamed the twisting prisoner. 'It was in a bloody sheath!'

'Bloody, eh? Used it already, have you, sir?' said Vimes. He thrust a hand into a pocket of the man's black coat. 'And . . . what's this? A little black velvet roll with, I do believe, a complete set of lock picks? That's Going Equipped for Burglary, that is.'

'They're not mine and you know it!' the man snarled.

'Are you sure, sir?' said Vimes.

'Yes! Because I keep *mine* in my inside pocket, you bastard.'

'That's Using Language liable to cause a Breach of the Peace,' said Vimes.

'Huh? You idiots have scared everyone away! Who's going to be offended?'

'Well, *I* might be. I'm sure you don't want that, sir.'

'You're that stupid sergeant we've been told about, aren't you,' growled the man. 'Too thick to see what's going on, right? Well, this is where you find out, mister . . .'

He twisted out of Vimes's grip, and there were a couple of sliding, metallic noises in the gloom. Wrist knives, thought Vimes. Even Assassins think they're an idiot's weapon.

He took a couple of steps back as the man danced towards him, both knives waving.

'Can't think of a dumb answer to this one, eh, brownjob?'

To his horror Vimes saw, behind the man, the shape of Sam raising his bell very slowly.

'Don't hit him!' he shouted, and then lashed out with his boot as the man's head turned.

'If you're going to fight, fight,' he said, as the man toppled forward. 'If you're going to talk, talk. Don't try to talk *and* fight. And right now, I caution you to do neither.'

'I could have got him easily, sarge,' Sam complained, as Vimes fished out his handcuffs and knelt down. 'I could have blown him out like a light.'

'Head injuries can be fatal, lance-constable. We serve the public trust.'

'But you kicked him in the privates, sarge!'

Because I don't want you to be a target, thought Vimes, as he tightened the cuffs. That means you don't belt one of them over the head. You stay as the dim sidekick, in the background. That way you survive, and *that* way, maybe I do too.

'You don't have to fight the way the other bloke wants you to fight,' he said, hefting the man on to his shoulders. 'Give me a hand here . . . up weee *go*. Okay, I've got him. You lead the way.'

'Back to the Watch House?' said Sam. 'You're *arresting* an *Unmentionable*?'

'Yes. I just hope we'll meet some of our lads on the way. Let this be a lesson, lad. There aren't any rules. Not when there's knives out. You take him down, quietly if possible, without hurting him much if possible, but you take him down. He comes at you with a knife, you bring your stick down on his arm. He comes at you with his hands, you use your knee or your boot or your helmet. Your job is to keep the peace. You make it peaceful as quickly as you can.'

'Yes, sir. But there's going to be trouble, sarge.'

'Straightforward arrest. Even coppers have to obey the law, what there is of it . . .'

'Yes, sarge, but I mean there's going to be trouble right now, sarge.'

They'd neared the end of the street, and there was a group of figures there. They looked like men with a purpose; there was something about the stance, the way they were standing in the road, and, of course, the occasional glint of light on a weapon also gave a hint. There was a snapping of little doors as dark lanterns were opened.

Of course he wouldn't have been alone, Vimes scolded himself. His job was just to watch until they'd all gone in. And then he'd just shlep away to call in the heavy gang. There must be a dozen of 'em. We're going to get *cheesed*.*

'What'll we do, sarge?' whispered Sam.

'Ring your bell.'

'But they've spotted us!'

'Ring the damn bell, will you? And keep walking! And don't stop ringing!'

The Unmentionables spread out now, and as Vimes trudged towards them he saw several figures at each end of the line slip around behind him. That's how it'd go. They'd be like the muggers up in Scoone Avenue, talking nice and friendly while their eyes said, hey, you know our mates are right behind you and we know you know and it's fun watching you trying to pretend that this is just a civilized conversation when you know that any minute you're going to get it right in the kidneys. We feel your pain. And we like it . . .

He stopped walking. It was that or walk into someone. And all along the street doors and windows were opening as the clanging of the bell roused the neighbourhood.

' 'evenin',' he said.

' 'evenin', your grace,' said a voice out of history. 'Nice to see an old friend, eh?'

Vimes groaned. The worst that could happen had happened. 'Carcer?'

'That's *Sergeant* Carcer, thank you. Funny how things work out, eh? Turns out I'm prime copper material, haha. They gave me a new suit and a sword and twenty-five dollars a month, just like that. Lads, this is the man I told you about.'

'Why d'you call him your grace, sarge?' said one of the shadowy men.

Carcer's eyes never left Vimes's face. 'It's a joke. Where we come from, everyone used to call him Duke,' he said. Vimes saw him slip a hand into a pocket. It came out holding something

* Like creamed, but it goes on for a lot longer.

that had a brassy glint. 'It was a sort of nickname, eh . . . Duke? Stop the kid ringing the damn bell, will you?'

'Knock it off, lance-constable,' Vimes muttered. The noise had worked, anyway. This little tableau had a silent audience now. Not that an audience would make any difference to Carcer. He'd cheerfully stab you to death in the centre of a crowded arena and then look around and say, 'Who, me?' But the men behind him were edgy, like cockroaches wondering when the light was going to go on.

'Don't you worry, Duke,' Carcer said, sliding his fingers into the brass knuckles, 'I've told the boys about you and me. How we, hah, go back a long way and all that, haha.'

'Yeah?' said Vimes. It wasn't prizewinning repartee, but Carcer obviously wanted to talk. 'And how did you get made a sergeant, Carcer?'

'I heard where they were looking for coppers with fresh ideas,' said Carcer. 'And that nice Captain Swing hisself talked to me and said he was in no doubt I was an honest man who had been unlucky. Measured me up, he did, with his calipers and his rules and jommetry and he said it *proved* I was not a criminal type. It was all the fault of my environment, he said.'

'What, you mean all those dead bodies everywhere you went?' said Vimes.

'Nice one, Duke, haha.'

'And you *had* fresh ideas, did you?'

'Well, he liked one of 'em,' said Carcer, narrowing his eyes. 'Turned out he didn't know the ginger beer trick.'

The ginger beer trick. Well, that just about put the tin lid on it. Torturers down the ages hadn't found the ginger beer trick, and Carcer had handed it over to a patent maniac like Captain Swing.

'The ginger beer trick,' said Vimes. 'Well done, Carcer. You're just what Swing's been looking for. The complete bastard.'

Carcer grinned as if he'd been awarded a small prize. 'Yeah, I already told 'em how you got a down on me for stealing a loaf of bread.'

'Come on, Carcer,' said Vimes. 'That's not you. You never pinched a loaf of bread in your life. Murdering the baker and stealing the bakery, that'd be your style.'

'He's a card, eh?' said Carcer, winking at his men and nodding towards Vimes. Then, in one movement, he spun around and punched the man beside him in the stomach.

'You *don't* call me sarge,' he hissed. 'It's sergeant, understand?'

On the floor, the man groaned.

'I'll take that as a yes, then, haha,' said Carcer, slipping the brass knuckles back into his pocket. 'Now the thing is . . . Duke . . . what you have there is one of my men, so how about you hand him over and we'll say no more about it?'

'What's happening, sarge?'

The voice was coming from some way behind Vimes. He turned. It was Wiglet and Scutts. They looked like men who'd been running but were now trying to affect a nonchalant swagger. It was getting less nonchalant and considerably less swaggery as they eyed up the Unmentionables.

The frantically ringing bell. That's what they'd always used. All the coppers who heard it would converge on it, because an Officer was in Trouble.

Of course, they wouldn't necessarily help him get out of trouble, not if the odds weren't right. This was the old Night Watch, after all. But at least they could fish him out of the river or cut him down and see he got a decent burial.

There was a rumble from further up the street and the rattling bulk of the hurry-up turned the corner, with Fred Colon at the reins and Constable Waddy hanging on behind. Vimes heard the shouts.

'What's up, Bill?'

'It's Keel and Vimesy,' Wiglet called back. 'Hurry up!'

Vimes tried to avoid Carcer's eyes, tried to appear as if nothing had happened, tried to pretend that the world had not suddenly cracked open and let in the cold winds of infinity. But Carcer was smart.

He glanced at Vimes, looked at Sam.

'Vimesy?' he said. 'Your name Sam Vimes, mister?'

'I ain't saying *anything*,' said Lance-Constable Vimes stoutly.

'Well, well, well, well, *well*,' said Carcer happily. 'Now *here*'s a nice how-d'yer-do, eh? Something for a chap to think about, and *no* mistake, haha.'

There was a creak as the hurry-up wagon rolled to a stop. Carcer glanced up at the round, pale face of Corporal Colon.

'You just go about your business, corporal,' said Carcer. 'You just leave *now*.'

Colon swallowed. Vimes could *see* his Adam's apple bob as it tried to hide.

'Er . . . we heard the ringing,' he said.

'Just a bit of high spirits,' said Carcer. 'Nothing that need worry you. We're all coppers here, right? I wouldn't like there to be any trouble. There's just been a bit of a misunderstanding, that's all. Sergeant Keel here was just going to hand over my friend there, right, sergeant? No hard feelings, eh? You just happened to blunder into a little operation of ours. Best not to talk about it. Just you hand him over and we'll call it quits.'

Every head turned to Vimes.

The sensible thing would be to hand the man over. He knew it. And then – probably – Carcer would go away, and he didn't want that man any closer to young Sam than he could help.

But Carcer would come back. Oh, yes. Things like Carcer always came back, especially when they thought they'd found a weakness.

That wasn't the worst part. The worst part was that Vimes had changed things.

There had *been* the Morphic Street Conspiracy. The Unmentionables *had* raided it. Several people had died but some had got away, and then there had been a few days of horrible confusion and then it ended when—

But young Sam Vimes hadn't been anywhere near Morphic Street that night. Keel had been teaching him to shake hands with doorknobs over on the other side of the Shades.

But you wanted to be *clever*, Duke. You wanted to put a spoke in the wheel and smack a few heads, didn't you?

And now Carcer's in it as well and you're out of the history books and travelling without a map . . .

Carcer was still grinning his cheerful grin. Here and now, more than anything else, Vimes wanted to see the end of that grin.

'Well, I'd like to oblige, *sarge*,' he said. 'I really would. But I've pinched him now, so I've got to take him back to my nick and do the paperwork. He might well be able to help us with our inquiries into a number of unsolved crimes.'

'Such as?' said Carcer.

'Dunno,' said Vimes. 'Depends on what we've got. We'll take him down the cells, give him a cup of tea, chat to him about this and that . . . *you* know how it is. A man can get quite chatty after a cup of tea. Or carbonated beverage of his choice, of course.'

There was a snigger from among the members of the Night Watch, although Vimes hoped none of them knew what the last sentence meant.

Carcer's smile dissolved. 'I *said* he's one of my men, on official business, and I am a sergeant,' he said.

'And I am Sergeant-at-Arms and *I* said we'll hand him over to you at the nick, Sergeant Carcer. Officially.'

Carcer nodded towards the lance-constable, so imperceptibly that only Vimes saw it. And he lowered his voice.

'But suddenly *I've* got all the aces, Duke,' he said.

'But suddenly *I'm* not playing cards, Carcer. Now, we could have a barney right here and now and, y'know, I'm not sure which way it'd go. But I'm sure as hell that you wouldn't be a sergeant tomorrow. And if you think you've got all the aces, you can afford to raise the stakes.'

Carcer stared at him for a moment. Then he winked, and half turned away.

'I told you he's a caution, eh?' he said to the multitude. He gave Vimes a conspiratorial dig in the ribs. 'Always trying it on! Okay, sergeant . . . at-arms, we'll do it your way. Got to give you brownjobs something to do, haha, eh? I'll send a couple of the lads down for him in an hour or so.'

That's right, give me time to sweat on whether I'll pop into non-existence if you cut the lad's throat, Vimes thought. Trouble is, I *am* sweating.

He straightened up, and beckoned to the hurry-up wagon.

'Me and my lads will *all* take him back,' he said. 'Time for our cocoa break, see? Give me a hand up with him, Waddy. Got any other passengers, Fred?'

'Just a drunk, sarge. Been spewing everywhere.'

'Okay. We'll put the prisoner in the back and we'll all hang on to the outside.' Vimes nodded at Carcer. 'I'm sure we'll meet again soon, sergeant.'

'Yeah,' said Carcer, and there was that impish grin again. 'And you be sure to look after yourself, d'you hear?'

Vimes leapt on to the side of the wagon as it rattled past, and didn't even look back. That was one thing about Carcer, at least – he wouldn't shoot you in the back if he thought there was a reasonable chance, pretty soon, of cutting your throat.

After a while, Constable Wiglet, hanging on beside him as the wagon rocked, said: 'What happened back there, sarge? You know that bloke?'

'Yes. He's killed two coppers. One that tried to arrest him and one who was off duty and eating a pie. Killed other people, too.'

'But he's a copper!'

'Swing gave him a job, Wiglet.'

Suddenly, the rattle of the wheels sounded much louder. All the other watchmen were listening very intently.

'You been in the Watch long, constable?' said Vimes.

'Two years, sarge,' said Wiglet. 'Used to be a fruit porter down

160

the market but I got a bad back and a bad chest what with all the cold mornings.'

'I never heard about coppers being killed,' said Lance-Constable Vimes.

'It wasn't here, kid. It was a long way away.'

'You were there?'

'They were coppers I knew, yes.'

Again, the mood on the cart changed. There was no obvious sound from the watchmen but over the wagon hung the word: 'Ah-*hah* . . .'

'So you came here to track him down . . . ?' said Wiglet.

'Something like that.'

'*We* heard you came from Pseudopolis, sarge,' said Sam.

'I've come from a lot of places.'

'Wow!' said Sam.

'He killed a copper who was eating a pie?' said Fred Colon, from the box.

'Yep.'

'What a bastard! What kind of pie was it?'

'Witnesses didn't say,' Vimes lied. This was *old* Ankh-Morpork. The dwarfs here right now were a tiny minority who kept their heads down . . . well, further down than usual. There certainly were no all-night rat pie shops.

Wiglet had something on his mind. 'They're going to come for that bloke you picked up,' he said.

'Want the rest of the night off, constable?' said Vimes. There was some nervous laughter from the rest of the crew. Poor devils, thought Vimes. You joined up 'cos the wages were good and there was no heavy lifting, and suddenly it's going to be *difficult*.

'What're you going to charge our man with, sarge?' said Sam.

'Attempted assault on a copper. You saw the knives.'

'You did kick him, though.'

'Right, I forgot. We'll do him for resisting arrest, too.'

There was some more laughter. We who think we are about to die will laugh at anything.

What a bunch. I know you well, gentlemen. You're in it for the quiet life and the pension, you don't hurry too much in case the danger is still around when you get there, and the most you ever expected to face was an obstreperous drunk or a particularly difficult cow. Most of you aren't even coppers, not in your head. In the sea of adventure, you're bottom-feeders.

And now, it's war . . . and you're in the middle. Not on either side. You're the stupid little band of brownjobs. You're beneath contempt. But believe me, boys – you'll rise.

For a minute or two after Morphic Street went quiet nothing moved and nothing happened.

Then a coach came around the corner. It was a particularly fine one, drawn by two horses. Its lamps were torches, and as the coach bounced on the cobbles the zig-zagging flames seemed to trail for a moment in the air, and appeared to have a smoky quality.

In so far as they revealed anything, these suggested that the coach had been done up in purple livery. It also seemed to be rather heavy on its wheels.

It pulled to a halt at the next doorway down from the one where Vimes had performed his arrest. Vimes, who thought he knew a lot about being a shadow, would have been surprised to see two dark figures step out of the doorway's darkness into the light of the torch.

The coach door swung open.

'Strange news, kind lady,' said one of the shadows.

'Very strange news, dearie,' said the other shadow.

They climbed up into the coach, which sped off.

Vimes was impressed at the way the men reacted back at the Watch House, despite the lack of any command from him. Wiglet and Scutts jumped down as soon as the wagon was in the yard and dragged the gates across.

Inside, Colon and Waddy pulled the shutters across the

windows. Waddy went into the armoury and came out with an armful of crossbows. It was all done with speed and, for the men concerned, precision.

Vimes nudged his younger self. 'Make the cocoa, will you, kid?' he said. 'I don't want to miss the show.'

He sat down at his desk and put his feet up as Colon locked the door and Waddy pulled the bar across.

This is happening, he thought, but it didn't happen before. Not exactly like this. This time, the Morphic Street mob did a runner. They weren't ambushed in their meeting. There wasn't a fight. The sight of all those coppers must've scared them rigid. They weren't much anyway, just sloganeers and skivers and me-too-ists, the people who crowd behind the poor slob who's the spokesman shouting 'yeah, right' and leg it up an alley when the law gets rough. But some had died in the ambush, and some fought back, and one thing led, as always, to another. Except, this time, there was no ambush, because some thick sergeant made too much noise . . .

Two different presents. One past, one future . . .

I don't know what's going to happen next.

However, I've got a damn good idea.

'Well done, lads,' he said, standing up. 'You finish trapping us inside and I'll go and tell the old man what's happening.'

He heard the puzzled muttering behind him as he climbed the stairs.

Captain Tilden was sitting at his desk, staring at the wall. Vimes coughed loudly, and saluted.

'Had a bit of—' he began, and Tilden turned his ashen face to him. He looked as though he had seen a ghost, and it had been in the mirror.

'You've heard the news too?'

'Sir?'

'The riot up at Dolly Sisters,' said Tilden. 'It was only a couple of hours ago.'

I'm too close, Vimes thought, as the words sank in. All those things were just names, it all seemed to happen at once. Dolly Sisters, yeah. They were a right mob of hotheads up there . . .

'The lieutenant of the Day Watch called in one of the regiments,' said Tilden. 'Which he was duly authorized to do. Of course.'

'Which one?' said Vimes, for the look of the thing. The name was in the history books, after all.

'Lord Venturi's Medium Dragoons, sergeant. My old regiment.'

That's right, thought Vimes. And cavalry are *highly trained* at civilian crowd control. Everyone knows that.

'And, er, there were some, er, accidental deaths . . .'

Vimes felt sorry for the man. In truth, it was never proved that anyone was given an order to ride people down, but did it matter? Horses pushing, and people unable to get away because of the press of people behind them . . . it was too easy for small children to lose grip of a hand . . .

'But, in fairness, missiles were thrown at the officers and one soldier was badly injured,' said Tilden, as if reading the words off a card.

That's all right, then? Vimes thought.

'What kind of missiles, sir?'

'Fruit, I gather. Although there may have been some stones as well.' Vimes realized that Tilden's hand was shaking. 'The riot was over the price of bread, I understand.'

No. The *protest* was over the price of bread, said Vimes's inner voice. The *riot* was what happens when you have panicking people trapped between idiots on horseback and other idiots shouting 'yeah, right!' and trying to push forward, and the whole thing in the charge of a fool advised by a maniac with a steel rule.

'The feeling of the palace,' said Tilden slowly, 'is that revolutionary elements may attack the Watch Houses.'

'Really, sir? Why?'

'It's the sort of thing they do,' said Tilden.

'As a matter of fact, sir, the men are putting up shutters and—'

'Do whatever you feel necessary, sergeant,' said Tilden, waving a hand with a scrawled letter in it. 'We are told we must be mindful of the curfew regulations. That has been underlined.'

Vimes paused before answering. He'd bitten back the first answer. He contented himself with 'Very well, sir,' and left.

The man wasn't a bad man, he knew; he must have been badly affected by the news to give such a stupid, dangerous order. 'Do what you feel necessary.' Give an order like that to a man who's liable to panic when he sees a bunch of people waving their fists and you got the Dolly Sisters Massacre.

He walked back down the stairs. The squad were standing around looking nervous.

'Prisoner in the cells?' said Vimes.

Corporal Colon nodded. 'Yessir. Sarge, Snouty says that up at Dolly Sisters—'

'I know. Now here's what I feel is necessary. Take the shutters down, unbar the door, leave it open and light all the lamps. Why isn't the blue lamp over the door lit?'

'Dunno, sarge. But what if—'

'Get it lit, corporal. And then you and Waddy go and stand guard outside, where you can be seen. You're friendly-looking local lads. Take your bells but, and I want to make this very clear, no swords, right?'

'No swords?' Colon burst out. 'But what if a bloody great mob comes round the corner and I'm not armed?'

Vimes reached him in two swift strides and stood nose to nose.

'And if you have got a sword, what will you do, eh? Against a bloody great mob? What do you want 'em to see? Now what *I* want 'em to see is Fatty Colon, decent lad, not too bright, I knew 'is dad, an' there's ol' Waddy, he drinks in my pub. 'cos if they just see a couple of men in uniform with swords you'll be

165

in trouble, and if you draw those swords you'll be in real trouble, and if by any chance, corporal, you draw swords tonight without my order and survive then you'll wish you hadn't done *either* because you'll have to face me, see? And then you'll know what trouble *is*, 'cos everything up until then will look like a bleedin' day at the soddin' seaside. Understand?'

Fred Colon goggled at him. There was no other word for it.

'Don't let my sugary sweet tones lead you to believe that I'm not damn well giving you orders,' said Vimes, turning away. 'Vimes?'

'Yes, sarge?' said young Sam.

'Have we got a saw in this place?'

Snouty stepped forward. 'I've got a toolbox, sarge.'

'Nails, too?'

'Yessir!'

'Right. Rip the door off my locker and hammer a lot of nails right through it, will you? Then lay it down on the upstairs landing, points up. I'll take the saw, 'cos I'm going to the privy.'

After the silence that followed, Corporal Colon obviously felt he had to make a contribution. He cleared his throat and said, 'If you've got a problem in that area, sarge, Mrs Colon's got a wonderful medicine she—'

'I won't be long,' said Vimes. In fact, he was four minutes.

'All done,' he said, returning to the sound of hammering from the locker room. 'Come with me, lance-constable. Time for a lesson in interrogation. Oh . . . and bring the toolbox.'

'Fred and Waddy don't like being outside,' said Sam, as they went down the stone steps. 'They say what if that bunch of Unmentionables turn up?'

'They needn't worry. Our friends at Cable Street are not front-door kind of people.'

He pushed open the door to the cells. The prisoner stood up and grabbed the bars.

'Okay, they've come, now you let me out,' he said. 'Come on, and I'll put in a good word for you.'

166

'No one's come for you, sir,' said Vimes. He locked the main door behind him, and then unlocked the cell.

'It's probably a busy time for them,' he added. 'Been a bit of a riot over in Dolly Sisters. A few deaths. Might be a while before they get around to you.'

The man eyed the toolbox that the lance-constable was holding. It was only a flicker, but Vimes saw the moment of uncertainty.

'I get it,' said the prisoner. 'Good Cop, Bad Cop, eh?'

'If you like,' said Vimes. 'But we're a bit short staffed, so if I give you a cigarette would you mind kicking *yourself* in the teeth?'

'Look, this is a game, right?' said the prisoner. 'You *know* I'm one of the Particulars. And you're new in town and want to impress us. Well, you have. Big laugh all round, haha. Anyway, I was only on stake-out.'

'Yes, but that's not how it works, is it,' said Vimes. 'Now we've got you, we can decide what you're guilty of. You know how it's done. Fancy a ginger beer?'

The man's face froze.

'Y'know,' said Vimes, 'it turns out that after the riot this evening we've been warned to expect revolutionary attacks on the Watch Houses. Now personally I wouldn't expect that. What I'd expect is a bunch of ordinary people turning up, you know, because they've heard what happened. But – and you can call me Mr Suspicious if you like – I've got a feeling that there *will* be something a bit worse. You see, apparently we've got to be mindful of the curfew regulations. What that means, I suppose, is that if we get people coming to complain about unarmed citizens being attacked by soldiers, which personally I would consider to be Assault With A Deadly Weapon, we've got to arrest them. I find that rather—'

There was a commotion from above. Vimes nodded to young Sam, who disappeared up the stairs.

'Now that my impressionable assistant has gone,' said Vimes

quietly, 'I'll add if any of my men get hurt tonight then I'll see to it that for the rest of your life you scream at the sight of a bottle.'

'I haven't done anything to you! You don't even know me!'

'Yes. Like I said, we're doing it your way,' said Vimes.

Sam reappeared, in a hurry. 'Someone's fallen in the privy!' he announced. 'They were climbing on the roof and it had been sawn through and gave way!'

'It must be one of those revolutionary elements,' said Vimes, watching the prisoner's face. 'We've been *warned* about them.'

'He says he's from Cable Street, sarge!'

'That's just the kind of thing I'd say, if I was a revolutionary element,' said Vimes. 'All right, let's take a look at him.'

Upstairs, the front door was still open. There were a few people outside, just visible in the lamplight. There was also Sergeant Knock inside, and he was not happy.

'Who said we open up like this?' he was saying. 'It looks nasty out on those streets! Very dangerous—'

'I said we stay open,' said Vimes, coming up the stairs. 'Is there a problem, sergeant?'

'Well . . . look, sarge, I heard on the way over, they're throwing stones at the Dimwell Street House,' said Knock, deflating. 'There's people in the streets! Mobs! I hate to think what's happening downtown.'

'So?'

'We're coppers! We should be getting prepared!'

'What? To bar the doors and listen to the stones rattle off the roof?' said Vimes. 'Or maybe we should go out and arrest everyone? Any volunteers? No? I'll tell you what, sergeant, if you want to do some coppering you can go and arrest the man in the privy. Do him for Breaking and Entering—'

There was a scream from upstairs.

Vimes glanced up.

'And I reckon if you go up on to the attic landing you'll find there's a man who dropped through the skylight right on to a

168

doorful of nails that was accidentally left there,' he went on. He looked at Knock's puzzled face. 'It's the Cable Street boys, sergeant,' he said. 'They thought they could come across the roofs and scare the dumb brownjobs. Chuck 'em both in the cells.'

'You're arresting *Unmentionables*?'

'No uniform. No badge. Carrying weapons. Let's have a bit of law around here, shall we?' said Vimes. 'Snouty, where's that cocoa?'

'We'll get into trouble!' Knock shouted.

Vimes let Knock wait until he'd lit a cigar. 'We're in trouble anyway, Winsborough,' he said, shaking out the match. 'It's just a case of deciding what kind we want. Thanks, Snouty.'

He took the mug of cocoa from the jailer and nodded at Sam. 'Let's take a stroll outside,' he said.

He was aware of the sudden silence in the room, except for the whimpering coming from upstairs and the distant yelling from the privy.

'What're you all standing around for, gentlemen?' he said. 'Want to ring your bells? Anyone fancy shouting out that all's well?'

With those words hanging in the room all big and pink, Vimes stepped out into the evening air.

There were people hanging around out there, in little groups of three or four, talking among themselves and occasionally turning to look at the Watch House.

Vimes sat down on the steps, and took a sip of his cocoa.

He might as well have dropped his breeches. The groups opened up, became an audience. No man drinking a non-alcoholic chocolate beverage had ever been the centre of so much attention.

He'd been right. A closed door is an incitement to bravery. A man drinking from a mug, under a light, and apparently enjoying the cool night air, is an incitement to pause.

169

'We're breaking curfew, you know,' said a young man, with a quick dart forward, dart back movement.

'Is that right?' said Vimes.

'Are you going to arrest us, then?'

'Not me,' said Vimes cheerfully. 'I'm on my break.'

'Yeah?' said the man. He pointed to Colon and Waddy. 'They on their break too?'

'They are now.' Vimes half turned. 'Brew's up, lads. Off you go. No, no need to run, there's enough for everyone. And come back out when you've got it . . .'

When the sound of pounding boots had died away, Vimes turned back and smiled at the group again.

'So when do you come *off* your break?' said the man.

Vimes paid him some extra attention. The stance was a give-away. He was ready to fight, even though he didn't look like a fighter. If this were a bar room, the bartender would be taking the more expensive bottles off the shelf, because amateurs like that tended to spread the glass around. Ah, yes . . . and now he could see why the words 'bar room' had occurred to him. There was a bottle sticking out of the man's pocket. He'd been drinking his defiance.

'Oh, around Thursday, I reckon,' said Vimes, eyeing the bottle. There was laughter from somewhere in the growing crowd.

'Why Thursday?' said the drinker.

'Got my day off on Thursday.'

There were a few more laughs this time. When the tension is drawing out, it doesn't take much to snap it.

'I demand you arrest me!' said the drinker. 'Come on, try it!'

'You're not drunk enough,' said Vimes. 'I should go home and sleep it off, if I was you.'

The man's hand grasped the neck of the bottle. Here it comes, thought Vimes. By the look of him, the man had one chance in five . . .

Fortunately, the crowd wasn't too big yet. What you didn't

need at a time like this was people at the back, craning to see and asking what was going on. And the lit-up Watch House was fully illuminating the lit-up man.

'Friend, if you take my advice you'll not consider that,' said Vimes. He took another sip of his cocoa. It was only lukewarm now, but along with the cigar it meant that both his hands were occupied. That was important. He wasn't holding a weapon. No one could say afterwards that he had a weapon.

'I'm no friend to you people!' snapped the man, and smashed the bottle on the wall by the steps.

The glass tinkled to the ground. Vimes watched the man's face, watched the expression change from drink-fuelled anger to agonizing pain, watched the mouth open . . .

The man swayed. Blood began to ooze from between his fingers and a low, thin animal sound escaped from between his teeth.

That was the tableau, under the light – Vimes sitting down with his hands full, the bleeding man several feet away. No fight, no one had touched anyone . . . he knew the way rumour worked, and he wanted this picture to fix itself in people's minds. There was even ash still on the cigar.

He stayed very still for a few seconds, and then stood up, all concern.

'Come on, one of you help me, will you?' he said, tugging off his breastplate and the chain-mail shirt underneath it. He grabbed his shirt sleeve and tore off a long strip.

A couple of men, jerked into action by the voice of command, steadied the man who was dripping blood. One of them reached for the hand.

'Leave it,' Vimes commanded, tightening the strip of sleeve around the man's unresisting wrist. 'He's got a handful of broken glass. Lay him down as gently as you can before he falls over but don't touch *nothing* until I've got this tourniquet on. Sam, go into the stable and pinch Marilyn's blanket for the boy. Anyone here know Doctor Lawn? Speak up!'

171

Someone among the awed bystanders volunteered that they did, and was sent running for him.

Vimes was aware of the circle watching him; a lot of the watchmen were peering around the doorway now.

'Saw this happen once,' he said aloud, and added mentally 'in ten years' time'. 'It was in a bar fight. Man grabbed a bottle, didn't know how to smash it, ended up with a hand full of shards and the other guy reached down and *squeezed*.' There was a satisfying groan from the crowd. 'Anyone know who this man is?' he added. 'Come on, *someone* must . . .'

A voice in the crowd volunteered that the man could well be Joss Gappy, an apprentice shoemaker from New Cobblers.

'Let's hope we can save his hand, then,' said Vimes. 'I need a new pair of boots.'

It wasn't funny at all but it got another of those laughs, the ones people laugh out of sheer frightened nervousness. Then the crowd parted as Lawn came through.

'Ah,' he said, kneeling down by Gappy. 'You know, I don't know why I own a bed. Trainee bottle fighter?'

'Yes.'

'Looks like you've done the right things but I need light and a table,' said Lawn. 'Can your men take him into the Watch House?'

Vimes had hoped it wouldn't come to that. Oh well, you had to make the best of it . . .

He pointed randomly at figures in the crowd. 'You and you and you and you and you too, lady,' he said. 'You can help Fred and Waddy take this young man inside, okay? And you're to stop with him, and we'll leave the doors open, right? All you lot out here'll know what's going on. We've got no secrets here. Everyone understand?'

'Yeah, but you're a copper—' a voice began.

Vimes darted forward and hauled a frightened young man out of the crowd by his shirt.

'Yeah, I am,' he said. 'And see that lad over there? He's a

copper, too. His name's Sam Vimes. He lives in Cockbill Street with his mum. And that's Fred Colon, just got married, got a couple of rooms in Old Cobblers. And Exhibit C there is Waddy, everyone round here knows Waddy. Billy Wiglet there, he was *born* in this street. Have I asked you *your* name?'

'N-no . . .' the man mumbled.

'That's 'cos I don't care who you are,' said Vimes, letting the man go and looking round at the crowd. 'Listen to me, all of you! My name's John Keel! No one gets taken into this Watch House without me knowing why! You're all here as witnesses! Those of you I pointed out, you come on inside to see fair play all round. Do the rest of you want to hang around to see what happens to Gappy? Fine, I'll get Snouty to bring you out some cocoa. Or you can go home. It's a cold night. You ought to be in your beds. I know I'd like to be in mine. And, yes, we know about Dolly Sisters and we don't like it any more than you do. And we've heard about Dimwell Street and we don't like *that*, either. And that's all I've got to say tonight. Now . . . anyone who still wants to take a swing at a copper can step right up, if they want to. I've got my uniform off. We'll have a go, here and now, fair and square, in front of everyone. Anyone?'

Something brushed his shoulder and clattered on the Watch House steps.

Then there was the sound of slipping tiles from a roof on the other side, and a man fell off the roof and into the pool of light. There were gasps from the crowd, and one or two short screams.

'Looks like you got a volunteer,' said someone. There was the horrible nervous sniggering again. The crowd parted to let Vimes view the sudden arrival.

The man was dead. If he hadn't been when he fell off the roof he was after he'd hit the ground, because no neck normally looked like that. A crossbow had fallen down with him.

Vimes remembered the draught across his shoulder, and went back to the Watch House steps. It didn't take long to find the arrow, which had broken into several pieces.

173

'Anyone know this man?' he said.

The crowd, even those members of it who hadn't been able to get a good look at the fallen bowman, indicated definite ignorance.

Vimes went through the man's pockets. Every single one was empty, which was all the evidence of identification he needed.

'Looks like it's going to be a long night,' he said, signalling Colon to take this body inside, too. 'I've got to get on with my work, ladies and gentlemen. If anyone wants to stay, and frankly I'll be obliged if you do, I'll send some lads out to build a fire. Thank you for your patience.' He picked up his mail and breastplate and went back inside.

'What're they doing?' he said to Sam, without turning round.

'Some of them are wandering off but most of 'em are standing around, sarge,' said Sam, peering around the door. 'Sarge, one of them shot at you!'

'Really? Who says the man on the roof was one of them? That's an expensive bow. And he didn't have anything in his pockets. *Nothing*. Not so much as a used hanky.'

'Very odd, sarge,' said Sam loyally.

'Especially since I was expecting a piece of paper saying something like "I am definitely a member of a revolutionary cadre, trust me on this",' said Vimes, looking carefully at the corpse.

'Yes, that'd tell us he was a revolutionary all right,' said Sam.

Vimes sighed and stared at the wall a moment. Then he said: 'Anyone notice anything about his bow?'

'It's the new Bolsover A7,' said Fred Colon. 'Not a bad bow, sarge. Not an Assassin's weapon, though.'

'That's true,' said Vimes, and twisted the dead man's head so they could see the tip of the little metal dart behind the ear. 'But *this* is. Fred, you know everyone. Where can I get some ginger beer at this time of night?'

'Ginger beer, sarge?'

'Yes, Fred.'

174

'Why do—' Colon began.

'Don't ask, Fred. Just get half a dozen bottles, all right?'

Vimes turned to the desk on which, surrounded by a fascinated crowd, Dr Lawn was at work on the stricken Gappy.

'How's it going?' said Vimes, pushing through.

'Slower than it'd go if people got out of the damn light,' said Lawn, carefully moving his tweezers to a mug by Gappy's hand and dropping a bloody fragment of glass therein. 'I've seen worse on a Friday night. He'll keep the use of his fingers, if that's what you want to know. He just won't be making any shoes for a while. Well done.'

There was general crowd approval. Vimes looked around at the people and the coppers. There were one or two muted conversations going on; he heard phrases like 'bad business' and 'they say that—' above the general noise.

He'd played the cards well enough. Most of the lads here lived within a street or two. It was one thing to have a go at faceless bastards in uniform, but quite another to throw stones at old Fred Colon or old Waddy or old Billy Wiglet, who you'd known since you were two years old and played Dead Rat Conkers with in the gutter.

Lawn put the tweezers down and pinched the bridge of his nose. 'That's it,' he said wearily. 'A bit of stitching and he'll be fine.'

'And there's some others I need you to take a look at,' said Vimes.

'You know, that comes as no surprise,' said the doctor.

'One's got a lot of holes in his feet, one dropped through the privy roof and has got a twisted leg, and one's dead.'

'I don't think I can do much about the dead one,' said the doctor. 'How do you know he's dead? I realize that I may regret asking that question.'

'He's got a broken neck from falling off a roof and I reckon he fell off because he got a steel crossbow bolt in his brain.'

'Ah. That sounds like dead, if you want my medical opinion. Did you do it?'

175

'No!'

'Well, you're a busy man, sergeant. You can't be everywhere.' The doctor's face cracked into a grin when he saw Vimes go red, and he walked over to the corpse.

'Yes, I'd say that life is definitely extinct,' he said. 'And?'

'I want you to write that down, please. On paper. With official-sounding words like "contusion" and "abrasions". I want you to write that down, and I want you to write down what time you found he was dead. And then if you don't mind two lads'll take you down to look at the other two, and after you've treated them, thank you, I'd like you to sign another piece of paper saying you did and I called you in. Two copies of everything, please.'

'All right. Dare I ask why?'

'I don't want anyone to say I did it.'

'Why should anyone say that? You told me he fell off a roof!'

'These are suspicious times, doctor. Ah, here's Fred. Any luck?'

Corporal Colon was carrying a box. He put it down on his desk with a grunt.

'Old Mrs Arbiter didn't like being knocked up in the middle of the night,' he announced. 'I had to give her a dollar!'

Vimes didn't dare look at Lawn's face. 'Really?' he said, as innocently as possible. 'And you got the ginger beer?'

'Six pints of her best stuff,' said Colon. 'There's three pence back on the bottles, by the way. And . . . er . . .' He shuffled uneasily. 'Er . . . I heard they set fire to the Watch House at Dolly Sisters, sarge. It's very bad up at Nap Hill, too. And, er . . . the Chittling Street House got all its windows broke, and up at the Leastgate House some of the lads went out to stop kids throwing stones and, er, one of them drew his sword, sarge . . .'

'And?'

'He'll probably live, sarge.'

Dr Lawn looked about him at the crowded office, where people were still talking. Snouty was going round with a tray of cocoa. Out in the street, some of the watchmen were standing around a makeshift fire with the remnant of the crowd.

'Well, I must say I'm impressed,' he said. 'Sounds like you're the only Watch House not under siege tonight. I don't want to know how you did it.'

'Luck played a part,' said Vimes. 'And I've got three men who carry no personal identification whatsoever in the cells, and another anonymous would-be assassin who has been assassinated.'

'Quite a problem,' said Lawn. 'Now me, I just have to deal with simple mysteries like what the rash means.'

'I intend to solve mine quite quickly,' said Vimes.

The Assassin moved quietly from roof to roof until he was well away from the excitement around the Watch House.

His movements could be called cat-like, except that he did not stop to spray urine up against things.

Eventually he reached one of the upper world's many hidden places, where several thickets of chimneys made a little sheltered space, invisible from the ground and from most of the surrounding roofscape. He didn't enter it immediately, but circled it for a while, moving with absolute silence from one vantage point to another.

What would have intrigued a watcher who knew the ways of Ankh-Morpork's Guild of Assassins was how *invisible* this one was. When he moved, you saw movement; when he stopped, he wasn't there. Magic would have been suspected and, in an oblique way, the watcher would have been right. Ninety per cent of most magic merely consists of knowing one extra fact.

At last the figure appeared satisfied, and dropped into the space. He picked up a bag from its nesting place between the smoking pots, and there was some faint swishing and heavier breathing that suggested clothes were being changed.

After a minute or so he emerged from the hidden niche and now, somehow, he was visible. Hard to see, yes, one shadow among others, but nevertheless *there* in a way that he had not been before, when he'd been as visible as the breeze.

He dropped lightly on to a lean-to roof and thence to the ground, where he stepped into a handy shadow. Then there was a further transformation.

It was done quite easily. The evil little crossbow was disassembled and slipped into the pockets of a clink-free velvet bag, the soft leather slippers were exchanged for a pair of heavier boots that had been stashed in the shadow, and the black hood was pushed back.

He walked lightly around the corner and waited a few minutes.

A coach came along, its torches trailing flame. It slowed briefly, and its door opened and shut.

The Assassin settled back in his seat as the coach picked up speed again.

There was a very faint lamp in the carriage. Its glow revealed a female figure relaxing in the shadows opposite. As the coach passed a torch there was a suggestion of lilac silk.

'You've missed a bit,' said the figure. It produced a lilac-coloured handkerchief and held it in front of the young man's face. 'Spit,' came the command.

Reluctantly, he did so. A hand wiped his cheek, and then held the cloth up to the light.

'Dark green,' said the woman. 'How strange. I understand, Havelock, that you scored zero in your examination for stealthy movement.'

'May I ask how you found that out, Madam?'

'Oh, one hears things,' Madam said lightly. 'One just has to hold money up to one's ear.'

'Well, it was true,' said the Assassin.

'And why was this?'

'The examiner thought I'd used trickery, Madam.'

'And did you?'

'Of course. I thought that was the idea.'

'And you never attended his lessons, he said.'

'Oh, I did. Religiously.'

'He says he never saw you at any of them.'

Havelock smiled. 'And your point, Madam, is . . . ?'

Madam laughed. 'Will you take some champagne?' There was the sound of a bottle moving in an ice bucket.

'Thank you, Madam, but no.'

'As you wish. I shall. And now . . . report, please.'

'I can't believe what I saw. I thought he was a thug. And he *is* a thug. You can see his muscles thinking for him. But he over-rules them moment by moment! I think I saw a genius at work, but . . .'

'What?'

'He's just a sergeant, Madam.'

'Don't underestimate him on that account. It is a very useful rank for the right man. The optimum balance of power and responsibility. Incidentally, they say he can read the street through the soles of his boots and keeps them very thin for that purpose.'

'Hmm. There are plenty of different surfaces, that's true, but . . .'

'You're always so solemn about these things, Havelock. Not at all like your late father. Think . . . mythologically. He can read the *street*. He can hear its voice, take its temperature, read its mind; it talks to him through his boots. Policemen are just as superstitious as other people. Every other Watch House was attacked tonight. Oh, Swing's people egged it on, but it was malice and stupidity that did the most damage. But not in Treacle Mine Road. No. Keel opened the doors and let the street inside. I wish I knew more about him. I'm told that in Pseudopolis he was considered to be slow, thoughtful, sensible. He certainly seems to have bloomed here.'

'I inhumed a man who attempted to nip him in the bud.'

'Really? That doesn't sound like Swing. How much do I owe you?'

179

The young man called Havelock gave a shrug. 'Call it a dollar,' he said.

'That's very cheap.'

'He wasn't worth more. I should warn you, though. Soon you may want me to deal with Keel.'

'Surely someone like him wouldn't side with people like Winder and Swing?'

'He's a side all by himself. He is a complication. You may think it best if he . . . ceased to complicate.'

The rattling of the coach underlined the silence this remark caused. It was moving through a richer part of the city now, where there was more light and the curfew, being for poorer people, was less rigorously observed. The figure opposite the Assassin stroked the cat on her lap.

'No. He'll serve some purpose,' said Madam. 'Everyone is telling me about Keel. In a world where we all move in curves he proceeds in a straight line. And going straight in a world of curves makes things happen.'

She stroked the cat. It yowled softly. It was ginger and had an expression of astonishing smugness, although periodically it scratched at its collar.

'On a different subject,' she said, 'what was that business with the book? I did not like to take too much notice.'

'Oh, it was an extremely rare volume I was able to track down. On the nature of concealment.'

'That stupid hulk of a boy burned it!'

'Yes. That was a piece of luck. I was afraid he might try to read it, although,' Havelock smiled wanly, 'someone would have had to help him with the longer words.'

'Was it valuable?'

'Priceless. Especially now it has been destroyed.'

'Ah. It contained information of value. Possibly involving the colour dark green. Will you tell me?'

'I *could* tell you.' Havelock smiled again. 'But then I would have to find someone to pay me to kill you.'

'Then don't tell me. But I do think Dog-botherer is an unpleasant nickname.'

'When your name is Vetinari, Madam, you're happy enough if it's merely Dog-botherer. Can you drop me off a little way from the Guild, please? I'll go in via the roof. I have a tiger to attend to before I go up to . . . you know.'

'A tiger. How exciting.' She stroked the cat again. 'You've found your way in yet?'

Vetinari shrugged. 'I've known my way for years, Madam. But now he has half a regiment around the palace. Four or five guards on each door, with irregular patrols and spot checks. I can't get through them. Only let me get inside, please, and the men there are no problem.'

The cat pawed at its collar.

'Is it possible that he is allergic to diamonds?' said Madam. She held up the cat. 'Is oo allergic to diamonds, den?'

Havelock sighed, but inwardly, because he respected his aunt. He just wished she was a bit more sensible about cats. He felt instinctively that if you were going to fondle a cat while discussing matters of intrigue, then it should be a long-haired white one. It shouldn't be an elderly street tom with irregular bouts of flatulence.

'What about the sergeant?' he said, shifting along the seat as politely as possible.

The lady all in lilac lowered the cat gently on to the seat. There was a distressing smell.

'I think I should meet Mr Keel as soon as possible,' she said. 'Perhaps he can be harnessed. The party is tomorrow night. Uh . . . do you mind opening the window?'

A little later that night, Downey was walking unsteadily back to his study after a convivial time in the Prefects' Common Room when he noticed that a torch had gone out.

With a swiftness that might have surprised someone who saw no further than his flushed face and unsteady walk, he pulled out a dagger and scanned the corridor. He glanced up at the ceiling, too. There were grey shadows everywhere, but nothing more than that. Sometimes, torches *did* go out all by themselves.

He stepped forward.

When he woke up in his bed next morning he put the headache down to some bad brandy. And some scag had painted orange and black stripes on his face.

It started to rain again. Vimes liked the rain. Street crime went down when it rained. People stayed indoors. Some of the best nights of his career had been rainy, when he'd stood in the shadows in the lee of some building, head tucked in so that there was barely anything showing between his helmet and his collar, and listened to the silvery rustle of the rain.

Once he'd been standing so quietly, so withdrawn, so *not there* that a fleeing robber, who'd evaded his pursuers, had leaned against him to catch his breath. And, when Vimes put his arms around him and whispered 'Gotcha!' into his ear, the man had apparently done in his trousers what his dear mother, some forty years before, had very patiently taught him not to do.

The people had gone home. The sewn-up Gappy had been escorted to New Cobblers, where Fred Colon had patiently explained events to the man's parents with his round red face radiating honesty. Lawn was possibly getting some use out of his bed.

And the rain gurgled in the downpipes and gushed from the gargoyles and swirled in the gutters and deadened all sound.

Useful stuff, rain.

Vimes picked up the bottle of Mrs Arbiter's best ginger beer. He remembered it. It was as gassy as hell and therefore hugely popular. A young boy could, with encouragement and training, eventually manage to belch the whole first verse of the national anthem after just one swig. This is an important social attribute when you're eight years old.

He'd chosen Colon and Waddy for this task. He wasn't going

182

to involve young Sam. It wasn't that what he was planning was illegal, as such, it was just that it had the same colour and smell as something illegal and Vimes didn't want to have to explain.

The cells were old, much older than the building above them. The iron cages were fairly new, and didn't take up all the space. There were other cellars beyond an arch, containing nothing more than rats and rubbish but, importantly, they couldn't be seen from the cages.

Vimes got the men to carry the dead bowman through. Nothing wrong with that. It was the middle of the night, filthy weather, no sense in waking up the people at the mortuary when there was a nice cold cellar.

He watched through the spy hole in the door as the body was taken past the cells. It caused a certain stir, especially in the first man he'd brought in. The other two had the look of men who'd seen a lot of bad stuff in the name of making money; if they were hired to steal or murder or be a copper it was all the same to them, and they'd learned not to react too readily to deaths that were not their own.

The first man, though, was getting nervous.

Vimes had nicknamed him Ferret. He was the best-dressed of the three, all in black; the dagger had been expensive and, Vimes had noticed, he had a silver Death's Head ring on one finger. The other two had dressed nondescript and their weapons had been workmanlike, nothing much to look at but well used.

No real Assassin would wear jewellery at work. It was dangerous and it shone. But Ferret wanted to be a big man. He probably checked himself in the mirror before he went out, to make sure he looked cool. He was the sort of little twerp that got a kick out of showing his dagger to women in bars.

Ferret, in short, had big dreams. Ferret had an imagination.

Well, that was *fine*.

The watchmen returned, and picked up the packages Vimes had prepared.

'Remember, we do it fast,' he said. 'They're worried, they're tired, no one's come for them and they've just seen a very dead colleague. We don't want to give the first two time to think. Understand?'

They nodded.

'And we leave the little one until last. I want him to have *lots* of time . . .'

Ferret was considering his prospects. Regrettably, this didn't take long.

He'd already had a row with the other two. Some rescue team they'd been. They weren't even dressed right. But the brown-jobs hadn't done things as per spec. Everyone knew they backed away. They weren't supposed to fight back or show any kind of *intelligence*. They—

The main cell door was flung back.

'It's *ginger beer* time!' roared someone.

And a watchman ran through with a box of bottles, and disappeared into the rooms beyond.

There wasn't much light in here. Ferret cowered against the wall and saw two watchmen unlock the cell next door, drag the shackled occupant upright and out into the cellar and then hustle him around the corner.

The voices had a slight echo.

'Hold him down. Mind his legs!'

'Right! Let's have the bottle! Give it a proper shake, otherwise it won't work!'

'Okay, friend. Anything you want to tell us? Your name? No? Well, it's like this. Right now, we don't care a whole lot if you talk or not . . .'

There was a loud pop, a hiss and then . . . a scream, an explosion of agony.

After it had died away the trembling Ferret heard someone say, 'Quick, get the next one, before the captain catches us.'

He cringed back as two watchmen rushed into the next cell,

184

dragged out the struggling prisoner and hustled him into the darkness.

'All right. One chance. Are you going to talk? Yes? No? Too late!'

Once again the pop, once again the hiss, once again the scream. It was louder and longer this time, and ended in a kind of bubbling sound.

Ferret crouched against the wall, fingers in his mouth.

Around the corner, sitting in the light of one lantern, Colon nudged Vimes, wrinkled his nose and pointed down.

There was a gully that ran between all the cells, as a primitive sop to hygiene. Now a thin trickle was inching its way along it. Ferret was nervous.

Gotcha, thought Vimes. But a good imagination needs a little more time. He leaned forward, and the other two moved closer expectantly.

'So,' he said in a low whisper, 'have you boys had your holidays yet?'

After a few minutes of very small talk he stood up, strode round to the last occupied cell, unlocked the door, and grabbed Ferret, who was trying to squeeze into a corner.

'No! Please! I'll tell you whatever you want to know!' the man yelled.

'Really?' said Vimes. 'What's the orbital velocity of the moon?'

'What?'

'Oh, you'd like something simpler?' said Vimes, dragging the man out of the cell. 'Fred! Waddy! He wants to talk! Bring a notebook!'

It took half an hour. Fred Colon wasn't a fast writer. And when the painful sound of his efforts concluded with the stab of his last full stop, Vimes said: 'Okay, sir. And now you write down at the end: I, Gerald Leastways, currently staying at the Young Men's Pagan Association, am making this statement of my own free will and not under duress. And then you sign it. Or else. Got it?'

'Yes, sir.'

The initials GL had been inscribed on the dagger. Vimes believed them. He'd met plenty of Leastwayses in his career, and they tended to spill their guts at the mere thought of spilling their guts. And when they did, you got everything. Anyone who had seen the ginger beer trick used on someone else would confess to *anything*.

'Well, now,' he said cheerfully, standing up. 'Thank you for your co-operation. Want a lift to Cable Street?'

Ferret's expression, if not his mouth, said 'huh?'

'We've got to drop off your friends,' Vimes went on, raising his voice slightly. 'Todzy and Muffer. We'll drop the dead one off at the mortuary. Just a bit of paperwork for you.' He nodded at Colon. 'One copy of your helpful statement. One certificate of death from the pox doctor for the late mystery man, and rest assured we'll try to track down his murderer. A chitty from Mossy about the ointment he put on Muffer's feet. Oh . . . and a receipt for six bottles of ginger beer.'

He put a hand on Ferret's shoulder and gently walked him round into the next cellar, where Todzy and Muffer were sitting gagged, bound and livid with rage. On a table near by was a box containing six flagons of ginger beer. The corks were heavily wired down.

Ferret stared at Vimes, who inserted a finger in his mouth, blew up his cheeks and flicked out the finger with a loud pop.

Waddy hissed between his teeth.

Fred Colon opened his mouth but Vimes clamped his hand over it.

'No, don't,' he said. 'Funny thing, Gerald, but Fred here just screams out loud at times for no reason at all.'

'You *tricked* me!' Ferret wailed.

Vimes patted him on the shoulder. 'Tricked?' he growled. 'How so, Gerald?'

'You made me think you were doing the ginger beer trick!'

'Ginger beer trick?' said Vimes, his brow wrinkling. 'What's that?'

'You know! You brought the stuff down here!'

'We don't drink alcohol on duty, Gerald,' said Vimes severely. 'What's wrong with a little ginger beer? We don't know any tricks with the stuff, Gerald. What tricks do you know? Seen any good tricks lately, Gerald? Do tell!'

At last it dawned on Ferret that he should stop talking. It was about half an hour too late. The expressions on what could be seen of the faces of Todzy and Muffer suggested that they wanted a very personal word with him.

'I demand protective custody,' he managed.

'Just when I'm letting you *go*, Gerald?' said Vimes. 'As you said in your statement . . . what was it, Fred? Something about just obeying orders? All that stuff about mixing with the mobs and throwing things at coppers and soldiers, you didn't want to do that, I know. You didn't like being round in Cable Street watching people being beaten up and being told what to confess to, 'cos it's plain to me that you're not that sort. You're small fry, I understand that. I say we call it quits, how about you?'

'Please! I'll tell you all I know!' Ferret squeaked.

'You mean you *haven't*?' Vimes roared. He spun round and grabbed a bottle.

'Yes! No! I mean, if I sit quiet I'm sure I'll remember some more!'

Vimes held his gaze for a moment, and then dropped the bottle back in the crate. 'All right,' he said. 'It'll be a dollar a day, meals extra.'

'Right you are, sir!'

Vimes watched Ferret scuttle back into his cell and shut the door behind him, then he turned to Fred and Waddy.

'Go and wake up Marilyn,' he said. 'Let's deliver the other three.'

The rain was falling steadily and a thin mist filled Cable Street.

The wagon came out of nowhere. Fred had urged Marilyn

into something approaching a canter down the street, and when the horse came around the corner she was trying to keep ahead of the heavy, rumbling cart behind.

As the hurry-up wagon passed the station the rear door was flung open and two bodies were tumbled out on to the wet cobbles.

The guards rushed forward. One or two of them fired after the retreating cart but the arrows clattered harmlessly off the black iron strips.

The other men approached the tied-up bodies with some care. There were groans, punctuated by swearwords. And, pinned to one man, some paperwork.

They read the note. They did not laugh.

Vimes unharnessed the old horse, rubbed her down and checked on her feed. Perhaps it was his imagination, but the feed bins seemed fuller than they had been. Guilty consciences were at work, maybe.

Then he walked out into the cool night air. The lights were on in the Watch House. It was a beacon, now that the street lamps had been doused. Beyond the walls of the yard the real night had closed in, the old night with its tendrils of fog and crawling shadows. He relaxed, and wore it like an overcoat.

A shadow near the gate was deeper than it ought to be.

He felt for his cigar case again, cursed, and pulled a cigar out of his shirt sleeve. He cupped his hands when he lit it, but kept his eyes tight shut to hold the night vision.

Then he looked up, and blew a smoke ring. *Yes. Everyone thought black didn't show up at night. They were wrong.*

He walked over to shut the gate and then pulled out his sword in one fluid movement.

Sadie raised her head, revealing a pale oval of a face in the depths of her bonnet. 'Good morning, kind sir,' she said.

'Good morning, Sadie,' said Vimes wearily. 'To what do I owe this pleasure?'

'Madam wants to see you, kind sir.'

'If you mean Rosie, I've been a bit busy—'

Dotsie's handbag hit him on the back of the head.

'Madam doesn't like waiting, dearie,' were the last words he heard before night closed in all the way.

The Aunts were experts. Probably not even Mossy Lawn could turn someone off with such precision.

Vimes drifted awake. He was in an armchair. It was extremely comfortable. And someone was shaking him.

It was Sandra the Real Seamstress. She stared at him and said, 'He looks okay . . .' Then she stepped back, sat down in another chair, and aimed a crossbow at him.

'You know,' said Vimes – it really *was* a comfortable chair, and reminded him of the softness that had gone from his life in the past few days; it hadn't been all bad – 'if someone wants to talk to me, they only have to bloody well *ask*.'

'Sadie said you'd only be out for ten minutes, but then you started to snore so we thought we'd let you sleep for a while,' said Rosie Palm, stepping into view. She was wearing a red off-the-shoulder evening dress, an impressively large wig and quite a lot of jewellery.

'Yes, it costs a lot of money to look as cheap as this, sergeant,' she said, catching his expression. 'I can't stop, I must go and talk to people. Now, if you—'

'Snapcase has promised you ladies that you'll be allowed to form a Guild, right?' said Vimes. It was another cheating move, but he was fed up with waking up in odd places. 'Yes, I thought so. And you believe him? It's not going to happen. When he's the Patrician he'll look right through you.'

He'll end up looking through everything, he added to himself. Mad Lord Snapcase. Just another Winder, but with fancier waistcoats and more chins. Same cronyism, same piggy ways, same stupid arrogance, one more leech in a line of leeches that'd make Vetinari seem like a breath of clean air. Ha . . . Vetinari. Yes, he'd be around here somewhere too, no doubt, learning that little expression he had which never, ever gave you a clue what he was thinking . . . But he'll be the one to give you the Guild you want so much. He's here somewhere. I know it.

'Don't expect anything from Snapcase,' he said aloud. 'Remember, there were people who thought Winder was the future, too.'

He derived some minor pleasure from seeing the look on Rosie Palm's face. At last she said: 'Give him a drink, Sandra. If he moves, shoot an eye out. I'll let Madam know.'

'Do you expect me to believe that she'll fire that?' said Vimes.

'Sandra has a very useful streak of belligerence,' said Rosie. 'A gentleman was being . . . impolite yesterday and she came running in and . . . you'll be surprised at what she did with her mushroom.'

Vimes eyed the crossbow. The girl had a very steady hand. 'I don't think I quite under—' he began.

'It's a wooden thing to make it easier to darn socks,' said Sandra. 'I hit him behind the ear with it.'

Vimes gave her a blank look for a while and then said: 'Fine. Fine. I'm sitting very still, believe me.'

'Good,' said Rosie.

She swept out and it was a real sweep, the dress brushing the ground. There were big, expensive double doors. When she opened them, the noise of a meeting filled the room. There was conversation, the smell of cigar smoke and alcohol, and a voice said '—to change the dominant episteme—' before the doors breathed shut.

Vimes stayed seated. He was getting attached to the chair and on current showing someone was likely to hit him again soon.

Sandra, still holding the bow, placed a very large glass of whiskey beside him.

'You know,' he said, 'in times to come people will wonder how all those weapons got smuggled around the city.'

'I'm sure I don't know what you're talking about.'

'And it's because the lads in the Watch never bother about the seamstresses, curfew or no curfew,' said Vimes, staring at the whiskey. 'Or posh coaches,' he added. 'A watchman can get into real trouble if he tries that.' He could smell the stuff from here. It was the good stuff from the mountains, not the local rubbish.

'You didn't tell anyone about the basket,' said Sandra. 'Or hand us over to the Unmentionables. Are you one of us?'

'I doubt it.'

'But you don't know who *we* are!'

'I still doubt it.'

And then he was aware of the doors opening and shutting, and the rustle of a long dress.

'Sergeant Keel? I've heard so much about you! Please leave us, Sandra. I'm sure the good sergeant can be trusted with a lady.'

Madam was only a little shorter than Vimes. Could be from Genua, he thought, or spent a lot of time there. Trace of it in the accent. Brown eyes, brown hair – but a woman's hair could be any colour tomorrow – and a purple dress that looked more expensive than most. And an expression that said quite clearly that the owner knew what was going to happen and was going along with things just to make sure—

'Don't forget the intricately painted fingernails,' she said. 'But if you're trying to guess my weight, don't expect to get any help from me. You can call me Madam.'

She sat down in a chair opposite him, put her hands together and stared at him over the top of them. 'Who are you working for?' she said.

'I'm an officer of the City Watch,' said Vimes. 'Brought here under duress . . . madam.'

The woman waved a hand. 'You're free to go whenever you wish.'

191

'It's a comfy chair,' said Vimes. He was damned if he'd be dismissed. 'Are you really from Genua?'

'Are you really from Pseudopolis?' Madam smiled at him. 'I find, personally, that it pays never to be from somewhere close at hand. It makes life so much easier. But I have spent a lot of time in Genua, where I have . . . business interests.' She smiled at him. 'And now you're thinking "old seamstress", no doubt?'

'Actually I was thinking bespoke tailoring,' said Vimes, and she burst out laughing. 'But mostly,' he added, 'I was thinking "revolutionary".'

'Continue, sergeant.' Madam stood up. 'Do you mind if I have some champagne? I'd offer you some, but I understand that you don't drink.'

Vimes glanced at the brimming whiskey glass beside him.

'We were just checking,' said Madam, hauling a large bottle out of an industrial-capacity ice bucket. 'You're not a sergeant. Rosie was right. You've been an officer. More than just any old officer, too. You're so *composed*, Sergeant Keel. Here you are, in a big house, in a lady's boudoir, with a woman of uneasy virtue,' Madam up-ended the bottle into what appeared to be a blue mug with a teddy bear on it, 'and you appear unfussed. Where *are* you from? You may smoke, by the way.'

'Somewhere a long way off,' said Vimes.

'Uberwald?'

'No.'

'I have . . . business interests in Uberwald,' said Madam. 'Alas, the situation there is becoming quite unstable.'

'Right. I see,' said Vimes. 'And you'd like to have the significant pause type of business interests in Ankh-Morpork, I expect. If it can be stabilized.'

'*Very* good. Let us say that I think this city has a wonderful future and that I would like to be part of it, and that you are remarkably perspicacious.'

'No,' said Vimes. 'I'm very simple. I just know how things work. I just follow the money. Winder is a madman, and that's

192

not good for business. His cronies are criminals, and that's not good for business. A new Patrician will need new friends, far-sighted people who want to be part of a wonderful future. One that's good for business. That's how it goes. Meetings in rooms. A little diplomacy, a little give and take, a promise here, an understanding there. That's how real revolutions happen. All that stuff in the streets is just froth . . .' Vimes nodded to the doors. 'Guests for a late supper? That was Doctor Follett's voice. A clever man, they used to— they call him. He'll pick the right side. If you've got the big Guilds with you, Winder is a dead man walking. But Snapcase won't do you much good.'

'Many people have great hopes of him.'

'What do you think?'

'I think he's a scheming, self-serving fool. But he's the best there is, at the moment. And where do you come in, sergeant?'

'Me? I'm staying outside. You've got nothing that I want.'

'You don't want *anything*?'

'I want lots of things, my lady. But you can't give them to me.'

'How would you like to be back in command?'

The question hit him like a hammer. This was *history*. She couldn't know! How could she know?

'Ah,' said Madam, who had watched his expression. 'Rosemary did say thieves took some *very* expensive armour off you. Fit for a general, I hear.'

She opened another bottle. Properly, too, Vimes noticed, through the shock. None of that amateur business with rocketing corks and wasted bubbles.

'Wouldn't that be strange if it was true?' Madam mused. 'A street-fighting man with the manner of a commander and the breastplate of a leader.'

Vimes stared straight ahead.

'And who needs to know how he got here?' said Madam, to the air in general. 'We could take the view that here at last is a man who could truly take command of the City Watch.'

The first thought that fizzed in Vimes's head like champagne was: bloody hell, I could do it! Chuck Swing out on his arse, promote some decent sergeants—

The second thought was: in this city? Under Snapcase? Now? We'd just be another gang. The third thought was: this is insane. It can't happen. It never *did* happen. You want to go home to Sybil.

Thoughts one and two shuffled out of the way, feeling ashamed of themselves and mumbling *yeah, right . . . Sybil . . . yeah, obviously . . . right . . . sorry . . .* until they faded into silence.

'I've always had a talent for seeing promise,' said Madam, while he still stared at nothing.

The fourth thought rose in the darkness like some ugly creature from the depths.

You didn't think about Sybil until thought three, it whispered.

He blinked.

'You know the city needs—' Madam began.

'I want to go home,' said Vimes. 'I'm going to finish the job that's in front of me, and then I'm going home. That's what I'm going to do.'

'There are those who would say that if you are not for us, you're against us,' said Madam.

'For you? For what? For *anything*? No! But I'm not for Winder, either. I'm not supposed to be "for" people. And I don't take bribes. Not even if Sandra threatens me with a toadstool!'

'I believe it was a mushroom. Oh dear.' The lady gave him a smile. 'You are incorruptible?'

Oh dear, here we go again, thought Vimes. Why did I wait until I was married to become strangely attractive to powerful women? Why didn't it happen to me when I was sixteen? I could have done with it then.

He tried to glare, but that probably only made it worse.

'I've met a few incorruptible men,' said Madam Meserole. 'They tend to die *horrible* deaths. The world balances out, you see. A corrupt man in a good world, or a good man in a corrupt

194

one . . . the equation comes out the same way. The world does not deal well with those who don't pick a side.'

'I like the middle,' said Vimes.

'That gives you *two* enemies. I'm amazed that you can afford so many, on a sergeant's pay. Please think of what you could be giving up.'

'I am. And I'm not going to help people to die just to replace one fool with another.'

'Then there is your door behind you, sergeant. I am very sorry we could not—'

'—do business?' said Vimes.

'I was *going* to say "reach a mutually beneficial agreement". We are not very far from your Watch House. I wish you . . . luck.'

She nodded towards the door. 'Such a shame,' she said, and sighed.

Vimes stepped out into the rainy night, and shifted his weight from foot to foot, and then took a few experimental steps.

Corner of Easy and Treacle Mine. A mix of flat-top cobbles and old bricks. Yeah.

He went home.

Madam stared at the closed door for a while, and then turned as the candles flickered slightly.

'You really are very good,' she said. 'How long have you been here?'

Havelock Vetinari stepped out of the shadow in the corner. He wasn't wearing official Assassin's black, but loose clothes that were . . . no real colour at all, just nondescript shades of grey.

'I've been here quite long enough,' he said, sprawling into the chair that Vimes had vacated.

'Not even the Aunts noticed you?'

'People look but don't see. The trick is to help them see nothing. But I think Keel would have seen me, if I hadn't been over here. He stares into shadows. Interesting.'

'He is a very angry man,' said Madam.

'You just made him angrier.'

'I believe you'll get your diversion,' said Madam.

'Yes. I believe so, too.'

Madam leaned over and patted him on the knee.

'There,' she said, 'your aunty thinks of everything . . .' She stood up. 'I'd better go and entertain my guests. I am a very entertaining person. By tomorrow night, Lord Winder will not have many friends.' She drained her mug of champagne. 'Doctor Follett is such a charming man, don't you think? Is that his own hair, do you know?'

'I have not sought the opportunity to find out,' said Havelock. 'Is he trying to get you drunk?'

'Yes,' said Madam. 'You have to admire him.'

'They say he can play a mean lute,' said Havelock.

'Fascinating,' said Madam.

She set her face into a genuine smile of pleasure and opened the big double doors at the other end of the room.

'Ah, doctor,' she said, stepping into the haze of smoke. 'A little more champagne?'

Vimes slept in a corner, standing up. It was an old trick, shared by night watchmen and horses. It wasn't *exactly* sleep, you'd die if you tried to keep it up for more than a few nights, but it took some of the tiredness away.

A few of the other men had already mastered the trick. Others made use of tables or benches. No one seemed inclined to go home, even when a sort of dawn suffused the rain and Snouty came in with a cauldron of fearsome porridge.

Vimes opened his eyes.

'Mug of tea, sarge?' said Snouty. 'Stewed for an hour and two sugars.'

'You're a lifesaver, Snouty,' said Vimes, clasping it like the elixir of life.

196

'An' there's some kid outside says he's got to speak to you, hnah, specially,' Snouty went on. 'Shall I give him a clip alongside the head?'

'What does he smell like?' said Vimes, sipping the scalding, corrosive tea.

'Bottom of a baboon's cage, sarge.'

'Ah, Nobby Nobbs. I'll go out and see him. Bring him a big bowl of porridge, will you?'

Snouty looked uncomfortable about this. 'If you'll, hnah, take my advice, sarge, it don't pay to encourage kids like—'

'See these stripes, Snouty? Well done. A big bowl.'

Vimes took his tea out into the damp yard, where Nobby was lurking against a wall.

There were hints that it was going to be a sunny day. That should bring things on, after the overnight rain. The lilacs, for example . . .

'What's happening, Nobby?'

Nobby waited a moment to see if a coin was forthcoming.

'Pretty bad everywhere, sarge,' he said, giving up for now but remaining hopeful. 'A constable got killed in Lobbin Clout. Hit by a stone, people say. Someone got their ear cut off 'cos of the fighting in Nap Hill. Cavalry charge, sarge. Running fights everywhere. All the Watch Houses got hit bad—'

Vimes listened gloomily to the list. It was the usual bloody business. Angry, frightened people on both sides, all crushed up together. It could only get worse. Nap Hill and Dolly Sisters sounded like war zones already.

. . . *see the little angels rise up high* . . .

'Anything happen in Cable Street?' he said.

'Just a few people,' said Nobby. 'A bit of shouting and running away, that sort of thing.'

'Right,' said Vimes. Even a mob wasn't that stupid. It was still only the kids and the hotheads and the drunks now. It'd get worse. You'd have to be really mad to attack the Unmentionables.

197

'There's bad stuff happening everywhere,' said Nobby. 'Except here, o'course. We're well out of it.'

No, thought Vimes. It'll pivot on us in the end.

Snouty emerged from the Watch House's rear door, carrying a big bowl of porridge with a spoon stuck in it. Vimes nodded towards Nobby, and the bowl was handed over with extreme reluctance.

'Sarge?' said Snouty, keeping his eye on the spoon as the boy ate or, more correctly, gobbled the stuff.

'Yes, Snouty?'

'Have we got any *orders*?'

'I don't know. Is the captain here?'

'That's it, sarge,' said Snouty. 'A runner come last night with an envelope for the captain, and I took it up and there was the captain waiting, so I thought, this is funny, haha, I thought, he's not normally in this early—'

'Faster please, Snouty,' said Vimes, as the man started to watch the oscillating spoon again.

'Well, when I took him up his cocoa later on he was jus' sittin' there, hnah, starin' right at nothing. He said "thank you, Snouty" when I give him the cocoa, hnah, though. Always very polite in that, hnah, respect. But when I went up just now he was gone.'

'He's an old man, Snouty, you can't expect him to be here all—'

'So's his inkwell, sarge. He never took it home before.' And Vimes saw that Snouty's eyes were more red-rimmed than usual.

He sighed. 'Any sign of the envelope?'

'No, sarge,' said Snouty, glancing again at the spoon in Nobby's hand. It was a very cheap one, Vimes noted, made of some pot metal.

'In that case we just keep the peace, Snouty,' he said.

'Not a lot of that about, sarge.'

'We'll have to see what we can find. Come with me.'

Snouty looked reluctant. 'Just want to keep an eye on the spoon, sarge; we've only got five left and kids like that one'll pinch the—'

'He can *keep* the damn spoon!' said Vimes. 'Spoons are not important at this point!'

Nobby downed the last scalding mouthful, stuck the spoon in his pocket, stuck out a porridge-laden tongue at Snouty, dropped the bowl on the ground and took to his heels.

Vimes strode back into the office, picked up the porridge ladle and rattled it on the sides of the empty cauldron. Heads looked up.

'All right, my sons! This is what we're going to do! All married men've got permission to nip home for an hour to stop your wives fretting! The rest of you, you're on unpaid overtime! Anyone surprised?'

Wiglet raised a hand. 'We've all got family, sarge,' he said.

'And the best thing you can do for them is make sure there's a bit of law around the place,' said Vimes. 'We don't know what's been happening in the other divisions, except that it sounds bad. So this House is staying open, understand? Day and night! Yes, lance-constable?'

'But our mum will be worrying, sarge,' said young Sam.

Vimes hesitated, but only for a moment. 'Snouty'll nip out with any messages you have, lad. The same goes for everyone else,' he said. 'We're going to go out on patrol soon. Yeah, I know we're Night Watch. So what? It's looking pretty black to me at the moment! Lance-constable, come on out in the yard, will you?'

Vimes walked back out into the morning.

In theory, one of the purposes of the yard was for training. It was seldom used for that. The Night Watch eschewed violence, as a rule. When threats or superior numbers had no effect, they preferred to run.

There were some mouldering targets in a shed, along with some straw men for stabbing practice. Vimes tugged them out

199

on to the cobbles as the lance-constable appeared behind him.

'I thought you said these things were useless, sarge.'

'They are,' said Vimes. 'I've put them here for you to land on. You're walking around, Sam, with a weapon you don't know how to use. That's worse than walking around knowing how to use a weapon and not having one. A man with a weapon he doesn't know how to use is likely to have it shoved where the sun does not shine.'

He took off his breastplate and helmet, and tossed his sword belt into a corner.

'All right, attack me,' he said. Out of the corner of his eye he saw that some of the men had wandered into the yard and were watching.

'I can't just stab you, sarge!' Sam wailed.

'No, but I'd like you to try.'

Sam hesitated again. I wasn't *entirely* stupid, Vimes thought.

'You're grinning, sarge,' said Sam.

'Well?'

'You're just grinning and standing there, sarge,' said Sam. 'I know I'm going to get a hiding, 'cos you haven't got a sword and you're grinning.'

'Worried about getting blood on your nice sword, lad? All right, throw it away. Feel better? You were in a gang, right? Of course you were. Everyone was. You're still alive. So you must've learned how to fight.'

'Yeah, sarge, but that was, you know, dirty fighting . . .'

'We're dirty people. Do your worst,' said Vimes.

'I don't want to hurt you, sarge!'

'That's your first mistake—'

Sam span and lashed out.

Vimes stepped back, caught the foot and helped it on its journey upwards.

I was quick too, he thought, as Sam landed flat on his back. And not too bad at cunning. But I've learned artful since then.

'It showed in your eyes,' he said to the sprawling Sam.

'But you've got hold of the basic idea. There's no rules.'

He sensed the change behind him. It included the very muffled sound of a chuckle. He glanced back at Sam, who was looking past him.

The blow was a neat one, to the back of where the head would have been if Vimes hadn't stepped smartly sideways. As it was, he turned and grabbed the arm and looked into the face of Ned Coates.

'Nice day off, Ned?' he said.

'Yes, sarge, thank you. Just wanted to see how good you were.'

He elbowed Vimes in the stomach and twisted away. There was some murmuring from the watchers but Vimes, bent double and with tears running from his eyes, raised a hand.

'No, it was fair enough, fair enough,' he panted. 'We've all got something to learn.' He put his hands on his knees, wheezing a little more theatrically than he needed to.

He was impressed that Ned wasn't falling for it. The man kept his distance, circling slowly. He was holding his truncheon. A less experienced fighter would have come to check that ol' sarge was all right, and would have suffered for it.

'That's right, sarge,' said Ned. 'I want to see what you can teach *me*. Sam's too trusting.'

Vimes's mind riffled desperately through options.

'So, sarge,' said Ned, still moving, 'what would you do, sarge, if you were unarmed and a man came at you with a truncheon?'

Get armed quick, thought Vimes, if I thought he was as good as you.

He ducked and rolled. Ned missed that. When Vimes started to move right he'd concentrated on the left, on the basis that from someone like Vimes the first move had to be a feint. By the time he caught himself and turned, Vimes had grabbed his scabbard and was rising, sword sliding out.

'Ah, raising the stakes. Good lesson, sarge,' said Ned. He drew his own sword. It gleamed; most of the Watch swords would have had difficulty cutting butter. 'Now we're level again. What next, sarge?'

They circled. Blimey, thought Vimes, who taught him? And he's grinning, and no wonder. This isn't a contest. He knows I can't cut him, not like this, not in front of everyone. He can accidentally hit me and get away with it, but a sergeant's supposed to know better. And we can't raise the stakes any higher.

Hold on . . .

He hurled the sword at the wall. It stuck in, by sheer luck. That impressed the watchers.

'Got to give you a chance, Ned,' he said, moving away.

You can always learn, Vimes thought. He remembered Gussie Two Grins. Sam wouldn't run into him for five years or so. It would be a real education. Two Grins was the dirtiest fighter Vimes had ever met. Anything was a weapon, anywhere was a target. Two Grins was a kind of genius in that limited area. He could see the weapon in *anything* – a wall, a cloth, a piece of fruit . . .

He wasn't even a big man. He was small and wiry. But he liked fighting big men, on the basis that there was more of them to bite. After a few drinks, though, it was hard to know what Two Grins was fighting. He'd fight the man next to him simply as a substitute for kneeing the whole universe in the groin.

He'd been called Two Grins ever since someone glassed him in the face; Gussie had been so marinated in adrenalin at that point that he regarded this as a mere detail. The scar had left a happy smiley face. Sam had learned a lot from Gussie Two Grins.

'What's this about?' he murmured, just loud enough for Ned to hear.

'Just want to find out what you know, sarge,' said Ned, still circling. 'Seems to me you know too much.'

He lunged. Vimes darted back, flailed with the scabbard like a man with no hope and, as Ned laughed and leaned out of his way, shifted his grip on the stiff leather.

'I've got the helmet on, as per regulations,' said Ned. 'And the armour. Hard to punch me out, sarge.'

Even with Detritus yelling at them, not one watchman in seven really used a sword properly. Ned did. There weren't many openings.

Oh, well . . . time for artful.

He took a step back, stopped, and saw what was happening behind Coates. He tried to hide it, but he couldn't stop the momentary flash of relief in his eyes.

Coates couldn't stop the momentary flicker of attention.

Vimes punched up, the scabbard an extension of his arm. The stiff leather caught the man under the chin, thrusting his head back. Then the leather was brought down on the sword hand and, as an afterthought, Vimes kicked Ned on the shin just enough to make him collapse. He'd always had an allergy to edged weapons too near his face.

'Well done, nice try,' he said, and turned his back and faced the crowd. To the sound of gurgling behind him, he said, 'Anything's a weapon, used right. Your bell is a club. Anything that pokes the other man hard enough to give you more time is a good thing. Never, ever threaten anyone with your sword unless you really mean it, because if he calls your bluff you suddenly don't have many choices and they're all the wrong ones. Don't be frightened to use what you learned when you were kids. We don't get marks for playing fair. And for close-up fighting, as your senior sergeant I explicitly forbid you to investigate the range of coshes, blackjacks and brass knuckles sold by Mrs Goodbody at No. 8 Easy Street, at a range of prices and sizes to suit all pockets, and should any of you approach me privately I absolutely will not demonstrate a variety of specialist blows suitable for these useful yet tricky instruments. Right, let's limber up. I want you all out here with your truncheons in two minutes. You think it's just a silly club. I will show you otherwise. Jump to it!'

He turned to the stricken Ned, who'd raised himself to a sitting position.

'Nice moves, Mr Coates. You didn't learn them in the Watch, I know that. Anything we need to discuss? Care to tell me where you were last night? Morphic Street, maybe?'

'Day off,' muttered Ned, rubbing his jaw.

'Right, right. None of my business. Seems to me we've failed to hit it off, Ned.'

' 'sright.'

'You think I'm some kind of spy.'

'I know you're not John Keel.'

Vimes kept his face perfectly impassive – which was, he realized, a complete giveaway in itself.

'Why d'you say that?' he said.

'I don't have to tell you. You ain't a Watch sergeant, either. And you were lucky just now, and that's all I'm saying.' Ned got to his feet as the other watchmen filed out into the yard again.

Vimes let him go, and turned his attention to the men.

None of them had ever been taught anything. They'd learned, to a greater or usually a lesser extent, from one another. And Vimes knew where that road went. On that road coppers rolled drunks for their small change and assured one another that bribes were just perks, and it got worse.

He was all for getting recruits out on the street, but you had to train them first. You needed someone like Detritus bellowing at them for six weeks, and lectures about duty and prisoners' rights and the 'service to the public'. And *then* you could hand them over to the street monsters who told them all the *other* stuff, like how to hit someone where it wouldn't leave a mark and when it was a good idea to stick a metal soup-plate down the front of your trousers before attending to a bar brawl.

And if you were lucky and they were sensible, they found somewhere between impossible perfection and the Pit where they could be real coppers – slightly tarnished, because the job did that to you, but not rotten.

He formed them into twos and set them attacking and defending. It was dreadful to watch. He let it go on for five minutes.

'All right, all right,' he said, clapping his hands. 'Very good indeed. When the circus comes to town I'll definitely recommend you.' The men sagged, and grinned sheepishly as he went on: 'Don't you know *any* of the moves? The Throat Slam, the Red Hot Poker, the Ribrattler? Say I'm coming at you with a big, big club . . . what do you do?'

'Run away, sarge,' said Wiglet. There was laughter.

'How far can you run?' said Vimes. 'Got to fight sometime. Lance-Corporal Coates?'

Ned Coates had not been taking part. He'd been leaning against the wall in a sort of stationary swagger, watching the sad show with disdain.

'Sarge?' he said, propelling himself upright with the minimum of effort.

'Show Wiglet how it's done.'

Coates pulled out his truncheon. It was, Vimes saw, custom-made, slightly longer than the general issue. He took up station in front of the constable, with his back very expressively towards Vimes.

'What do you want me to do, sarge?' he said, over his shoulder.

'Show him a few decent moves. Take him by surprise.'

'Right you are, sarge.'

Vimes watched the desultory clatter of sticks. One, two, three . . .

—and around Ned came, truncheon whistling through the air.

But Vimes ducked under the blow and caught the man's arm in both hands, twisting it up behind his back and bringing his ear into immediate conjunction with Vimes's mouth.

'Not quite unexpected, sunshine,' he whispered. 'Now, we'll both keep grinning because the lads are laughing at our Ned, isn't he a card, who keeps having another go at the ol' sarge, and we don't want to spoil their fun. I'm letting you go now, but

205

you try it on one more time and you'll have to use both hands to pick up a spoon and you'll need to pick up a spoon, Ned, 'cos of living off soup by reason of having no damn *teeth*!' He relaxed his grip. 'Who taught you all this stuff, anyway?'

'Sergeant Keel, sarge,' said Ned.

'You're doing a good job, Sergeant Keel!'

Vimes turned to see Captain Swing advancing across the yard.

He was smaller and slimmer in daylight and he looked like a clerk, and a clerk who was only erratically careful about his appearance; his hair was lank, and the thick black strands plastered across a central bald spot suggested that the man either had no mirror or completely lacked a sense of humour.

His coat, in the light, was old-fashioned but well cared for, but his buckled shoes were scuffed and generally downtrodden. Vimes's mother would have had something to say about that. A man ought to look after his boots, she always said. You could tell a man by the shine of his shoes.

Swing also carried a walking stick or, rather, an opera cane. It was just possible that he thought it made him look sophisticated rather than, say, like a man carrying an unnecessary length of wood. It was certainly a swordstick, because it rattled when it hit the pavement, and it did so now as he primly picked his way through the old targets and straw debris.

'Keeping the men up to scratch, I see,' he said. 'Very well done. Is your captain here?'

'I believe not,' said Vimes, letting Coates go, 'sir.'

'Ah? Well, perhaps you will give him this, Sergeant Keel.' Swing gave him a faint smile. 'You had a successful night . . . I am given to understand.'

'We had a few visitors,' said Vimes, 'sir.'

'Ah, yes. Misplaced zeal. It does not pay to . . . underestimate you, sergeant. You are a man of resource. Alas, the other Houses were not so—'

'—resourceful?'

'Ah. Yes. I am afraid, sergeant, that some of my keener men

feel you are anobstacle . . . to our very needful work. I, onthecontrary . . . believe that you are a man of iron adherence to the law and, while this hasledto . . . elements of friction because of your lack of full understanding of the exigencies of the situation, I know that you are a man after my own heart.'

Vimes considered the anatomical choices.

'That would be broadly correct, sir,' he said, 'although I would not aspire that high.'

'Capital. I lookforwardto . . . our future co-operation, sergeant. Your new captain willundoubtedly . . . inform you of other matters, as he sees fit. Good day.'

Swing swivelled, and walked his jerky walk back to the gate. His men turned to follow him but one of them, who was wearing a plaster cast on one arm, made a gesture.

'Morning, Henry,' said Vimes.

He examined the letter. It was quite thick, and had a big embossed seal. But Vimes had spent too much time in the company of bad men, and knew exactly what to do with a sealed envelope.

He also knew how to listen. New captain. So . . . it was starting.

The men were watching him.

'They calling in more, hnah, soldiers, sarge?' said Snouty.

'I expect so,' said Vimes.

'They gave Captain Tilden the push, didn't they . . .'

'Yes.'

'He was a *good captain*!' Snouty protested.

'Yes,' Vimes said. No, he thought. He wasn't. He was a decent man and he did his best, that's all. He's well out of it now.

'What're we gonna do *now*, sarge?' said Lance-Constable Vimes.

'We'll patrol,' said Vimes. 'Close in. Just these few streets.'

'What good'll that do?'

'More good than if we didn't, lad. Didn't you take the oath when you joined up?'

'What oath, sarge?'

He didn't, Vimes remembered. A lot of them hadn't. You just got your uniform and your bell and you were a member of the Night Watch.

A few years ago Vimes wouldn't have bothered about the oath either. The words were out of date and the shilling on a string was a joke. But you needed something more than the wages, even in the Night Watch. You needed something else to tell you that it wasn't just a job.

'Snouty, nip up to the captain's office and get the Shilling, will you?' said Vimes. 'Let's get this lot sworn in. And where's Sergeant Knock?'

'Pushed off, sarge,' said Wiglet. 'Dunno if it helps, but he said "to hell with him" when he went out the door.'

Vimes counted heads.

It'd be said, later on, that all the Watch House stayed on. They hadn't, of course. Some had slipped away, some hadn't come back on duty at all. But it was true about Keel and the Line.

'Okay, lads,' he said, 'it's like this. We know what's been going on. I don't know about you, but I don't like it. Once you get troops on the streets, it's only a matter of time before it goes bad. Some kid throws a stone, next minute there's houses on fire and people getting killed. What we're going to do is keep the peace. That's our job. We're not going to be heroes, we're just going to be . . . normal. Now,' he shifted position, 'it might just be that someone will say we're doing something wrong. So I'm not going to order you.'

He drew his sword and scratched a line across the mud and stones.

'If you step over the line, then you're in,' he said. 'If you don't, then that's fine. You didn't sign up for this and I doubt that there'll be any medals, whatever happens. I'll just ask you to go, and the best of luck to you.'

It was almost depressing how quickly Lance-Constable Vimes crossed the line. Fred Colon came next, and Waddy, and Billy

Wiglet. And Spatchcock, Culweather and Moist and Leggy Gaskin and Horace Nancyball and . . . Curry, wasn't it? . . . and Evans and Pounce . . .

A dozen crossed the line, the last few with the reluctance caused by a battle between peer pressure and a healthy regard for their skin. A few others, more than Vimes had hoped, evaporated at the back.

That left Ned Coates. He crossed his arms. 'You're all bloody mad,' he said.

'We could use you, Ned,' said Vimes.

'I don't want to die,' said Ned, 'and I don't intend to. This is stupid. There's barely a dozen of you. What can you do? All that stuff about "keeping the peace" – it's rubbish, lads. Coppers do what they're told by the men in charge. It's always like that. What'll you do when the new captain comes in, eh? And who're you doing this for? The people? They attacked the other Houses, and what's the Night Watch ever done to hurt them?'

'Nothing,' said Vimes.

'There you are, then.'

'I mean the Watch did nothing, and that's what hurt them,' said Vimes.

'What could you do, then? Arrest Winder?'

Vimes felt he was building a bridge of matchsticks over a yawning abyss, and now he could feel the chilly winds below him.

He'd arrested Vetinari, back in the future. Admittedly the man had walked free, after what passed for the due process of law, but the City Watch had bee— was going to be big enough and strong enough and well-connected enough to actually arrest *the ruler of the city*. How had they ever got to that stage? How had he even *dreamed* that a bunch of coppers could slam the cell door on the boss?

Well, perhaps it had started here. Lance-Constable Vimes was watching him intently.

'Of course we can't,' he said, 'but we ought to be able to.

209

Maybe one day we will. If we can't then the law isn't the law, it's just a way of keeping people down.'

'Looks like you've woken up and smelled the cacky,' said Coates, 'because that's exactly what you're in. Sorry, lads, but you're going to *die*. That's what'll happen if you tangle with real soldiers. Hear about Dolly Sisters last night? Three dead and they weren't even trying.'

'Come on, Ned, no one's going to have a go at us if we're just patrolling,' mumbled Colon.

'Patrolling for *what*?' said Coates. 'To keep the peace? What'll you do when there's no peace left to keep? Well, I'm not going to stand around and see you get killed. I'm off.'

He turned and strode out of the yard and into the Watch House. You bloody fool, you're right, Vimes thought. I just wish you weren't so right.

'Still with us, lads?' he said, to the group caught behind the line.

'That's right, sarge!' said Lance-Constable Vimes. The rest of the volunteers seemed slightly less certain.

'*Are* we gonna get killed?' said Wiglet.

'Who said it's going to come to a fight?' said Vimes, watching Coates's retreating back. 'Wait a moment, I want a word with Ned—'

'Got the Shilling, sarge,' Snouty announced, advancing across the yard. 'And the captain wants a word with you.'

'Tell him I'll be up in just a few—'

'It's the new captain,' said Snouty quickly. 'He's here already, hnah. Keen. *Milit'ry*. Not the patient type, sarge.'

I used to have Carrot and Detritus and Angua and Cheery for this, Vimes thought bitterly. I'd say you do this, and *you* do that, and all I had to do was fret and deal with the soddin' politics . . .

'Get Fred to swear the men in,' he said. 'And tell the officer I'll be with him shortly.'

He ran through the Watch House and out of the front door. There were a lot of people in the street, more than usual. It wasn't a mob as such, but it was Ankh-Morpork's famous ur-mob, the state you got just before a real mob happened. It spread across the city like web and spider and, when some triggering event happened, twanged its urgent message through the streets and thickened and tightened around the spot. The Dolly Sisters Massacre had got around and the numbers had grown in the telling. Vimes could sense the tension in the web. It was just waiting for some idiot to do the wrong thing, and Nature is bountiful where idiots are concerned.

'Coates!' he yelled.

To his surprise, the man stopped and turned.

'Yeah?'

'I know you're with the revolutionaries.'

'You're just guessing.'

'No, you had the password in your notebook,' said Vimes. 'The same one Dibbler was passing out in pies. You must *know* I was able to get into the lockers. Look, do you think you and Dibbler'd still be walking around if I was a spy for Swing?'

'Sure. You're not after us, we can be mopped up later. Swing wants the leaders.'

Vimes stood back. 'Okay. Why haven't you told the lads?'

'Things are moving, that's why. It's all starting,' said Ned. 'Who you are doesn't matter any more. But you're going to get the lads killed. They'd have been on *our* side, if it wasn't for you. I was working on 'em. You know Spatchcock always drops his sword on his foot and Nancyball wets himself when he's threatened and Vimesy is simple, and now you're going to stick 'em all right in the middle and they're gonna *die*. And all for no reason!'

'Why haven't you told them?' Vimes repeated.

'Maybe you've got friends in high places,' Ned snarled.

Vimes glanced up at the rooftops.

'Have we finished?' said Ned.

'Give me your badge,' said Vimes.

'You what?'

'You're quitting. Fair enough. Give me your badge.'

Coates recoiled as if he'd been stung. 'Blow that!'

'Then leave the city,' said Vimes. 'It'd be for your own good.'

'Is that a threat?'

'Not from me. But here's some advice, boy. Don't put your trust in revolutions. They always come around again. That's why they're called revolutions. People die, and nothing changes. I'll see *you* later.'

He turned his back and hurried away, so that the man wouldn't see his face.

Okay. Now it was time. It had to be now, or he'd burst like Mr Salciferous. He had wanted to do this, hadn't dared try it, because those monks could probably do a man a lot of no good if he crossed them, but it had all gone too far now . . .

A sense of duty told him there was an officer waiting to see him. He overruled it. It was not in possession of all the facts.

Vimes reached the entrance to the Watch House, and stopped. He shut his eyes. If anyone had bothered to look at him, they'd have seen a man apparently trying to grind two cigarette stubs into the road, one with each foot. Thank you, Rosie, for those cardboard soles. He smiled.

He thought with the brains in his feet. And as young Sam had noticed, the feet had a memory of their own . . .

Rounded cathead cobbles, the usual kind. They hadn't been well set in this part of the city and moved very slightly under-foot . . . then twice before getting to the Watch House his feet had felt larger cobbles, narrow bands of them, where the road surface had been replaced after drains had been laid. And before that, there'd been a similar band but of soft brick rubble, so crushed by cartwheels that it was practically a gully.

A few dozen steps earlier they'd twirled him round a couple of times, but the last surface before that had been . . . mud.

Vimes, who had been walking with his eyes shut, bumped into a cart.

Mud, he thought, getting up and ignoring the strange looks of

212

passers-by. That meant an alley. Let's see . . . ah, yes, over there . . .

It took twenty minutes.

People turned as he walked through the streets, closing his eyes when he dared so that his feet could see better. Sometimes he did look around, though, and there it was again, the thunderstorm sensation of tensions building up, waiting for the first little thing. People were uneasy – the *herd* was restless – and they didn't quite know why. Everyone he looked at returned his gaze blankly.

He stepped onwards. Rough flagstones between two stretches of the ancient cobbles they called trollheads . . . the only place where you got that in this part of the city was here, where Pewter Street crossed Elm, and before that it had been . . . yeah, big stones, some of the most ancient in the city, rutted by hundreds and hundreds of years of iron-bound cartwheels, that was a road that had been right behind a city wall . . . yes; he crossed the Pitts, still on Elm, and then lost his thread. A metal grating on the pavement gave it back to him. Cellar grating. *Cool* cellar. Coat of arms on it, worn down. Buttermarket. Yeah. Go, feet!

The monks had turned him again here but . . . long bricks, hard-fired in the kiln, and a stretch of quite modern flagstones, well dressed and fitted. It could trick you if you didn't know you were in . . . yeah, Masons Road, and there *were* masons here and they looked after the surface. Now find an alley, mud but with a lot of gravel in it, because the stonemasons dumped their waste here but this one has occasional hummocks across it, where pipes have been laid. Yeah. Now find square-head cobbles . . .

He opened his eyes.

Yeah.

Away on his left, on Clay Lane, was a block of three buildings. A temple sandwiched between two cheapjack corner shops. It was . . . just a temple, slightly foreign-looking, but weren't they

213

all? It looked High Hublandish, where everyone lived on yaks or something.

The temple doors were locked. He rattled the handle impotently, and then hammered on the woodwork with his sword. It had no effect. He didn't even leave a mark on the wood.

But the door of the shonky shop next door was open. It was a familiar place. Once upon a time, it was his tailor and boot-maker. And, like a pawn shop, a shonky shop was *always* open. Vimes stepped inside, and was immediately enveloped in dusty darkness.

It was a cave of cloth. Racks of old suits hung from the ceiling. Ancient shelves bent under piles of shirts and vests and socks. Here and there old boxes loomed in the gloom and caught his knees. Piles of derelict boots slipped and slid under his feet. And there was the smell. If poverty had a smell, this was it. If humbled pride had a smell, this was it. And there was a touch of disinfectant as well.

Within a few feet of the door, Vimes was already lost. He turned and shoved his way through grey aisle after grey aisle of suffocating cloth and wondered if anyone had ever died in here and how anyone could ever find out. He pulled aside a hanger containing a greasy, threadbare suit—

'You want?'

He turned.

There was no one there, until his gaze fell slightly and met that of a small, glossy little man, totally bald, very small and thin, and wearing some vague clothing that presumably even a shonky shop hadn't been able to unload on a customer. Who was he? who was he? . . . surprisingly, the name seemed quite fresh in the memory . . .

'Ah, er, yeah . . . Mr Shine—'

'Soon Shine Sun,' said Mr Soon. He grabbed the suit Vimes was still holding. 'Good eye, good eye, lovely cloth, lovely cloth, owned by priest, very good, fifty pence to you, shame to sell it, times are hard.'

Vimes hastily put the suit back on the rack and pulled out his badge. Soon glared at it.

'I pay already other copper,' he said. 'One dollar, one month, no trouble. Already I pay other copper.'

'Pay?' said Vimes.

'Two-stripe copper already I pay. One dollar, one month, no trouble!'

'Corporal Quirke,' muttered Vimes. 'You don't have to pay coppers, Mr Soon. We're here for your protection.'

Despite his barely basic grasp of the language, Mr Soon's expression suggested very clearly that the three-stripe, one-crown copper in front of him had dropped in from the planet Idiot.

'Look, I haven't got time for this,' said Vimes. 'Where's the back door? This is Watch business!'

'I pay! I *pay* protection! One month, no trouble!'

Vimes grunted and set off along another narrow, cloth-lined tunnel.

A glint of glass caught his eye, and he sidled crabwise up a choked aisle until he found a counter. It was piled with more hopeless merchandise, but there was a bead-curtained doorway behind it. He half clambered, half swam over the piles and scrambled into the tiny room beyond.

Mr Soon pushed his way to an ancient tailor's dummy; it was so scratched, chipped and battered it looked like something dug up from the volcanic ash of an ancient city.

He pulled on an arm, and the eyes lit up.

'Number Three here,' he said, into its ear. 'He's just gone through. And, boy, is he angry . . .'

The back door was locked but yielded under the weight of Vimes's body. He staggered into the yard, looked up at the wall separating this greasy space from the temple's garden, jumped, scrabbled his boots on the brickwork and dragged himself on to the top, feeling a couple of bricks crumble away underneath him.

He landed on his back, and looked up at a thin, robed figure sitting on a stone seat.

'Cup of tea, commander?' said Sweeper cheerfully.

'I don't want any damn tea!' shouted Vimes, struggling to his feet.

Sweeper dropped a lump of rancid yak butter in the tea bowl beside him. 'What *do* you want, then, Mister Vimes with the very helpful feet?'

'I can't deal with this! You know what I mean!'

'You know, some tea really would calm you down,' said Sweeper.

'Don't tell me to be calm! When are you going to get me home?'

A figure stepped out of the temple. He was a taller, heavier man than Sweeper, white-haired and with the look of a good-natured bank manager about him. He held out a cup.

Vimes hesitated a moment, and then took the cup and poured the tea out on to the ground.

'I don't trust you,' he said. 'There could be *anything* in this.'

'I can't imagine what we could put in tea that would make it any worse than the way you normally drink it,' said Sweeper calmly. 'Sit *down*, your grace. Please?'

Vimes sagged on to the seat. The rage that had been driving him sank a little, too, but he could feel it bubbling. Automatically, he pulled out a half-smoked cigar and put it in his mouth.

'Sweeper said you'd find us, some way or other,' said the other monk, and sighed. 'So much for secrecy.'

'Why should you worry?' said Vimes, lighting the stub. 'You can just play around with time and it won't have happened, right?'

'We don't intend to do that,' said the other monk.

'What could I do, anyway? Go around telling everyone that those loony monks you see in the streets are some kind of time shifters? I'd get locked up! Who are you, anyway?'

'This is Qu,' said Sweeper, nodding at the other monk.

'When the time comes, he'll get you back. But not yet.'

Vimes sighed. The anger had drained, leaving only a hopeless, empty feeling. He stared blankly at the strange rockery that occupied most of the garden. It looked oddly familiar. He blinked.

'I've been talking to people today who are going to *die*,' he said. 'How do you think that makes me feel? Do you know what that feels like?'

The monks gave him a puzzled look.

'Er . . . yes,' said Qu.

'We do,' said Sweeper. 'Everyone we talk to is going to die. Everyone you talk to is going to die. Everyone dies.'

'I've been changing things,' said Vimes, and added defensively: 'Well, why shouldn't I? Carcer is! I have no idea how things are going to turn out! I mean, doesn't it change history even if you just tread on an ant?'

'For the ant, certainly,' said Qu.

Sweeper waved a hand. 'I told you, Mister Vimes. History finds a way. It's like a shipwreck. You're swimming to the shore. The waves will break whatever you do. Is it not written: "The big sea does not care which way the little fishes swim"? People die in their due time—'

'Keel didn't! Carcer mugged the poor devil!'

'His due time in *this* present, commander,' said Qu. 'But he *will* play his part in the other one, Mister Vimes. Eventually. You'll reach the shore. You must. Otherwise—'

'—there's no shore,' said Sweeper.

'No,' said Vimes. 'There's got to be more. I'm not swimming, I'm drowning. It was fun, d'you know? At first? Like a boys' night out? Feeling the street under my boots again? But now . . . what about Sybil? Are my memories real? What I *know* is she's a girl living with her dad. *Is* there somewhere where she's my wife, having my child? I mean, really? Is it all in my mind? Can you *prove* it? Is it happening? Will it happen? What is *real*?'

The monks were silent. Sweeper glanced at Qu, who

217

shrugged. He glanced rather more meaningfully and, this time, Qu made that dismissive little wave of the hand which is someone signifying 'all right, all right, against my better judgement . . .' Then Sweeper said: 'Ye-es,' very slowly. 'Yes, I think we can help, commander. You want to know there's a future waiting. You want to hold it in your hand. You want to feel the weight of it. You want one point to navigate by, one point to steer for. Yes. I think we can help you there . . . but . . .'

'Yes?'

'But you climb back over that wall and Sergeant Keel plays his part. He sees it through to the end. He gives the orders he feels are right and *they will be* the right orders. He holds the line. He does the job.'

'He's not the only one,' said Vimes.

'Yes, Commander Vimes has a job in hand, too.'

'Don't worry, I'm not leaving Carcer behind,' growled Vimes.

'Good. We'll be in touch.'

Vimes tossed the stump of his cigar aside, and looked up at the wall.

'All right,' he said. 'I'll see it through. But when the time comes—'

'We will be ready,' said Sweeper. 'Just so long as you—'

He stopped. There was another subtle sound, scaly in its way, a sort of silicon slither.

'My goodness,' said Qu.

Vimes looked down.

The cigar butt still smouldered. But around it the Garden of Inner City Tranquillity was moving, pebble sliding over tiny pebble. A large, water-rounded rock floated gently around, spinning. And then Vimes became aware that the *whole* garden was spinning, turning on the little wisp of smoke. A spent match sailed past, rolling from stone to stone like a scrap of food passed from ant to ant.

'Is it meant to do that?' he said.

'In theory, yes,' said Sweeper. 'I should leave right *now*, Mister Vimes.'

Vimes took one last look at the moving garden, shrugged, and then heaved himself over the wall.

The two monks stared. The tide of little stones was gently pushing the stub into the centre.

'Astonishing,' said Qu. 'He's part of the pattern now. I don't know how you manage it.'

'I'm not doing it,' said Sweeper. 'Qu, can we—'

'No more time shifting,' said Qu. 'It's caused enough trouble.'

'Fair enough,' said Sweeper. 'Then I'll need to send out search parties. The fences, the bent jewellers, the pawnshops . . . we'll find it. I understand our friend. The job's not enough. He needs one real thing. And I know what it is.'

They looked again at the turning, shifting garden, and felt the fingers of history spreading out and into the world.

Vimes tried not to run back to the Watch House, because too many people were standing around in nervous groups and even a running uniform could be risky.

Besides, you didn't run for officers. He was a sergeant. Sergeants walked with a measured tread.

To his mild surprise, the men were still out in the yard. Someone had even hung up the swordsmanship targets, which would certainly be helpful if the watchmen were faced with an enemy who was armless and tied to a pole.

He climbed the stairs. The captain's door was open, and he saw that the new man had repositioned his desk so that he could see out on to the landing and down the stairs. Not a good sign, not a good sign at all. An officer shouldn't see what was going on, he should rely on his sergeants to *tell* him what was going on. That way things ran smoothly.

This man was keen. Oh, dear . . .

The new captain looked up. Oh, good grief, Vimes thought. It's bloody Rust this time round! And it was indeed the Hon.

Ronald Rust, the gods' gift to the enemy, any enemy, and a walking encouragement to desertion.

The Rust family had produced great soldiers, by the undemanding standards of 'Deduct your own casualties from those of the enemy, and if the answer is a positive number, it was a glorious victory' school of applied warfare. But Rust's lack of any kind of military grasp was matched only by his high opinion of the talent he in fact possessed only in negative amounts.

It hadn't been Rust last time. He vaguely remembered some other dim captain. All these little changes . . . what would they add up to?

I bet he's only just been made a captain, thought Vimes. Just think of the lives I could save by accidentally cutting his head off now. Look at those blue eyes, look at that stupid curly moustache. And he's only going to get worse.

'Are you Keel?' The voice was a bark.

'Yessir.'

'I sent an order for you to come up here an hour ago, man.'

'Yessir. But I've been on duty all night and morning and there's been rather a lot to attend to—'

'I expect an order to be obeyed promptly, sergeant.'

'Yessir. So do I, sir. That's why—'

'Discipline starts at the top, sergeant. The men obey you, you obey me, I obey my superiors.'

'Glad to hear it, sir.' Rust had the same firm grip of common politeness, too.

'What is all that going on in the yard?'

Vimes steered according to the prevailing wind . . .

'A bit of morale building, sir. Instilling a bit of esprit de corps.'

. . . and hit a reef. Rust raised his eyebrows.

'Why?' he said. 'The men's job is to do what they are told, as is yours. A group hug is not part of the arrangement, is it?'

'A bit of camaraderie helps the job along, sir. In my experience.'

'Are you eyeballing me, Keel?'

'No, sir. I am wearing an expression of honest doubt, sir. "Eyeballing" is four steps up, right after "looking at you in a funny way", sir. By standard military custom and practice, sir, sergeants are allowed to go all the way up to an expression of acute—'

'What's that pip over your stripes, man?'

'Means sergeant-at-arms, sir. They were a special kind of copper.'

The captain grunted, and glanced at the papers in front of him. 'Lord Winder has received an extraordinary request that you be promoted to lieutenant, sergeant. It has come from Captain Swing of the Particulars. And his lordship listens to Captain Swing. Oh, and he wants you to be transferred to the Particulars. Personally, I think the man is mad.'

'I'm one hundred per cent behind you there, sir.'

'You do not wish to be a lieutenant?'

'No, sir. Too long for Dick and too short for Richard, sir,' said Vimes, focusing on a point a few inches above Rust's head.

'What?'

'Neither one thing nor t'other, sir.'

'Oh, so you'd like to be a *captain*, eh?' said Rust, grinning evilly.

'Nosir. Don't want to be an officer, sir. Get confused when I see more'n one knife and fork on the table, sir.'

'You certainly don't look like officer material to *me*, sergeant.'

'Nosir. Thank you, sir.' Good old Rust. Good *young* Rust. The same unthinking rudeness masquerading as blunt speaking, the same stiff-neckedness, the same petty malice. Any sergeant worth his salt would see how to make use of that.

'Wouldn't mind transferring to the Particulars though, sir,' he volunteered. It was a bit of a gamble, but not much. Rust's mind was reliable.

'I expect you *would* like that, Keel,' said Rust. 'No doubt you ran rings round that old fool Tilden and don't fancy the idea of a captain with his finger on the pulse, eh? No, you can damn well stay here, understand?'

Wonderful, thought Vimes. Sometimes it's like watching a wasp land on a stinging nettle: someone's going to get stung and you don't care.

'Yessir,' he said, eye still staring straight ahead.

'Have you *shaved* today, man?'

'Excused shaving, sir,' Vimes lied. 'Doctor's orders. Been sewn up onna face, sir. Could shave one half, sir.'

He remained at eye front while Rust grudgingly stared at him. The cut was still pretty livid, and Vimes hadn't dared look under the patch yet.

'Hit yourself in the face with your own bell, did you?' grunted the captain.

Vimes's fingers twitched. 'Very funny, sir,' he said.

'Now go and get the men fell in, Keel. Look sharp. I shall inspect them in a moment. And tell that idiot with the flat nose to clear the stable.'

'Sir?'

'My horse will be arriving shortly. I don't want to see that disgusting screw in there.'

'What, turn out Marilyn, sir?' said Vimes, genuinely shocked.

'That was an order. Tell him to jump to it.'

'What do you want us to *do* with her, sir?'

'I don't care! You are a sergeant, you've had an order. Presumably there are knackermen? People around here must eat *something*, no doubt?'

Vimes hesitated for a moment. Then he saluted. 'Right you are, sir,' he said.

'Do you know what I saw on the way here, sergeant?'

'Couldn't say, sir,' said Vimes, staring straight ahead.

'People were building *barricades*, sergeant.'

'Sir?'

'I *know* you heard me, man!'

'Well, it's to be expected, sir. It's happened before. People get jumpy. They hear rumours of mobs and out-of-control soldiers. They try to protect their street—'

'It is a flagrant challenge to government authority! People can't take the law into their own hands!'

'Well, yes. But these things generally run their course—'

'My gods, man, how did you manage to get promoted?'

Vimes knew he should leave it at that. Rust was a fool. But at the moment he was a young fool, which is more easily excused. Maybe it was just possible, if caught early enough, that he could be upgraded to idiot.

'Sometimes it pays to—' he began.

'Last night every Watch House in the city was mobbed,' said Rust, ignoring him. 'Except this one. How do you account for that?' His moustache bristled. Not being attacked was definite proof of Vimes's lack of moral fibre.

'It was just a case of—'

'Apparently a man attempted an assault on you. Where is he now?'

'I don't know, sir. We bandaged him up and took him home.'

'You *let him go*?'

'Yessir. He was—' But Rust was always a man to interrupt an answer with a demand for the answer he was in fact interrupting.

'Why?'

'Sir, because at that time I thought it prudent to—'

'Three watchmen were killed last night, did you know that? There were gangs roaming the streets! Well, martial law has been declared! Today we're going to show them a firm hand! Get your men together! Now!'

Vimes saluted, turned about, and walked slowly down the stairs. He wouldn't have run for a big clock.

A firm hand. Right. Gangs roaming the streets. Well, we sure as hell never did anything when they were criminal gangs. And when you've got madmen and idiots on either side, and everything hangs in the balance . . . well, trouble is always

223

easy to find, when you have enough people looking for it.

One of the hardest lessons of young Sam's life had been finding out that the people in charge weren't in charge. It had been finding out that governments were not, on the whole, staffed by people who had a grip, and that plans were what people made instead of thinking.

Most of the watchmen were clustered around the stairs. Snouty was quite good at internal communications of the worrying kind.

'Tidy yourselves, lads,' said Vimes. 'Captain'll be down in a few minutes. Apparently it's time for a show of strength.'

'What strength?' said Billy Wiglet.

'Ah, Billy, what happens is, the vicious revolutionaries take one look at us and scuttle off back to their holes,' said Vimes. He was immediately sorry he'd said that. Billy hadn't learned irony.

'I mean we just give the uniforms an airing,' he translated.

'We'll get cheesed,' said Fred Colon.

'Not if we stick together,' said Sam.

'Right,' said Vimes. 'After all, we're heavily armed men going on patrol among civilians who are, by law, unarmed. If we're careful, we shouldn't get *too* badly hurt.'

Another bad move. Dark sarcasm ought to be taught in schools, he thought. Besides, armed men *could* get into trouble if the unarmed civilians were angry enough, especially if there were cobblestones on the streets.

He heard the distant clocks strike three. Tonight, the streets would explode.

According to the history books it would be one shot that did it, round about sunset. One of the foot regiments would be assembled in Hen and Chickens Field, awaiting orders. And there would be people watching them. Troops always drew an audience: impressionable kids, the inevitable Ankh-Morpork floating street crowd and, of course, the ladies whose affection was extremely negotiable.

The crowd shouldn't have been there, people said afterwards.

But where should they have been? The field was a popular spot. It was the only vaguely green space in that part of the city. People played games there and, of course, there was always the progress of the corpse on the gibbet to inspect. And the men were troops, ordinary foot soldiers, people's sons and husbands, taking a bit of a rest and having a drink.

Oh, that was right – afterwards, it was said that the troops were drunk. And that they shouldn't have been there. Yep, that was the reason, Vimes reflected. *No one* should have been there.

But they were, and when that captain got an arrow in his stomach and was groaning on the ground, some of the crossbowmen fired in the direction of the shot. That's what the history books said. They fired at the house windows, where people had been watching. Perhaps the shot *had* come from one of them.

Some arrows fell short, some did not. And there were people who fired back.

And then, one after another, horrible things would happen. By then it was too late for them not to. The tension would unwind like a huge spring, scything through the city.

There *were* plotters, there was no doubt about it. Some had been ordinary people who'd had enough. Some were young people with no money who objected to the fact that the world was run by old people who were rich. Some were in it to get girls. And some had been idiots as mad as Swing, with a view of the world just as rigid and unreal, who were on the side of what they called 'the people'. Vimes had spent his life on the streets, and had met decent men and fools and people who'd steal a penny from a blind beggar and people who performed silent miracles or desperate crimes every day behind the grubby windows of little houses, but he'd never met The People.

People on the side of The People always ended up disappointed, in any case. They found that The People tended not to be grateful or appreciative or forward-thinking or obedient. The People tended to be small-minded and conservative and not very clever and were even distrustful of cleverness. And so the children of the revolution were faced with the age-old problem: it wasn't that you had the wrong kind of government, which was obvious, but that you had the wrong kind of people.

As soon as you saw people as things to be measured, they didn't measure up. What would run through the streets soon enough wouldn't be a revolution or a riot. It'd be people who were frightened and panicking. It was what happened when the machinery of city life faltered, the wheels stopped turning and all the little rules broke down. And when that happened, humans were worse than sheep. Sheep just ran; they didn't try to bite the sheep next to them.

By sunset a uniform would automatically be a target. Then it wouldn't matter where a watchman's sympathies lay. He'd be just another man in armour—

'What?' he said, snapping back to the present.

'You all right, sarge?' said Corporal Colon.

'Hmm?' said Vimes, as the real world returned.

'You were well away,' said Fred. 'Staring at nothing. You ought to have had a proper sleep last night, sarge.'

'There's plenty of time to sleep in the grave,' said Vimes, looking at the ranks of the Watch.

'Yeah, I heard that, sarge, but no one wakes you up with a cup of tea. I got 'em lined up, sarge.'

Fred had made an effort, Vimes could see. So had the men themselves. He'd never seen them looking quite so . . . formal. Usually they had a helmet and breastplate apiece. Beyond that, equipment was varied and optional. But today, at least, they looked neat.

Shame about the heights. No man could easily inspect a row that included Wiglet at one end and Nancyball at the other. Wiglet was so short that he'd once been accused of navelling a sergeant, being far too short to eyeball anyone, while Nancyball was always the first man on duty to know when it was raining. You had to stand well back to get both of them into vision without eyestrain.

'Well done, lads,' he managed, and heard Rust coming down the stairs.

It must have been the first time the man had seen his new command in full. In the circumstances, he bore up quite well. He merely sighed.

He turned to Vimes and said: 'I require something to stand on.'

Vimes looked blank. 'Sir?'

'I wish to address the men in order to inspire them and stiffen their resolve. They must understand the political background to the current crisis.'

'Oh, we know all about Lord Winder being a loony, sir,' said Wiglet cheerfully.

Frost nearly formed on Rust's forehead.

Vimes drew himself up. 'Squad diiiiismiss!' he shouted, and then leaned towards Rust as the men scuttled away. 'A quiet word, sir?'

'Did that man really say—' Rust began.

'Yes, sir. These are simple men, sir,' said Vimes, thinking quickly. 'Best not to disturb them, if you take my meaning.'

Rust inserted this into his range of options. Vimes could see him thinking. It was a way out, and it suited his opinion of the Watch in general. It meant that he hadn't been cheeked by a constable, he'd merely dealt with a simpleton.

'They know their duty, sir,' Vimes added, for reinforcement.

'Their duty, sergeant, is to do what they are told.'

'Exactly, sir.'

Rust stroked his moustache. 'There is something in what you say, sergeant. And you trust them?'

'As a matter of fact, sir, yes.'

'Hmm. We will make a circuit of the surrounding streets in ten minutes. This is a time for action. Reports are disturbing. We must hold the line, sergeant.'

And he believes it, thought Vimes. He really does.

*

227

The watchmen marched out into the afternoon sunshine, and did so badly. They were not used to marching. Their normal method of progress was the stroll, which is not a recognized military manoeuvre, or the frantic withdrawal, which is.

In addition, the convection currents of prudent cowardice were operating in the ranks. There was a definite sideways component to each man's progress as he sought to be in the middle. The watchmen had shields, but they were light wicker-work things intended to turn blows and deflect stones; they wouldn't stand up to anything with an edge. The advance, therefore, was by means of a slowly elongating huddle.

Rust didn't notice. He had a gift for not seeing things he did not want to see and not hearing things he did not want to hear. But he could not ignore a barricade.

Ankh-Morpork wasn't really a city, not when the chips were down. Places like Dolly Sisters and Nap Hill and Seven Sleepers had been villages once, before they were absorbed by the urban sprawl. On some level, they still held themselves separate. As for the rest . . . well, once you got off the main streets it was all down to neighbourhoods. People didn't move around much. When tension was high, you relied on your mates and your family. Whatever was going down, you tried to make sure wasn't going down your street. It wasn't revolution. It was quite the reverse. It was defending your doorstep.

They were building a barricade in Whalebone Lane. It wasn't a particularly good one, being made up mostly of overturned market stalls, a small cart and quite a lot of household furniture, but it was a Symbol.

Rust's moustache bristled. 'Right in our faces,' he snapped. 'Absolute defiance of constituted authority, sergeant. Do your duty!'

'And what would that be at this point, sir?' said Vimes.

'Arrest the ringleaders! And your men will pull the barricade down!'

Vimes sighed. 'Very well, sir. If you will stand back, I shall seek them out.'

He walked up to the domestic clutter, aware of eyes watching him before and behind. When he was a few feet away he cupped his hands. 'All right, all right, what's going on here?' he shouted.

He was aware of whispering. And he was ready for what happened next. When the stone flew over the top of the furniture he caught it in both hands.

'I asked a civil question,' he said. 'Come on!'

There was more whispering. He distinctly heard '—that's the sergeant from last night—' and some sort of sotto voce argument. Then a voice shouted, 'Death to the Fascist Oppressors!'

This time the argument was more frantic. He heard someone say 'oh, all right', and then 'Death to the Fascist Oppressors, Present Company Excepted! There, is everyone *happy* now?'

He knew that voice. 'Mr Reginald Shoe, is it?' he said.

'I regret that I have only one life to lay down for Whalebone Lane!' the voice shouted, from somewhere behind a wardrobe.

If only you knew, Vimes thought.

'I don't think that will be necessary,' he said. 'Come *on*, ladies and gentlemen. Is this any way to behave? You can't take . . . the law . . . into your own . . . hands . . .' His voice faltered.

Sometimes it takes the brain a little while to catch up with the mouth.

Vimes turned and looked at the squad, who'd needed no prompting at all to hang back. And then he turned to look at the barricade.

Where, exactly, *was* the law? Right now?

What did he think he was doing?

The Job, of course. The one that's in front of you. He'd always done it. And the law had always been . . . *out there*, but somewhere close. He'd always been pretty sure where it was, and it definitely had something to do with the badge.

The badge was important. Yes. It was shield-shaped. For

229

protection. He'd thought about that, in the long nights in the darkness. It protected him from the beast, because the beast was waiting in the darkness of his head.

He'd killed werewolves with his bare hands. He'd been mad with terror at the time, but the beast had been there inside, giving him strength . . .

Who knew what evil lurked in the hearts of men? A copper, that's who. After ten years you thought you'd seen it all, but the shadows always dished up more. You saw how close men lived to the beast. You realized that people like Carcer were not mad. They were incredibly sane. They were simply men without a shield. They'd looked at the world and realized that all the rules didn't have to apply to them, not if they didn't want them to. They weren't fooled by all the little stories. They shook hands with the beast.

But he, Sam Vimes, had stuck by the badge, except for that time when even that hadn't been enough and he'd stuck by the bottle instead . . .

He felt as if he'd stuck by the bottle now. The world was spinning. Where *was* the law? There was the barricade. Who was it protecting from what? The city was run by a madman and his shadowy chums so *where was the law*?

Coppers liked to say that people shouldn't take the law into their own hands, and they thought they knew what they meant. They were thinking about the normal times, and men who went round to sort out a neighbour with a club because his dog had crapped once too often on their doorstep. But at times like *this*, who did the law belong to? If it shouldn't be in the hands of people, where the hell *should* it be? People who knew better? Then you got Winder and his pals, and how good was that?

What was supposed to happen next? Oh yes, he had a badge, but it wasn't *his*, not really . . . and he'd got orders, and they were the wrong ones . . . and he'd got enemies, for all the wrong reasons . . . and maybe there was *no future*. It didn't exist

230

any more. There was nothing real, no solid point on which to stand, just Sam Vimes where he had no right to be . . .

It was as if his body, trying to devote as many resources as possible to untangling the spinning thoughts, was drawing those resources from the rest of Vimes. His vision darkened. His knees were weak.

There was nothing but bewildered despair.

And a lot of explosions.

Havelock Vetinari knocked politely on the window of the little office just inside the Assassins' Guild main gate.

The duty porter raised the hatch.

'Signing out, Mr Maroon,' said the Assassin.

'Yessir,' said Maroon, pushing a big ledger towards him. 'And where are we off to today, sir?'

'General reconnoitring, Mr Maroon. Just generally looking around.'

'Ah, I said to Mrs Maroon last night, sir, that you are a great one for looking around,' said Maroon.

'We look and learn, Mr Maroon, we look and learn,' said Vetinari, signing his name in the book and putting the pen back in its holder. 'And how is your little boy?'

'Thank you for asking, sir, he's a lot better,' said the porter.

'Glad to hear it. Oh, I see the Hon. John Bleedwell is out on a commission. To the palace?'

'Now, now, sir,' said Maroon, grinning and waving a finger. 'You know I couldn't tell you that, sir, even if I knew.'

'Of course not.' Vetinari glanced at the back wall of the office where, in an old brass rack, were a number of envelopes. The word 'Active' was inscribed at the top of the rack.

'Good afternoon, Mr Maroon.'

' 'afternoon, sir. Good, er, looking around.'

He watched the young man walk out into the street. Then Maroon went into the cubbyhole next to the office to put the kettle on.

He rather liked young Vetinari, who was quiet and studious and, it had to be said, a generous young man on appropriate occasions. But a bit weird, all the same. Once Maroon had watched him in the foyer, standing still. That was all he was doing. He wasn't making any attempt at concealing himself. After half an hour Maroon had wandered over and said, 'Can I help you, sir?'

And Vetinari had said, 'Thank you, no, Mr Maroon. I'm just teaching myself to stand still.'

To which there wasn't really any sensible comment that could be made. And the young man must have left after a while, because Maroon didn't remember seeing him again that day.

He heard a creak from the office, and poked his head around the door. There was no one there.

As he made the tea he thought he heard a rustle from next door, and went to check. It was completely empty. Remarkably so, he thought later on. It was almost as if it was even more empty than it would be if there was just, well, no one in it.

He went back to his comfy armchair in the cubbyhole, and relaxed.

In the brass rack, the envelope marked 'Bleedwell, J.' slid back slightly.

There were a *lot* of explosions. The firecrackers bounced all over the street. Tambourines thudded, a horn blared a chord unknown in nature, and a line of monks danced and twirled around the corner, all chanting at the tops of their voices.

Vimes, sagging to his knees, was aware of dozens of sandalled feet gyrating past and grubby robes flying. Rust was yelling something at the dancers, who grinned and waved their hands in the air.

Something square and silvery landed in the dirt.

And the monks were gone, dancing into an alleyway, yelling and spinning and banging their gongs . . .

'Wretched heathens!' said Rust, striding forward. 'Have you been hit, sergeant?'

Vimes reached down and picked up the silver rectangle.

A stone clanged off Rust's breastplate. As he raised his mega-phone, a cabbage hit him on the knee.

Vimes stared at the thing in his hand. It was a cigar case, slim and slightly curved.

He fumbled it open and read:

To Sam with love from your Sybil

The world moved. But now Vimes no longer felt like a drift-ing ship. Now he felt the tug of the anchor, pulling him round to face the rising tide.

A barrage of missiles was coming over the barricade. Throwing things was an old Ankh-Morpork custom, and there was something about Rust that made him a target. With what dignity he could muster, he raised the megaphone again and got as far as 'I hereby warn you—' before a stone spun it out of his hand.

'Very well, then,' he said, and marched stiffly back to the squad. 'Sergeant Keel, order the men to fire. One round of arrows, over the top of the barricade.'

'No,' said Vimes, standing up.

'I can only assume you've been stunned, sergeant,' said Rust. 'Men, prepare to execute that order.'

'First man that fires, I will personally cut that man down,' said Vimes. He didn't shout. It was a simple, confident statement of precisely what the future would hold.

Rust's expression did not change. He looked Vimes up and down.

'Is this mutiny, then, sergeant?' said the captain.

'No. I'm not a soldier, sir. I can't mutiny.'

'Martial law, sergeant!' snapped Rust. 'It is *official*!'

'Really?' said Vimes, as another rain of rocks and old vegetables came down. 'Shields up, lads.'

Rust turned to Fred Colon. 'Corporal, you will put this man under arrest!'

Colon swallowed. 'Me?'

'You, corporal. *Now*.'

Colon's pink face mottled with white as the blood drained from it. 'But he—' he began.

'You won't? Then it seems I must,' said the captain. He drew his sword.

At that Vimes heard the click of a crossbow's safety catch going off, and groaned. He didn't remember *this* happening.

'You just put that sword away, sir, please,' said the voice of Lance-Constable Vimes.

'You will not shoot me, you young idiot. That would be murder,' said the captain calmly.

'Not where I'm aiming, sir.'

Bloody *hell*, thought Vimes. Maybe the lad *was* simple. Because one thing Rust wasn't, was a coward. He thought idiot stubbornness was bravery. He wouldn't back down in the face of a dozen armed men.

'Ah, I think I can see the problem, captain,' Vimes said brightly. 'As you were, lance-constable. There's been a slight misunderstanding, sir, but this should sort it out—'

It was a blow he'd remember for a long time. It was sweet. It was textbook. Rust went down like a log.

In the light of all his burning bridges, Vimes slipped his hand back into his hip pocket. Thank you, Mrs Goodbody and your range of little equalizers.

He turned to the watchmen, who were a tableau of silent horror.

'Let the record show Sergeant-at-Arms John Keel did that,' he said. 'Vimes, what did I tell you about waving weapons around when you're not going to use them?'

'You laid him out, sarge!' Sam squeaked, still staring at the sleeping captain.

Vimes shook some life back into his hand. 'Let the record show that I took command after the captain's sudden attack of insanity,' he said. 'Waddy, Wiglet . . . drag him back to the House and lock him up, will you?'

'What we gonna *do*, sarge?' wailed Colon.

Ah . . .

Keep the peace. That was the thing. People often failed to understand what that meant. You'd go to some life-threatening disturbance like a couple of neighbours scrapping in the street over who owned the hedge between their properties, and they'd both be bursting with aggrieved self-righteousness, both yelling, their wives would either be having a private scrap on the side or would have adjourned to a kitchen for a shared pot of tea and a chat, and they all expected you to *sort it out*.

And they could never understand that it wasn't your job. Sorting it out was a job for a good surveyor and a couple of lawyers, maybe. *Your* job was to quell the impulse to bang their stupid fat heads together, to ignore the affronted speeches of dodgy self-justification, to get them to stop shouting and to get them off the street. Once that had been achieved, your job was over. You weren't some walking god, dispensing finely tuned natural justice. Your job was simply to bring back peace.

Of course, if your few strict words didn't work and Mr Smith subsequently clambered over the disputed hedge and stabbed Mr Jones to death with a pair of gardening shears, then you had a different job, sorting out the notorious Hedge Argument Murder. But at least it was one you were trained to do.

People expected all kinds of things from coppers, but there was one thing that sooner or later they all wanted: make this not be happening.

Make this not be happening . . .

'What?' he said, suddenly noticing a voice that had, in fact, been on the edge of awareness for some time.

'I said, was he insane, sarge?'

But when you're falling off the cliff it's too late to wonder if there might have been a better way up the mountain . . .

'He asked you to shoot at people who weren't shooting back,' growled Vimes, striding forward. 'That makes him insane, wouldn't you say?'

'They *are* throwing stones, sarge,' said Colon.

'So? Stay out of range. They'll get tired before we do.'

In fact the barrage of missiles from the barricade had ceased; even in a time of crisis, the people of Ankh-Morpork would stop for a decent piece of street theatre. Vimes walked back towards them, stopping on the way to retrieve Rust's bent megaphone.

As he approached he cast his eye over faces just visible through the chair legs and junk. There would be Unmentionables somewhere, he knew, helping matters along. With luck they wouldn't have bothered with Whalebone Lane.

There was muttering from the defenders. Most of them had a look Vimes recognized, because it was the one he was trying to keep off his own face. It was the look of people whose world had suddenly been swept from under them, and now they were trying to tap-dance on quicksand.

He tossed away the stupid pompous megaphone. He cupped his hands.

'Some of you know me!' he shouted. 'I'm Sergeant Keel, currently in command of the Treacle Mine Road Watch House! And I order you to dismantle this barricade—'

There was a chorus of jeers and one or two badly thrown missiles. Vimes waited, stock still, until they'd died away. Then he raised his hands again.

'I repeat, I order you to dismantle this barricade.' He took a breath, and went on: 'And rebuild it on the other side on the corner with Cable Street! And put up another one at the top of Sheer Street! Properly built! Good grief, you don't just pile stuff up, for gods' sake! A barricade is something you *construct*! Who's in charge here?'

There were sounds of consternation behind the overturned

furniture, but a voice called out, 'You?' There was nervous laughter.

'Very funny! Now laugh this one off! No one's interested in us yet! This is a quiet part of town! But when things really go bad you're going to have cavalry on your backs! With sabres! How long would you last? But if you shut off this end of Treacle Mine and the end of Sheer then they're left with alleyways, and they don't like that! It's up to you, of course! We'd like to protect you, but me and my men'll be behind the barricades over *here* . . .'

He turned on his heel and marched back to the waiting watchmen.

'Right, lads,' he said. 'You heard. Pounce and Gaskin, you take the hurry-up wagon up to the bridge and turn it over. Waddy and Nancyball and you too, Fred . . . go and nick some carts. You grew up round here, so don't tell me you've never done *that* before. I want a couple blocking the streets down here, and the rest, I want you to run them into the alley mouths until they wedge. You men know the area. Block up all the little back ways.'

Colon rubbed his nose. 'We could do that on the river side, sarge, but it's all alleys on the Shades side. Can't block 'em all.'

'I wouldn't worry about those,' said Vimes. 'Cavalry can't come through there. You know what they call a horse in the Shades?'

Colon grinned. 'Yeah, sarge. Lunch.'

'Right. The rest of you, get all the benches and tables out of the Watch House—'

It dawned on him that none of the men had moved. There was a certain . . . problem in the air.

'Well?'

Billy Wiglet removed his helmet and wiped his forehead. 'Er . . . how far is this going to go, sarge?'

'All the way, Billy.'

'But we took the oath, sarge, and now we're disobeying

237

orders and helping rebels. Doesn't seem right, sarge,' said Wiglet, wretchedly.

'You took an oath to uphold the law and defend the citizens without fear or favour,' said Vimes. 'And to protect the innocent. That's all they put in. Maybe they thought those were the important things. Nothing in there about orders, even from me. You're an officer of the law, not a soldier of the government.'

One or two of the men looked longingly at the other end of the street, empty and inviting.

'But I won't stop anyone who wants to walk,' said Vimes. They stopped looking.

' 'ullo, Mister Keel,' said a sticky voice behind him.

'Yes, Nobby?' he said, without turning round.

' 'ere, how did you detect it was me, sergeant?'

'It's an amazing talent, kid,' said Vimes, turning, against all wisdom, to look at the urchin. 'What's been happening?'

'Big riot in Sator Square, sarge. And they say people've broke into the Dolly Sisters Watch House and thrown the lieutenant out the window. An' there's lootin' all over the place, they say, an' the Day Watch are out chasin' people only most of 'em are hidin' now 'cos—'

'Yeah, I get the picture,' sighed Vimes. Carcer had been right. Coppers were always outnumbered, so being a copper only *worked* when people let it work. If they refocused and realized you were just another standard idiot with a pennyworth of metal for a badge, you could end up a smear on the pavement.

He could hear shouting now, a long way off.

He looked around at the hesitant watchmen.

'On the other hand, gentlemen,' he said, 'if you *are* going to leave, where are you going to go *to*?'

The same thought had clearly occurred to Colon and the others.

'We'll get the carts,' he said, hurrying off.

'And I wants a penny,' said Nobby, holding out a grubby

hand. To the boy's amazement, Vimes gave him a dollar, saying, 'And just keep telling me everything, will you?'

Tables and benches were already being dragged out of the Watch House and after only a couple of minutes Waddy arrived with a cartload of empty barrels. Barricades were easy in these streets; it was keeping them clear that had always been the problem.

The watchmen set to work. This was something they understood. They'd done it when they were kids. And perhaps they thought, hey, this time we're wearing uniforms. We can't be in the wrong.

While Vimes was struggling to wedge a bench into the growing wall he was aware of people behind him. He worked steadily, however, until someone gave a delicate cough. Then he turned.

'Yes? Can I help you?'

There was a small group of people, and it was clear to Vimes that it was a group pushed together out of shared terror because, by the look of them, they'd have nothing to do with one another if they could possibly avoid it.

The spokesman, or at least the one in front, looked almost exactly like the kind of person Vimes had pictured when thinking about the Hedge Argument Murder.

'Erm, officer . . .'

'Yes, sir?'

'What, er, are you doing, exactly?'

'Keeping the peace, sir. This piece, to be exact.'

'You said that there's, er, rioting and soldiers on the way . . .'

'Very likely, sir.'

'You don't have to *ask* him, Rutherford, it's his *duty* to protect us,' snapped the woman who was standing beside the man with an air of proprietorship. Vimes changed his mind about the man. Yes, he had that furtive look of a timid domestic poisoner about him, the kind of man who'd be appalled at the idea of divorce but would plot womanslaughter every day. And you could see why.

He gave the lady a nice warm smile. She was holding a blue vase. 'Can I help you, ma'am?' he said.

'What are you intending to do about us being murdered in our beds?' she demanded.

'Well, it's not four o'clock yet, ma'am, but if you'll let me know when you want to retire—'

Vimes was impressed at the way the woman drew herself up. Even Sybil, in full Duchess mode, with the blood of twenty generations of arrogant ancestors behind her, could not have matched her.

'Rutherford, are you going to *do* something about this man?' she said.

Rutherford looked up at Vimes. Vimes was aware that he was villainously unshaven, dishevelled, dirty and probably starting to smell. He decided not to load more troubles on the man's back.

'Would you and your lady care to assist with our barricade?' he said.

'Oh, yes, thank you very—' Rutherford began, but was outgunned again.

'Some of that furniture looks very dirty,' said Mrs Rutherford. 'And aren't those *beer* barrels?'

'Yes, ma'am, but they're empty ones,' said Vimes.

'Are you *sure*? I refuse to cower behind alcohol! I have never approved of alcohol, and neither has Rutherford!'

'I can assure you, ma'am, that any beer barrel in the presence of my men for any length of time will be empty,' said Vimes. 'You may rest assured on that score.'

'And are your men sober and clean-living?' the woman demanded.

'Whenever no alternative presents itself, ma'am,' said Vimes. This seemed acceptable. Mrs Rutherford was like Rust in that respect. She listened to the tone of voice, not the words.

'I think perhaps it would be a good idea, dear, if we made haste to—' Rutherford began.

'Not without Father!' said his wife.

'No problem, ma'am,' said Vimes. 'Where is he?'

'On our barricade, of course! Which was, let me tell you, a rather better barricade altogether.'

'Jolly good, ma'am,' said Vimes. 'If he'd like to come over here we'll—'

'Erm, you don't quite understand, sir,' murmured Rutherford. 'He is, erm, *on* the barricade . . .'

Vimes looked at the other barricade, and then looked harder. It was just possible to see, near the top of the piled-up furniture, an overstuffed armchair. Further examination suggested that it was occupied by a sleeping figure in carpet slippers.

'He's very attached to his armchair,' sighed Rutherford.

'It's going to be an *heirloom*,' said his wife. 'Be so kind as to send your young men to collect our furniture, will you? And be careful with it. Put it at the back somewhere where it won't get shot at.'

Vimes nodded at Sam and a couple of the other men as Mrs Rutherford picked her way over the debris and headed for the Watch House.

'Is there going to be any fighting?' said Mr Rutherford anxiously.

'Possibly, sir.'

'I'm not very good at that sort of thing, I'm afraid.'

'Don't worry about that, sir.' Vimes propelled the man over the barricade, and turned to the rest of the little group. He'd been aware of eyes boring into him, and now he traced the rays back to source, a young man with black trousers, a frilly shirt and long curly hair.

'This is a ruse, isn't it,' said the man. 'You'll get us in your power and we'll never be seen again, eh?'

'Stay out then, Reg,' said Vimes. He cupped his hands and turned back to the Whalebone Lane barricade. 'Anyone else wants to join us had better get a move on!' he shouted.

'You don't know that's my name!' said Reg Shoe.

Vimes stared into the big protruding eyes. The only difference between Reg now and the Reg he'd left back in the future was that Constable Shoe was rather greyer and was held together in places by stitches. Zombiehood would come naturally to Reg. He was *born* to be dead. He believed so strongly in things that some kind of inner spring kept him going. He'd make a good copper. He didn't make a very good revolutionary. People as meticulously fervent as Reg got real revolutionaries worried. It was the way he stared.

'You're Reg Shoe,' he said. 'You live in Whalebone Lane.'

'Aha, you've got secret files on me, eh?' said Reg, with terrifying happiness.

'Not really, no. Now if you'd be so good—'

'I bet you've got a big file on me a mile long,' said Reg.

'Not a whole mile, Reg, no,' said Vimes. 'Listen, Reg, we—'

'I demand to see it!'

Vimes sighed. 'Mr Shoe, we don't have a file on you. We don't have a file on *anyone*, understand? Half of us can't read without using a finger. Reg, we are not *interested* in you.'

Reg Shoe's slightly worrying eyes remained fixed on Vimes's face for a moment, and then his brain rejected the information as contrary to whatever total fantasy was going on inside.

'Well, it's no good you torturing me because I won't reveal any details about my comrades in the other revolutionary cells!' said Reg.

'Okay. I won't, then. Now perhaps—'

'That's how we work, see? None of the cadres knows about the other ones!'

'Really. Do they know about you?' said Vimes.

For a moment, Reg's face clouded. 'Pardon?'

'Well, you said you don't know about them,' said Vimes. 'So . . . do they know about you?' He wanted to add: you're a cell of one, Reg. The real revolutionaries are silent men with poker-player eyes and probably don't know or care if you exist. You've got the shirt and the haircut and the sash and you know all the

242

songs, but you're no urban guerrilla. You're an urban dreamer. You turn over rubbish bins and scrawl on walls in the name of The People, who'd clip you round the ear if they found you doing it. But you *believe*.

'Ah, so you're a secret operative,' he said, to get the poor man off the hook.

Reg brightened. 'That's right!' he said. 'The people are the sea in which the revolutionary swims!'

'Like swordfishes?' Vimes tried.

'Pardon?'

And you're a flounder, thought Vimes. *Ned*'s a revolutionary. He knows how to fight and he can think, even if he is on the skew. But Reg, you really ought to be indoors . . .

'Well, I can see you're a dangerous individual,' he said. 'We'd better have you where we can keep an eye on you. Hey, that's right. You can undermine the enemy from within.'

The relieved Reg raised a fist in salute and carried a table to the new barricade with revolutionary speed. There was some hurried conversation behind the old makeshift barricade, already being denuded of Mrs Rutherford's furniture. This was interrupted by the clatter of hoofbeats from the far end of Treacle Mine Road and a sudden burst of instant decisiveness on the part of the remainder of the crowd.

They poured towards the new *official* barricade, with Lance-Constable Vimes bringing up the rear, fairly well hampered by a dining-room chair.

'Mind out for that!' shouted a female voice from somewhere behind him. 'It's one of a set!'

Vimes put his hand on the young man's shoulder. 'Just give me your crossbow, will you?' he said.

The horsemen came closer.

Vimes was not good at horsemen. Something in him resented being addressed by anyone eight feet above the ground. He didn't like the sensation of being looked at by nostrils. He didn't like being talked down to.

By the time they'd reached the barricade he'd clambered around to the front of it and was standing in the middle of the street.

They slowed down. It was probably the way he didn't move, and held the crossbow in the nonchalant manner of someone who knows how to use it but has decided not to, for the moment.

'You, there!' said a trooper.

'Yes?' said Vimes.

'Are you in charge?'

'Yes. Can I help you?'

'Where are your men?'

Vimes jerked a thumb towards the growing barricade. On the top of the heap, Mrs Rutherford's father was snoring peacefully.

'But that's a barricade!' said the trooper.

'Well done.'

'There's a man waving a *flag*!'

Vimes turned. Surprisingly, it was Reg. Some of the men had brought out the old flag from Tilden's office and stuck it on the barricade, and Reg was the sort to wave any flag going.

'Probably high spirits, sir,' said Vimes. 'Don't worry. We're all fine.'

'It's a damn *barricade*, man. A rebel barricade!' said the second trooper. Oh boy, thought Vimes. They have shiny, shiny breast-plates. And wonderfully fresh pink faces.

'Not exactly. In fact it's—'

'Are you stupid, fellow? Don't you know that all barricades are to be torn down by order of the Patrician?'

The third horseman, who had been staring at Vimes, urged his horse a little closer.

'What's that pip on your shoulder, officer?' he said.

'Means I'm Sergeant-at-Arms. Special rank. And who're you?'

'He doesn't have to tell you that!' said the first trooper.

244

'Really?' said Vimes. The man was getting on his nerves. 'Well, you're just a trooper and I'm a bleedin' sergeant and if you dare speak to me like that again I'll have you down off that horse and thump you across the ear, understand?'

Even the horse took a step backwards. The trooper opened his mouth to speak, but the third horseman raised a white-gloved hand.

Oh dear, thought Vimes, focusing on the sleeve of the red jacket. The man was a captain. Not only that, he was an intelligent one, by the look of him. He hadn't mouthed off until he'd had a chance to assess the situation. You got them sometimes. They could be dangerously bright.

'I note, sergeant-at-arms,' said the captain, enunciating the rank with care and without apparent sarcasm, 'that the flag over the barricade is the flag of Ankh-Morpork.'

'It's the one out of our Watch House,' said Vimes, and added, 'sir.'

'You know that the Patrician has declared that the building of barricades is an act of rebellion?'

'Yessir.'

'And?' said the captain patiently.

'Well, he would say that, sir, wouldn't he . . .'

The faintest hint of a smile skimmed across the captain's face. 'We can't allow lawlessness, sergeant-at-arms. If we all disobeyed the law, where would we be?'

'There's more coppers per person behind that barricade than anywhere else in the city, sir,' said Vimes. 'You could say it's the most law-abiding place around.'

Now there was the sound of raised voices from behind the barricade.

'—*we own all your helmets, we own all your shoes, we own all your generals, Touch us and you'll loooose . . . Morporkia, Morporkia, Morpooroorooorooooorrroorrr—*'

'Rebel songs, sir!' said trooper number one. The captain sighed.

'If you *listen*, Hepplewhite, you might note that it is the national anthem sung very badly,' he said.

'We can't allow rebels to sing *that*, sir!'

Vimes saw the captain's expression. It had a lot to say about idiots.

'Raising the flag and singing the anthem, Hepplewhite, are, while somewhat suspicious, not in themselves acts of treason,' said the captain. 'And we are urgently required elsewhere.' He saluted Vimes, who found himself returning the salute. 'We shall leave you, sergeant-at-arms. I trust your day will be full of interest. I fact, I *know* it.'

'But it's a *barricade*, sir,' the trooper insisted, glaring at Vimes.

'It's just a pile of furniture, man. People have been spring cleaning, I expect. You'll never be an officer if you can't see straight. Follow me, if you please.'

With a last nod to Vimes, the captain led his men away at a trot.

Vimes leaned against the barricade, put the crossbow on the ground, and fished out the cigar case. He fumbled in his pocket, pulled out the battered carton of little cigars and, with some delicacy, slotted them into place.

Hmm. To the left was Cable Street. In front, Treacle Mine Road stretched all the way to Easy Street.

Now, if a man could get barricades all the way up to Easy Street, there'd be quite a slice of the Lower Rimside behind it, which'd be a lot easier to protect . . .

We'll do it. After all, we did it.

Of course, that'd mean having the Unmentionables' head-quarters in here with us. That's like pitching your tent over a nest of vipers.

We'll handle that. We handled it.

A couple of elderly people pushing a cart full of miscellaneous belongings approached the barricade. They gave Vimes a look of mute pleading. He nodded towards it and they scuttled through.

All we need now is—

'Sarge?' Fred Colon was leaning over the top of the heap.

He looked more out of breath than usual.

'Yes, Fred?'

'There's lots of people coming across the Pon's bridge. There's things happening everywhere, they say. Shall we let 'em in?'

'Any soldiers?'

'I don't reckon so, sarge. It's mostly old people and kids. And my granny.'

'Trustworthy?'

'Not when she's had a few pints.'

'Let them in, then.'

'Er . . .' said Colon.

'Yes, Fred?'

'Some of 'em is watchmen. A few of the lads from Dimwell and a lot from Kings Way. I know most of 'em, and those I don't are known to the ones I do, if you catch my meanin'.'

'How many?'

'About twenty. One of 'em's Dai Dickins, sergeant at Dimwell. He says they were told they'd got to shoot people and most of 'em deserted on the spot.'

'Quit, Fred,' said Vimes. 'We don't desert. We're civilians. Now, I want young Vimes and you and Waddy and maybe half a dozen others out here fully kitted up in two minutes, understand? And tell Wiglet to organize squads ready to move the barricades forward at my signal.'

'*Move* them, sarge? I thought barricades stood still!'

'And tell Snouty he's got two minutes to find me a bottle of brandy,' said Vimes, ignoring this. 'A big one.'

'Are we taking the law into our own hands again, sarge?' said Colon.

Vimes stared at the entrance to Cable Street, and was aware of the weight of the cigar case in his pocket.

'Yes, Fred,' he said. 'Only this time we're going to squeeze.'

The two guards on the Unmentionables' headquarters watched with interest as the small contingent of watchmen

247

marched up the street and came to a halt in front of them.

'Oo, look, it's the army,' said one of them. 'What do *you* want?'

'Nothing, sir,' said Corporal Colon.

'Then you can push off!'

'Can't do that, sir. I'm under orders.'

The guards stepped forward. Fred Colon was sweating, and they liked to see things like that. It was a dull job, and most of the Unmentionables were out on more interesting assignments. They entirely failed to hear the soft tread behind them.

'Orders to do *what*, mister,' said one of them, looming over Colon.

There was a sigh and a soft thud behind him.

'Be a decoy?' quavered Colon.

The remaining guard turned, and met a Mrs Goodbody No. 5 'Negotiator' coming the other way.

As the man slipped to the ground Vimes winced and massaged his knuckles.

'Important lesson, lads,' he said. 'It hurts, no matter what you do. You two, drag these into the shadows to sleep it off. Vimes and Nancyball, you come with me.'

The key to winning, as always, was looking as if you had every right, nay, *duty* to be where you were. It helped if you could also suggest in every line of your body that no one else had any rights to be doing anything, anywhere, whatsoever. It came easily to an old copper.

Vimes led the way into the building. There were a couple of guards inside, heavily armed, behind a stone barrier that made them ideally placed to ambush any unwise intruders. They put their hands on the hilts of their swords when they saw Vimes.

'What's happening out there?' said one.

'Oh, people are getting restless,' said Vimes. 'Getting very bad across the river, they say. That's why we've come for the prisoners in the cells.'

'Yeah? On whose authority?'

Vimes swung his crossbow up. 'Mr Burleigh and Mr Stronginthearm,' he said, and grinned.

The two guards exchanged glances. 'Who the hell are they?' said one.

There was a moment of silence followed by Vimes saying, out of the corner of his mouth: 'Lance-Constable Vimes?'

'Yessir?'

'What make are these crossbows?'

'Er . . . Hines Brothers, sir. They're Mark Threes.'

'Not Burleigh and Stronginthearm?'

'Never heard of them, sir.'

Damn. Five years too early, thought Vimes. And it was such a good line, too.

'Let me put it another way,' he said to the guards. 'Give me any trouble and I will shoot you in the head.' That *wasn't* a good line, but it did have a certain urgency, and the bonus that it was simple enough even for an Unmentionable to understand.

'You've only got one arrow,' said a guard.

There was a click from beside Vimes. Sam had raised his bow, too.

'There's two now, and since my lad here is in training he might hit you *anywhere*,' said Vimes. 'Drop your swords on the floor! Get out of the door! Run away! Do it now! Don't come back!'

There was a moment of hesitation, just a moment, and then the men ran for it.

'Fred will watch our backs,' said Vimes. 'Come on . . .'

All the Watch Houses were pretty much the same. Stone steps led down to the cellars. Vimes hurried down them, swung open a heavy door—

And stopped.

Cells never smelled that good at the best of times. At the best of times, even at Treacle Mine Road, hygiene consisted of a bucket per cell and as much slopping-out as Snouty felt inclined to do. But, at the worst of times, the cells below Treacle Mine Road never smelled of blood.

The beast stirred.

In this room there was a big wooden chair. In this room there was, by the chair, a rack. The chair was bolted to the floor. It had wide leather straps. The rack held clubs and hammers. In this room, that was all the furnishings.

The floor was dark and sticky. Down the length of it, a gully ran to a drain.

Boards had been nailed over the tiny window at street level. This wasn't a place where light was welcomed. And all the walls, and even the ceiling, were padded heavily with sacks stuffed with straw. Sacks had even been nailed to the door. This was a very *thorough* cell. Not even sound was meant to escape.

A couple of torches did nothing at all for the darkness except make it dirty.

Behind him, Vimes heard Nancyball throw up.

In a strange kind of dream, he walked across the floor and bent down to pick up something that gleamed in the torchlight. It was a tooth.

He stood up again.

A closed wooden door led off on one side of the cellar; on the other, a wider tunnel almost certainly led to the cells. Vimes took a torch out of its holder, handed it to Sam and pointed along the tunnel—

There were footsteps accompanied by a jingle of keys heading towards the door, and a light growing brighter underneath it.

The beast tensed . . .

Vimes dragged the largest club out of the rack and stepped swiftly to the wall beside the door. Someone was coming, some-one who knew about this room, someone who called themselves a copper . . .

Getting a firm two-handed grip, Vimes raised the club—

And looked across the stinking room, and saw young Sam

watching him, young Sam with his bright shiny badge and face full of . . . strangeness.

Vimes lowered the club, leaned it delicately against the wall, and pulled the leather cosh from his pocket.

Shackled, not quite understanding, the beast was dragged back into the night . . .

A man stepped through the door, whistling under his breath, took a few steps into the room, saw young Sam, opened his mouth and then fell fast asleep. He was a big man, and hit the cobbles heavily. He had a leather hood over his head, and was naked to the waist. A big ring of keys hung from his belt.

Vimes darted into the corridor behind the door, ran around a corner, burst into a small, brightly lit room, and grabbed a man he found in there.

This one was a lot smaller, and suppressed a scream as Vimes dragged him up out of his chair.

'And what does daddy do at work all day, mister?' Vimes roared.

The little man was suddenly clairvoyant. One look at Vimes's eyes told him how short his future might be.

'I'm just a clerk! A clerk! I just write things down!' he protested. He held up a pen by way of desperate demonstration.

Vimes looked at the desk. There were compasses there, and other geometer's tools, symbols of Swing's insane sanity. There were books, and folders stuffed with paperwork. And there was a yard-long steel ruler. He grabbed it in his spare hand and slammed it on the desktop. The heavy steel made a satisfying noise.

'And?' he said, his face a few inches from the struggling man.

'And I measure people! It's all in the captain's book! I just measure people! I don't do anything wrong! I'm not a bad man!'

Again the ruler slammed into the desk. But this time Vimes had twisted it, and the steel edge chopped into the wood.

'Want me to cut you down to size, mister?' The little man's eyes rolled.

'Please!'

251

'Is there another way out of here?' Vimes slapped the rule down on the desk.

The flicker of eyes was enough. Vimes saw a doorway in the wall, almost lost in the wooden panelling.

'Good. Where does it come out?'

'Er—'

Now Vimes was nose to nose with the man who, in police parlance, was helping him with his inquiries.

'You're all alone here,' he said. 'You have no friends here. You sat and took notes for a torturer, a bloody torturer! And I see a desk, and it's got a desk drawer, and if you ever, *ever* want to hold a pen again you'll tell me everything I want to know—'

'Warehouse!' the man gasped. 'Next door!'

'Right, sir. Thank you, sir. You've been very helpful,' said Vimes, lowering the limp body to the floor. 'Now, sir, I'm just handcuffing you to this desk for a moment, sir, for your protection.'

'Who . . . who from?'

'Me. I'll kill you if you try to run away, sir.'

Vimes hurried back to the main chamber. The torturer was still out cold. Vimes hauled him up into the chair, with great effort, and pulled off his hood, and recognized the face. The face, yes, but not the person. That is, it was the kind of face you saw a lot of in Ankh-Morpork: big, bruised, and belonging to someone who'd never quite learned that hitting people long after they'd lost consciousness was a wicked thing to do. He wondered if the man actually liked beating people to death. They often didn't think about it. It was just a job.

Well, he wasn't about to ask him. He buckled him in, with every strap, even the one that went across the forehead, pulling the last one tight just as the man came round. The mouth opened, and Vimes stuffed the hood into it.

Then he took the key ring and locked the main door. That should ensure a little extra privacy.

He met young Sam coming the other way as he headed

for the cells. The boy's face was white in the gloom.

'Found anyone?' said Vimes.

'Oh, sarge . . .'

'Yes?'

'Oh, sarge . . . sarge . . .' Tears were running down the lance-constable's face.

Vimes reached out and steadied himself. Sam felt as though there were no bones left in his body. He was trembling.

'There's a *woman* in the last cell, and she . . . sarge . . . oh, sarge . . .'

'Try taking deep breaths,' said Vimes. 'Not that this air is fit to breathe.'

'And there's a room right at the end, sarge . . . oh, sarge . . . Nancyball fainted again, sarge . . .'

'You didn't,' said Vimes, patting him gently on the back.

'But there's—'

'Let's rescue what we can, shall we, lad?'

'But we were on the hurry-up wagon, sarge!'

'What?' said Vimes, and then it dawned. Oh, yes . . .

'But we didn't hand anyone over, lad,' he said. 'Remember?'

'But I've been on it before, sarge! All the lads have! We just handed people over and went back to the Watch House for cocoa, sarge!'

'Well, you'd had orders . . .' said Vimes, for what good that did.

'We didn't *know*!'

Not exactly, thought Vimes. We didn't *ask*. We just shut our minds to it. People went in through that front door and some of the poor devils came out through the secret door, not always in one box.

They hadn't measured up.

Nor did we.

He heard a low, visceral sound from the boy. Sam had spotted the torturer in the chair. He shook himself away from Vimes, ran over to the rack, and snatched up a club.

253

Vimes was ready. He grabbed the boy, swung him round, and twisted the thing out of his hand before murder was done.

'No! That's not the way! This is not the time! Hold it back! Tame it! Don't waste it! Send it back! It'll come when you call!'

'You know he did those things!' shouted Sam, kicking at his legs. 'You said we had to take the law into our own hands!'

Ah, thought Vimes. This is *just* the time for a long debate about the theory and practice of justice. Here comes the shortened version.

'You *don't* bash a man's brains out when he's tied to a chair!'

'*He* did!'

'And you don't. That's because you're not him!'

'But they—'

'Stand to attention, lance-constable!' shouted Vimes, and the straw-covered ceiling drank and deadened the sound. Sam blinked through reddened eyes.

'Okay, sarge, but—'

'Are you going to snivel all day? *Forget* about this one. Let's get the living out, right?'

'Hard to tell with—' Sam began, wiping his nose.

'Do it! Follow me!'

He knew what was going to be in the dark arches of the cell tunnels, but that didn't make it any better. Some people could walk, or maybe hop. One or two had just been beaten up, but not so badly that they couldn't hear what was going on just out of sight, and dwell on it. They cringed when the gates were opened, and whimpered as he touched them. No wonder Swing got his confessions.

And some were dead. Others were . . . well, if they weren't dead, if they'd just gone somewhere in their heads, it was as sure as hell that there was nothing for them to come back to. The chair had broken them again and again. They were beyond the help of any man.

Just in case, and without any feeling of guilt, Vimes removed his knife, and . . . gave what help he could. There was not a twitch, not a sigh.

He stood up, black and red stormclouds in his head.

You could almost understand a thug, simple as a fist, being paid decent money for doing something he didn't mind doing. But Swing had *brains* . . .

Who *really* knew what evil lurked in the heart of men?

ME.

Who knew what sane men were capable of?

STILL ME, I'M AFRAID.

Vimes glanced at the door of the last room. No, he wasn't going in there again. No wonder it stank here.

YOU CAN'T HEAR ME, CAN YOU? OH. I THOUGHT YOU MIGHT, said Death, and waited.

Vimes went to help young Sam bring Nancyball round. Then they half carried, half walked the prisoners out along the passage up into the warehouse. They laid them down, and went back and dragged out the clerk, whose name was Trebilcock. Vimes explained to him the advantages of turning King's Evidence. They were not *major* advantages, except when they were compared with the huge disadvantages that would follow swiftly if he refused to do so.

And Vimes stepped out into the early evening. Colon and the squad were still waiting; the whole business had taken only twenty minutes or so.

The corporal saluted, and then his nose wrinkled.

'Yes, we stink,' said Vimes. He unbuckled his belt and pulled off his breastplate and chain-mail undershirt. The filth of the place had crawled everywhere. 'Okay,' he said, when he no longer felt that he was standing in a sewer, 'I want a couple of men at the entrance over there in the warehouse, a couple round the back with truncheons, and the rest ready out here. Just like we talked about, okay? Wallop them first, arrest them later.'

'Right, sir.' Colon nodded. Men set off.

'And now give me that brandy,' Vimes added.

He unwrapped his neckerchief, soaked it in spirit, and tied it around the neck of the bottle. He heard the angry murmur from the squad. They'd just seen Sam and Nancyball bringing out some of the prisoners.

'There was worse,' said Vimes, 'believe me. Top middle window, Fred.'

'*Right*, sarge,' said Fred Colon, dragging his eyes away from the walking wounded. He raised his crossbow, and neatly took out two window panes and a glazing bar.

Vimes located his silver cigar case, removed a cigar, lit it, applied the match to the brandy-soaked rag, waited for it to catch, and hurled the bottle through the window.

There was a tinkle, a whoomph of exploding spirit, and a flame that rapidly grew.

'Nice one, sarge,' said Fred. 'Er, I don't know if this is the right time, sarge, but we brought an extra bottle while we were about it . . .'

'Really, Fred? And what d'you say?'

Fred Colon glanced at the prisoners again. 'I say we use it,' he said.

It went through one of the ground-floor windows. Smoke was already curling out from under the eaves.

'We haven't seen anyone go in or out apart from those guards,' said Fred, as they watched it. 'I don't reckon there's many left in there.'

'Just so long as we destroy the nest,' said Vimes.

The front door opened slightly, increasing the draught to the fires. Someone was checking.

'They'll wait until the last minute and come out fighting, Fred,' Vimes warned.

'Good, sarge. It's getting darker,' said Colon grimly. He pulled out his truncheon.

Vimes walked around to the back of the building, nodded at the watchmen waiting there, and locked the door with his stolen key ring. It was a narrow door, anyway. Anyone inside would surely go for the big doors at the front, where they could spread out quickly and an ambush wasn't so easy.

He checked on the warehouse. But that was an unlikely exit for the same reason. Besides, he'd locked the door to the cellar, hadn't he?'

Young Sam grinned at him. 'That's why you left the torturer tied up, eh, sarge?' he said.

Damn! That hadn't occurred to him. He'd been so angry with the clerk he'd forgotten all about the brute in the chair.

Vimes hesitated. But burning was a horrible death. He reached for his knife, and remembered it was back in its sheath on his sword belt. Smoke was already drifting up the passage into the warehouse.

'Give me your knife, Sam,' he said. 'I'll just go and . . . check on him.'

The lance-constable handed over the knife with some reluctance.

'What're you going to do, sarge?'

'You just get on with your job, lance-constable, and I'll do mine . . .'

Vimes slipped down into the passage. I'll cut one strap, he thought. They're fiddly to undo. And then . . . well, he'll have a chance, even in the smoke. That's more than anyone else got.

He crept through the office and into the chamber.

One torch was still alight, but the flame was just a nimbus in the yellow haze. The man was trying to rock the heavy chair, but it had been secured firmly to the floor.

Some thought had gone into that chair. The straps on the buckles were hard to reach. Even if a prisoner got one hand free, and that hand had not yet felt the professionalism of the torturer, they'd have a job to get out of the chair in a hurry.

He reached down to cut a strap, and heard a key in the lock.

Vimes stepped swiftly into the darker shadows.

The door opened, letting in the noise of distant shouting and the crackle of burning timber. It sounded as though the Unmentionables were making a run for the clear air of the street.

Findthee Swing stepped delicately into the room, and locked the door behind him. He stopped when he saw the seated figure, and examined it carefully. He walked to the office doorway and looked inside. He peered into the cells, but by then Vimes had moved soundlessly around a wall.

He heard Findthee sigh. There was the familiar sound of moving steel, followed by a small, organic sort of noise, and a cough.

Vimes reached down for his sword. But it was up on the road, too, wasn't it . . .

Down here, the song in his head came back louder, with the background clink of metal that was always part of it . . . *see how they rise up, rise up, rise up* . . .

He shook his head, as if that'd dislodge the memory. He had to *concentrate*. Vimes ran into the room and made a leap.

It seemed to him that he stayed in the air a long time. There was the torturer, blood on his shirt. There was Swing, just sliding the blade back into the stick. And Vimes, airborne, armed with just a knife.

I'm going to get out of this, he thought. I know, because I remember this. I remember Keel coming out and saying it was all over.

But that was the real Keel. This is me. *It doesn't have to happen the same way.*

Swing jerked aside with surprising speed, trying to tug his blade out again. Vimes hit the sacks on the wall, and had the sense to roll away immediately. The blade slashed down beside him, spilling straw on to the floor.

He'd expected Swing to be a bad swordsman. That ridiculous stick suggested it. But he was a street swordsman – no finesse, no fancy tricks, just some talent at moving the blade quickly and sticking it where you hoped it wasn't going to go.

Fire crackled in the corner of the ceiling. Dripping spirit or sheer heat had worked itself through the heavy floorboards. A couple of the sacks began to blossom thick white smoke, which rolled above the men in a spreading cloud.

He circled the chair, watching Swing intently.

'I believe you are making a gravemistake,' said Swing.

Vimes concentrated on avoiding the sword.

'Hard times demand hard measures. Every leader knows that . . .' said Swing.

Vimes dodged, but continued circling, knife at the ready.

'History needs its butchers as well as its shepherds, sergeant.'

Swing jabbed, but Vimes had been watching his eyes, and swayed away in time. The man wasn't pleading. He didn't understand what had been done to require it. But he could see Vimes's face. There was no emotion in it at all.

'You must understand that in times of nationalemergency we cannot be too concerned with the so-called rights of—'

Vimes darted sideways and along the haze-filled corridor to the office. Swing lurched after him. The blade sliced Vimes on the back of the leg. He sprawled on to the clerk's desk, knife skittering from his fingers.

Swing circled to find a stabbing point. He drew back the sword . . .

Vimes's hand came up holding the steel ruler. The smack of its flat steel knocked the sword right out of the captain's grasp.

Vimes pulled himself upright as though in a dream, following on the curve of the stroke.

Send it back into the dark until you need it . . .

He turned the ruler as the backstroke began and it whispered through the air edge-first, leaving the hazy smoke rolling and coiling behind it. The tip caught Swing across the neck.

Behind Vimes the white smoke tumbled out of the corridor. The ceiling of the bloody chamber was falling in.

But he stayed, watching Swing with the same blank, intent expression. The man had raised his hands to his throat, blood spurting from between his fingers. He rocked, gasping for a breath that couldn't come, and fell backwards.

Vimes tossed the ruler on top of him and limped away.

Outside, there was the thunder of moving barricades.

Swing opened his eyes. The world around him was grey, except for the black-clad figure in front of him.

He sought, as he always did, to learn more about the new person by carefully examining their features.

'Um, your eyes are . . . er . . . your nose is . . . your chin . . .' He gave up.

YES, said Death, I'M A BIT OF A TRICKY ONE. THIS WAY, MR SWING.

Lord Winder was, thought Vetinari, impressively paranoid. He'd even put a guard on the top of the whisky distillery that overlooked the palace grounds. Two guards, in fact.

One of them was clearly visible as you rose over the parapet, but the other was lurking in the shadows by the chimneys.

The late Hon. John Bleedwell had spotted only the first one.

Vetinari watched impassively as the young man was dragged away. If you were an Assassin, being killed in the pursuit of your craft was all part of the job, albeit the last part. You couldn't complain. And it meant there was only one guard now, the other one taking Bleedwell, who had lived up to his name, downstairs.

Bleedwell had worn black. Assassins always did. Black was cool and, besides, it was the rules. But only in a dark cellar at midnight was black a sensible colour. Elsewhere, Vetinari preferred dark green, or shades of dark grey. With the right colouring, and the right stance, you vanished. People's eyes would *help* you vanish. They erased you from their vision, they fitted you into the background.

Of course, he'd be expelled from the Guild if caught wearing such clothing. He'd reasoned that this was much better than being expelled from the land of the upright and breathing. He'd rather not be cool than be cold.

The guard, three feet away, lit a cigarette with no consideration for other people.

What a genius Lord Winstanleigh Greville-Pipe had been. What an observer. Havelock would love to have met him, or even to have visited his grave, but apparently that was inside a tiger somewhere which, to Greville-Pipe's gratified astonishment, he hadn't spotted until it was too late.

Vetinari had done him a private honour, though. He had hunted down and melted the engraver's plates of *Some Observations on the Art of Invisibility*.

He tracked down the other four extant copies, too, but had felt unable to burn them. Instead he'd had the slim volumes bound together inside the cover of *Anecdotes of the Great Accountants, Vol. 3*. He felt that Lord Winstanleigh Greville-Pipe would rather appreciate that.

Vetinari lay comfortably on the lead of the roof, patient as a cat, and watched the palace grounds below.

Vimes lay face down on a table in the Watch House, wincing occasionally.

'*Please* hold still,' said Dr Lawn. 'I've nearly finished. I suppose you'd laugh if I told you to take it easy?'

'Ha. Ha. Uh!'

'It's only a flesh wound, but you ought to get some rest.'

'Ha. Ha.'

'You've got a busy night ahead of you. So have I, I suspect.'

'We should be okay if we've got the barricades all the way to Easy Street,' said Vimes, and was aware of a telling silence.

He sat up on the table that Lawn was using as a bench. 'We *have* got them to Easy Street, haven't we?' he demanded.

'The last I heard, yes,' said the doctor.

'The last you heard?'

'Well, technically no,' said Lawn. 'It's all getting . . . bigger,

John. The *actual* last I heard was someone saying "why stop at Easy Street?"'

'Oh, good *grief* . . .'

'Yes. I thought so, too.'

Vimes dragged his breeches up, fastened his belt and limped out into the road and also into an argument.

There was Rosie Palm, and Sandra, and Reg Shoe and half a dozen others sitting around another table, in the middle of the street. As Vimes stepped out into the evening, a plaintive voice said, 'You cannot fight for "reasonably priced love".'

'You can if you want me and the rest of the girls on board,' said Rosie. ' "Free" is not a word we wish to see used in these circumstances.'

'Oh, very well,' said Reg, making a note on a clipboard. 'We're all happy with Truth, Justice and Freedom, are we?'

'And better sewers.' This was the voice of Mrs Rutherford. 'And something done about the rats.'

'I think we should be thinking about higher things, comrade Mrs Rutherford,' said Reg.

'I am not a comrade, Mr Shoe, and nor is Mr Rutherford,' said Mrs Rutherford. 'We've always kept ourselves to ourselves, haven't we, Sidney?'

'I've got a question,' said someone in the crowd of onlookers. 'Harry Supple's my name. Got a shoe shop in New Cobblers . . .'

Reg seized on this as an opportunity to avoid talking to Mrs Rutherford. Revolutionaries should not have to meet someone like Mrs Rutherford on their first day.

'Yes, comrade Supple?' he said.

'Nor are we boyjoys,' said Mrs Rutherford, not willing to let things go.

'Er, bourgeoisie,' said Reg. 'Our manifesto refers to bourgeoisie. That's like bore, er, shwah, er, zee.'

'Bourgeoisie, bourgeoisie,' said Mrs Rutherford, turning the word over on her tongue. 'That . . . doesn't sound *too* bad. What, er, sort of thing do they do?'

'Anyway, it says here in article seven of this here list—' Mr Supple ploughed on.

'—People's Declaration of the Glorious Twenty-fourth of May,' said Reg.

'Yeah, yeah, right . . . well, it says we'll seize hold of the means of production, sort of thing, so what I want to know is, how does that work out regarding my shoe shop? I mean, I'm in it anyway, right? It's not like there's room for more'n me and my lad Garbut and maybe one customer.'

In the dark, Vimes smiled. Reg could never see stuff coming.

'Ah, but after the revolution all property will be held in common by the people . . . er . . . that is, it'll belong to you but *also* to everyone else, you see?'

Comrade Supple looked puzzled. 'But I'll be the one making the shoes?'

'Of course. But everything will *belong* to the people.'

'So . . . who's going to pay for the shoes?' said Mr Supple.

'Everyone will pay a reasonable price for their shoes and you won't be guilty of living off the sweat of the common worker,' said Reg, shortly. 'Now, if we—'

'You mean the cows?' said Supple.

'What?'

'Well, there's only the cows, and the lads at the tannery, and frankly all they do is stand in a field all day, well, not the tannery boys, obviously, but—'

'Look,' said Reg. 'Everything will belong to the people and everyone will be better off. Do you understand?'

The shoemaker's frown grew deeper. He wasn't certain if he was part of the people.

'I thought we just didn't want soldiers down our street and mobs and all that lot,' he said.

Reg had a hunted look. He made a dive for safety. 'Well, at least we can agree on Truth, Freedom and Justice, yes?'

There was a chorus of nods. Everyone wanted those. They didn't cost anything.

A match flared in the dark, and they turned to see Vimes light a cigar.

'You'd like Freedom, Truth and Justice, wouldn't you, comrade sergeant?' said Reg encouragingly.

'I'd like a hard-boiled egg,' said Vimes, shaking the match out.

There was some nervous laughter, but Reg looked offended.

'In the circumstances, sergeant, I think we should set our sights a little higher—'

'Well, yes, we could,' said Vimes, coming down the steps. He glanced at the sheets of paper in front of Reg. The man cared. He really did. And he was serious. He really was. 'But . . . well, Reg, tomorrow the sun will come up again, and I'm pretty sure that whatever happens we won't have found Freedom, and there won't be a whole lot of Justice, and I'm *damn* sure we won't have found Truth. But it's just possible that I might get a hard-boiled egg. What's this all about, Reg?'

'The People's Republic of Treacle Mine Road!' said Reg proudly. 'We are forming a government!'

'Oh, good,' said Vimes. 'Another one. Just what we need. Now, does any one of you know where my damn barricades have gone?'

''ullo, Mr Keel,' said a glutinous voice.

He looked down beside him. There, still wearing his hugely oversize coat but now with the addition of a helmet much too large for him, was Nobby Nobbs.

'How did you get there, Nobby?'

'My mum says I'm insidious,' said Nobby, grinning. A concertina sleeve rose to the vicinity of Nobby's head, and Vimes realized that somewhere in there was a salute.

'She's right,' said Vimes. 'So, where—'

''m a acting constable now, sarge,' said Nobby. 'Mr Colon said so. Gave me a spare helmet. 'm carvin' meself a badge out of, of— what's that, like, waxy, kind of like candles but you can't eat it?'

'Soap, Nobby. Remember the word.'

'Right, sarge. Then I'm gonna carve a—'

'Where have the barricades gone, Nobby?'

'That'll cost—'

'I am your *sergeant*, Nobby. We are not in a financial relation-ship. Tell me where the bloody barricades are!'

'Um . . . prob'ly nearly to Short Street, sarge. It's all got a bit . . . metaphysical, sarge.'

Major Clive Mountjoy-Standfast stared blankly at the map in front of him, trying to find some comfort. He was, tonight, the senior officer in the field. The commanders had gone to the palace for some party or other. And he was in charge.

Vimes had conceded that the city's regiments had quite a few officers who weren't fools. Admittedly they got fewer the higher you went, but by accident or design every army needs, in key if unglamorous posts, men who can reason and make lists and arrange for provisions and baggage wagons and, in general, have an attention span greater than a duck. It's their job to actually run things, leaving the commanding officer free to concentrate on higher matters.

And the major was, indeed, not a fool, even though he looked like one. He was idealistic, and thought of his men as 'jolly good chaps' despite the occasional evidence to the contrary, and on the whole did the best he could with the moderate intelligence at his disposal. When he was a boy he'd read books about great military campaigns, and visited the museums and looked with patriotic pride at the paintings of famous cavalry charges, last stands and glorious victories. It had come as rather a shock, when he later began to participate in some of these, to find that the painters had unaccountably left out the intestines. Perhaps they just weren't very good at them.

The major hated the map. It was the map of a city. A city wasn't a place for cavalry, for heavens' sake! Of course there had been casualties among the men. Three of them had been deaths. Even a cavalry helmet is not a lot of use against a ballistic cobblestone. And a trooper had been pulled off his horse in Dolly Sisters and, bluntly, mobbed to death. And that was tragic and terrible and, unfortunately, inevitable, once fools had decided to use cavalry in a city with as many alleys as Ankh-Morpork.

The major didn't think of his superiors as fools, of course, since it would follow that everyone who obeyed them was a fool. He used the term 'unwise', and felt worried when he used it.

As for the rest of the casualties, three of them had been men knocked senseless by riding into hanging shop signs while pursuing . . . well, people, when it came down to it, because with the smoke and darkness who could tell who the real enemy was? The idiots had apparently assumed that anyone running away was the enemy. And they'd been the luckier idiots, because men who rode their horses into dark alleys which twisted this way and that and got narrower and narrower, and then realized that it had all gone quiet and their horse couldn't turn round, well, they were men who learned how fast a man could run in cavalry boots.

He totted up the reports. Broken bones, bruises, one man suffering from 'friendly stab' by a comrade's sabre . . .

He looked across the makeshift table at Captain Tom Wrangle of Lord Selachii's Light Infantry, who glanced up from his own paperwork and gave him a weak smile. They'd been at school together and Wrangle, the major knew, was a lot brighter than him.

'What's it look like to you, Tom?' said the major.

'We've lost nearly eighty men,' said the captain.

'What? That's terrible!'

'Oh, about sixty of them are deserters, as far as I can see. You tend to get that in this sort of mess. Some have probably just popped home to see dear ol' mum.'

'Oh, *deserters*. We've had some of those, too. In the cavalry! What would you call a man who leaves his horse behind?'

'An infantryman? As for the rest, well, as far as I can see only six or seven of them went down to definite enemy action. Three men got stabbed in alleyways, for example.'

'Sounds like enemy action to *me*.'

'Yes, Clive. But you were born in Quirm.'

'Only because my mother was visiting her aunt and the coach was late!' said the major, going red. 'If you cut me in half you'd find Ankh-Morpork written on my heart!'

'Really? Well, let's hope it doesn't come to that,' said Tom. 'Anyway, getting murdered in alleyways is just part of life in the big city.'

'But they were armed men! Swords, helmets—'

'Valuable loot, Clive.'

'But I thought the City Watch took care of the gangs—'

Tom looked at his friend over the top of his paperwork.

'Are you suggesting that we ask for police protection? Anyway, there isn't any, not any more. Some of the watchmen are with us, for what good they are, and the rest either got beaten up or ran away—'

'More deserters?'

'Frankly, Clive, everyone's drifting away so fast that by tomorrow we'll be feeling pretty lonely.'

The men paused as a corporal brought in some more messages. They thumbed through them gloomily.

'Well, it's gone quiet, anyway,' said the major.

'Suppertime,' said the captain.

The major threw up his hands. 'This isn't war! A man throws a rock, walks around the corner and he's an upstanding citizen again! There's no *rules*!'

The captain nodded. Their training hadn't covered this sort of thing. They'd studied maps of campaigns, with broad sweeping plains and the occasional patch of high ground that had to be taken. Cities were to be laid siege to, or defended. They weren't for fighting in. You couldn't see, you couldn't group, you couldn't manoeuvre and you were always going to be up against people who knew the place like their own kitchen. And you *definitely* didn't want to fight an enemy that had no uniform.

'Where's your lordship?' said the captain.

'Gone to the ball, the same as yours.'

'And what were your orders, may I ask?'

'He told me to do whatever I considered necessary to carry out our original objectives.'

'Did he write that down?'

'No.'

'Pity. Neither did mine.'

They looked at one another. And then Wrangle said, 'Well . . . there's no actual *unrest* at the moment. As such. My father said all this happened in his time. He said it's best just to keep the lid on it. There's only a limited number of cobblestones, he said.'

'It's almost ten,' said the major. 'People will be going to bed soon, surely?'

Their joint expression radiated the fervent hope that it had all calmed down. No one in their right mind wanted to be in a position where he was expected to do what he thought best.

'Well, Clive, provided there's no—' the captain began.

There was a commotion outside the tent, and then a man stepped inside. He was bloodstained and smoke-blackened, his face lined with pink where sweat had trickled through the dreadful grime. A crossbow was slung across his back, and he'd acquired a bandolier of knives.

And he was mad. The major recognized the look. The eyes were too bright, the grin too fixed.

'Ah, right,' he said, and removed a large brass knuckleduster from his right hand. 'Sorry about your sentry, gen'lemen, but he didn't want to let me in even though I gave him the password. Are you in charge?'

'Who the hell are you?' said the major, standing up.

The man seemed unimpressed. 'Carcer. *Sergeant* Carcer,' he said.

'A sergeant? In that case you can—'

'From Cable Street,' Carcer added.

Now the major hesitated. Both the soldiers knew about the Unmentionables, although if asked they probably wouldn't have been able to articulate exactly what it was that they knew. Unmentionables worked in secret, behind the scenes. They were a lot more than just watchmen. They reported directly to the Patrician; they had a lot of pull. You didn't mess with them. They were not people to cross. It didn't matter that this man was only a sergeant. He was an Unmentionable.

And, what was worse, the major realized that the creature could see what he was thinking and was enjoying the view.

'Yeah,' said Carcer. 'That's right. And it's lucky for you that I'm here, soldier boy.'

Soldier boy, thought the major. And there were men listening, who'd remember that. Soldier boy.

'How so?' he said.

'While you and your shiny soldiers have been prancing around chasing washerwomen,' said Carcer, pulling up the tent's only vacant chair and sitting down, 'the *real* trouble's been happening down in Treacle Mine Road. You know it?'

'What are you talking about? We haven't had any reports about any disturbances down there, man!'

'Yeah, right. Don't you think that's strange?'

The major hesitated. A vague memory bobbed at the back of his mind . . . and there was a grunt from the captain, who pushed a piece of paper across to him. He glanced at it, and recalled.

'One of my captains was down there this afternoon and said everything was under control,' he said.

'Really? Whose control?' said Carcer. He leaned back in his chair and put his boots on the desk.

The major stared at them, but the boots showed no sign of embarrassment. 'Remove your feet from my desk,' he said coldly.

Carcer's eyes narrowed. 'You an' whose army?' he said.

'Mine, as a matter of fact . . .'

The major looked into Carcer's eyes, and wished he hadn't. Mad. He'd seen eyes like that on the battlefield.

Very slowly, with exaggerated care, Carcer swung his feet off the table. Then he pulled out a handkerchief made grimy with unguessable humours, huffed theatrically on the wood, and polished it industriously.

'I do beg your pardon so very much,' he said. 'However, while you *gentlemen* have been keeping your desk nice and clean, a canker, as they say, haha, is eating at the very heart of the city. Has anyone told you that the Cable Street Watch House has been burned to the ground? With, we believe, the loss of the lives of poor Captain Swing and at least one of our . . . technical people.'

'Swing, bigods,' said Captain Wrangle.

'That is what I said. All the scum your lads have been driving out of Dolly Sisters and all the other nests, well, they've ended up down there.'

The major looked at the report. 'But our patrol said that everything seemed to be in hand, the Watch were very visible on the streets, and people were showing the flag and singing the national anthem,' he said.

'There you are, then,' said Carcer. 'Do *you* ever sing the national anthem in the street, major?'

'Well, no—'

'Who did his lordship send down there?' said Wrangle.

Major Mountjoy-Standfast thumbed through his papers. His face fell. 'Rust,' he said.

'Oh dear. That's a blow.'

'I daresay the man is dead,' said Carcer, and the major tried not to look slightly more cheerful. 'The person in charge down there now calls himself Sergeant Keel. But he is a impostor. The real Keel is in the mortuary.'

'How do you know all this?' said the major.

'We in the Particulars have ways of finding things out,' said Carcer.

'I've heard,' murmured the captain.

'Martial law, gentlemen, means that the military comes to the aid of the civil power,' said Carcer. 'And that's me, right now. O'course, you could send a couple of runners up to the ball, but I don't reckon that would be a good career move. So what I'm asking is for your men to assist us with a little . . . surgical strike.'

The major stared at him. There was now no limit to the distaste he had for Carcer. But he hadn't been a major for very long, and when you've just been promoted you hope to stay that way long enough for the braid to get a tarnish.

He forced himself to smile. 'You and your men have had a long day, sergeant,' he said. 'Why don't you go along to the mess tent while I consult with my fellow officers?'

Carcer stood up with a suddenness that made the major flinch, then leaned forward with his knuckles on the desk.

'You do that, sonny Jim,' he said, with a grin like the edge of a rusty saw. Then he turned and strode out into the night.

In the silence that followed Wrangle said, 'His name is on the list of officers that Swing sent us yesterday, I'm afraid. And, er, he's technically correct about the law.'

'You mean we have to take orders from him?'

'No. But he's entitled to request assistance from you.'

'Am I entitled to refuse?'

'Oh, yes. Of course. But . . .'

'. . . I'd have to tell his lordship why?'

'Exactly.'

'But that man's an evil bastard! You know the sort. The kind that joins up for the pillaging? The kind you have to end up hanging as an example to the men?'

'Um . . .'

'What now?'

'Well, he's right about one thing. I've been looking at the reports and, well, it's odd. It's all been very quiet down towards Treacle Mine Road.'

'That's good, isn't it?'

'It's unbelievable, Clive, when you put it all together. Even the Watch House didn't get attacked, it says here. Er . . . and your Captain Burns says he met this Keel chap, or someone who said he was Keel, and he says that if the man's a Watch sergeant then he, Burns, is a monkey's uncle. He says the man is used to *serious* command. I think he rather took to him, to tell you the truth.'

'Ye gods, Tom, I need some *help* here!' said the major.

'Then send out some gallopers right away. A little informal patrolling, perhaps. Get some proper intelligence. You can afford to wait half an hour.'

'Right! Right! Good idea!' said the major, steaming with relief. 'See to it, could you?'

After the flurry of orders, he sat back and stared at the map. Some things at least made sense. All these barricades looked inward. People were barricading themselves against the palace and the centre of the city. No one would be bothered much about the outside world. If you *had* to take an outlying part of the city in those circumstances, then the thing to do would be to go in via a gatehouse in the city wall. They might not be quite so guarded as they ought to be.

'Tom?'

'Yes, Clive?'

'Have you ever sung the national anthem?'

'Oh, lots of times, sir.'

'I don't mean officially.'

'You mean just to show I'm patriotic? Good gods, no. That would be a rather odd thing to do,' said the captain.

'And how about the flag?'

'Well, obviously I salute it every day, sir.'

'But you don't wave it, at all?' the major enquired.

'I think I waved a paper one a few times when I was a little boy. Patrician's birthday or something. We stood in the streets as he rode by and we shouted "Hurrah!" '

'Never since then?'

'Well, *no*, Clive,' said the captain, looking embarrassed. 'I'd be very worried if I saw a man singing the national anthem and waving the flag, sir. It's really a thing foreigners do.'

'Really? Why?'

'*We* don't need to show *we're* patriotic, sir. I mean, this is Ankh-Morpork. We don't have to make a big fuss about being the best, sir. We just *know*.'

It was a beguiling theory that might have arisen in the minds of Wiglet and Waddy and, yes, even in the not overly exercised mind of Fred Colon, and as far as Vimes could understand it, it went like this.

1 Supposing the area *behind* the barricades was bigger than the area in *front* of the barricades, right?

2 Like, sort of, it had more people in it and more of the city, if you follow me.

3 Then, correct me if I'm wrong, sarge, but that'd mean in a manner of speaking we are now in *front* of the barricades, am I right?

4 Then, as it were, it's not like *we're* rebellin', is it? 'cos there's *more* of us, so the majority can't rebel, it stands to reason.

5 So that makes us the good guys. Obviously we've been the good guys all along, but now it'd be kind of official, right? Like, mathematical?

6 So we thought we'd push on to Short Street and then we could nip down into Dimwell and up the other side of the river . . .

7 Are we going to get into trouble for this, sarge?

8 You're looking at me in a funny way, sarge.

9 Sorry, sarge.

Vimes, with an increasingly worried Fred Colon in front of him, and some of the other barricadeers standing around as if caught in an illicit game of Knocking On Doors And Running Away, thought about this. The men watched him carefully, in case of explosion.

And it actually made a weird kind of logic, if you didn't factor in considerations like 'real life' and 'common sense'.

They'd worked hard. It was easy enough to block a city street, heavens knew. You just nailed planks around a couple of wagons and piled it high with furniture and junk. That took care of the main streets, and with enough pushing you could move it forwards.

As for the rest, it really hadn't been that hard. There had been lots of small barricades in any case. The lads had simply joined them up. Without anyone really noticing, The People's Republic of Treacle Mine Road now occupied almost a quarter of the city.

Vimes took a few deep breaths. 'Fred?' he said.

'Yes, sarge?'

'Did I *tell* you to do this?'

'No, sarge.'

'There's too many alleys. There's too many *people*, Fred.'

Colon brightened. 'Ah, well, there's more coppers too, sarge. A lot of the lads found their way here. Good lads, too. And Sergeant Dickins, he knows about this stuff, he remembers the *last* time this happened, sarge, so he asked every able-bodied man who knew how to use a weapon to muster up, sarge. There's a *lot* of 'em, sarge! We got an *army*, sarge!'

This is how the world collapses, thought Vimes. I was just a young fool, I didn't see it like this. I thought Keel was leading the revolution. I wonder if that's what he thought, too?

But *I* just wanted to keep a few streets safe. I just wanted to keep a handful of decent, silly people away from the dumb mobs and the mindless rebels and the idiot soldiery. I really, really hoped we could get away with it.

Maybe the monks were right. Changing history is like damming a river. It'll find its way round.

274

He saw Sam beaming among the men. Hero worship, he thought. That sort of thing can turn you blind.

'Any trouble?' he said to Colon.

'Don't think anyone's worked out what's happening here, sarge. There's been a lot happening around Dolly Sisters and over that way. Cavalry charges and what have you— hold on, here come some more.'

A watchman had signalled from the top of the barricade. Vimes heard the commotion on the other side of the pile.

'More people runnin' away from Dolly Sisters, by the look of it,' said Colon. 'What d'you want us to do, sarge?'

Keep them out, thought Vimes. We don't know who they are. We can't let everyone in. Some of them *will* be trouble.

The trouble is, I know what's going on out there. The city is a little slice of Hell, and there's no real safety anywhere.

And I know what I'm going to decide, because I watch me decide it.

I don't believe this. I'm standing over there now, a kid who's still clean and pink and full of ideals, looking at me as if I'm some kind of hero. I don't dare not be. I'm going to make the stupid decision because I don't want to look bad in front of *myself*. Try explaining *that* to anyone who hasn't had a couple of drinks.

'All right, let them through,' he said. 'But no weapons. Pass the word around.'

'Take weapons off people?' said Colon.

'Think about it, Fred. We don't want Unmentionables in here, do we, or soldiers in disguise? A man's got to be vouched for before he can carry arms. I ain't going to be stabbed in the back and the front at the same time. Oh, and Fred . . . I don't know if I can do this, and probably it won't last, but as far as I'm concerned you're promoted to sergeant. Anyone who wants to argue about the extra stripe, tell 'em to argue with me.'

Fred Colon's chest, already running to fat, swelled visibly. '*Right*, sarge. Er . . . does that mean I still take orders from you? Right. Right. Right. I still take orders from you. Right.'

'Don't move any more barricades. Fill up the alleys. Hold this line. Vimes, you come with me, I'll need a runner.'

'I'm pretty runny, sarge,' Nobby volunteered, from somewhere behind him.

'Then what I want *you* to do, Nobby, is get out there and find out what's happening now.'

Sergeant Dickins turned out to be younger than Vimes remembered. But he was still close to retirement. He'd maintained a flourishing sergeant's moustache, waxed to points and clearly dyed, and the proper sergeant shape, occasioned by means of undisclosed corsetry. He'd spent a lot of time in the regiments, Vimes recalled, although he came from Llamedos originally. The men found that out because he belonged to some druid religion so strict that they didn't even use standing stones. And they were strongly against swearing, which is a real handicap in a sergeant. Or would be, if sergeants weren't so good at improvising.

He was currently in Welcome Soap, a continuation of Cable Street. And he had the army.

It wasn't much of one. No two weapons were exactly alike and most of them were not, strictly speaking, weapons. Vimes shuddered when he saw the crowd and had a flashback, which was probably a flash forward, to all the domestic disputes he'd attended over the years. You knew where you were with strictly-speaking weapons when they came at you. It was the not-strictly-speaking ones that scared the cacky out of a new recruit. It was the meat cleavers tied to poles. It was the long spikes, and the meathooks.

This was, after all, the area of small traders, porters, butchers and longshoremen. And so standing in raggedy lines in front of Vimes were men who, every day, peacefully and legally, handled things with blades and spikes that made a mere sword look like a girl's hatpin.

There *were* classic weapons, too. Men had come back from

276

wars with their sword or their halberd. Weapons? Gods bless you, sir, no! Them's *mementoes*. And the sword had probably been used to poke the fire, and the halberd had done duty as a support for one end of the washing line, and their original use had been forgotten . . .

. . . until now.

Vimes stared at the metalwork. All this lot would have to do to win a battle would be to stand still. If the enemy charged them hard enough, he'd come out the other side as mince.

'Some of 'em are retired watchmen, sah,' Dickins whispered. 'A lot of them have been in the regiments at one time or another, see. There's a few kids wanting to see some action, you know how it is. What d'you think?'

'I'd certainly hate to fight them,' said Vimes. At least a quarter of the men had white hair, and more than a few were using their weapons as a means of support. 'Come to that, I'd hate to be responsible for giving them an order. If I said "about turn!" to this lot, it'd be raining limbs.'

'They're resolute, sah.'

'Fair enough. But I don't want a war.'

'Oh, it won't come to that, sah,' said Dickins. 'I've seen a few barricades in my time. It generally ends peaceful. The new man takes over, people get bored, everyone goes home, see.'

'But Winder is a nutter,' said Vimes.

'Tell me one that wasn't, sah,' said Dickins.

Sir, thought Vimes. Or 'sah', at least. And he's older than me. Oh well, I might as well be good at it.

'Sergeant,' he said, 'I want you to pick twenty of the best, men that have seen action. Men you can trust. And I want them down at the Shambling Gate, and alert.'

Dickins looked puzzled. 'But that's barred, sah. And it's right down behind us, it is. I thought maybe—'

'Down at the gate, sergeant,' Vimes insisted. 'They're to watch for anyone sneaking up to unbar it. And I want the guard on the bridges to be strengthened. Put down caltrops on the bridge,

277

string wires . . . I want anyone who tries to come at us over the bridge to have a really bad time, understand?'

'Do you know something, sah?' said Dickins, with his head on one side.

'Let's just say I'm thinking like the enemy, shall we?' said Vimes. He took a step closer and lowered his voice. 'You know some history, Dai. No one with an ounce of sense goes up against a barricade. You find the weakness.'

'There's other gates down there, sah,' said Dickins doubtfully.

'Yes, but if they take Shambling they get into Elm Street and have a nice long gallop, right into where we're not expecting them,' said Vimes.

'But . . . you *are* expecting them, sah.'

Vimes just gave him a blank look, which sergeants are quite good at deciphering.

'As good as done, sah!' said Dickins happily.

'But I want a decent presence at all the barricades,' said Vimes. 'And a couple of patrols that can go wherever there's trouble. Sergeant, you *know* how to do it.'

'Right, sah.' Dickins saluted smartly, and grinned.

He turned to the assembled citizenry. 'All right, you shower!' he yelled. 'Some of you has been in a regiment, I know it! How many of you knows "All The Little Angels"?'

A few of the more serious class of mementoes rose in the air.

'Very good! Already we has a choir! Now, this is a soldiers' song, see? You don't look like soldiers but by the gods I'll see you sounds like 'em! You'll pick it up as we goes along! Right turn! March! "All the little angels rise up, rise up, All the little angels rise up high!" Sing it, you sons of mothers!'

The marchers picked up the response from those who knew it.

'How do they rise up, rise up, rise up, how do they rise up, rise up high?'

'They rise *heads* up, *heads* up, *heads* up—' sang out Dickins, as they turned the corner.

Vimes listened as the refrain died away.

'That's a nice song,' said young Sam, and Vimes remembered that he was hearing it for the first time.

'It's an old soldiers' song,' he said.

'Really, sarge? But it's about angels.'

Yes, thought Vimes, and it's amazing what bits those angels cause to rise up as the song progresses. It's a *real* soldiers' song: sentimental, with dirty bits.

'As I recall, they used to sing it after battles,' he said. 'I've seen old men cry when they sing it,' he added.

'Why? It sounds cheerful.'

They were remembering who they were not singing it with, thought Vimes. You'll learn. I *know* you will.

After a while, the patrols came back. Major Mountjoy-Standfast was bright enough not to ask for written reports. They took too long and weren't very well spelled. One by one, the men told the story. Sometimes Captain Wrangle, who was plotting things on the map, would whistle under his breath.

'It's huge, sir. It really is! Nearly a quarter of the city's behind barricades down there!'

The major rubbed his forehead and turned to Trooper Gabitass, the last man in and the one who seemed to have taken pains to get the most information.

'They're all on a sort of line, sir. So I rode up to the one in Heroes Street, with me helmet off and looking off-duty, sort of thing, and I asked what it was all about. A man shouted down that everything was all right, thank you very much, and they'd finished all the barricades for now. I said what about law and order, and they said we've got plenty, thank you.'

'No one fired at you?'

'No, sir. Wish I could say the same about round here. People were throwing stones at me and an old lady emptied a pissp— a utensil all over me from her window. Er . . . there's something else, sir. Er . . .'

'Out with it, man.'

'I, er, think I recognized a few people. Up on the barricades. Er . . . they were some of ours, sir . . .'

Vimes shut his eyes, in the hope that the world would be a better place. But when he opened them, it was still full of the pink face of only-just Sergeant Colon.

'Fred,' he said, 'I wonder if you fully understand the basic idea here? The soldiers – that's the *other* people, Fred – they stay on the *outside* of the barricade. If they are on the *inside*, Fred, we don't, in any real sense, *have* a bloody barricade. Do you understand?'

'Yes, sir. But—'

'You want to do a spell in a regiment, Fred, and one of the things I think you'll find they're very hot on indeed is knowing who's on your side and who is not, Fred.'

'But, sir, they are—'

'I mean, how long have I known you, Fred?'

'Two or three days, sir.'

'Er . . . right. Yeah. Of course. Seems longer. So *why*, Fred, do I arrive here and find you've let in what seems like a platoon? You haven't been thinking metaphysically again, have you?'

'It started with Billy Wiglet's brother, sir,' said Colon nervously. 'A few of his mates came with him. All local lads. And there's a lad Nancyball grew up with and a bloke who's the son of Waddy's next-door neighbour who he used to go out drinking with, and then there's—'

'How many, Fred?' said Vimes wearily.

'Sixty, sir. Might be a few more by now.'

'And it doesn't occur to you that they might be part of some clever plan?'

'No, sarge, it never did. 'cos I can't see Wally Wiglet being part of a clever plan, sarge, on account of him not being much of a thinker, sir. They only allowed him to be in the regiment after he got someone to paint L and R on his boots. See, we *know* 'em all,

280

sarge. Most of the lads join up for a bit, just to get out of the city and maybe show Johnny Foreigner who's boss. They never expected to have old grannies spitting on them in their own city, sarge. That can get a lad down, that sort of thing. And getting cobblestones chucked at them too, of course.'

Vimes gave in. It was all true. 'All right,' he said. 'But if this goes on, everyone is going to be inside the barricade, Fred.'

And there could be worse ways of ending it, he thought.

People had lit fires in the streets. Some cooking pots had been brought out. But most of the people were engaging in Ankh-Morpork's traditional pastime, which was hanging around to see what'd happen next.

'What's going to happen next, sarge?' said Sam.

'I think they'll attack in two places,' said Vimes. 'The cavalry will go right outside the city and try to come in through the Shambling Gate because that'll look easy. And the soldiers and . . . the rest of the Watch who aren't on our side will probably creep across Misbegot Bridge under cover.'

'Are you sure, sir?'

'Positive,' said Vimes. After all, it had already happened . . . or something . . .

He pinched the bridge of his nose. He couldn't quite remember when he'd slept last. *Slept*, not dozed or been unconscious. He knew his thinking was a little fuzzy around the edges. But he did know how the Treacle Mine Road barricade had been broken. It had been only one sentence in the history book, but he remembered it. Sieges that weren't broken via treachery were breached via some small door around the back. It was a fact of history.

'But it won't be for an hour or two,' he said aloud. 'We're not important enough. It's all been quiet down here. It's when they start to wonder why that the midden will hit the windmill.'

'Lots of people are getting through, sarge. Some of the men said they could hear screaming in the distance. People are just piling in. There's robberies and everything going on out there . . .'

'Lance-constable?'

'Yes, sarge?'

'You know when you wanted to swing a club at that torturing bastard and I stopped you?'

'Yes, sarge?'

'That's why, lad. Once we break down, it all breaks down.'

'Yes, sarge, but you do bop people over the head.'

'Interesting point, lance-constable. Logical and well made, too, in a clear tone of voice bordering on the bloody cheeky. But there's a big difference.'

'And what's that, sarge?'

'You'll find out,' said Vimes. And privately thought: the answer is, It's Me Doing It. I'll grant that it is not a *good* answer, because people like Carcer use it too, but that's what it boils down to. Of course, it's also to stop me knifing them and, let's be frank, them knifing me. That's quite important, too.

Their walk had brought them to a big fire in the centre of the street. A cauldron was bubbling on it, and people were queuing up, holding bowls.

'Smells good,' he said, to the figure gently stirring the cauldron's contents with a ladle. 'Oh, it's you, er, Mr Dibbler . . .'

'It's called Victory Stew, sergeant,' said Dibbler. 'Tuppence a bowl or I'll cut my throat, eh?'

'Close enough,' said Vimes, and looked at the strange (and, what was worse, occasionally hauntingly familiar) lumps seething in the scum. 'What's in it?'

'It's stew,' explained Dibbler. 'Strong enough to put hairs on your chest.'

'Yes, I can see that some of those bits of meat have got bristles on them already,' said Vimes.

'Right! That's how good it is!'

'It looks . . . very nice,' said Sam weakly.

'You'll have to excuse the lance-constable, Mr Dibbler,' said Vimes. 'The poor lad was brought up not to eat stew that winks at him.'

He sat down with his bowl and his back against the wall and looked up at the barricade. People had been busy. In truth, there wasn't much else to do. The one here, from side to side of Heroes Street, was fourteen feet high and even had a crude walkway. It looked businesslike.

He leaned back and shut his eyes.

There was a hesitant slurping sound beside him as young Sam tried the stew, and then: 'Is it going to come down to fighting, sarge?'

'Yes,' said Vimes, without opening his eyes.

'Like, really fighting?'

'Yep.'

'But won't there be some talking first?'

'Nope,' said Vimes, trying to make himself comfortable. 'Maybe some talking afterwards.'

'Seems the wrong way round!'

'Yes, lad, but it's a tried and tested method.'

There was no further comment. Slowly, with the sounds of the street in his ears, Vimes slid into sleep.

Major Mountjoy-Standfast knew what would happen if he sent a message to the palace. 'What do I do now, sir?' was not something his lordship wanted to hear. It was not the sort of question a major was supposed to ask, given that the original orders had been very clear. Barricades were to be torn down, rebels were to be repelled. Grasp the nettle firmly and all that. He had, as a child, grasped nettles firmly, and had sometimes had a hand the size of a small pig.

There were deserters behind the barricade. Deserters! How did that happen?

It was a huge barricade, it was lined with armed men, there were deserters on it, and he had his orders. It was all clear.

If only they'd, well, *rebel*. He'd sent Trooper Gabitass down there again, and by his account it seemed very peaceful. Normal city life appeared to be going on behind the barricade, which was more than you could say for the chaos outside it. If they'd fired on Gabitass, or thrown things, that would have made it so much easier. Instead they were acting . . . well . . . *decently*. That was no way for enemies of the state to behave!

An enemy of the state was in front of the major now. Gabitass had not come back empty-handed.

'Caught it sneakin' after me,' he said. To the captive he said, 'Been behind the barricade, haven't we, my lad!'

'Can it speak?' said the major, staring at the thing.

'There's no need to be like that,' said Nobby Nobbs.

'It's a street urchin, sir,' said the trooper.

The major stared at all he could see of the prisoner, which was an oversized helmet and a nose.

'Get it something to stand on, will you, captain?' he said, and waited while a stool was found. It did not, all things considered, improve matters. It just gave rise to questions.

'It's got a Watch badge, trooper. Is it some kind of mascot?'

'Carved it meself out of soap,' said Nobby. 'So I can be a copper.'

'Why?' said the major. There was something about the apparition that, despite the urgency, called for a kind of horrified yet fascinated study.

'But I'm thinking of going for a soldier if I grow up,' Nobby went on, giving the major a happy grin. 'Much better pickin's, the way things are going.'

'I'm afraid you're not tall enough,' said the major quickly.

'Don't see why not, the enemy reaches all the way to the ground,' said Nobby. 'Anyway, people're lyin' down when you get their boots off. Ol' Sconner, he says the money's in teeth and earrings but I say every man's bound to have a pair of boots, right? Whereas there's a lot of bad teeth around these days and the false-teeth makers always demand a decent set—'

'Do you mean to tell me that you want to join the army just to loot the battlefields?' said the major, completely shocked. 'A little . . . lad like you?'

'Once when ol' Sconner was sober for two days together he made me a little set of soldiers,' said Nobby. 'An' they had these little boots that you could—'

'Shut up,' said the major.

'—take off, and tiny tiny little wooden teeth that you could—'

'Will you *shut up*!' said the major. 'Have you no interest in honour? Glory? Love of city?'

'Dunno. Can you get much for 'em?' said Nobby.

'They are *priceless*!'

'Oh, well, in that case I'll stick with the boots, if it's all the same to you,' said Nobby. 'You can sell them for ten pence a pair if you know the right shop—'

'Look at Trooper Gabitass there!' said the major, now quite upset. 'Twenty years' service, a fine figure of a soldier! He wouldn't stoop to stealing the boots of a fallen enemy, would you, trooper?'

'No, sir! Mug's game, sir!' said Trooper Gabitass.*

'Er . . . yes. Right!' said the major. 'You could learn a lot from men like Trooper Gabitass, young man. By the sound of it, your time with the rebels has filled your head with very wrong ideas *indeed*.'

'I ain't a rebel!' Nobby shouted. 'Don't you go calling me a rebel, I ain't a rebel, I'm an Ankh-Morpork lad, I am, and proud of it! Hah, you are wrong, I've never been a rebel and you're cruel to say so! I'm an honest lad, I am!'

Big tears began to run down his cheeks, washing aside the grime to reveal the lower strata of grime beneath.

---

* And this was true. Don't bother with the boots, would have been Trooper Gabitass's advice, had he been inclined to part with it. You need to bribe someone on the baggage carts to build up stock and when all's said and done you'll only make a few dollars. Stick to jewellery. It's portable. Trooper Gabitass had seen too many battlefields up close to use the word 'glory' without wincing.

The major had no experience of this sort of thing. Every available orifice on the little lad's face seemed to be gushing. He looked for help to Gabitass.

'You're a married man, aren't you, trooper? What are we supposed to do now?'

'I could give him a clout alongside the ear, sir,' said Trooper Gabitass.

'That's very unfeeling, trooper! Look here, I had a handkerchief on me somewhere . . .'

'Huh, I have my own wiper, thank you very much, I don't have to be condescended at,' sniffed Nobby, and pulled one out of his pocket. In fact, he pulled several dozen, including one with the initials C. M.-S. on it. They were tangled together like a conjuror's flags-of-all-nations, and dragged with them several purses and half a dozen spoons.

Nobby wiped his face with the first one, and thrust the entire collection back into his pocket. At this point he realized that all the men were staring at him.

'What? What?' he said defiantly.

'Tell us about this man Keel,' said the major.

'I don't know nuffin',' said Nobby automatically.

'Aha, that means you *do* know something,' said the major, who was indeed the sort of person who liked this kind of little triumph.

Nobby looked blank. The captain leaned forward to whisper to his superior officer.

'Er, only under the rules of mathematics, sir,' he said. 'Under the rules of common grammar, he is merely being emphat—'

'Tell us about Keel!' the major shouted.

'Tell you what, major, why not leave that sort of thing to the experts?' said a voice.

The major looked up. Carcer and his men had entered the tent. The sergeant was grinning again.

'Got yourself a little prisoner, have you?' he said, stepping forward to examine Nobby. 'Reckon you've got a ringleader here, yeah. Told you anything, has he? I shouldn't think so. You need special training to get the best out of lads like this, haha.'

He slipped his hand into his pocket. When it came out, the knuckles were ringed with brass.

'Now then, lad,' he said, as the soldiers watched in horror, 'you know who I am, do you? I'm in the Particulars, me. And I can see two of you. One of them's a lively lad who's going to help the proper authorities with their business and the other is a lippy little bugger who's going to try to be clever. One of these lads has a future, and all his teeth. Now the funny thing about me, it's a little habit of mine, is that I never ask a question twice. So . . . you're not a criminal, are you?'

Nobby, his eyes huge and fixed on the brass knuckles, shook his head.

'You just do what you have to to survive, right?'

Nobby nodded.

'In fact you were probably a decent lad before you fell in with the rebels, I expect. Sang hymns and that.'

Nobby nodded.

'This man who calls himself Sergeant Keel is the ringleader of the rebels, yes?'

There was a moment of hesitation, and then Nobby raised a hand. 'Um . . . everyone does what he tells them, is that the same thing?' he said.

'Yep. Is he charismatic?'

Nobby kept staring at the brass knuckles. 'Um, um, um, I don't know. I haven't heard him cough much.'

'And what do they talk about beyond the barricade, my little lad?'

'Um . . . well, Justice an' Truth an' Freedom and stuff,' said Nobby.

'Aha. Rebel talk!' said Carcer, straightening up.

'Is it?' said the major.

'Take it from me, major,' said Carcer. 'When you get a bunch of people using words like that, they're up to no good.' He looked down at Nobby. 'Now, I wonder what I've got in my pocket for a good boy, eh? Oh, yes . . . someone's ear. Still warm. Here you go, kid!'

'Cor, thanks, mister!'

'Now run a long way away or I'll gut yer.'

Nobby fled.

Carcer glanced at the map spread on the desk. 'Oh, you're planning a little sortie. That's *nice*. Don't want to upset the rebels, do we? Why aren't you bloody well *attacking*, major?'

'Well, they're not—'

'You're losing your troops to 'em! They hold a quarter of the city! And you're gonna sneak round the back. Across the bridge, I see, and up Elm Street. Quiet, like. Like you are *frightened*!' Carcer's hand smashed down on to the table, making the major jump.

'I'm frightened of no man!' he lied.

'You're the city right now!' said Carcer, a little speck of white foam appearing at the corner of his mouth. '*They* sneak. *You* don't. You ride right up to them and damn them to hell, that's what you do. They're stealing the streets from you! You take 'em back! They've put 'emselves beyond the Law! You take the Law to 'em!'

He stepped back, and the manic rage subsided as quickly as it had arrived.

'That's my advice,' he said. 'Of course, you know your own business best. Me and what's left of my poor lads, we're going to go out and fight. I'm sure their lordships will appreciate anything you feel you can do.'

He strode out, the Particulars falling in behind him.

'Er . . . you all right, Clive?' said the captain. Only the whites of the major's eyes were showing.

'What a *horrible* man,' said the major quietly.

'Er . . . yes, of course. On the other hand—'

'Yes, yes, yes. I know. We have no *choice*. We have orders. That . . . *weasel* is right. If the damn thing is there in the morning, I've got no career and nor have you. Show of strength, bold front, take no prisoners . . . that's what our orders are. Stupid, stupid orders.' He sighed.

'I suppose we could disobey . . .' said the captain.

'Are you mad? And then what would we do? Don't be a fool, Tom. Muster the men, get the ox teams hitched up, let's make a bit of a show for the sake of it. Let's just get it *over* with!'

Vimes was shaken awake. He looked up into his own face, younger, less lined, more terrified.

'Wha'?'

'They're bringing up siege weapons, sarge! They're coming down the *street*, sarge!'

'What? That's stupid! The barricade is highest here! A couple of men could defend it!'

Vimes leapt to his feet. It must be a feint. A stupid feint, too. Just here Waddy and his mates had wedged two big carts across the road, and they'd become the nucleus of a solid wall of wood and rubble. But there was a narrow, low entrance for people to come through, which let them into the Republic with their head at just the right height for a gentle tap if they turned out to be a soldier. People were scrambling through now like rats.

Vimes climbed up the barricade and looked over the top. At the far end of the street a big metal wall was advancing, surrounded by flaming torches. That was all there was to see, in a city without lights. But he knew what it was.

It was called Big Mary and it was mounted on a heavy cart. Vimes had seen it before. There would be a couple of oxen behind the cart, pushing it. The walls weren't solid metal, but merely a skin to stop defenders throwing fire at the wooden planks underneath. And the whole thing was simply to defend the men who, behind that cosy shelter, had the big, *big* hooks on the end of the long chains . . .

They'd fix them in the barricade, and the oxen would be turned around in the traces, and maybe another four beasts would be added and then there was *nothing* you could build of wood that wouldn't be pulled apart.

Between the cart and the barricade, struggling to escape from the crush, was a mass of frightened people.

'You got any orders, sarge?' said Fred Colon, pulling himself up alongside Vimes. He looked up the street. 'Oh dear,' he said.

'Yeah, this is when you need a couple of trolls on the force,' said Vimes. 'I reckon Detr—'

'Trolls? Huh, wouldn't work with any trolls,' said Colon. 'Too fick to take orders.'

You'll find out one day, thought Vimes, and said aloud: 'Okay. Anyone that can't or shouldn't have a weapon, they get back as far as possible, right? Get a message to Dickins, tell him we'll need anyone he can spare, but— blast it!'

What'd happened before? There'd been a lot of activity against the barricades, but it had been a feint while the cavalry were sneaking around outside. He didn't remember *this*.

He glanced at the oncoming wagon. At the top of the wobbling wall, on the other side, there was generally a narrow ledge for bowmen to stand and fire down at anyone trying to interfere with the demolition men.

In the treacherous light of the torches, Vimes thought he saw the features of Carcer. Even at this distance, there was something horribly recognizable about that expression.

Swing was dead. And when everyone's running around in confusion a man who is firm of purpose can push his way up by sheer nerve. After all, Vimes thought, *I* did.

He clambered down the barricade and looked at the men.

'I want a volunteer *no, not you, Sam*. Wiglet, you'll do. Your dad's a carpenter, right? Well, there's a carpenter's shop round the corner. *Run* and get me a couple of mallets and some wooden wedges, or long nails . . . something spiky. Go, go, go!'

Wiglet nodded and ran off.

'And . . . let's see, yeah, I need two-pennyworth of fresh ginger. Nancyball, nip around the corner to the apothecary, will you?'

'What's that any good for, sarge?' said Sam.

'Gingering things up.'

Vimes removed his helmet and armour, and nodded to the gap through which people were streaming.

'Fred, we'll be going out that way. Think you can push us a path?'

'I'll give it a go, sarge.' Fred squared his shoulders.

'We're going to stop that thing. They can't move it fast and with all this noise and confusion no one will notice a thing— that was quick, Billy . . .'

'I just grabbed everything, sarge,' panted Wiglet, running up with a small sack. 'I know what you want to do, sarge, I did it sometimes out of mischief when I was a kid—'

'Me too,' said Vimes. 'And here's my ginger. Ah, lovely. It brings tears to my eyes. Okay, Billy? Ready, Fred.'

It took all of Colon's bulk, with Vimes pushing behind him, to thrust a way through the desperate mob into the world beyond the barricade. In the darkness Vimes forced his way between the bodies, up to the side of the siege engine. It was like a huge slow ram pushing its way down the street, but jerking forward more slowly than a walking pace because of the press of people. Vimes fancied that Carcer probably enjoyed this ride.

He ducked under the cart, unseen in the mob, and grabbed a mallet and a wedge from Wiglet's bag.

'You do the left rear wheel and then make a run for it, Billy,' he said.

'But sarge—'

'That was an order. Get out, get back, get people off the street as fast as possible. Do it!'

Vimes crawled up to one of the front wheels and held the wedge ready between wheel and axle. The cart stopped for a moment, and he thrust the wedge into the gap and thumped it with the hammer. He had time for another blow before the cart gave a creak that suggested the oxen were pushing again. Then he crawled back quickly and took the sack from Billy before the

291

little man, with a reluctant glance, scuttled out into the forest of legs.

Vimes got a third wedge in before loud voices somewhere behind him indicated that the lack of progress had been noticed. The wheels rocked, and bound even further on the wedges. The wheels would have to come off before they could be got out.

Even so, oxen were powerful beasts. Enough of them would have no problem at all in dragging the cart as well as the barricade. But the nice thing, the *nice* thing, was that people thought of a barricade as something people tried to get into, not out of . . .

Vimes slipped out into the noisy, confusing night. There were soldiers, and watchmen, and refugees, all cursing at cross purposes. In the flickering shadows, Vimes was just another shape. He pushed his way confidently around to the straining oxen and their driver, who was prodding them with a stick. He was heartened by the fact that the man looked the kind of man who'd get six out of ten when answering the question: 'What is your name?'

Vimes didn't even stop. The important thing was not to let the other person have a chance to say 'But—', let alone 'Who the *hell* do you think you are?' He pushed the man aside and glared at the sweating beasts.

'Ah, right, I can see your problem right here,' he said, in the voice of one who knows everything there is to know about oxen. 'They've got the glaggies. But we can fix that. Hold up that one's tail. Hurry up, man!'

The ox poker responded to the voice of authority. Vimes palmed a lump of ginger. Here goes, he thought. At least it's somewhere warm on a cold night . . .

'Okay. Now the other one . . . right. Okay. Now, I'll just go around and, er . . . just go round . . .' said Vimes, hurrying back into the shadows.

He shouldered his way through the throng and dived through the tiny hole.

'It's all right, sarge, I spied you coming through Mrs Rutherford's dining-room chairs,' said Fred Colon, hauling him upright. 'Well, you stopped it, sarge, and no mistake. You really . . . urrrhg . . .'

'Yes, don't shake hands with me until I've had a wash,' said Vimes, heading for the pump.

He kept an ear cocked for any strange noises on the other side of the barricade. There were none for several seconds. And then he heard it . . .

Nothing much had happened for some while after his visit to the oxen except that, very slowly, their eyes had begun to cross and then, also quite slowly, turn red. It takes a long time for anything to happen inside the head of an ox, but, when it does, it happens extensively.

The moo started off low and rose slowly. It was a visceral sound that had rolled across the ancient tundra and told early man that here came dinner or death, and either way it was pissed off. It was the sound of a big beast that was still too small to restrain all the emotions that were welling up inside it. And it was a duet.

Vimes, hauling himself up the barricade, saw people running. Then the whole of Big Mary shuddered. That didn't look too impressive unless you knew that a couple of tons of wood had just jumped sideways. Then there was the sound of splintering, two of Big Mary's locked wheels collapsed, and she toppled side-ways in a mass of flame, splinters, smoke and dust.

Vimes counted under his breath, and had only reached two when a cartwheel rolled out of the smoke and away down the road. This always happens.

It wasn't over, though. The oxen, tangled in the remains of the shafts and harness, and now an enraged joint creature that could get only six legs out of eight on the ground, headed erratically but with surprising speed in the opposite direction.

The other oxen, which had been waiting for the big pull, watched it approach. They were already spooked by the crash, and now they caught the stink of terror and fury and began a slow stampede away from it and towards, as it turned out, the waiting bowmen behind them who, in turn, tried to run into the cavalry. The horses were not inclined to be well behaved towards armed men in any case and were also in a state of some apprehension. They relieved this by kicking the hell out of anyone close.

It was hard for the watchers along the barricade to see much of what happened after that, but the noises were very interesting for quite some time.

Sergeant Colon's mouth shut. 'Bloody hell, sarge,' he said, admiringly. In the distance, glass shattered.

'They'll be back,' said Vimes.

'Yeah, but not all of 'em,' said Wiglet. 'Well done, sarge.'

Vimes turned, and saw Sam staring at him in wide-eyed hero worship.

'I was lucky, lad,' he said. 'But it helps to remember little details and not mind getting your hands dirty.'

'But we could *win* now, sarge,' said Sam.

'No, we can't. But we can put off losing until it doesn't hurt too much.' Vimes turned to the others. 'Right, lads, back to work. We've had some fun, but dawn's a long way off.'

The news had got around even before he'd climbed down from the barricade. There was a cheer from the crowd, and a general struttiness about the armed men. We'd shown them, eh? They don't like the taste of cold steel, those . . . er . . . other people from Ankh-Morpork! We'll show 'em, eh?

And it had taken a few wedges, some raw ginger and a lot of luck. That wouldn't happen twice.

Maybe it wouldn't need to. He remembered hearing about the assassination. It was all very mysterious. Winder had been killed in a room full of people, and no one saw a thing. Magic had been suggested, and hotly denied by the wizards. Some historians had said that it happened because troops around the palace had been sent to attack the barricades, but that didn't answer the question. Anyone who could stab a man to death in a brightly lit room full of people surely wouldn't find some guards in the darkness any kind of obstacle . . .

Of course, with Snapcase as new Patrician, no one had tried very hard to establish the facts in any case. People said things like 'quite possibly we shall never know the truth' which meant, in Vimes's personal lexicon, 'I know, or think I know what the truth is, and hope like hell it doesn't come out, because things are all smoothed over now.'

Supposing we don't lose?

Keel hadn't killed Big Mary. She hadn't been used in the other present. The soldiers hadn't been stupid enough to try it. That sort of thing was okay to deal with little local affairs manned by civilians, but it was a joke if you put it up against stout defences manned by professionals. Now she was a wreck, the attackers would have to think up a new plan in a hurry, and time was moving on . . .

Supposing we don't lose?

All they had to do was hold out. The people at the top had very short memories. Winder is mysteriously dead, long live Lord Snapcase! And suddenly all the rebels become glorious freedom fighters. And there's seven unfilled graves in the cemetery . . .

Would he be *able* to go back, then? Supposing Madam was right and he got offered the post of Commander, not as a bribe, but because he'd earned it? That'd change history!

He took out the cigar case and stared hard at the inscription.

Let's see, he thought . . . if I never met Sybil, we wouldn't get married and she wouldn't buy me this, and so I couldn't be looking at it . . .

He stared hard at the curly engraving, almost willing it to disappear. It didn't.

On the other hand, that old monk had said that whatever happens, stays happened. And now Vimes had a mental picture of Sybil and Carrot and Detritus and all the rest of

295

them, frozen in a moment that'd never have a next moment.

He wanted to go home. He wanted it so much that he trembled at the thought. But if the price of that was selling good men to the night, if the price was filling those graves, if the price was not fighting with every trick he knew . . . then it was too high.

It wasn't a decision that he was making, he knew. It was happening far below the areas of the brain that made decisions. It was something built in. There was no universe, anywhere, where a Sam Vimes would give in on this, because if he did then he wouldn't be Sam Vimes any more.

The writing stayed on the silver but it was blurred now because of the tears welling up. They were tears of anger, mostly at himself. There was not a thing that he could do. He hadn't bought a ticket and he hadn't wanted to come, but now he was on the ride and couldn't get off until the end.

What else had the old monk said? History finds a way? Well, it was going to have to come up with something good, because it was up against Sam Vimes now.

He glanced up, and saw young Sam watching him.

'You okay, sarge?'

'Fine, fine.'

'Only you've been sitting there for twenty minutes looking at your cigars.'

Vimes coughed, and tucked the case away, and pulled himself together.

'Half the pleasure's in the anticipation,' he said.

The night wore on. News came through, from barricades at bridges and gates. There were forays, more to test the defenders' strength of will than make a serious dent in the defences. And there were even more deserters.

One reason for the desertion rate was that those people of a practical turn of mind were working out the subtle economics. The Republic of Treacle Mine Road lacked all the big, important buildings in the city, the ones that traditional rebels were

296

supposed to take. It had no government offices, no banks and very few temples. It was almost completely bereft of important civic architecture.

All it had was the unimportant stuff. It had the entire slaughterhouse district, and the butter market, and the cheese market. It had the tobacco factors and the candlemakers and most of the fruit and vegetable warehouses and the grain and flour stores. This meant that while the Republicans were being starved of important things like government, banking services and salvation, they were self-sufficient in terms of humdrum, everyday things like food and drink.

People are content to wait a long time for salvation, but prefer dinner to turn up inside an hour.

'A present from the lads down at the Shambles, sarge,' said Dickins, arriving with a wagon. 'They said it'd only spoil otherwise. Is it okay for me to dish 'em out to the field kitchens?'

'What've you got?' said Vimes.

'Steaks, mostly,' said the old sergeant, grinning. 'But I liberated a sack of onions in the name of the revolution!' He saw Vimes's expression change. 'No, sarge, the man gave them to me, see. They need eating, he said.'

'What did I tell you? Every meal will be a feast in the People's Republic!' said Reg Shoe, striding up. He still hung on to his clipboard; people like Reg tend to. 'If you could just take it along to the official warehouse, sergeant?'

'What warehouse?'

Reg sighed. 'All food must go into the common warehouse and be distributed by my officials according to—'

'Mr Shoe,' said Dickins, 'there's a cart with five hundred chickens coming up behind me, and there's another full of eggs. There's nowhere to send 'em, see? The butchers have filled up the ice-houses and smoke-rooms and the only place we can store this grub is in our guts. I ain't particularly bothered about officials.'

'On behalf of the Republic I order you—' Reg began, and Vimes put his hand on his shoulder.

'Off you go, sergeant,' he said, nodding to Dickins. 'A word in your ear, Reg?'

'Is this a military coop?' said Reg uncertainly, holding his clipboard.

'No, it's just that we're under siege here, Reg. This is not the time. Let Sergeant Dickins sort it out. He's a fair man, he just doesn't like clipboards.'

'But supposing people get left out?' said Reg.

'There's enough for everyone to eat themselves sick, Reg.'

Reg Shoe looked uncertain and disappointed, as though this prospect was less pleasing than carefully rationed scarcity.

'But I'll tell you what,' said Vimes. 'If this goes on, the city will see to it the deliveries come in by other gates. We'll be hungry then. *That's* when we'll need your organizational skills.'

'You mean we'll be in a famine situation?' said Reg, the light of hope in his eyes.

'If we aren't, Reg, I'm sure you could organize one,' said Vimes, and realized he'd gone just a bit too far. Reg was only stupid in certain areas, and now he looked as though he was going to cry.

'I just think it's important to be fair—' the man began.

'Yeah, Reg. I understand. But there's a time and a place, you know? Maybe the best way to build a bright new world is to peel some spuds in this one? Now, off you go. And you, Lance-Constable Vimes, you go and help him . . .'

Vimes climbed back up the barricade. The city beyond was dark again, with only the occasional chink of light from a shuttered window. By comparison the streets of the Republic were ablaze.

In a few hours the shops out there were expecting deliveries, and they weren't going to arrive. The government couldn't sit this one out. A city like Ankh-Morpork was only two meals away from chaos at the best of times.

Every day, maybe a hundred cows died for Ankh-Morpork. So did a flock of sheep and a herd of pigs and the gods alone knew how many ducks, chickens and geese. Flour? He'd heard it was eighty tons, and about the same amount of potatoes and maybe twenty tons of herring. He didn't particularly *want* to know this kind of thing, but once you started having to sort out the everlasting traffic problem these were facts that got handed to you.

Every day, forty thousand eggs were laid for the city. Every day, hundreds, *thousands* of carts and boats and barges converged on the city with fish and honey and oysters and olives and eels and lobsters. And then think of the horses dragging this stuff, and the windmills . . . and the wool coming in, too, every day, the cloth, the tobacco, the spices, the ore, the timber, the cheese, the coal, the fat, the tallow, the hay *EVERY DAMN DAY* . . .

And that was *now*. Back home, the city was twice as big . . .

Against the dark screen of night, Vimes had a vision of Ankh-Morpork. It wasn't a city, it was a *process*, a weight on the world that distorted the land for hundreds of miles around. People who'd never see it in their whole life nevertheless spent their life working for it. Thousands and thousands of green acres were part of it, forests were part of it. It drew in and consumed . . .

. . . and gave back the dung from its pens and the soot from its chimneys, and steel, and saucepans, and all the tools by which its food was made. And also clothes, and fashions and ideas and interesting vices, songs and knowledge and something which, if looked at in the right light, was called civilization. That's what civilization *meant*. It meant the city.

Was anyone else out there thinking about this?

A lot of the stuff came in through the Onion Gate and the Shambling Gate, both now Republican and solidly locked. There'd be a military picket on them, surely. Right now, there were carts on the way that'd find those gates closed to them. Yet

299

no matter what the politics, eggs hatch and milk sours and herds of driven animals need penning and watering and where was that going to happen? Would the military sort it out? Well, would they? While the carts rumbled up, and then were hemmed in by the carts behind, and the pigs escaped and the cattle herds wandered off?

Was anyone *important* thinking about this? Suddenly the machine was wobbling, but Winder and his cronies didn't think about the machine, they thought about money. Meat and drink came from servants. They happened.

Vetinari, Vimes realized, thought about this sort of thing all the time. The Ankh-Morpork back home was twice as big and four times as vulnerable. He wouldn't have let something like this happen. Little wheels must spin so that the machine can turn, he'd say.

But now, in the dark, it all spun on Vimes. If the man breaks down, it all breaks down, he thought. The whole machine breaks down. And it goes on breaking down. And it breaks down the people.

Behind him, he heard a relief squad marching down Heroes Street.

'—how do they rise? They rise *knees* up! *knees* up! *knees* up! They rise *knees* up, knees up high. All the little angels—'

For a moment Vimes wondered, looking out through a gap in the furniture, if there wasn't something in Fred's idea about moving the barricades on and on, like a sort of sieve, street by street. You could let through the decent people, and push the bastards, the rich bullies, the wheelers and dealers in people's fates, the leeches, the hangers-on, the brown-nosers and courtiers and smarmy plump devils in expensive clothes, all those people who didn't know or care about the machine but stole its grease, push them into a smaller and smaller compass and then leave them in there. Maybe you could toss some food in every couple of days, or maybe you could leave 'em to do what they'd always done, which was live off other people . . .

There wasn't much noise from the dark streets. Vimes wondered what was going on. He wondered if anyone out there was taking care of business.

Major Mountjoy-Standfast stared empty-eyed at the damn, damn map.

'How many, then?' he said.

'Thirty-two men injured, sir. And another twenty probable desertions,' said Captain Wrangle. 'And Big Mary is firewood, of course.'

'Oh gods . . .'

'Do you want to hear the rest, sir?'

'There's more?'

'I'm afraid there is, sir. Before the remains of Big Mary left Heroes Street, sir, she smashed twenty shop windows and various carts, doing damage estimated at—'

'Fortunes of war, captain. We can't help that!'

'No, sir.' The captain coughed. 'Do you want to know what happened next, sir?'

'Next? There was a next?' said the major, beginning to panic.

'Um . . . yes, sir. Quite a lot of next, actually, sir. Um. The three gates through which most of the agricultural produce comes into the city are picketed, sir, on your orders, so the carters and drovers are trying to bring their stuff along Short Street, sir. Fortunately not too many animals at this time of night, sir, but there were six millers' wagons, one wagon of, er, dried fruits and spices, four dairymen's wagons and three hegglers' carts. All wrecked, sir. Those oxen really were *very* feisty, sir.'

'Hegglers? What the hell are hegglers?' said the major, bewildered.

'Egg marketers, sir. They travel around the farms, pick up the eggs—'

'Yes, all right! And what are we supposed to do?'

'We could make an enormous cake, sir.'

'Tom!'

'Sorry, sir. But the city doesn't *stop*, you see. It's not like a battlefield. The best place for urban fighting is right out in the countryside, sir, where there's nothing else in the way.'

'It's a bloody big barricade, Tom. Too well defended. We can't even set fire to the damn thing, it'll take the city up with it!'

'Yes, sir. And the point is, sir, that they're not actually *doing* anything, sir. Except being there.'

'What do you mean?'

'They're even putting old grannies up on the barricades, shouting down to the lads. Poor Sergeant Franklin, sir, his granny saw him and said that if he didn't turn it up she'd tell everyone what he did when he was eleven, sir.'

'The men are armed, aren't they?' said the major, wiping his forehead.

'Oh, yes. But we've kind of advised them not to shoot unarmed old ladies, sir. We don't want another Dolly Sisters, do we, sir?'

The major stared at the map. There was a solution, he felt. 'Well, what *did* Sergeant Franklin do when he was—' he said absent-mindedly.

'She didn't say, sir.'

A sudden feeling of relief stole over the major. 'Captain, you know what this is now?'

'I'm sure you'll tell me, sir.'

'I will, Tom, I will. This is *political*, Tom. We're soldiers. Political goes higher up.'

'You're *right*, sir. Well done, sir!'

'Dig out a lieutenant who has been a bit slack lately and send him up to tell their lordships,' said the major.

'Isn't that a bit cruel, sir?'

'Of course it is. This is *politics* now.'

Lord Albert Selachii didn't much like parties. There was too much politics. And he particularly didn't like this one because it meant he was in the same room as Lord Winder, a man who, deep down, he believed to be A Bad Sort. In his personal vocabulary, there was no greater condemnation. What made it worse was that, while seeking to avoid him, he also had to try at the same time to avoid Lord Venturi. Their families cordially detested one another. Lord Albert wasn't sure, now, what event in history had caused the rift, but it must have been important, obviously, otherwise it would be silly to go on like this. Had the Selachii and the Venturi been hill clans, they would have been a-feudin' and a-fightin'; since they were two of the city's leading families they were chillingly, viciously, icily polite to each other whenever social fate forced them together. And right now his careful orbit of the less dangerously political areas of the damn party had brought him face to face with Lord Charles Venturi. It was bad enough having to campaign with the feller, he thought, without being forced to talk to him over some rather inferior wine, but currently the party's tides offered no way of escape without being impolite. And, curiously, upper-class etiquette in Ankh-Morpork held that, while you could snub your friends any time you felt like it, it was the height of bad form to be impolite to your worst enemy.

'Venturi,' he said, raising his glass a carefully calculated fraction of an inch.

'Selachii,' said Lord Venturi, doing the same thing.

'This is a party,' said Albert.

'Indeed. I see you are standing upright.'

'Indeed. So are you, I see.'

'Indeed. Indeed. On that subject, I notice many others are doing the same thing.'

'Which is not to say that the horizontal position does not have its merits when it comes to, for example, sleeping,' said Albert.

'Quite so. Obviously that would not be done here.'

'Oh, indeed. Indeed.'*

---

* The Selachii and the Venturi made a point, on occasions like this, to talk only about things on which there was no possibility of disagreement. Given the history of the two families, this had become a very small number of things.

A brisk lady in a magnificent purple dress advanced across the ballroom floor, her smile travelling in front of her.

'Lord Selachii?' she said, proffering a hand. 'I hear you have been doing sterling work defending us from the mob!'

His lordship, on social automatic pilot, bowed stiffly. He wasn't used to forward women, and this one was all forward. However, all safe topics of conversation with a Venturi had been exhausted.

'I fear you have the advantage of me, madam . . .' he murmured.

'I certainly expect so!' said Madam, giving him such a radiant smile that he didn't analyse her actual words. 'And who is this imposing military gentleman? A comrade in arms?'

Lord Selachii floundered. He'd been brought up knowing that you always introduced men *to* women, and this smiling lady hadn't told him her—

'Lady Roberta Meserole,' she said. 'Most people who know me call me Madam. But my friends call me Bobbi.'

Lord Venturi clicked his heels. He was quicker on the uptake than his 'comrade in arms' and his wife told him more of the current gossip.

'Ah, you must be the lady from Genua,' he said, taking her hand. 'I have heard so much about you.'

'Anything good?' said Madam.

His lordship glanced across the room. His wife appeared to be deep in conversation. He knew to his cost that her wifely radar could fry an egg half a mile away. But the champagne had been good.

'Mostly expensive,' he said, which didn't sound quite as witty as he intended. She laughed anyway. Perhaps I *was* witty, he thought. I say, this champagne really is excellent . . .

'A woman has to make her way in the world as best she can,' she said.

'May I make so bold as to ask if there is a Lord Meserole?' he said.

'So early in the evening?' said Madam, and laughed again. Lord Venturi found himself laughing with her. My word, he told himself, this wit is a lot easier than I thought!

'No, of course I meant—' he began.

'I'm sure you did,' said Madam, tapping him lightly with her fan. 'Now, I mustn't monopolize you, but I really must drag both of you away to talk to some of my friends . . .'

She took Lord Venturi by the unresisting arm and piloted him across the floor. Selachii followed morosely, being of the opinion that when respectable women called themselves Bobbi the world was about to end, and ought to.

'Mr Carter has extensive interests in copper and Mr Jones is very interested in rubber,' she whispered.

There were about six men in the group, talking in low voices. As their lordships approached they caught '—and at a time like this one really must ask oneself where one's true loyalties lie . . . oh, good evening, Madam . . .'

On her apparently random walk to the buffet table Madam happened to meet several other gentlemen and, like a good hostess, piloted them in the direction of other small groups. Probably only someone lying on the huge beams that spanned the hall high above would spot any pattern, and even then they'd have to know the code. If they had been in a position to put a red spot on the heads of those people who were not friends of the Patrician, and a white spot on those who were his cronies, and a pink spot on those who were perennial waverers, then they would have seen something like a dance taking place.

There were not many whites.

They would have seen that there were several groups of reds, and white spots were being introduced into them in ones, or twos if the number of reds in the group was large enough. If a white left a group, he or she was effortlessly scooped up and shunted into another conversation which might contain one or two pinks but was largely red.

Any conversation entirely between white spots was gently

broken up with a smile and an 'oh, but now you must meet—', or was joined by several red spots. Pinks, meanwhile, were delicately passed from red group to red group until they were *deeply* pink, and then they were allowed to mix with other pinks of the same hue, under the supervision of a red.

In short, the pinks met so many reds, and so few whites, that they probably forgot about whites at all, while the whites, constantly alone or hugely outnumbered by reds or deep pinks, appeared to be going red out of embarrassment or a desire to blend in.

Lord Winder was entirely surrounded by reds, leaving the few remaining whites out in the cold. He looked like all the Patricians tended to look after a certain time in office – unpleasantly plump, with the pink jowliness of a man of normal build who had too much rich food. He was sweating slightly in this quite cool room, and his eyes swivelled this way and that, looking for the flaws, the clues, the angles.

At last Madam reached the buffet, where Dr Follett was helping himself to the devilled eggs and Miss Rosemary Palm was debating with herself as to whether the future should contain strange pastry things with a green filling that hinted mysteriously of prawn.

'And how are we doing, do we think?' said Dr Follett, apparently to a swan carved out of ice.

'We are doing well,' Madam told a basket of fruit. 'There's four, however, that are still proving awkward.'

'I know them,' said the doctor. 'They'll fall into place, trust me. What else can they do? We're used to this game here. We know that if you complain too loudly when you lose, you might not be asked to play again. But I shall station some stout friends near them, just in case their resolve needs a little . . . bolstering.'

'He is suspicious,' said Miss Palm.

'When isn't he?' said Dr Follett. 'Go and talk to him.'

'Where is our new best friend, doctor?' said Madam.

'Mr Snapcase is dining quietly but visibly, in impeccable company, some way away.'

They turned when the double doors opened. So did several of the other guests, who then turned back hastily. But it was only a servant, who hurried over to Madam and whispered something. She indicated the two military commanders, and the man went to hover anxiously beside them. There was a brief exchange and then, without even a bow towards Lord Winder, all three men went out.

'I shall just go and see to the arrangements,' said Madam, and, without in any sense following the men, headed towards the doors.

When she stepped into the hall the two servants waiting by the cake stopped lounging and snapped to attention, and a guard who was patrolling the corridor gave her a quick glance of interrogation.

'Now, madam?' said one of the servants.

'What? Oh. No! Just wait.' She glided over to where the commanders were in animated conversation with a couple of junior officers, and took Lord Venturi's arm.

'Oh dear, Charles, are you leaving us so soon?'

Lord Venturi didn't think of wondering how she knew his first name. The champagne had been plentiful, and he saw no reason at the moment why any attractive woman of a certain age shouldn't know his name.

'Oh, there are one or two pockets of resistance left,' he said. 'Nothing to concern you, Madam.'

'Bloody big pocket,' murmured Lord Selachii, into his moustache.

'They destroyed Big Mary, sir,' said the luckless messenger. 'And they—'

'Major Mountjoy-Standfast can't outthink a bunch of gormless watchmen and civilians and some veterans with garden forks?' said Lord Venturi, who had no idea of how much damage a garden fork could do if hurled straight down from an elevation of twenty feet.

'That's just it, sir, they are veterans and they know all—'

'And the civilians? Unarmed civilians?' said Venturi.

The messenger, who was a sub-lieutenant and very nervous, couldn't find the right words to explain that 'unarmed civilian' was stretching a point when it was a 200lb slaughterhouse man with a long hook in one hand and a flensing knife in the other. Young men who'd joined up for the uniform and a bed all to themselves did not expect that kind of treatment.

'Permission to speak freely, sir?' he tried.

'Very well!'

'The men haven't got the heart for it, sir. They'd kill a Klatchian in a wink, sir, but . . . well, some of the old soldiers are from the regiment, sir, and they're shouting down all kinds of stuff. A lot of the men come from down there, and it's not good for them. And what some of the old ladies shout, sir, well, I've never heard such language. Dolly Sisters was bad enough, sir, but this is a bit too much. Sorry, sir.'

Their lordships looked out of the window. There was half a regiment in the palace grounds, men who'd had nothing to do for several days but stand guard.

'Some backbone and a quick thrust,' said Selachii. 'That's what's needed, by Io! Lance the boil! This is not a cavalry action, Venturi. And I'll take *those* men. Fresh blood.'

'Selachii, we do have orders—'

'We have all kinds of orders,' said Selachii. 'But we know where the enemy is, don't we? Aren't there enough guards here? How many guards does one fool need?'

'We can't just—' Lord Venturi began, but Madam said, 'I'm sure Charles will see that no harm comes to his lordship,' and took his arm. 'He does have his sword, after all . . .'

A few minutes later, Madam glanced out of the window and saw that the troops were quietly moving out.

She also noticed, after watching for some time, that the guard patrolling in the hall seemed to have vanished.

There were rules. When you had a Guild of Assassins, there had to be rules which everyone knew and which were never, ever broken.*

An Assassin, a real Assassin, had to look like one – black clothes, hood, boots and all. If they could wear any clothes, any disguise, then what could anyone do but spend all day sitting in a small room with a loaded crossbow pointed at the door?

And they couldn't kill a man incapable of defending himself (although a man worth more than AM$10,000 a year was considered automatically capable of defending himself or at least of employing people to do it for him).

And they had to give the target a chance.

But there was no helping some people. It was regrettable how many rulers of the city had been inhumed by the men in black because they didn't recognize a chance when they saw it, didn't know when they'd gone too far, didn't care that they'd made too many enemies, didn't read the signs, didn't know when to walk away after embezzling a moderate and acceptable amount of cash. They didn't realize it when the machine had stopped, when the world was ripe for change, when it was time, in fact, to spend more time with their family in case they ended up spending it with their ancestors.

Of course, the Guild didn't inhume their rulers on their own behalf. There was a rule about that, too. They were simply there when needed.

There was a tradition, once, far back in the past, called the King of the Bean. A special dish was served to all the men of the clan on a certain day of the year. It contained one small hard-baked bean, and whoever got the bean was, possibly after some dental attention, hailed as King. It was quite an inexpensive system and it worked well, probably because the clever little bald men who actually ran things and paid some attention to

---

* Sometimes, admittedly, for a given value of 'never'.

possible candidates were experts at palming a bean into the right bowl.

And while the crops ripened and the tribe thrived and the land was fertile the King thrived too. But when, in the fullness of time, crops failed and the ice came back and animals were inexplicably barren, the clever little bald men sharpened their long knives, which were *mostly* used for cutting mistletoe.

And on the due night, one of them went into his cave and carefully baked one small bean.

Of course, that was before people were civilized. These days, no one had to eat beans.

People were *still* working on the barricade. It had become a sort of general hobby, a kind of group home improvement. Fire buckets, some full of water, some of sand, had turned up. In places the barricade was more impregnable than the city walls, considering how often the latter had been pillaged for stone.

There were occasional drumbeats down in the city, and the sound of troop movements.

'Sergeant?'

Vimes looked down. A face had appeared at the top of the ladder leading down to the street.

'Ah, Miss Battye? I didn't know you were with us.'

'I didn't intend to be, but suddenly there was this big wall . . .'

She climbed all the way up. She was holding a small bucket.

'Doctor Lawn presents his compliments and says how come you haven't beaten up anyone yet?' she said, putting it down. 'He says he's got three tables scrubbed, two buckets of tar on the boil, six ladies rolling bandages and all he's had to deal with so far is a nose-bleed. You've let him down, he says.'

'Tell him ha, ha, ha,' said Vimes.

'I've brought you up some breakfast,' said Sandra, and Vimes realized that down below, doing their not-very-best to remain unseen, were some of the lads. They were sniggering.

'Mushrooms?' he said.

'No,' said the girl. 'I was told to tell you that since it's to-morrow, you're going to get everything you wished for . . .'

For a moment Vimes tensed, not certain where the world was taking him.

'A hard-boiled egg,' said Sandra. 'But Sam Vimes said you probably like the yolk runny and some toast cut up into soldiers.'

'Just like he does,' said Vimes weakly. 'Good guess, that man.'

Vimes tossed the egg up into the air, expecting to catch it when it came down. Instead, there was a noise like scissors closing and the air rained runny yolk and bits of shell. And then it rained arrows.

The noise level of the conversation had gone up. Madam moved in on the group around Lord Winder. Magically, within ten seconds they were left alone as all the other people in the group saw people across the room that they really had to talk to.

'Who are yer?' said Winder, his eyes surveying her with that care a man takes when he fears that a woman is carrying concealed weaponry.

'Madam Roberta Meserole, my lord.'

'The one from Genua?' Winder snorted, which was his attempt at a snigger. 'I've heard stories about Genua!'

'I could probably tell you a few more, my lord,' said Madam. 'But, right now, it's time for the cake.'

'Yeah,' said Winder. 'Did you know we got another assassin tonight? They keep trying, you know. Eleven years, and still they try. But I get 'em, every time, sneak about though they may.'

'Well done, my lord,' said Madam. It did help that he was an unpleasant person, ugly clear to the bone. In some ways, it made things easier. She turned, and clapped her hands. Surprisingly, this small noise caused a sudden cessation in the chatter.

The double doors at the end of the hall opened, and two

trumpeters appeared. They took up positions on either side of the door—

'Stop 'em!' Winder yelled, and ducked. His two guards ran down the hall and grabbed the trumpets from the frightened men. They handled them with extreme care, as if expecting them to explode or issue a strange gas.

'Poison darts,' said Winder in a satisfied voice. 'Can't be too careful, madam. In this job you learn to watch every shadow. All right, let 'em play. But no trumpets. I 'ate tubes pointed at me.'

There was some bewildered conversation at the other end of the hall, and then the bereft trumpeters stood back and whistled as best they could.

Lord Winder laughed as the cake was pushed in. It was in tiers, about man-height, and heavily iced.

'Lovely,' he said, as the crowd clapped. 'I do like some entertainment at a party. And I cut it, do I?'

He took a few steps back and nodded at the bodyguards. 'Off you go, boys,' he said.

Swords stabbed into the top tier several times. The guards looked at Winder and shook their heads.

'There's such a thing as dwarfs, you know,' he said.

They stabbed at the second layer, again meeting no more resistance than can be offered by dried fruit and suet and a crust of marzipan with sugar frosting.

'He could be kneeling down,' said Winder.

The audience watched, their smiles frozen. When it became clear that the cake was solid and unoccupied, the food taster was sent for. Most of the guests recognized him. His name was Spymould. He was said to have eaten so much poison in his time that he was proof against anything, and that he ate a toad every day to keep in condition. It was also rumoured that he could turn silver black by breathing on it.

He selected a piece of cake and chewed it thoughtfully, staring intently upwards while he did so.

'Hmm,' he said, after a while.

'Well?' said Winder.

'Sorry, milord,' said Spymould. 'Nuffin'. I thought there was a touch of cyanide there but, no luck, it's just the almonds.'

'No poison at all?' said the Patrician. 'You mean it's edible?'

'Well, yes. It'd be all the better for some toad, o'course, but that's just one man's opinion.'

'Perhaps the servants can serve it now, my lord?' said Madam.

'Don't trust servants serving food,' said Winder. 'Sneakin' about. Could slip somethin' in.'

'Do you mind if I do it, then, my lord?'

'Yeah, all right,' said Lord Winder, watching the cake carefully. 'I'll have the ninth piece you cut.' But in fact he snatched the fifth piece, triumphantly, as if saving something precious from the wreckage.

The cake was disassembled. Lord Winder's objection to servants handling food withered once the food was headed for other people, and so the party spread out a little as the guests pondered the ancient question of how to hold a plate and a glass and eat at the same time without using one of those little glass-holding things that clip on the side of the plate and make the user look as though they're four years old. This takes a lot of concentration, and that might have been why everyone was so curiously self-absorbed.

The door opened. A figure walked into the room. Winder looked up, over the top of his plate.

It was a slim figure, hooded and masked, all in black.

Winder stared. Around him, the conversation rose, and a watcher above might have noticed that the drift of the party tides was such that they were leaving a wide empty path, stretching from the door all the way to Winder, whose legs didn't want to move.

As it strolled towards him the figure reached both hands behind it and they came back each holding a small pistol bow. There were a couple of small *tic* noises and the bodyguards collapsed gently towards the floor. Then it tossed the bows behind it, and kept coming. Its footfalls made no sound.

'Brw?' said Winder, staring. His mouth was open, and stuffed with cake. People chattered on. Somewhere, someone had told a joke. There was laughter, perhaps a shade shriller than might normally be the case. The noise level rose again.

Winder blinked. Assassins didn't do this. They snuck around. They used the shadows. This didn't happen in real life. This was how it happened in dreams.

And now the creature was in front of him. He dropped his spoon, and there was a sudden silence after it clanged on the ground.

There was another rule. Wherever possible, the inhumed should be told who the Assassin was, and who had sent him. It was felt by the Guild that this was only fair. Winder did not know this, and it was not widely advertised, but nevertheless, in the midst of terror, eyes wide, he asked the right questions.

'Who sent yer?'

'I come from the city,' said the figure, drawing a thin, silvery sword.

'Who are yer?'

'Think of me as . . . your future.'

The figure drew the sword back, but it was too late. Terror's own more subtle knife had done its work. Winder's face was crimson, his eyes were staring at nothing, and coming up from the throat, through the crumbs of cake, was a sound that merged a creak with a sigh.

The dark figure lowered its sword, watched for a moment in the echoing silence, and then said: 'Boo.'

It reached out one gloved hand and gave the Patrician a push. Winder went over backwards, his plate dropping from his hand and shattering on the tiles.

The Assassin held his bloodless sword at arm's length and let it drop on the floor beside the corpse. Then he turned and walked slowly back across the marble floor. He shut the double doors behind him, and the echoes died away.

Madam counted slowly to ten before she screamed. That seemed long enough.

Lord Winder got to his feet, and looked up at the black-clad figure.

'Another one? Where did you creep in from?'

I DO NOT CREEP.

Winder's mind felt even fuzzier than it had done over the past few years, but he was certain about cake. He'd been eating cake, and now there wasn't any. Through the mists he saw it, apparently close but, when he tried to reach it, a long way away.

A certain realization dawned on him.

'Oh,' he said.

YES, said Death.

'Not even time to finish my cake?'

NO. THERE IS NO MORE TIME, EVEN FOR CAKE. FOR YOU, THE CAKE IS OVER. YOU HAVE REACHED THE END OF CAKE.

A grapnel thudded into the wall beside Vimes. There were shouts along the barricade. More hooks snaked up and bit into the wood.

Another rain of arrows clattered on the roofs of the houses. The attackers weren't ready to risk hitting their own side, but arrows were snapping and bouncing in the street below. Vimes heard shouts, and the clang of arrows on armour.

A sound made him turn. A helmeted head rose level with his and the face beneath it blanched in terror when it saw Vimes.

'That was my *egg*, you bastard!' he screamed, punching the nose. 'With soldiers!'

The man fell back, by the sound of it, on to other climbers. Men were yelling all along the parapet.

Vimes pulled out his truncheon. 'At 'em, lads,' he yelled.

315

'Truncheons! Nothing fancy! Bop 'em on the fingers and let gravity do the work! They're goin' *down*!'

He ducked, pressing close to the wood, and tried to find a spyhole—

'They're using big catapults,' said Sandra, who'd found a gap a few feet away. 'There's a—'

Vimes pulled her away. 'What are you doing still up here?' he roared.

'It's safer than the street!' she yelled back, nose to nose with him.

'Not if one of those grapnels hits you it isn't!' He grabbed his knife. 'Here, take this . . . you see a rope anywhere, cut it!'

He scurried along behind the shelter of the wobbling parapet, but the defenders were doing very well. It wasn't exactly rocket magic, in any case. The people at ground level were firing out through any crack they could find and, while aiming was not easy, it didn't need to be. There is nothing like the zip and zing of arrows around them to make people nervous at their work.

And the climbers were too bunched up. They had to be. If they tried attacking on a broad front there'd be three defenders to greet each man. So they were in one another's way, and every falling man would take a couple more down with him, and the barricade was full of little gaps and holes where a defender with a spear could seriously prod those trying to climb up the outside.

This is *stupid*, Vimes thought. It'd take a thousand men to break through, and that'd only be when the last fifty ran up the slope made of the bodies of all the rest of them. Someone out there is doing the old 'hit them at their strongest point to show 'em we mean business' thinking. Ye gods, is this how we won our wars?

So how would I have dealt with this? Well, I'd have said 'Detritus, remove the barricade' and made sure that the defenders heard me, that's what I'd have done. End of problem.

There was a scream from further along the parapet. A grapnel had caught one of the watchmen and pulled him hard against the wood. Vimes reached him in time to see a hook dragged into the man's body, through breastplate and mail, as an attacker hauled himself up—

Vimes caught the man's sword arm in one hand and punched him with the other, letting him tumble into the mêlée below.

The stricken watchman was Nancyball. His face was blue-white, his mouth opened and shut soundlessly, and blood pooled around his feet. It dripped through the planks.

'Let's get the bloody thing out—' Wiglet said, grabbing the hook. Vimes pushed him away, as a couple of arrows hummed overhead.

'That could do *more* damage. Call up some lads, take him down really *carefully* and get him to Lawn.' Vimes snatched up Nancyball's truncheon and brought it down on the helmet of another struggling climber.

'He's still breathing, sarge!' said Wiglet.

'Right, right,' said Vimes. It was amazing how willing people were to see life in the corpse of a friend. 'So make yourself useful and get him down to the doctor.' And, speaking as one who'd seen some stricken men in his time, he mentally added: *and if Lawn can sort* him *out, he can start his own religion.*

A lucky attacker, who'd achieved the top of the barricade and then found himself horribly alone, slashed desperately at Vimes with his sword. Vimes turned back to business.

Ankh-Morpork was good at this, and had become good at it without anyone ever discussing it. Things *flowed* rather than happened; that is, you'd sometimes have to look quite hard to find the point of change between 'hasn't been done yet' and 'already taken care of, old boy'. And that was how it was done. Things were taken care of.

It was twenty minutes before Mr Snapcase arrived and twenty-five minutes before he was duly sworn in as Patrician, had magically become Lord Snapcase and was sitting in the

Oblong Office; this included the one minute's silence for the late Lord Winder, whose body had been taken care of.

A number of servants were shown the door without any great unpleasantness, and even Spymould was allowed to remove his toad farm in peace. But those who filled the grates and dusted the furniture and swept the floors stayed on, as they had stayed on before, because they seldom paid any attention to, or possibly didn't even know, who their lord was, and in any case were too useful and knew where the brooms were kept. Lords come and go, but dust accumulates.

And it was the morning of a new day which looked, seen from below, quite like the old ones.

After a while, someone raised the question of the fighting, which clearly needed to be taken care of.

There were scuffles all along the barricade now, but they were going only one way. Siege ladders had been brought up and at several places along the parapet men had managed to climb in. But they could never get enough in one place. There were far more defenders than attackers, and they weren't all men under arms. One thing Vimes was learning fast was the natural vindictiveness of old ladies, who had no sense of fair play when it came to fighting soldiers; give a granny a spear and a hole to jab it through, and young men on the other side were in big trouble.

And then there was Reg Shoe's inspired idea of the use of steak dinners as a weapon. The attackers did not come from homes where steak was ever on the table. Meat tended to be the flavouring, not the meal. But here and there men who'd achieved the top of the ladders, in darkness, with the groans and yells of their unsuccessful comrades below them, had their weapons dragged from their hands by well-fed former colleagues who were not unkind and who directed them down the ladder inside for steak and eggs and roast chicken and a promise that every day would be like this, come the revolution.

Vimes didn't want that news to get out, in case there was a rush to invade.

But the grannies, oh, the grannies . . . The neighbourhoods of the Republic were a natural recruiting ground for the regiments. It was also an area of big families and matriarchs whose word was family law. It had almost been cheating, putting them on the parapet with a megaphone during the lulls.

'I knows you're out there, our Ron! This is your Nan! You climb up one more time and you'll feel the back of my hand! Our Rita sends her love and wants you to hurry home. Grandpa is feeling a lot better with the new ointment! Now stop being a silly boy!'

It was a dirty trick, and he was proud of it. Messages like that sapped a fighting spirit better than arrows.

And then Vimes realized there were no more men on the ropes and ladders. He could hear yells and groans below, but those soldiers who could stand were withdrawing to a safe distance.

Now me, thought Vimes, I'd have gone down to the cellars of the houses near the street. Ankh-Morpork is *all* cellars. And I'd have chipped my way through the rotten walls, and half the cellars on *this* side of the barricades would have men in them now, nice and snug.

Admittedly last night I had the men nail up and bar every cellar door they could find but, after all, I wouldn't be fighting *me*, now, would I?

He peered through a gap between planks, and was amazed to see a man walking gingerly forward among the wreckage and the groaning men. He was carrying a white flag, and stopped occasionally to wave it but not to shout 'Hurrah!'

When he was as close as possible to the barricade, he called up: 'I say?'

Behind his planking, Vimes shut his eyes. *Oh gods*, he thought.

He called down: 'Yes? Can we help you?'

'Who are you?'

'Sergeant Keel, Night Watch. And you?'

'Sub-lieutenant Harrap. Er . . . we ask for a brief truce.'

'Why?'

'Er . . . so that we can recover our wounded.'

The rules of war, Vimes thought. The field of honour. Good grief . . .

'And then?' he said.

'Sorry?'

'What happens after that? We start fighting again?'

'Um . . . hasn't anyone told you?' said the sub-lieutenant.

'Told us what?'

'We've just heard. Lord Winder is dead. Um. Lord Snapcase is Patrician.'

A cheer began among the nearby defenders, and was taken up below. Vimes felt the relief rise. But he wouldn't be Vimes if he just let things lie.

He called out: 'So would you like to change ends?'

'Er . . . sorry?'

'I mean, would your chaps like to have a go at defending the barricade and we can try attacking it?'

Vimes heard laughter from the defenders.

There was a pause. Then the young man said: 'Um . . . why?'

'Because, correct me if I am wrong, we are now the loyal supporters of the official government and you are the rebellious rump of a discredited administration. Am I right?'

'Um . . . I think we did have, um, legitimate orders—'

'Heard of a man called Captain Swing?'

'Um . . . yes . . .'

'He thought he had legitimate orders, too,' said Vimes.

'Um . . . yes?'

'Boy, was he surprised. All right, all right. A truce. We agree. Would you like my lads to give you a hand? We've got a doctor here. Very good. I've yet to hear screaming.'

'Um . . . thank you, sir.' The young man saluted. Vimes saluted back.

Then he relaxed, and turned to the defenders. 'Okay, lads,' he said. 'Stand down. Steal 'em if you haven't got 'em.'

He shinned down the ladder. Well, then, that was it. It was over. Ring out bells, dance in streets . . .

'Sarge, did you mean that about helping them others with their wounded?' said Sam, who was standing at the bottom of the ladder.

'Well, it makes as much sense as anything else that's been happening,' said Vimes. 'They're city lads just like us, not their fault they were given the wrong orders.' And it messes with their heads, he thought, makes 'em wonder why all this is happening . . .

'Only . . . Nancyball's dead, sarge.'

Vimes took a deep breath. He'd known it anyway, up there on the wobbling ramparts, but hearing it said aloud was still a shock.

'I daresay there's a few of theirs who won't make it through to morning,' he said.

'Yes, but they were the *enemy*, sarge.'

'It's always worth thinking about who your enemy really is,' said Vimes, tugging at the barricade.

'How about the man who's trying to stick a sword into you?' said Sam.

'That's a good start,' said Vimes. 'But there are times when it pays to be a little less tightly focused.'

In the Oblong Office, Snapcase put his hands together and tapped his front teeth with his forefingers. Quite a lot of paperwork was spread in front of him.

'What to do, what to do,' he said thoughtfully.

'A general amnesty is usual, my lord,' said Mr Slant. Mr Slant, as Head of the Guild of Lawyers, had advised many leaders of the city. He was also a zombie, although this had if anything benefited his career. He *was* precedent. He knew how things should go.

'Yes, yes, of course,' said Snapcase. 'A clean start. Of course. No doubt there is a traditional form of words?'

'In fact, my lord, I happen to have a copy right here—'

'Yes, yes. Tell me about this barricade, though, will you? The one that was still standing?' He looked up at the crowd assembled in the office.

'You know about that, sir?' said Follett.

'I *do* have my own informants, you know,' said Snapcase. 'It has caused rather a stir, has it not? Some fellow put together a rather smart defence force, cut us off from the vital organs of the city, broke up Captain Swing's organization and has withstood the best attacks that could be made against him. And he is a sergeant, I hear.'

'May I suggest that a promotion is in order?' said Madam.

'I was thinking *exactly* the same thing,' said Snapcase, his little eyes gleaming. 'And then there is the question of his men. Loyal, are they?'

'Apparently, sir,' said Madam. She exchanged a puzzled glance with Dr Follett.

Snapcase sighed. 'On the other hand, a soldier can hardly be punished for loyalty to a senior officer, especially in these difficult times. There is no reason to take formal action against them.'

Eyes met again. They all felt it, the sense of the world slipping.

'But not Keel, however,' said Snapcase, standing up and removing a snuffbox from his waistcoat pocket. '*Think* about it, I pray you. What ruler could tolerate the existence of such a man? He did all that in just a few days? I dread to think what he might take it into his head to do tomorrow. These are delicate times. Are *we* to be hostage to every whim of a mere sergeant? We do not need someone like Keel doing things *his* way. Besides, you know, the Particulars could have been useful to us. Suitably re-educated, obviously.'

'I thought you said you wanted to promote him?' said Dr Follett bluntly.

Lord Snapcase took a pinch of snuff, and blinked once

or twice. 'Yes,' he said. 'Promote him, as they say, to glory.'

The crowd in the room were silent. One or two of its members were horrified. Some were impressed. You didn't stay at the top in Ankh-Morpork without developing a certain pragmatic approach to life, and Snapcase seemed to have got a grip on that with commendable speed.

'The barricade is coming down?' said the Patrician, shutting the snuffbox with a click.

'Yes, my lord,' said Dr Follett. 'Because of the general amnesty,' he added, just to make sure the word was repeated. The Guild of Assassins had a code of honour as well as rules; it was an odd code, carefully constructed to fit their needs, but it was a code none the less. You didn't kill the unprotected, or servants, you did it up close, and you kept your word. This was appalling.

'Capital,' said Snapcase. 'Ideal time. Streets full. Much confusion. Unreconstructed elements, vital message not passed on, left hand not knowing what right hand doing, difficulties of the situation, regrettable. No, my dear doctor, I do not intend to make any demands of your guild. Fortunately, there are those whose loyalty to the city is a little less . . . conditional. Yes. And now, please, there is much to be done. I shall look forward to meeting you again later.'

The crowd were ushered politely but firmly out of the room, and the doors shut behind them.

'It seems we're back at school,' muttered Dr Follett, as they were swept along the corridor.

'Ave! Duci novo, similis duci seneci,' murmured Mr Slant, drily as only a zombie can manage. 'Or, as we used to say at school, "Ave! Bossa nova, similis bossa seneca!"' He gave a little schoolmasterly laugh. He felt at home with dead languages. 'Of course, grammatically that is completely—'

'And that means . . .?' said Madam.

'Here comes the new boss, same as the old boss,' muttered Dr Follett.

'I counsel patience,' said Slant. 'He's new in the job. He may settle into it. The city is good at working around problems. Give him time.'

'And we want someone who is decisive,' said someone in the hurrying crowd.

'We wanted someone who decides the right things,' said Madam. She elbowed her way to the front of the crowd, hurried down the main staircase and darted into an anteroom.

Miss Palm stood up as she came in. 'Have they—' she began.

'Where's Havelock?' Madam demanded.

'Here,' said Vetinari, detaching himself from a shadow by the curtains.

'Take my coach. Find Keel. Warn him. Snapcase wants him dead!'

'But where is—'

Madam pointed a threatening, trembling finger. 'Do it now or receive an aunt's curse!'

When the doors were shut Lord Snapcase stared at them for some moments, and then pressed the bell for his chief secretary. The man insinuated himself into the room via the private door.

'Everyone is settling in?' said Snapcase.

'Yes, my lord. There are a number of matters for your attention.'

'I am sure people would like to believe there are,' said Snapcase, leaning back in the chair. He shifted his weight from side to side. 'Does this thing swivel?'

'I believe not, sir, but I shall have a skilled swiveller here within the hour.'

'Good. Now, what was the other thing . . . oh, yes. Tell me, are there any up and coming men in the Guild of Assassins?'

'I am sure there are, my lord. Would you like me to prepare dossiers on, say, three of them?'

'Do it.'

'Yes, my lord. My lord, various people are urgently seeking an audience with—'

'Let them wait. Now that we have the Patricianship, we mean to enjoy it.' Snapcase drummed his fingers on the edge of the desk for a moment, still staring at the doors. Then he said:

'My inaugural speech is prepared? Very sorry hear unexpected death Winder, overwork, new direction, et cetera, keep best of old while embracing best of new, beware dangerous elements, sacrifices must be made, et cetera, pull together, good of city?'

'Exactly, sir.'

'Add that I was particularly sad to hear tragic death Sergeant Keel, hope that fitting memorial to him would be the uniting of citizens of all shades of opinion in an effort to, et cetera, et cetera.'

The secretary made a few notes. 'Quite, sir,' he said. Snapcase smiled at him.

'I expect you're wondering why I've taken you on even though you worked for my predecessor, eh?' he said.

'No, sir,' said the secretary, without looking up. He wasn't wondering firstly because he had a pretty good idea and secondly because there were in any case things he found it safest not to wonder about.

'It is because I recognize talent whenever it presents itself,' said Snapcase.

'It is good of you to say so, sir,' said the secretary smoothly.

'Many a rough stone can be polished into a gem.'

'Exactly, my lord,' said the secretary, and he was thinking *Exactly, my lord* too, because he'd also found there were things he found it safest not to think, either, and these included phrases like *what a little tit.*

'Where *is* my new Captain of the Guard?'

'I believe Captain Carcer is in the rear courtyard, my lord, exhorting the men in no uncertain terms.'

'Tell him I want to see him here *now*,' said Snapcase.

'Certainly, sir.'

The barricade was taking some while to dismantle. Chair legs and planks and bedsteads and doors and baulks of timber had settled into a tangled mass. Since every piece belonged to someone, and Ankh-Morpork people care about that sort of thing, it was being dismantled by collective argument. This was not least because people who had donated a three-legged stool to the common good were trying to take away a set of dining chairs, and similar problems.

And then there was the traffic. Carts that had been held up outside the city were trying to make their way to their destinations before eggs hatched or milk got so rotten it could get out and walk the rest of the way. If Ankh-Morpork had a grid, there would have been gridlock. Since it did not it was, in the words of Sergeant Colon, 'a case of no one being able to move because of everyone else'. Admittedly, this phrase, while accurate, did not have the same snap.

Some of the watchmen had joined in the dismantling work, mostly to stop the fights that were breaking out among irate householders. But a group of them had congregated at the end of Heroes Street, where Snouty had set up a mess and a cocoa urn. There wasn't, in fact, much to do. A few hours ago they'd been fighting. Now the streets were so crowded that even patrols were impossible. Every good copper knows that there are times when the wise man keeps out of the way, and the conversation had turned to the kind of questions that follow victory, such as 1) is there going to be any extra money? and 2) are there going to be any medals? With an option on 3) which was never far from the watchmen's thoughts: are we going to get into trouble about this?

'An amnesty means we ain't,' said Dickins. 'It means everyone pretends nothing really happened.'

'All right, then,' said Wiglet. 'Are we going to get medals? What I mean is, if we've been . . .' he concentrated '. . . val-i-ant defenders of freedom, that sounds like medal time to me.'

'I reckon we should simply have barricaded the whole city,' said Colon.

'Yeah, Fred,' said Snouty, 'but then that'd mean the bad people, hnah, would be in here with us.'

'Right, but we'd be in charge,' said Fred.

Sergeant Dickins puffed on his pipe, and said: 'Lads, you're just flapping your mouths. There's been fighting, and here you are with all your arms and legs and walking around in the gods' good sunlight. That's winning, that is. You've won, see. The rest is just gravy.'

No one spoke for a while until young Sam said: 'But Nancyball didn't win.'

'We lost five men in all,' said Dickins. 'Two got hit by arrows, one fell off the barricade and one cut his own throat by accident. It happens.'

They stared at him.

'Oh, you thought it didn't?' said Dickins. 'You get a lot of worried people and edged weapons and a lot of scurrying, all in one place. You'd be amazed at the casualties you can get even when you're fifty miles from an enemy. People die.'

'Did Nancyball have a mum?' said Sam.

'He was brought up by his gran, but she's dead,' said Wiglet.

'No one else?'

'Dunno. He never talked about them. He never talked about anything much,' said Wiglet.

'What you do is, you have a whip-round,' said Dickins firmly. 'Wreath, coffin, the lot. You don't let anyone else do it. And another thing . . .'

Vimes sat a little way from the men, watching the street. There were groups of former defenders and veterans and watchmen everywhere. He watched a man buy a pie from Dibbler, and shook his head, and grinned. On a day when you couldn't give steak away, some people would still buy a pie from Dibbler. It was a triumph of salesmanship and the city's famously atrophied taste buds.

The song began. Whether it was a requiem or a victory chant he didn't know, but Dickins started it and the rest joined in, each man singing as though he was all by himself and unaware of the rest.

'—*see the little angels rise up high . . .*' Others were picking up the tune.

Reg Shoe was also sitting all alone, on a piece of barricade currently not in dispute, still clutching the flag and looking so miserable that Vimes felt moved to go and speak to him.

'—*do they rise up, rise up, rise up, how do they rise up, rise up high?*'

'It could have been good, sergeant,' said Reg, looking up. 'It really could. A city where a man can breathe free.'

'—*they rise ARSE up, arse up, arse up, see the little angels rise up high . . .*'

'Wheeze free, Reg,' said Vimes, sitting down next to him. 'This is Ankh-Morpork.' And they all hit that line together, thought the part of him that was listening with the other ear. Strange that they should do that, or maybe not.

'Yeah, make a joke of it. Everyone thinks it's funny,' said Reg, looking at his feet.

'I don't know if this'll help, Reg, but I didn't even get my hard-boiled egg,' said Vimes.

'And what's going to happen next?' said Reg, far too sunk in misery to sympathize or, for that matter, notice.

'*All the little angels rise up, rise up—*'

'I really don't know. Things'll get better for a while, I expect. But I don't know what I'm—'

Vimes stopped. On the far side of the street, oblivious of the traffic, a little wizened old man was sweeping dust out of a doorway.

Vimes stood up and stared. The little man saw him, and gave him a wave. And at that moment yet another cart rumbled down the road, piled high with former barricade.

Vimes flung himself flat and stared between the legs and wheels. Yes, the slightly bandy legs and the battered sandals

328

were still there, and still there too when the cart had passed, and still there when Vimes started to run across the street, and may have been there when the unregarded following cart almost knocked him over, and were completely not there when he straightened up.

He stood where they had been, in the busy street, on the sunny morning, and felt the night sweep over him. He felt the hairs stand up on his neck. The conversations around him grew louder, became a clamour in his ears. And the light was too bright. There were no shadows, and he was looking for shadows now.

He dodged and jinked across the street to the singing men, and waved them into silence.

'Get ready,' he growled. 'Something's going to happen . . .'

'What, sarge?' said Sam.

'Something not good, I think. An attack, maybe.' Vimes scanned the street for . . . what? Little old men with brooms? If anything, the scene was less menacing than before the troubles, because now the other shoe had dropped. People weren't standing around waiting for it any more. There was a general bustle.

'No offence, sarge,' said Dickins, 'but it all looks peaceful enough to me. There's an *amnesty*, sarge. No one's fighting anyone.'

'Sarge! Sarge!'

They all turned. Nobby Nobbs was sidling and skipping down the street. They saw his lips shape a message, completely drowned out by the squeals from a wagonload of pigs.

Lance-Constable Sam Vimes looked at the face of his sergeant. 'Something *is* wrong,' he said. 'Look at sarge!'

'Well, what?' said Fred Colon. 'A giant bird's going to drop out of the sky or something?'

There was a thud, and a gasp from Wiglet. An arrow had hit him in the chest and had gone right through.

Another one smacked into the wall above Vimes's head, showering dust.

'In here!' he yelled. The door to the shop behind them was open, and he plunged through. People piled in behind him. He heard the noise of arrows outside, and one or two screams.

'Amnesty, sergeant?' he said. Outside, the rumbling carts had stopped, blocking out the light to the bullseye panes of the shop windows and temporarily shielding it.

'Then it's got to be some idiots,' said Dickins. 'Rebels, maybe.'

'Why? There were never that many rebels, we *know* that! Anyway, they won!' Now there was shouting outside, beyond the carts. Nothing like a cart for blocking the road . . .

'Counter-revolutionaries, then?' Dickins suggested.

'What, people who want to put Winder back in charge?' said Vimes. 'Well, I don't know about you, but *I'd* join.' He looked around the shop. It was packed wall to wall. 'Who are all these people?'

'You said "in here", sergeant,' said a soldier.

'Yeah, and we didn't need telling 'cos it was raining arrows,' said another soldier.

'I didn't mean to come but I couldn't swim against the tide,' said Dibbler.

'I want to show solidarity,' said Reg.

'Sarge, sarge, it's me, sarge!' said Nobby, waving his hands.

A firm, authoritative voice, thought Vimes. It's amazing the trouble it can get you into. There were about thirty people crowded into the shop, and he didn't recognize half of them.

'Can I help any of you gentlemen?' said a thin, querulous little voice behind him. He turned and saw a very small, almost doll-like old lady, all in black, cowering behind her counter.

He looked desperately at the shelves behind her. They were piled with skeins of wool.

'Er, I don't think so,' he said.

'Then do you mind if I finish serving Mrs Soupson? Four ounces of grey two-ply was it, Mrs Soupson?'

'Yes please, Ethel!' quavered a tiny, frightened voice somewhere in the middle of the crowd of armed men.

'We'd better get out of here,' muttered Vimes. He turned to the men and waved his hands frantically to suggest that, as far as possible, no one should upset any old ladies. 'Do you have a back way, please?'

The shopkeeper's innocent old eyes looked up at him. 'It helps if people buy something, sergeant,' she said meaningfully.

'Er, we, um . . .' Vimes looked around desperately, and inspiration struck. 'Ah, right, yes . . . I'd like a mushroom,' he said. 'You know, one of those wooden things for—'

'Yes, sergeant, I know. That will be sixpence, thank you, sergeant. I always like to see a gentleman ready to do it for himself, I must say. Could I interest you in a—'

'I'm in a big hurry, please!' said Vimes. 'I've got to darn all my socks.' He nodded at the men, who responded heroically.

'Me, too—'

'Full of holes, it's disgusting!'

'Got to patch them up right now!'

'It's me, sarge, Nobby, sarge!'

'You could use mine for fishing nets!'

The lady unhooked a big key ring. 'I think it's this one, no, I tell a lie, I think it's, no . . . wait a moment . . . ah, yes, this is the one . . .'

'Here, sarge, there's a bunch of men with crossbows in the street,' said Fred Colon, from the window. 'About fifty of 'em!'

'. . . no, that's the one, dear me, that's for the lock we used to have . . . does this one look right to you? Let's try this one . . .'

Very carefully, and very slowly, she unlocked and unbolted the door.

Vimes poked his head out. They were in an alley, filled with trash and old boxes and the horrible smell of alleys everywhere. No one seemed to be around.

'Okay, everybody out,' he said. 'We need a bit of space. Who's got a bow?'

'Just me, sarge,' said Dickins. 'It's not like we were expecting trouble, see.'

331

'One bow against fifty men, that's bad odds,' said Vimes. 'Let's get out of here!'

'Are they after us, sarge?'

'They shot Wiglet, didn't they? Let's move!'

They scuttled along the alleyway. As they crossed a wider one, there was the distant sound of the shop door being kicked open again, and a gleeful shout.

'I got you now, Duke!'

Carcer . . .

An arrow clattered off a wall and pinwheeled end over end along the alley.

Vimes had run before. Every watchman knew about running. They called it the Backyard Handicap. Vimes had taken that route many times, ducking through alleys, leaping on wings of terror over the walls from one dog-infested yard to the next, falling into the chicken runs and slipping down privy roofs, looking for safety or his mates or, failing that, somewhere to stand with his back to the wall. Sometimes you had to run.

And, like the herd, you stayed together by instinct. In a crowd of thirty or so, you were harder to hit.

Fortunately, Dickins had taken the lead. The old coppers were best at running, having run so much during their lives. As on the battlefield, only the cunning and the fast survived.

And so he didn't bother to stop as the cart appeared at the end of the alley. It was a heggler's wagon, probably trying to take a short cut and escape the 'no one being able to move because of everyone else' chaos in the main streets. The man, the back of his wagon piled ten feet high with boxes, his vehicle scraping the walls, looked in horror at the stampede heading for him. No one had any brakes and absolutely no one was going to go backwards.

Vimes, in the rear, watched the group flow over and under the wagon, to the splintering of boxes and the pop of exploding eggs. The horse danced in the shafts and men dived through its legs or clear over its back.

When Vimes reached it he clambered on to the box just as an arrow hit the woodwork. He grinned desperately at the driver.

'Jump,' he suggested, and smacked the horse on the flank with the flat of his sword. Both men were thrown back as it reared and sent the remains of the stricken load sliding off the wagon.

Vimes hauled the driver upright as soon as the debris stopped falling. He was covered in egg.

'Sorry about that, sir. Watch business. Ask for Sergeant Keel. Got to rush!'

Behind them the wagon rattled up the alley, wheel rims knocking sparks off the walls. There were doorways and side alleys to escape into, but Carcer's crew would certainly be slowed down.

The rest of *his* crew had stopped when they heard the noise, but Vimes piled into them and forced them on until they reached a road, blocked with carts and thronged with people.

'Well, you got your soldiers covered in egg, sarge,' said Sam, with a worried grin. 'What's all that about?'

'It's some of the Unmentionables,' said Vimes. 'Probably want to settle the score.' Well, that was close enough.

'But I saw watchmen and soldiers with 'em,' said Fred Colon.

'Sarge, it's me, sarge! *Please*, sarge!' Nobby elbowed his way through the men.

'Is this a good time, Nobby?' said Vimes.

'There's men after you, sarge!'

'Well done, Nobby!'

'Carcer, sarge! He's got a job with Snapcase! Captain of the Palace Guard, sarge! And they gonna *get* you! Snapcase told 'em to, sarge! My mate Scratch'n'Sniff is the under-bootboy at the palace and he was in the yard and heard 'em talking, sarge!'

I should have known, Vimes thought. Snapcase was a devious devil. And now Carcer's got his feet under another bastard's table. Captain of the Guard . . .

'I haven't been making a lot of friends lately,' said Vimes.

'Okay, gentlemen, I'm going to run. If you lot melt away into the crowd you'll be fine, I expect.'

'No fear, sarge,' said Sam, and there was a general murmur of agreement.

'We had an *amnesty*,' said Dickins. 'They can't do this!'

'Anyway, they were shooting at everyone,' said one of the soldiers. 'Bastards! They need a good going-over!'

'They've got bows,' said Vimes.

'So we ambush 'em, sarge,' said Dickins. 'Choose your ground and fight up close and a crossbow's just a piece of wood.'

'Did any of you hear me?' said Vimes. 'They're after *me*. Not you. You do *not* want to mix it with Carcer. You, Snouty, you shouldn't be doing this at your time of life.'

The old jailer glared at him through runny eyes. 'That's a hell of a thing for you, hnah, to say to me, sarge,' he said.

'How do we know he won't decide to come after us anyway?' said Dickins. 'An amnesty's an amnesty, right? They can't do this!' There was a general chorus on the lines of 'Yeah, that's right!'

It's happening, Vimes thought. They are talking themselves right into it. But what can I do? We've got to face 'em. *I've* got to face 'em. I've got to face Carcer. The thought of leaving him here, with all he knows . . .

'How about if we head down Cable Street?' said Dickins. 'Lots of little alleyways off there. They'll go rushing along, thinking we've bolted for the Watch House, and we'll 'ave 'em! We ain't standing for this, sarge.'

Vimes sighed. 'Okay,' he said. 'Thank you. You're of one mind?'

There was a cheer.

'Then I won't make a speech,' said Vimes. 'There isn't time. I'll just say this. If we don't win this, if we don't see them off . . . well, we've got to, that's all. Otherwise it'll be . . . very bad for this city. Very bad.'

'That's right,' Dickins cut in, insistently. 'There was an *amnesty*.'

'But, look,' said one of the soldiers. 'I don't know half the men here. If we're going to close in, we want to know who's on our side . . .'

'That's right, hnah,' said Snouty. 'I mean, some of them chasing us was *watchmen*!'

Vimes raised his eyes. The wide alley in front of them, known as Lobsneaks, stretched all the way to Cable Street. It was lined with gardens, and there were purple flowers on the bushes.

The morning air smelled of lilac.

'I recall a battle once,' said Dickins, looking up at a tree. 'In history, it was. And there was this company, see, and they was a ragtag of different squads and all covered in mud in any case, and they found themselves hiding in a field of carrots. So as a badge they all pulled up carrots and stuck them on their helmets, so's they'd know who their friends were and incidentally have a nourishing snack for later, which is never to be sneezed at on a battlefield.'

'Well? So what?' said Dibbler.

'So what's wrong with a lilac flower?' said Dickins, reaching up and pulling down a laden branch. 'Makes a spanking plume, even if you can't eat it . . .'

And now, Vimes thought, it ends.

'I think they are very bad men!' said a high, rather elderly but nevertheless determined voice from somewhere in the crowd, and there was a glimpse of a skinny hand waving a knitting needle.

'And I shall need a volunteer to escort Mrs Soupson home,' he said.

Carcer surveyed the length of Lobsneaks.

'Looks like we just follow the trail of egg,' he said. 'Looks like Keel has a yellow streak.'

It didn't get quite the laugh he'd expected. A lot of the men he'd been able to collect had a more physical sense of humour. But Carcer had, in his own way, some of Vimes's qualities, only they were inverted. A certain kind of man looks up to someone who's brave enough to be really bad.

'Are we going to get into trouble for this, captain?'

And of course, you got those who were just along for the ride. He turned to Sergeant Knock, with Corporal Quirke lurking behind him. He fully shared Vimes's view of them although he approached it, as it were, from the other direction. You couldn't trust either of them. But they hated Keel with that gnawing, nerve-sapping hatred that only the mediocre can really bring to bear, and that was useful.

'How do you think we're going to get into *trouble*, sergeant?' he said. 'We're working for the *government*.'

'He's a devious devil, sir!' said Knock, as if this was a character flaw in a copper.

'Now you lot listen to me, right?' said Carcer. 'No mess-ups this time! I want Keel alive, okay? And that kid Vimes. You can do what the hell you like to the rest of them.'

'Why d'you want him taken alive?' said a quiet voice behind Carcer. 'I thought Snapcase wanted him dead. And what's the kid done that's so wrong?'

Carcer turned. To his mild surprise, the watchman behind him didn't flinch.

'What's your name, mister?' he said.

'Coates.'

'Ned's the one I told you about, sir,' said Knock urgently, leaning over Carcer's shoulder. 'Keel gave him the push, sir, after—'

'Shut up,' said Carcer, without taking his eyes off Coates. There wasn't a hint of fear there, not even a glimmer of bravado. Coates just stared back.

'Did you just come along for the ride, Coates?' he said.

'No, captain. I don't like Keel. But Vimesy is just a kid that got dragged along. What're you going to do to him?'

Carcer leaned forward; Coates did not lean back.

'You were a rebel, weren't you?' he said. 'Don't like to do what you're told, eh?'

336

'They're going to get a big bottle of ginger beer!' said a voice drunk with evil delight.

Carcer turned and looked down at the skinny, black-clad Ferret. He was somewhat battered, partly because he'd put up a fight when the watchmen had tried to pry him out of his cell, and mostly because Todzy and Muffer had been waiting outside. But he'd been allowed to live; beating something like Ferret to death was, to the other two, an embarrassing and demeaning waste of fist.

He certainly flinched under Carcer's gaze. His whole body was a flinch.

'Did I ask you to speak, you little dog's tonker?' Carcer enquired.

'Nosir!'

'Right. Remember that. It could save your life one day.' Carcer turned his attention back to Ned. 'Okay, sunshine, this is the bright new dawn you wanted. You asked for it, you got it. We've just got to sweep away a few of yesterday's leftovers. By order of Lord Snapcase, your mate. And it ain't your job to ask why and who, but young Vimesy? Why, I think he's a game lad who'll be a credit to the city if he's kept out of the way of bad company. Now, Knock says you're good at thinking. So now you tell me what you think Keel's gonna do.'

Ned gave him a look that went on for slightly longer than Carcer felt comfortable with.

'He's a defender,' he said, eventually. 'He'll be back at the Watch House. He'll set a few traps, get the men tooled up and wait for you.'

'Hah?' said Carcer.

'He doesn't like to see his men hurt,' said Ned.

'This is not going to be his day, then,' said Carcer.

Halfway down Cable Street was a barricade. It wasn't much. A few doors, a table or two . . . by the standards of the big one that was even now being turned back into unbelligerent dining-room furniture, it barely existed at all.

Carcer's informal crew walked slowly, staring up at buildings and into the mouths of alleys. People in the street fled at their approach. Some men walk in a way that projects bad news ahead of them.

Vimes crouched behind the makeshift wall and peered through a crack. They'd snatched a few crossbows from aimless soldiers on the way here, but by the look of it Carcer's men had at least fifteen between them. And they outnumbered the lilac lads two to one.

If push came to shove, he'd take Carcer out right now. It wasn't the way it ought to go. He wanted people to see the man hang, he wanted *the city* to execute him. Going back empty-handed would leave a loose end flapping.

He heard the sound of sobbing from further along the barricade. It wasn't young Sam, he knew, and Nobby Nobbs had probably cried all the tears a body was capable of some time ago. It was Reg. He sat with his back to the makeshift defence, the threadbare flag across his knees, and tears dripping off his chin.

'Reg, you ought to go,' Vimes hissed. 'You don't even have a weapon.'

'What's the good of it, eh?' said Reg. 'You were bloody right, sarge! Things just go round and round! You got rid of the bloody Unmentionables and here they are again! What's the point, eh? This city could be such a great place but *no*, oh no, the bastards always end up on top! Nothing ever bloody changes! They just take their money and mess us around!'

Carcer had stopped twenty yards from the barricade, and was watching it carefully.

'Way of the world, Reg,' murmured Vimes, counting enemies under his breath.

And a big covered cart came around the corner, rocking under its load. It rolled to a halt a little way from Carcer's crew, partly because the way was blocked but mostly, perhaps, because one of the men had walked up to the driver and aimed a crossbow at his head.

'And now the bloody bastards have won,' moaned Reg.

'Every day of the week, Reg,' said Vimes absently, trying to follow the movements of too many people at once.

The other men were spreading out. After all, they had the firepower.

The man holding up Mr Dibbler, the cart driver, wasn't paying too much attention. Now Vimes wished he'd put himself in the wagon. Oh, well, someone had to start the rumble—

'Yeah? You want to shoot something? Bastards!'

They all stared, Carcer too. Reg had stood up, was waving the flag back and forth, was clambering over the barricade . . .

He held the flag like a banner of defiance. 'You can take our lives but you'll never take our freedom!' he screamed.

Carcer's men looked at one another, puzzled by what sounded like the most badly thought-out war cry in the history of the universe. Vimes could see their lips moving as they tried to work it out.

Carcer raised his crossbow, gestured to his men, and said: 'Wrong!'

Reg was hit by five heavy bolts so that he did a little dance before falling to his knees. It happened in seconds.

Vimes opened his mouth to give the order to charge, and shut it when he saw Reg raise his head. In silence, using the flag pole as an aid, Reg got back to his feet.

Three more arrows hit him. He looked down at his skinny chest, bristling with feathers, and took a step forward. And another.

One of the crossbowmen drew his sword and ran at the stricken man, and was knocked into the air by a blow from Reg that must have felt like it had come from a sledgehammer. And in the ranks of the crew there was a fight. Someone in a copper's uniform had drawn his own sword and taken out two bowmen. And the man at the cart was running back to the action . . .

'Get them!' Vimes yelled, and leapt the barricade.

There was no plan any more. Dickins and his men poured out of the cart. There were still loaded crossbows out there, but a bow is suddenly not the weapon you want to be holding when angry swords are approaching from both directions.

It'll come when you call . . .

All plans, all futures, all politics . . . were elsewhere. Vimes scooped up a fallen sword and with a weapon in either hand screamed wordless defiance and launched himself at the nearest enemy. The man went down headless.

He saw Snouty go down in the mêlée, and sprang over him to catch his attacker in a windmill of blades. And then he spun around to confront Knock, who dropped his sword and fled. And Vimes ran on, not fighting but hacking, ducking strokes without seeing them, blocking attacks without turning his head, letting the ancient senses do their work. Someone was slicing towards young Sam; Vimes brought a sword down on the arm in true self-defence. He moved on, in the centre of a widening circle. He wasn't an enemy, he was a nemesis.

And as suddenly as it had come the beast withdrew, leaving an angry man with two swords.

Carcer had retreated to the side of the street, with his men – far fewer men now.

Colon was on his knees, throwing up. Dickins was down, and Vimes knew he was dead. Nobby was down too, but that was just because someone had kicked him hard and he'd probably decided that staying down was best. There were a lot of Carcer's men down, more than half. Some more had fled a maniac with two swords. Some had even fled Reg Shoe, who was sitting on the barricade, staring at the sheer weight of arrows in him. As he watched, his brain seemingly decided that he must be dead on this evidence, and he fell backwards. But in a few hours, his brain would be in for a surprise.

No one knew why some people became natural zombies, sub-stituting sheer stubborn will power for blind life force. But

340

attitude played a part. For Reg Shoe, life was only just beginning . . .

Young Sam was upright. He looked as though he'd thrown up, but he'd done well to survive his first real mêlée. He gave Vimes a weak smile.

'What's happening now, sarge?' he managed, taking off his helmet and wiping his forehead.

Vimes sheathed a sword and quietly slipped one of Mrs Goodbody's little friends out of his pocket.

'That depends on what happens over there,' he said, nodding towards the other end of the street. Sam obediently turned to look, and fell asleep.

Vimes pocketed the cosh, and saw Coates looking at him.

'Whose side are you on, Ned?' he said.

'What did you hit the kid for?' said Ned.

'So he's out of it. You got anything to say?'

'Not much, sarge.' Ned grinned. 'We're all learning a lot today, ain't we?'

'True enough,' said Vimes.

'There's even bigger bastards than you, for a start.'

This time Vimes grinned. 'But I try harder, Ned.'

'You know Carcer?'

'He's a murderer. And just about everything else, too. A stone-cold killer. With brains, said Vimes.'

'This is going to go the distance?'

'Yep. It's got to. We've got to stop this, Ned. This is the only chance. It stops here or not at all. Can you imagine him loose now he's pally with Snapcase?'

'Yes. I can,' said Ned. 'Just as well I wasn't planning anything this evening, eh? But you can tell me one thing, sarge. How do you know all this?'

Vimes hesitated. But at a time like this, what difference did it make?

'I'm from this city,' said Vimes. 'But, oh, there was a hole in time, something like that. You want to know? I travelled here in time, Ned, and that's the truth.'

Ned Coates looked him up and down. Blood covered Vimes's armour, and his hands, and half his face, and he was holding a bloody sword in his hand.

'From how far back?' he said.

Time stopped. Coates froze and faded in colour, into a world made up of shades of grey.

'Nearly there, your grace,' said Sweeper, behind Vimes.

'Ye gods!' yelled Vimes, flinging his sword to the ground. 'You are *not* making any friends here, you know?'

The sword hadn't *hit* the ground. It hung a few inches from his hands, and had faded to greyness.

'There's just a few things we need to tell you,' said Sweeper, as if a sword in mid-air was a minor consideration.

'What's happened to the bloody sword?' said Vimes, to whom it wasn't.

'Time has stopped for everyone but you,' said Sweeper patiently. 'Actually that sentence is wrong in every particular, but it's quite a useful lie. It'll just take us a moment to set things up . . .'

Now Vimes had time, of some kind, to look around. The whole street was darker, as if the fight had been taking place in the half-light just before dawn. The only colour was in the robes and faces of Sweeper and Qu as they manoeuvred a handcart out of an alley. It held a couple of small stone columns, and the body of John Keel, wrapped in a shroud.

'We have some good news,' said Sweeper.

'You have?' said Vimes weakly. He walked over to the body.

'Indeed,' said Qu, unshipping the stone cylinders. 'We thought we might have to persuade you to remove all your armour but you will not, I think, need to do this.'

'That's because it will stay here,' said Lu-Tze. 'Belongs here, see?'

'No,' said Vimes, 'I don't know what the hell you're talking about.' He touched the body. 'So cold,' he said. 'That's what I remember. He was so cold.'

'A morgue does that to people,' said Sweeper, in a matter-of-fact voice.

'Now please pay attention, commander,' said Qu. 'When we operate the—'

Vimes looked up, violence in his eyes. Sweeper laid a hand on Qu's arm.

'We've got things to do for a minute or two,' he said.

'Yes, but it's vital that he knows how—'

'We've got *things* to *do* for a *minute or two*,' Sweeper repeated, making a face.

'Oh? What? Oh. Yes. Er . . . we've got, er . . . things. To do. Things to do . . . er . . . things.'

They wandered away. Out of the corner of his eye Vimes saw them walking back and forth across the street, as if taking measurements.

He looked back at John Keel. But what could you say? Sorry you're dead? Keel had originally died on the barricades, not in a street fight. But he was just as dead, all the same.

Vimes was hazy on religion. He attended Watch funerals and went to such religious events as the proper fulfilling of the office of Commander entailed, but as for the rest . . . well, you saw things sometimes that made it impossible to believe not only in gods, but also in common humanity and your own eyes. From what he could remember, Keel had felt the same way. You got on with things. If there were any gods, you expected them to get on with things, too, and didn't interrupt them while they were working.

What could you say to a dead copper? What would *he* want said?

Ah . . .

He leaned closer. 'Carcer's going to bloody swing for this,' he said, and stood back.

Behind him, Sweeper coughed theatrically. 'Ready, your grace?' he said.

'Ready enough,' said Vimes.

'We were telling you about the armour,' said Sweeper. 'It'll—'

'The thing is, commander,' Qu interrupted, 'that you and this fellow Carcer and all the clothes and possessions you arrived with form an elongated trans-time anomaly, which is under considerable tension.'

Vimes turned and looked at Sweeper.

'It's very, very hard to move things out of the time where they belong but it takes much less effort to move them back to where they were,' Sweeper translated.

Vimes carried on staring.

'Everything really, really wants to stay where it should be,' Sweeper tried.

'You're right there,' said Vimes.

'All we do is . . . grease the way,' said Sweeper. 'We give a little push, and it'll all snap back. And away you go. Have you had anything to eat this morning?'

'No!'

'Shouldn't be too messy, then,' said Sweeper. When Vimes looked puzzled he went on: 'Undigested food. It'll stay here, you see.'

'You mean it'll come tearing out of—'

'No, no, no,' said Qu, quickly. 'You won't notice. But a nourishing meal when you get back would be a good idea.'

'And the armour stays here?'

Qu beamed. 'Yes, your grace. Everything. Eyepatch, socks, everything.'

'Boots, too?'

'Yes. Everything.'

'What about my drawers?'

'Yes, those too. Everything.'

'So I'll arrive in the *nuddy*?'

344

'The one costume that's in fashion anywhere,' said Sweeper, grinning.

'Then why did all my armour arrive with me when I came?' said Vimes. 'And damn Carcer had his knives, that's for sure!'

Qu opened his mouth, but Sweeper answered faster.

'It takes a thousand steps to get to the top of a mountain but one little hop'll take you all the way back to the bottom,' he said. 'Okay?'

'Well, I suppose it makes sen—' Vimes began.

'That isn't how it works at all, Lu-Tze!' wailed Qu.

'No,' said Sweeper, 'but it's another good lie. Look, commander, we don't have a damn great thunderstorm and we don't have enough stored time. This is a field operation. It's the best we can do. We'll get you back, and your prisoner, although you almost certainly won't arrive in the same place, 'cos of quantum. It's hard enough making sure you don't arrive two hundred feet in the air, believe me. Pushing all your clothes as well, when they belong here, that just takes too much power. Now, are you ready? You need to go back to where you were standing. Get to Carcer as soon as you can. You *must* grab him, otherwise he'll stay behind.'

'Okay, but I've changed lots of things!' said Vimes.

'Leave that to us,' said Sweeper.

'What about Keel?' said Vimes, walking away with reluctance.

'Don't *worry*. We told you at the temple. We'll put him in your armour. He'll have died in battle.'

'Make sure nothing happens to young Sam!' said Vimes, as Qu carefully prodded him into position. The little stone columns began to spin.

'We will!'

'Make sure Reg Shoe gets a decent burial!'

'We will!'

'Not too deep, he'll be wanting to come out again in a few hours!'

345

Qu gave him a last prod.

'*Goodbye*, commander!'

Time came back.

Ned was looking at him. 'What happened just then, sarge? You *blurred*.'

'You only get one question, Ned,' said Vimes, fighting the moment of nausea. 'Now, let's show Snapcase where the line's drawn, shall we? Let's finish it—'

They charged, the men falling in behind them.

Vimes remembered in slow motion. Some of Carcer's men ran at the sight of them, some raised their hastily reclaimed weapons, and Carcer stood there and grinned. Vimes headed for him, ducking and weaving through the fight.

The man's expression changed as Vimes approached. Vimes was speeding up, shoulder-charging and thrusting other bodies away. Carcer raised his sword and took a stance, but there was no room for finesse in the mêlée and Vimes closed like a bull, knocking the sword up and grabbing Carcer by the throat.

'You're *nicked*, my ol' chum,' he said. And then it all went black.

He felt, later on, that there should have been more to it. There should have been rushing blue tunnels, or flashes, or the sun should have shot round and round the sky. Even pages tearing off a calendar and fluttering away would have been *something*.

But it was just the blackness of the deepest sleep, followed by pain as he hit the floor.

Vimes felt arms reach down and haul him to his feet. He shook them off as soon as he was upright, and focused, through the bleary mist, on the face of Captain Carrot.

'Good to see you, sir. Oh, dear—'

'I'm fine,' croaked Vimes, through a throat that felt stuffed with sand. 'Where's Carcer?'

'You've got a nasty cut on—'

'Really? I'm amazed,' growled Vimes. 'Now, where the *hell* is *Carcer*?'

'We don't know, sir. You just appeared in mid-air and landed on the floor. In a lot of blue light, sir!'

'Ah,' muttered Vimes. 'Well, he's come back somewhere. Somewhere close, probably.'

'Right, sir, I'll tell the men to—'

'No, don't,' said Vimes. 'He'll keep. After all, where's he going to go?'

He wasn't too sure of his legs. They felt as though they belonged to someone with a very poor sense of balance.

'How long was I . . . away?' he said. Ponder Stibbons stepped forward.

'About half an hour, your grace. Er, we have, er, hypothesized that there was some temporal disturbance, which, coupled with the lightning stroke and a resonance in the standing wave of the Library, caused a space-time rupture—'

'Yeah, it felt something like that,' said Vimes hurriedly. 'Half an hour, did you say?'

'Did it feel longer?' said Ponder, taking out a notebook.

'A bit,' Vimes conceded. 'Now, has anyone here got a pair of drawers I—'

I can see your house from up here . . .

That was Carcer. He liked you to stew, to use your imagination.

And Vimes had said: where's he going to go?

'Captain, I want you and every man you can spare, every damn man, to get up to my house right now, understand,' he said. 'Just do it. Just do it *now*.' He turned to Ridcully. 'Archchancellor, can you get me there faster?'

'The Watch wants *magical* assistance?' said the Archchancellor, taken aback.

'Please,' said Vimes.

'Of course, but you realize that you have no clothes on—'

Vimes gave up. People always wanted *explanations*. He set off, overruling the jelly in his legs, running out of the octangle and across the lawns until he reached the University's Bridge of Size, where he sped past Nobby and Colon who were drawn into the wake of watchmen running to keep up.

On the other side of the bridge was the garden known as the Wizard's Pleasaunce. Vimes ploughed through it, twigs whipping at his bare legs, and then he was out and on to the old towpath, mud splashing up over the blood. Then right and a left, past amazed bystanders, and then there were the catshead cobbles of Scoone Avenue under his feet and he found the wind to accelerate a little. He didn't slow until he reached the gravel drive, and almost collapsed at the front door, hanging on to the bell pull.

There were hurrying feet, and the door was wrenched open.

'If you're not Willikins,' growled Vimes, focusing, 'there's going to be trouble!'

'Your grace! Whatever has happened to you?' said the butler, pulling him into the hall.

'Nothing!' said Vimes. 'Just get me a fresh uniform, nice and quietly, and don't let Sybil know—'

He read everything in the way the butler's face changed.

'What's happened to Sybil?'

Willikins backed away. A bear would have backed away.

'Don't go up there, sir! Mrs Content says it's . . . all rather difficult, sir. Things aren't, um, happening quite right . . .'

'Is the child born?'

'No sir, a-apparently not, sir. It's rather . . . Mrs Content says she's trying everything but maybe we . . . ought to send for the doctors, sir.'

'For a childbirth?'

Willikins looked down. After twenty unflappable years as butler, he was shaking now. No one deserved a confrontation with Sam Vimes at a time like this.

'Sorry, sir . . .'

348

'No!' snapped Vimes. 'Don't send for a doctor. I *know* a doctor! And he knows all about . . . this sort of thing! He'd better!'

He ran back outside in time to see a broomstick touch down on the lawn, piloted by the Archchancellor himself.

'I thought I'd better come along anyway,' said Ridcully. 'Is there anything—'

Vimes swung himself on to it before the wizard could get off.

'Take me to Twinkle Street. Can you do that?' he said. 'It's . . . important!'

'Hang on, your grace,' said Ridcully, and Vimes's stomach dropped into his legs as the stick climbed vertically. He made a small mental note to promote Buggy Swires and buy him the buzzard he'd always wanted. Anyone prepared to do this every day for the good of the city couldn't be paid too much.

'Try my left pocket,' said Ridcully, when they were well aloft. 'There's something that belongs to you, I believe.'

Nervously, well aware of what a wizard's pocket might hold, Vimes pulled out a bunch of paper flowers, a string of flags of all nations . . . and a silver cigar case.

'Landed on the Bursar's head,' said the Archchancellor, steering around a seagull. 'I hope it's not damaged.'

'It's . . . fine,' said Vimes. 'Thank you. Er . . . I'll put it back for now, shall I? Don't seem to have any pockets on me at the moment.'

It found its way back, Vimes thought. We're home.

'And a suit of ornamental armour landed in the High Energy Magic building,' Ridcully went on, 'and, I am happy to report, it is—'

'Very badly bent out of shape?' said Vimes. Ridcully hesitated. He was aware of Vimes's feelings of gilt.

'Excessively, your grace. Completely bent out of shape because of quantum thingummies, I suspect,' he said.

Vimes shivered. He was still naked. Even the hated formal uniform would have helped up here. But it didn't matter either way, now. Gilt and feathers and badges and feeling chilly . . .

349

there were other things that mattered more, and always would.

He jumped off the stick before it had stopped, stumbled in a circle and fell against Dr Lawn's door, hammering on it with his fists.

After a while it opened a crack and a familiar voice, changed only a little with age, said 'Yes?'

Vimes thrust the door fully open. 'Look at me, Doctor Lawn,' he said.

Lawn stared. 'Keel?' he said. In his other hand he was holding the world's biggest syringe.

'Can't be. They buried John Keel. You know they did,' said Vimes. He saw the huge instrument in the man's hand. 'What the hell were you going to do with that?'

'Baste a turkey, as a matter of fact. Look, who are you, then, because you look like—'

'Grab all your midwifing stuff and come with me now,' said Vimes. 'All those funny tools you said worked so well. Bring 'em all. Right now. And I'll make you the richest doctor that ever lived,' said Vimes, a man wearing nothing but mud and blood.

Lawn gestured weakly towards the kitchen. 'I'll just have to take the turkey out—'

'Stuff the turkey!'

'I already—'

'Come on!'

The broomstick did not fly well with three on board, but it was faster than walking and Vimes at this point knew he'd be incapable of anything else. He was out of breath and strength by the time he got home the first time. Now merely standing upright was a test of endurance. It was the broomstick or crawling.

It lumbered down out of the sky and landed unsteadily on the lawn.

'Lady upstairs, big bedroom on left,' said Vimes, pushing vaguely at the doctor. 'Midwife there, not got a clue. All the money you want. Go on.'

Lawn hurried off. Vimes, helped by Ridcully, followed rather more stiffly, but as they reached the door the doctor came out walking backwards very slowly. It became apparent, as he emerged, that this was because Detritus's huge crossbow was pressed against his nose.

When Vimes spoke his voice was slightly muffled, because he was lying flat on the ground.

'Put the bow *down*, sergeant,' he managed.

'He come rushin' in, Mister Vimes,' rumbled Detritus.

'That's because he's the *doctor*, sergeant. Let him go upstairs. That is an order, thank you.'

'Right, Mister Vimes,' said Detritus, stepping aside with reluctance and shouldering the bow. At which point, the bow discharged.

When the thunder had died away Vimes got up and looked around. He hadn't actually liked the shrubbery very much. That was just as well. Nothing remained but some tree trunks, and they were all stripped of bark down one side. There were a few small fires.

'Er, sorry about that, Mister Vimes,' said the troll.

'What did I tell you about Mister Safety Catch?' said Vimes weakly.

'When Mister Safety Catch Is Not On, Mister Crossbow Is Not Your Friend,' recited Detritus, saluting. 'Sorry, sir, but we all a bit tense at dis time.'

'I certainly am,' said Ridcully, picking himself off the lawn and pulling twigs out of his beard. 'I may not walk properly for the rest of the day. I suggest, sergeant, that we pick the doctor up, bring him round under the pump, and take him upstairs . . .'

The things that happened next were a waking dream for Vimes. He moved like a ghost through his own house, which was full of watchmen. No one wanted to be anywhere else.

He shaved himself very slowly, concentrating on every stroke. He was aware of noises off, which arrived via the pink clouds in his head.

'—he says he wants them boiled, the nasty horrid things! What's that for, to make them softer?'

'— trolls and dwarfs on tonight, every door and window covered and I mean covered—'

'— stood over me and said damn well boil them for twenty minutes! Like they were cabbage—'

'—now he's asked for a small brandy—'

'—Mrs Content stormed out and he said not to let her in again—'

'—Igor came and offered to help and Lawn took one look and said only if he's been boiled for twenty minutes—'

'— pox doctor, when all's said and done—'

'— old Stoneface'll cover him with gold if it all turns out right—'

'—yeah, and if it turns out wrong?'

Vimes got dressed in his street uniform, moving slowly and willing every limb into position. He brushed his hair. He went out into the hall. He sat down on an uncomfortable chair with his helmet on his knees, while ghosts both living and dead hurried around him.

Usually – always – there was a part of Vimes that watched the other parts, because he was at heart a policeman. This time it wasn't there. It was in here with the rest of him, staring at nothing, and waiting

'—someone take up more towels—'

'—now he's asked for a large brandy!'

'—he wants to see Mister Vimes!'

Vimes's brain lit up from whatever little pilot light of thought had been operating at the most basic level. He walked up the stairs, helmet under his arm, like a man going to take a statement. He knocked at the door.

Lawn opened it. He was holding a brandy glass in his other hand, and moved aside with a smile.

Sybil was sitting up. He saw, through the mist of exhaustion, that she was holding something wrapped in a shawl.

'He's called Sam, Sam,' she said. 'And no argument.'

The sun came out.

'I'll teach him to walk!' beamed Vimes. 'I'm *good* at teaching people to walk!'

And he fell asleep before he hit the carpet.

It was a pleasant stroll in the early evening air. Vimes trailed cigar smoke behind him as he walked down to Pseudopolis Yard, where he acknowledged the cheers and congratulations and thanked people for the lovely flowers.

His next stop was at Dr Lawn's house where he sat and spoke for a while, about such things as memory and how tricky it can be, and forgetfulness, and how profitable it could prove.

Then, with the doctor, he went to his bank. This institution was, not surprisingly, willing to open outside normal hours for a man who was a Duke, and the richest man in the city, and the Commander of the City Watch and, not least, quite prepared to kick the door down. There he signed over one hundred thousand dollars and the freehold of a large corner site in Goose Gate to one Dr J. Lawn.

And then, alone, he went up to Small Gods. Legitimate First, whatever his private feelings, knew enough not to shut the gates on this night, and he'd filled the lamps.

Vimes strolled over the moss-grown gravel. In the twilight, the lilac blooms seemed to shine. Their scent hung in the air like fog.

He waded through the grass and reached the grave of John Keel, where he sat on the headstone, taking care not to disturb the wreaths; he had a feeling that the sergeant would understand that a copper sometimes needed to take the weight off his feet. And he finished his cigar, and stared into the sunset.

After a while he was aware of a scraping noise to his left and could just make out the turf starting to sag on one of the graves. A grey hand was thrust out of the ground, clutching a shovel. A few pieces of turf were pushed aside and, with some effort, Reg Shoe rose from the grave. He was halfway out before he noticed Vimes, and nearly fell back.

'Oh, you frightened the life out of me, Mister Vimes!'

'Sorry, Reg,' said Vimes.

'Of course, when I say you frightened the life out of me—' the zombie began, gloomily.

'Yes, Reg, I understood you. Quiet down there, was it?'

'Very peaceful, sir, very peaceful. I think I'll have to get myself a new coffin before next year, though. They don't last any time at all these days.'

'I suppose not that many people look for durability, Reg,' said Vimes.

Reg slowly shovelled the soil back into place. 'I know everyone thinks it's a bit odd, but I think I owe it to them really,' he said. 'It's only one day a year, but it's like . . . solidarity.'

'With the downtrodden masses, eh?' said Vimes.

'What, sir?'

'No argument from me, Reg,' said Vimes happily. This was a perfect moment. Not even Reg, fussing around smoothing down earth and patting turf into place, could detract from it.

There'll come a time when it'll all be clear, Sweeper had said. A perfect moment.

The occupants of these graves had died for something. In the sunset glow, in the rising of the moon, in the taste of the cigar, in the warmth that comes from sheer exhaustion, Vimes saw it.

History finds a way. The nature of events changed, but the nature of the dead had not. It had been a mean, shameful little fight that ended them, a flyspecked footnote of history, but they hadn't been mean or shameful men. They hadn't run, and they could have run with honour. They'd stayed, and he wondered if the path had seemed as clear to them then as it did to him now. They'd stayed not because they wanted to be heroes, but because they chose to think of it as their job, and it was in front of them—

'I'll be off, then, sir,' said Reg, shouldering his shovel. He seemed a long way away. 'Sir?'

'Yeah, right. Right, Reg. Thank you,' mumbled Vimes, and in

the pink glow of the moment watched the corporal march down the darkening path and out into the city.

John Keel, Billy Wiglet, Horace Nancyball, Dai Dickins, Cecil 'Snouty' Clapman, Ned Coates and, technically, Reg Shoe. Probably there were no more than twenty people in the city now who knew all the names, because there were no statues, no monuments, nothing written down anywhere. You had to have been there.

He felt privileged to have been there twice.

The night was welling up as the sun set. It unfolded from the shadows where it had hidden from the day, and flowed and joined together. He felt his senses flow with it, spreading out like the whiskers of a dark, giant cat.

Beyond the gates of the cemetery the city noise died down a little, although Ankh-Morpork never truly slept. It probably didn't dare.

Vimes felt now, in this strange calm mood, that he could hear everything, *everything*, just as he had done back in that terrible moment in Heroes Street when history came to claim its own. He heard the tiny sounds in the stone wall as it cooled, the slither of dirt underground as Reg's vacated plot settled, the faint movement of the long grass around the graves . . . a thousand subtle sounds added up to a richly textured, localized silence. It was the song of the dark and in it, on the edge of detection, was a discord.

Let's see . . . he'd put a guard on his house and they were core people, ones he could trust not to stand around and get bored but to remain watchful, all night long. He hadn't had to explain how important that was. So the house was safe. And the Watch Houses had double guard, too—

There was something wrong with Keel's grave. There was always the egg, every year, a little joke out of history. But now, it looked as though there was nothing down there but bits of eggshell—

As he leaned forward to look, the blade went over his head.

But the beast had been ready. The beast didn't think about guards and defences. The beast didn't think at all. But it forever sniffed the air and eyed the shadows and sampled the night and almost before the swish of the sword it had sent Vimes's hand thrusting into his pocket.

Crouched, he swivelled and punched Carcer on the kneecap with one of Mrs Goodbody's finest items. He heard things crackle, he launched himself up and forward, he bore Carcer to the ground.

There was no science to this. The beast was off the chain and looking to kill. It was not often that Vimes was sure that he could make the world a better place, but he was sure now. It was all very clear now.

And also very hard. The sword had gone, tumbling into the grass as Carcer went down. But Carcer fought, and was as tough as teak. And it is very hard, with your hands, to kill a man who does not want to be killed.

Vimes shook off the brass knuckles because what he needed to do now was throttle. There was no room, though. Carcer was trying to stick a thumb in his eye.

They rolled across the graves, scrabbling and struggling for advantage. Blood filled Vimes's left eye. His rage needed just one second, and that second was being denied.

He rolled again, and flung out a hand.

And there was the sword. He rolled again, and again, and staggered up with the blade in his hand.

Carcer had rolled too, and was pulling himself up with remarkable speed for a man with only one good knee. Vimes saw that he was dragging himself upright by one of the lilac trees; blossoms and scent floated down in the darkness.

Metal slid. There was the momentary gleam of a knife. And a little chuckle, Carcer's little laugh that said, hey, this is all good fun, eh?

'So who's gonna arrest me?' he said, as they both gulped air. 'Sergeant Keel or Commander Vimes?'

'Who said you were going to be arrested?' said Vimes, trying to fill his lungs. 'I'm fighting an attacker, Carcer.'

'Oh, you *was*, Mister Vimes,' said the shadow. 'Only now I'm in front of you.' Metal clinked on the gravel path. 'And I ain't armed no more, haha. Thrown down my last weapon. Can't kill an unarmed man, Mister Vimes. You got to arrest me now. Drag me in front of Vetinari. Let me have my little say, haha. You can't *kill* me, just standin' here.'

'No one wants to hear anything you've got to say, Carcer.'

'Then you'd better kill me, Mister Vimes. I got no weapon. I can't run.'

'You've always got an extra knife, Carcer,' said Vimes, above the roar of the beast.

'Not this time, Mister Vimes. Come *on*, Mister Vimes. Can't blame a man for tryin', eh? A man's got to give it his best shot, right? No hard feelings?'

And that was Carcer. No hard feelings. His best shot. Can't blame a man for trying.

Innocent words got dirty in his mouth.

Vimes took a step closer.

'You got a nice home to go to, Mister Vimes. I mean, what've I got?'

And the man was *convincing*. He fooled everybody. You could almost forget the corpses.

Vimes glanced down.

'Whoops, sorry,' said Carcer, 'I walked over your grave there. No offence meant, eh?'

Vimes said nothing. The beast was howling. It wanted to shut that mouth up.

'You're not going to kill me, Mister Vimes. Not you. Not you with a badge. That ain't your way, Mister Vimes.'

Without looking, Vimes reached up and tore his badge off.

'Ah, well, I know you want to give me a fright, Mister Vimes, and many would say you've got a right. Look, here's what I'll do, I'll throw away my other knife, haha, you knew I'd got another one, right?'

It was the voice. It could make you think that what you *knew* was wrong.

'Okay, okay, I can see you're upset, haha, fair enough, and you *know* I've always got a third knife, well, I'm dropping it now, see, there it goes . . .'

Vimes was only a step or two away now.

'That's it, Mister Vimes. No more knives. I can't run. I surrender. No messing about this time. I give in, okay? Just arrest me? For old times' sake?'

The beast screamed inside Vimes. It screamed that no one would blame him for doing the hangman out of ten dollars and a free breakfast. Yeah, and you could say a swift stab now was the merciful solution, because every hangman knew you could go the easy way or the hard way and there wasn't one in the country that'd let something like Carcer go the easy way. The gods knew the man deserved it . . .

. . . but young Sam was watching him, across thirty years.

When we break down, it all breaks down. That's just how it works. You can bend it, and if you make it hot enough you can bend it in a circle, but you can't break it. When you break it, it all breaks down until there's nothing unbroken. It starts here and now.

He lowered the sword.

Carcer looked up, grinning, and said, 'Never tastes right, does it, haha, an egg without salt . . .'

Vimes felt his hand begin to move of its own accord—

And stopped. Red rage froze.

There was the beast, all around him. And that's what it was. A beast. Useful, but still a beast. You could hold it on a chain, and make it dance, and juggle balls. It didn't think. It was *dumb*. What you were, what *you* were, was not the beast.

You didn't have to do what it wanted. If you did, Carcer won.

He dropped the sword.

Carcer stared at him, the gleam of Vimes's sudden smile more worrying than the rictus of his rage. Then metal gleamed in his hand. But Vimes was already on him, grabbing the hand, slamming it again and again on John Keel's headstone until the fourth knife dropped from bleeding fingers. He dragged the man upright with both hands forced up behind his back and rammed him hard against the stone.

'See that up in the sky, Carcer?' he said, his mouth by the man's ear. 'That's the sunset, that is. That's the stars. And they'll shine all the better on my lad Sam tomorrow night 'cos they won't be shining down on you, Carcer, by reason of the fact that before the dew's off the leaves in the morning I'll drag you in front of Vetinari, and we'll have the witnesses there, lots of 'em, and maybe even a lawyer for you if there's any of 'em who could plead for you with a straight face and then, Carcer, we'll take you to the Tanty, one gallows, no waiting, and you can dance the hemp fandango. And then I'll bleedin' well go home and maybe I'll even have a hard-boiled egg.'

'You're hurting!'

'You know, you're right there, Carcer!' Vimes managed to get both the man's wrists in a steel grip, and ripped the sleeve off his own shirt. 'I'm hurting and I'm *still* doing it all by the book.' He wrapped the linen around the wrists a couple of times and knotted it firmly. 'I'll make sure there's water in your cell, Carcer. I'll make sure you get breakfast, anything you like. I'll make sure the hangman doesn't get sloppy and let you choke to death. I'll even make sure the trapdoor is greased.' He released the pressure. Carcer stumbled, and Vimes kicked his legs from under him.

'The machine ain't broken, Carcer. The machine is waiting for you,' he said, tearing a sleeve off the man's own shirt and fashioning it into a crude binding for his ankles. 'The city will kill you dead. The proper wheels'll turn. It'll be fair, I'll make sure of that. Afterwards you won't be able to say you didn't have a fair trial. Won't be able to say a thing, haha. I'll see to that, too . . .'

359

He stood back.

'Good evening, your grace,' said Lord Vetinari. Vimes spun around. There was a change of texture in the darkness, which could have been man-shaped.

Vimes snatched up his sword and peered into the night. The shape came forward, became recognizable.

'How long were *you* there?' he demanded.

'Oh . . . some little while,' said the Patrician. 'Like you, I prefer to come alone and . . . contemplate.'

'You were very quiet!' said Vimes accusingly.

'Is that a crime, your grace?'

'And you heard—?'

'A very neat arrest,' said Vetinari. 'Congratulations, your grace.'

Vimes looked at the unbloodied sword.

'I suppose so,' he said, temporarily derailed.

'On the birth of your son, I meant.'

'Oh . . . yes. Oh. Of course. Yes. Well . . . thank you.'

'A healthy lad, I am given to understand.'

'We'd have been just as happy with a daughter,' said Vimes, quickly.

'Quite so. These are modern times, after all. Oh, I see you have dropped your badge . . .'

Vimes glanced at the long grass. 'I'll come and find it in the morning,' he said. 'But *this*,' he picked up the moaning Carcer and slung him over his shoulder with a grunt, 'is going back to Pseudopolis Yard right now.'

They walked slowly down the gravel path, leaving the scent of lilac behind. Ahead was the everyday stink of the world.

'You know,' said Lord Vetinari, after a few moments, 'it has often crossed my mind that those men deserve a proper memorial of some sort.'

'Oh yes?' said Vimes, in a non-committal voice. His heart was still pounding. 'In one of the main squares, perhaps?'

'Yes, that would be a good idea.'

'Perhaps a tableau in bronze?' said Vimes sarcastically. 'All seven of them raising the flag, perhaps?'

'Bronze, yes,' said Vetinari.

'Really? And some sort of inspiring slogan?' said Vimes.

'Yes, indeed. Something like, perhaps, "They Did The Job They Had To Do"?'

'*No,*' said Vimes, coming to a halt under a lamp by the crypt entrance. 'How *dare* you? How dare you! At this time! In this place! They did the job they didn't have to do, and they died doing it, and you can't give them anything. Do you understand? They fought for those who'd been abandoned, they fought for one another, and they were betrayed. Men like them always are. What good would a statue be? It'd just inspire new fools to believe they're going to be heroes. They wouldn't want that. Just let them be. *For ever.*'

They walked in heavy silence, and then Vetinari said, as if there had been no outburst: 'Happily, it appears that the new deacon at the temple here has suddenly heard the call.'

'What call?' said Vimes, his heart still racing.

'I'm never very good at religious matters, but apparently he was filled with a burning desire to spread the good word to the benighted heathen,' said Vetinari.

'Where?'

'I suggested Ting Ling.'

'That's right on the other side of the world!'

'Well, a good word can't be spread too far, sergeant.'

'Well, at least it puts—'

Vimes stopped at the entrance gates. Overhead, another lamp flickered. He dropped Carcer to the ground.

'You knew? You bloody well knew, didn't you?'

'Not until, oh, one second ago,' said Vetinari. 'As one man to another, commander, I must ask you: did you ever wonder why I wore the lilac?'

'Yeah. I wondered,' said Vimes.

'But you never asked.'

'No. I never asked,' said Vimes shortly. 'It's a flower. Anyone can wear a flower.'

'At this time? In this place?'

'Tell me, then.'

'Then I'll recall the day I was sent on an urgent errand,' said Vetinari. 'I had to save the life of a man. Not a usual errand for an Assassin although, in fact, I had already saved it once before.' He gave Vimes a quizzical look.

'You'd shot a man who was aiming a crossbow?' said Vimes.

'An inspired guess, commander! Yes. I have an eye for the . . . unique. But now I was fighting time. The streets were blocked. Chaos and confusion were everywhere, and it wasn't as if I even knew where he could be found. In the end I took to the rooftops. And thus I came at last to Cable Street, where there was a different sort of confusion.'

'Tell me what you saw,' said Vimes.

'I saw a man called Carcer . . . vanish. And I saw a man called John Keel die. At least, I saw him dead.'

'Really,' said Vimes.

'I joined the fight. I snatched up a lilac bloom from a fallen man and, I have to say, held it in my mouth. I'd like to think I made some difference; I certainly killed four men, although I take no particular pride in that. They were thugs, bullies. No real skill. Besides, their leader had apparently fled, and what morale they had had gone with him. The men with the lilac, I have to say, fought like tigers. Not skilfully, I'll admit, but when *they* saw that *their* leader was down they took the other side to pieces. Astonishing.

'And then, afterwards, I took a look at John Keel. It *was* John Keel. How could there be any question about that? Blood on him of course. There was blood everywhere. His wounds looked somewhat old, I thought. And death, as we know, changes people. Yet I remember wondering: this much? So I put it down as half a mystery and today . . . sergeant . . . we find the other half of a mystery. It's wonderful, isn't it, how alike men can be? I can imagine that even your Sergeant Colon would not realise anything. After all, he saw Keel die and he watched you grow up—'

'Where is this leading?' Vimes demanded.

'Nowhere, commander. What could I prove? And to what end would I prove it?'

'Then I'm saying *nothing*.'

'I cannot imagine what you *could* say,' said Vetinari. 'No. I agree. Let us leave the dead alone. But for you, commander, as a little gift on the occasion of the birth of—'

'There's nothing I want,' said Vimes quickly. 'You can't promote me any further. There's nothing left to bribe me with. I've got more than I deserve. The Watch is working well. We don't even need a new bloody dartboard—'

'In memory of the late John Keel—' Vetinari began.

'I *warned* you—'

'—I can give you back Treacle Mine Road.'

Only the high-pitched squeak of bats, hunting around the poplars, broke the silence that followed.

Then Vimes muttered: 'A dragon burned it years ago. Some dwarfs live in the cellars now . . .'

'Yes, commander. But dwarfs . . . well, dwarfs are so refreshingly open about money. The more money the city offers, the less dwarf there is. The stable's still there, and the old mining tower. Stout stone walls all around. It could all be put back, commander. In memory of John Keel, a man who in a few short days changed the lives of many and, perhaps, saved some sanity in a mad world. Why, in a few months you could light the lamp over the door . . .'

Again, all that could be heard was the bats.

Perhaps they could even bring back the smell, Vimes thought. Perhaps there could be a window above the privy that'd spring open if you thumped it just right. Perhaps they could teach new coppers to learn old tricks—

'We could do with the space, it's true,' he conceded, with some effort.

'I can see you like the sound of it already,' said Vetinari. 'And if you care to come along to my office tomorrow we can settle the—'

'There's a trial tomorrow,' said Vimes sharply.

'Ah, yes. Of course. And it will be a fair one,' said the Patrician.

'It'd better be,' said Vimes. 'I want this bastard to hang, after all.'

'Well, then,' said Vetinari, 'afterwards we could—'

'Afterwards I'm going home to my family for a while,' said Vimes.

'Good! Well said,' said Vetinari, not missing a beat. 'You have a gift, I have noticed, for impressive oratory.' And Vimes heard the gentle note of warning as he added, 'At this time, commander, and in this place.'

'That's sergeant-at-arms, thank you,' said Vimes. 'For now.'

He grabbed Carcer's shirt collar, and dragged him to justice.

On the way back to Scoone Avenue, in the dark of night, Vimes walked along the alley behind Clay Lane and stopped when he reckoned he was at a point halfway between the backs of the pawn shop and the shonky shop, and therefore behind the temple.

He threw his cigar stub over the fence. He heard it land on gravel, which moved a little.

And then he went home. And the world turned towards morning.